THE YELLOW PAINTED MAN

Jason Roberts

To Ted and Betty Roberts, I wish you were here.

CONTENTS

*We Spaniards know a sickness of the
heart that only gold can cure.*

-Hernan Cortez

*The entire world is my temple, and a very fine
one too, if I'm not mistaken, and I'll never lack
priests to serve it as long as there are men.*

– Erasmus

September 2, 1603
Hembrillo Basin
New Spain

The blood pooled in halos of black mercury around the dead. Vincente LaRue stood washed in the moonlight, suppressing the prayers fighting to escape his lips. Instead, he pointed to the vertical rock leaning like a door into the mountain and the void beyond it.

The Chief passed between LaRue and the moonlight. Ash and blood cut jagged streaks down his face in violent pigments of red, at his mouth an equator of black; he turned his head to the lifeless company, piled together like the horrific catch of some mad fisherman. Behind him, his warriors came forward in pairs, still slick with the blood of LaRue's men. They took the bodies by hand or foot and dragged them to the edge of the void, then fed them into the gaping darkness.

From the mountain, looking north, the Jornada del Muerto was a darkened scab of tongue slashing outward from the jagged madness of fanged ridges. It was a star-haunted place where the moon ruled with an icy indifference. The morbid scraping of dead men's flesh against the rocks carried on the wind as LaRue shouldered his pack and took the trail down the mountain. He crossed himself quickly, allowing himself the brief indulgence of prayer before turning his back to them forever.

A thought manifested in his mind, quickly developing into a compulsion. When he reached the bed of the basin, LaRue went to the base of the rocky ledge on the west side of the valley and made his mark on a stone there. It was in the semblance of his Jesuit cross, with the northern facing arm emphasized, though he could not imagine who might find it and think to follow.

The mountain faded behind him in the sterile glow of the

lunar light as the miles of salt flat passed beneath his feet. He was joined by the smoldering breath of the dead wind, untethered from its golden palace to guide him into the unknown places. From his pocket he drew his mark, a triangle made of gold, embossed with a sunburst cross. It grew warm in his hands and began to gleam with the sunrise, as if one golden thing had spoken to another and bid it to rise out of the earth.

PART ONE
THE NEOPHYTES

glacier inverted
returning in increments
no eye can measure

-Matsuo Sogi

ONE

September 3, 1862
Bootheel Region, New Mexico Territory

B elow the ridge, a small rancheria smoldered in the valley, curdling smoke into the spoiled sunset. Turkey vultures, like greasy black angels, sifted through the haze in descending spirals. Nothing moved in the ruins.

"Chiricahua," said Jeffords.

"They're close," said Sheldon, urging his horse down the trail into the valley.

"This is where my road ends, Captain."

Sheldon pulled up on the reins, staring back over his shoulder at Tom Jeffords.

"Don't look so injured. I told you I'd track your Apache to the border and no further."

Sheldon lifted his hat and brushed back the rusty-blond tuffs of hair clinging to his brow. His face remained expressionless, his drained blue eyes focused on the scout.

"One more thing; I'd lose that uniform before you cross, it might impress your Yale friends, but down here, they'll just bury you in it."

Sheldon snapped the reins and continued down the ridge line.

"You got any last words? Anything you want me to tell

your kin?" Jeffords shouted after him.

He did not reply, and Jeffords vanished over the ridge.

The wind shifted as Samuel Sheldon reached the valley floor, carrying the stench of burnt flesh. He counted eight dead, scattered about the yard, all Mexicans. Most lay face down where they fell, their bodies rent by spears and blades, heads crushed with rocks. One unfortunate soul was lashed to two crossed lengths of split-rail fence over still smoldering coals. His ears and nose were sliced off, and his penis was shoved in his mouth. The remains of several slaughtered goats lay nearby as if they were cooked and eaten there while the man was tortured.

Sheldon secured his horse to a hitching post and investigated the rest of the ranch. The only structure still standing was an adobe ranch house, though the roof had burned off and collapsed. In a corner, there was a tangled pile of bodies, all women and small children. Their heads were so badly bludgeoned that their features could not be identified.

The sun glowed red over the horizon as the Turkey vultures gorged on carrion. Night was coming. Sheldon tore a couple rails from the smashed corral and built a fire at the edge of the compound, upwind and away from the carnage.

Hours passed, and stars filled the sky. Coyotes replaced the vultures, snarling and yipping as they feasted. Sheldon, unable to sleep through their predation, sat by the fire and watched the flames dance over the coals. In his left hand, he held a silver key, in the right, an ancient Roman coin struck from gold. The silver key was his mother's, a keepsake to remind him of home. The coin bore the face of the mad emperor Caligula and was more complicated. It was given to him by his mentor, Danfort Collins, with curious intent, shortly after being tapped into Skull and Bones.

"Of what use is gold?" Collins had asked him.

One year later, Sheldon still could not answer the riddle.

"Of what use, indeed," said a voice from beyond the light of the fire.

"Someone alive out there?" Sheldon drew his pistol and panned the darkness.

"You have nothing to fear from me, Mr. Sheldon."

"How do you know my name?"

The silhouette of a man took shape against the backdrop of stars as he stepped forward. Sheldon trained his gun on the interloper as he stepped into the glow of his campfire.

"I make it my business to know all who enter my service."

The man was tall and lean, his skin darker than the night sky. There was an abnormal elongation to his head, tapering toward his chin like the image of an Egyptian Pharoh. His suit was black, impeccably tailored, and miraculously clean, considering the wild and distant location.

"I'm quite certain I would recognize my own employer."

"Unlikely."

"That's close enough." Sheldon drew the hammer back.

The man smiled widely, his teeth gleaming white in the darkness. He extended his hands outward into the fire's light to show that he carried no weapon. His skeletal fingers were long and strangely segmented, each possessive of an extra knuckle. A large ring adorned his right hand, seemingly carved from a solid piece of milky green jade. It was ornamented by a golden orb, set inside the talon-like clasp of the ring.

"Who are you?"

"I am the Master, Morya," he said. "I've been following your progress for some time, Mr. Sheldon, long before Skull and Bones or even your days at Willaim Russell's academy. You were born for this Trust of ours."

"How do you know the Trust? Did Collins send you?"

"Danfort Collins has too much pride to seek my council in matters of his protégé. No, I've come as a courtesy to share my wisdom, perhaps offer some advice."

"You have my attention, sir," he said, holstering his pistol.

"The man you seek, Mangas Coloradas, is chosen. Even if he does not understand, it is important that you do. Like yourself, he has a role to play. How that unfolds has yet to be decided, although the end will always be the same."

"What does that mean?"

"Two sides, one coin."

"I can't say that I understand."

"In success or failure, you serve His purpose, and He holds no preference which."

"He? Mangas?"

"No, not Mangas. Even I have my master, Mr. Sheldon."

"What are you saying?"

"Whatever glory or fortune you might find, remember this; we are not kings. It's a warning that is seldom spoken more than once."

"On my honor, you needn't worry about the gold."

"I never worry about gold," he said, stepping back from the fire.

"Then what?" Sheldon asked, but Morya was no longer there.

◆ ◆ ◆

Sheldon followed the Chiricahua trail south, out of the valley, and toward the border. At first, their path was clear, marked by the tracks of stolen cattle and horses, but he lost them across a shelf of shale as he crossed into Chihuahua. Guessing, he continued south into the hill country north of Janos. Late in the afternoon, the Chiricahua found him at a place devoid of any noteworthy landmarks.

They rose up seemingly from nothing, appearing on the hills around him, armed with rifles, bows, and lances. Sheldon pulled back on the reins and brought his horse to a stop. He kept his hands high and his movements slow and deliberate.

"Mangas Coloradas!" Sam called out.

The stoic Apache did not respond.

At the crest of the hill before him, an older warrior stepped forward, dragging one foot in a subtle limp. He held something small in his hand that captivated his attention. Studying the item until satisfied, he deposited it in a pouch and descended the hill.

"Brave soldier," he said in Spanish. "Or stupid."

"I do not come as a soldier," Sheldon answered in Spanish.

"Why do you come?"

"I wish to speak to Mangas."

The lame Apache made a gesture, and two warriors joined him. Sheldon did not resist as they removed his sidearm and blindfolded him. One of them took his horse's lead and led him slowly into the Sonoran without ever acknowledging whether Mangas was indeed their destination.

Several hours later, he was pulled down from his horse and roughly pushed to the ground, where his hands were tied behind him. Someone put a water skin to his lips, and he drank. Somewhere in the periphery, a fire crackled, though he was too distant to feel its warmth. Eventually, night came, marked by the sinister mewling of coyotes.

Hours passed until he was forcefully jerked to his feet and instructed to march via the continuous probing of a rifle in his back. He stumbled along the rough terrain, occasionally falling to his knees on the unforgiving rocks. Each time being pulled to his feet by a disgruntled Chiricahua warrior.

"Torpe!" said his guide with some disgust.

Finally, after descending a steep trail, they stopped. Sheldon's blindfold was removed, and he found himself in the company of the limping old man and two other warriors. They were at the mouth of a small canyon with a small stream running its length. The old Apache pointed downstream, then turned back up the canyon trail, followed by the two warriors.

Halfway into the canyon, Sheldon found a wikiup flanked by two nude Apache women. They watched him with indifference as he continued past, following the stream. A short distance further, the stream came to a shallow pool just before it tumbled down a modest fall to a lower area of the canyon. Cross-legged on a flat, sunny rock was the largest human being Samuel Sheldon had ever seen there.

Mangas faced away, toward the falls, chanting a mournful song in his native tongue. His long hair was drawn back in a ponytail and cast over one of his massive shoulders. Below his opposite shoulder, an enormous exit wound gapped, glistening in the morning sun. So grievous and cavernous was the wound that Sheldon was certain that if he got close enough, he could see straight through the man's chest.

Sheldon listened as Mangas sang with low, rasping breaths. The tune flowed with an alien tonality, contrary to the western scale, yet harmonious and resonating. Delicate blood trickles seeped from his wound as he sang, meandering like raindrops down his powerful back.

"Mangas," Sheldon called out.

The song ended abruptly.

"You are not what I imagined," said Mangas, rising to his full height, a full head above Sheldon.

"You've imagined me?"

"Someone like you."

"The Army did not send me if that is what you think. This has nothing to do with the fight at Apache Pass."

"I know," said Mangas, arriving next to Sheldon with a few massive strides.

"Then you know that you possess something of ours?"

"You are the one that is possessed."

"Does this look familiar?"

Sheldon held up a small golden figurine molded into a Jaguar's shape.

"What do they call you?" Asked Mangas.

"My name is Samuel Sheldon," he answered.

"You have come a long way to die, Samuel Sheldon."

"No, you won't kill me, Mangas. I'm just the head of the Hydra."

"Hydra?"

"What is that?" He asked.

"A snake that, when it loses its head, grows two more to replace it."

"Then let the canyon be filled with heads," said Mangas.

"I didn't come here to fight you, Mangas."

"You don't know why you have come."

"The Aztec people called them ocelot, jaguar. Idols like this honored their war gods. They are all long dead now. Their Gods could not protect them. There are very few places where one of your people could have found one, yet somehow, they did. A warrior with a broad scar across his face brought this one to a trading post. I have come to see where he found it."

Mangas stared down the creek and to the sky beyond. He seemed to notice his wound for the first time, and a weariness filled his eyes.

"I have a dream; when the earth was born, it was covered in fire. A burning star falls. It cuts deep into the earth and falls beneath a tiny mountain. It is from this place that he speaks to me."

"Who?"

"The yellow painted man," said Mangas.

"Can you take me there?"

"I will not. One evil brings another. I have no cause to open that place."

"What if I promised you I could take the evil away?"

"You cannot take Him from his home if he wishes to stay. It is a hollow promise."

"What is evil for the Apache is not evil for my people, I

can make this promise to you."

"Every day, I sing the death song, it is the only promise I know."

"What then? What do you wish for more than all things?"

"Peace for my people."

"If that is your desire, I can easily see it done. It is well within my power to arrange for treaties to be made. The Army does not want the Apache for an enemy. They are already at war with the grey coats. You frightened them at Apache Pass, this is a good time to ask for peace."

Mangas looked away again as if somewhere beyond the horizon, a scale was weighing Sheldon's words. Then he turned and examined Sheldon. Finally, after a moment, he spoke.

"I have the power to read men's hearts, though I cannot read yours, it is not there. Still, I hear your words, I have no reason to doubt them. White eyes will do anything for the yellow metal, even make peace. Go, Sheldon, prepare your treaty. I will send word when I am well enough, and we will meet at Apache Tejo."

Mangas was joined by his wives, who draped a blanket over his massive shoulders and led him away toward the wiki up. Sheldon followed a few paces behind, continuing past them to the mouth of the canyon. The crooked-foot Apache waited there with his two companions. They blindfolded him once more and led him north away from their camps.

January 17, 1863
Apache Tejo, New Mexico Territory

Sheldon came to the small clearing between an arroyo and a stand of cottonwood, where he was meant to meet Mangas. To his horror, a small mob of miners, settlers, and ranchers had gathered there. Worse, a detachment of Union cavalry also occupied the clearing, currently restraining the crowd. The soldiers, mostly California volunteers, were led by a high-strung young lieutenant whose frustrations with the rabble were growing.

Sheldon looked down the clearing to where a torn white shirt twisted in the wind above a deep arroyo. Beyond that, there was no sign of Mangas. He hitched his horse to a cottonwood and approached the Lieutenant.

"Fucking cowards! Don't give two shits about the white man! Coddle those red bastards all you want, they just come back to slit your throat in the night!" One of the miners shouted.

"What's going on here, Lieutenant?" Asked Sheldon

"I'm here to arrest that filthy savage, Mangas Coloradas if this mob doesn't kill him first!"

"On whose command?"

"That would be General Joseph West, sir," said the Lieutenant. "Orders came straight from Washington."

"That cannot be right, only the General and I knew that Mangas was even expected. It was meant to be a peace negotiation, not an arrest!"

"I can't speak to that, sir, I'm just here to collect him, but if this mob has its way, there won't be anything left to arrest."

Sheldon drew his pistol and fired a shot into the air.

"The next cock sucker so much as opens his mouth gets a bullet in it! Now step off and let the Army do its work!"

With minimal mumbling, the dejected crowd backed away from the clearing.

"Keep those men back, and I'll try and salvage this debacle."

Sheldon walked halfway across the clearing. The wind picked up, and the white shirt twisted on its stick. Nothing else moved.

"Mangas!" Sheldon took another step forward. "Mangas, I've come!"

Above the arroyo, the withered grass twisted in the wind, and the mesquite shook. Three men came over the rocks, rising from the arroyo like ghosts. One of them dwarfed his companions like children. His red plaid shirt bulged at the shoulders and clung tight to his muscular arms and chest. Jet black hair with thin streaks of white draped nearly to his waist. His mouth was a slit across the width of his face, and his eyes were dark like the space between the stars. There was no mistaking Mangas Coloradas, the most fearsome man in all Apacheria.

Beside him stood the old warrior with the crooked foot and a younger one with a facial scar carved into his face like a scowl. The limping Apache held a gold pocket watch that he stared at with morbid fascination. None of them carried weapons.

"You look well, Mangas. How is your wound?" Sheldon asked.

"Healing."

"It is good that you have come."

"I have come."

Mangas glanced at the soldiers and miners trading insults in the distance. The younger warrior spoke softly to Mangas, who answered briefly before addressing the young captain.

"Those are violent men, Sheldon."

"They will not harm you. I promise."

"Another promise from your empty heart," said Mangas.

"I am good for my word. I have arranged for you to meet the Nantan, General West. He will talk peace. Are you good for your word, Mangas?"

"I told you, Sheldon, this is beyond your power to promise."

Mangas turned back to the arroyo, and the other warriors followed.

"You've come too far to quit now! If you walk away, the soldiers will keep coming till there are none of you left!"

"Let them come," said Mangas.

"Mangas, wait! The Nantan intends to make peace with the Chiricahua, to grant them land. Don't let that chance slip away."

Mangas stopped and discussed the matter with his companions.

After a brief deliberation, he responded, "We will go and speak to the Nantan."

"No, I'm sorry, you must come alone."

The two warriors beside him protested vehemently and urged Mangas to abandon the meeting. He acknowledged their pleas, then ended their arguments with a firm, "Enjuh!"

Turning back to Sheldon, he said, "I will go with you."

The Apache shared a silent exchange. Mangas' two companions looked as if they were staring into a grave. They backed away slowly, then turned toward the arroyo and disappeared. Sheldon heard the faint sound of horses, then only the wind in the grass.

"It is good that you will speak to the Nantan. He has power over this land and can make a lasting peace."

"No one has power over the land, Sheldon. Only Ussen."

"I meant, he has the authority of the Great Nantan in Washington, who now owns this land and makes the laws."

"The White Eyes think they own the sun and stars. It is not so. I have only come to make peace between our people."

"Yes, Mangas, let's do that."

Across the field, the soldiers waited as violent rhetoric rumbled among the miners. The sun, still only a light spot on the silver-gray canvass of sky, drifted to the west.

"Mangas, do you know what Manifest Destiny means?"

"No."

"It's a hunger," Sheldon said, reaching for his horse's reins. "A hunger that can never be sated. It means that my people will keep coming west until they do own the sun and the stars; this cannot be stopped."

"I know this hunger, it is a sickness. There is no medicine, only death."

"Maybe you do understand," said Sheldon. "You can save your people, protect them, make a place in this world for them if you help me. Tell me, where is the tiny mountain?"

"First, the Nantan, then we will speak of the mountain."

"Do I have your word, Mangas?"

"As I have yours."

They approached the assembled rabble of miners who, despite all their fury, gave Mangas a wide berth as he came near. A young corporal stepped down from his horse and went to his saddle bag, and retrieved a heavy set of manacles.

"Chains? Am I your prisoner, Sheldon?"

"Are those necessary, lieutenant?"

"I have my orders," he said.

The soldier hesitated, but the Lieutenant waved him forward. The private placed one hand on his sidearm. The mounted soldiers watched in a state of readiness.

"No, Mangas, you are not my prisoner. This is not how I wanted it, but you will wear those chains," said Sheldon.

Like all Chiricahua, Mangas valued his freedom above all else. Death was preferable to imprisonment. His lips curled, and a sickly pallor of disgust crossed his face. A chorus of hammers clicked among the soldiers' raised rifles. The wind blew the dead grass, and the chains rattled in the corporal's trembling hands.

"I allow this," Mangas said, "only for peace."

The soldiers applied the chains and then swiftly backed away.

The miners cheered at the sight of the Chiricahua in chains. Many of them directed their gratitude toward Sheldon, who ignored them entirely.

"I'm sorry we don't have an extra horse, but I will walk with you and keep you company," said Sheldon. He held his hand up and twirled his finger, directing his men to move out. They formed into two evenly spaced columns and moved toward the trail.

"Ride, Sheldon. I find your company foul."

Sheldon mounted his horse and rode beside Mangas, and four soldiers fell in behind them. They moved east on the old military trail towards Fort McLane with the faded silver sun at their back.

Above the arroyo, the white shirt twisted in the

breeze.

TWO

January 17, 1863
Fort Mclane, New Mexico Territory

T he sun was low in the sky, and Pedro needed to get this deal done. It seemed more and more likely that he and Andres would be camping at the fort. The prospect was less than ideal. Too many grifters and lowlifes sought the Army's protection there. This was fine for white men, but a Mexican's scalp looked the same as an Indian's and, just over the border, sold for ten dollars apiece.

"Please, mister, it's a good price!" Pedro said in poor English.

"I can't understand a goddamn word out of your goddamn mouth!" said the sergeant. "I ain't in the mood to be swindled by no goddamn Mexican!"

Regulations did not prohibit the sale of surplus, and for a considerable profit, the sergeant frequently supplied settlers and prospectors. While Sergeant Conny understood Pedro, his service was exclusive to white customers.

"Gold, señor! It's gold! Oro!" Pedro pleaded.

"Do I look like a goddamned assay to you? I don't want your fuckin' rocks!" The sergeant came around the counter of the commissary, intent on shooing them out the door.

"This is gold!" Pedro insisted as he and his brother were shoved out into the compound.

"Easy, Brother," Andres said. "We will be fine. Don't worry."

Pedro put the ore sample back in his knapsack. The ore was rich, and he had no doubt it would assay at a handsome price. This fact gave him little solace. They were far from home, and the sum of their worldly possessions consisted of the clothes on their backs, a knapsack full of unprocessed gold ore, a hand-drawn map, and a gun. Three nights prior, they had been run out of their camp by prospectors and forced to leave everything they couldn't carry behind.

"Don't look so sour, Pedro! Our fortunes have improved, this isn't a jail in Pinos Altos. The worm doth turn, Brother!" Andres put his hand on his brother's shoulder. "Have faith!"

No rain existed in Andres' world. He was optimistic to a fault. Of his time in the military stockade at Pinos Altos, he would speak of the tobacco he won gambling with guards without a mention of the loss of the deed to his mining claim, the forfeit of his gold, or the beating that put him near death. "Five cigarillos, it's the start of my empire, Jefe," he would tell his jailors. That's not to say he wasn't grateful when Pedro bribed three soldiers to look the other way and a judge to burn his warrant, but he considered it part of the plan. Fate. Even Jesus had to be crucified before he made it big. Hardships were part of the game, and that made winning all the sweeter.

"That fucking idiot has no idea what he refused!" Pedro fumed.

Pedro knew. Pedro appreciated. He was a man who knew the value of things. His first enterprise was copper scrap. As a child, he combed the dirt around the jewelry vendors in Parral and scavenged the bits of wire used to bind pieces of turquoise. Sometimes he found bits of silver, he kept that too. Pedro kept everything he found and understood its value. When he had enough of any one thing, he would trade it for something more precious. Gold is what he valued above all else. In his mind, there was a giant scale on which he would place any item and imagine the ballast point when gold was placed on the opposite side. By the age of nine, Pedro owned his first gold coin. The platform of that imaginary scale was big enough for a team of horses.

"Forget it. The air is fine, and it smells like treasure! Let's go find it!"

"With what? We have no horses, no tools. We don't even have food!"

"We don't have this, we don't have that," Andres mocked his brother, smiling. "But look at all we do have. We have our uncle's map! We have proof that it is real! We have blood in our veins and fire in our souls! Fortune awaits!"

Pedro couldn't help but smile at his older brother. Andres was the counterbalance that kept the minutia at bay. Not that Pedro would ever forget the details, though sometimes he needed reminding that a golden prize waited at the end.

"You're right, of course. You're right!" Pedro surrendered.

"I still have a little mescal. We can get a fire going and figure things out. Everything will work out. We just need to..."

Andres' words trailed off as he looked past Pedro to a group of soldiers passing through the compound's gates. Standing head and shoulders above the cavalrymen was a solitary prisoner of remarkable size. The prisoner was an Indian, Apache by the colors of his beaded necklace, and the largest human Pedro had ever seen. A baby-faced, blond captain walked beside the prisoner, sunburned and sweating but immaculately dressed. The escort stopped at the gates, but the guards on the promenade took notice and made their rifles ready. The captain and the Apache headed toward General West's office.

Two tufts of steely gray hair billowed out from either side of the general's shiny head, balanced in symmetry by the tendrils of beard shooting out from his chin. West's eyes were tiny clumps of dirt, and when he squinted, it was as if everything he viewed was also dirt. As he stepped out of his office to meet them, it was Mangas who was the object of the general's squinting stare.

"So, Captain Sheldon, this is that murderous red bastard I've heard so much about!" He said.

"This is Mangas Coloradas, Chief of the Mimbreno Apache," said Sheldon.

"This is the sonofabitch that's been raising hell all up and down the old Butterfield Line? Well, he's murdered his last white man!"

"I have kept my people from killing whites for five years!" Mangas argued in Spanish. He understood little English, though enough to know what "murder" meant.

"There are the bleached bones of five hundred white settlers up and down this country that beg to differ, Chief," West said. "Men, his trail of blood ends here! I want him dead, you hear? Dead!"

Spittle escaped the gravity of his beard as he spoke.

"Dead? Sir, when we last spoke, you agreed to hear this man out. You promised me that we would discuss a treaty!"

"My position has since changed, Captain, as have my orders."

"Sir, with due respect, my orders are direct from Washington, and they are very clear."

"I'm afraid you have your signals crossed, captain. My orders also come from Washington, straight from the office of Secretary of War Edwin Stanton. There will be no treaty, captain."

"General, there must be some mistake. Please, allow me to contact my superiors. I'm certain they can alleviate all confusion on the matter."

"There is no confusion, Captain Sheldon. However, if you feel it necessary to contact your 'superiors,' I'm happy to direct you to the telegraph officer," then, turning to the lieutenant, he said, "Lock that man up and keep an extra guard on him."

The general turned and walked back to his office. The captain watched as the lieutenant and several soldiers led the huge Apache away.

"It will be dark soon. We need to make camp," Pedro said.

"Good idea, these soldiers are none too friendly. We should be going."

The brothers skirted the edge of the spectacle and left the compound in the shadows of the setting sun.

West of the fort stood a collection of adobe buildings, small camps, and guard houses stretched over the terraced landscape. Soldiers called it the Skids. All manner of humanity camped there for the relative safety it afforded. Most were prospectors or the merchants that followed them like vultures. Settlers were less common, as most men able to carry a rifle found themselves suited in blue or gray. Some, though, still headed west, trying to outrun the war. Pedro picked a spot closest to the stream and away from the other camps.

They sat beside each other, leaning against the eroded embankment with their feet toward their fire. Andres produced his bottle of mescal, pulled the stopper, and took a pull.

"Tomorrow, our luck changes. You'll see! There are plenty of posts along the old stage line. We'll get what we need, no problem," Andres said, passing the bottle to Pedro.

"Yes, but I'm hungry now!" Pedro laughed.

"This land is crawling with food. I saw three rabbits just now at the creek!"

"Then why are there not three rabbits in the fire?"

"I felt sorry for them. But I am so quick that it would not be fair!"

Pedro laughed as he passed the bottle back.

"Good thinking, give them a head start. It's more sporting that way."

"I am grateful, you know that I am. Right, Pedro?"

"I know that you are, but it's Uncle Miguel that deserves your gratitude."

Pedro poked the fire with a stick and stirred the coals to coax more heat. Yellow flames shot up from the bed of red coals. Their meager pile of wood wouldn't last the night.

"How did you convince him to give up his map? That miserable old miser would just as soon bury every penny as buy a pinch of grain."

Pedro held the bottle to the light and swirled the liquid around.

"You've been gone a long time, Andres. Things changed. Anything of value was taken by the emperor, the governor,

Liberals, Republicans, or anyone with enough guns to demand a tax. All the mines in Sonora are played out, and even if they weren't, those, too, would be taken. If Don Miguel could come north, I believe he would. I don't think he has much time left, he's not well. It's all about family for him now. He is very proud."

A thin, pinkish-blue line defined the horizon, swiftly fading into the starless black sky.

"I thought it was all a bunch of bullshit, just a story he would tell," said Andres.

"I believed him. I followed the map."

"Oh, I believe now! My God that is the richest ore I've ever seen!"

"That partner of yours, he talked you up. He rode down and told Uncle Miguel you had found the biggest load in all of New Mexico. He just needed gold for your bail and a little more for a grubstake."

"Ha! Sounds like he believed too!" Andres hit the bottle. "What happened to Jake? Why didn't he come with you?"

"Uncle Miguel said he didn't know who you were." Pedro took the bottle and watched Andres' face slowly fade into a wounded frown. "Then he sent for me."

"Hey, I would have been alright, you know me. I always come up roses!"

"Andres, it took much more than five cigarillos to buy you out of that stockade. I followed the Rio Salado, and I found those mountains. I can tell you, it will take more than this bottle of mescal to get back there."

"Yes, Brother, I know. Just think of the adventure before us! I, for one, cannot wait for the sun to rise!" He held his hands up dramatically as if conjuring the sun.

"I don't know if our uncle will be there when we get back. I think not. He didn't want the secret to die with him. He is one of the last on the Peralta side and the only living man other than me who has been there. It's more than gold, Andres, it's family."

"I know," said Andres finishing the bottle.

In the distance, the disembodied voices of other camps, howling coyotes, and the faint babbling of the creek filled the darkness. Finally, the two wedged their shoulders together against the cold, dirt wall and faded to sleep as the last of their wood turned to coals on the fire.

An anguished cry of pain startled them awake. Pedro instinctively drew his pistol. The fire had gone out, and darkness covered the Skids. A single fire stood out against one of the adobe buildings where the soldiers had built a small fortification. It was too far and too dim to put form to the shadows moving through the fire's light.

Another scream, even more, pained than the last.

"What is happening?" Andres wondered, peering into the darkness.

"I don't know."

"I am no thing to be played with like a child!" shouted a voice in Spanish.

"I think it's that big Apache! It sounds like they are torturing him!" Pedro said.

Another scream came over the Skids, then several gunshots followed by silence.

The brothers turned to each other fearfully.

"What do you want to do?" Andres asked.

"We wait. When the sun comes up, we go."

They huddled together against the shelter of the dirt wall and did not speak. After the shots, they heard nothing and eventually returned to sleep.

At first light, Pedro woke to find Andres looking across the Skids with an expression of abject terror on his face. Pedro leaped to his feet to observe the danger.

The blond captain was hacking at something with a hatchet, something that looked vaguely human. Leveraging force with his boot, he ripped at the object and held his trophy high.

In the dull gray dawn, the captain held the severed head of

Mangas Coloradas.

January 18, 1863
New Mexico Territory

The hands of the golden watch were frozen at twenty-two minutes after three, although Nana could not tell time. Nevertheless, he knew that somewhere in the timepiece's pale bone face and strange markings, the secret habits of the sun and moon were revealed. That is not to say that Nana did not understand time, only that as it related to the golden watch, it was either time to live or time to die.

"There," Geronimo pointed to the brush-choked trail.

Nana closed the watch and slipped it into his medicine pouch, bound with a leather cord around his neck. He had consulted the watch, and the watch had spoken life. With rifle in hand, he stepped out into the wide part of the trail, his lame foot slightly dragging behind. He was shirtless, naked to his breechcloth and moccasins. Geronimo, Fun, and Chewawa followed close behind.

One of the Mexicans sang, "Bésame por suerta..."

Nana held his hand up.

"Bésame mi amor!"

The singing stopped abruptly as the two men noticed him on the road.

"Stop," Nana said in Spanish.

"Hello," said the non-musical of the pair, holding his hands up and carefully walking forward. The other followed suit.

"You have come from the bluecoats' fort," Nana said.

"Yes."

"Our chief went to the fort yesterday. He has not returned."

The two Mexicans shared a terrified glance.

"I'm sorry," the singer stammered.

Nana was unclear whether they were speaking to him or exchanging final goodbyes.

"Death!" Geronimo hissed.

"Tell me what you know, and I will let you live," said Nana, holding one hand out in front of the angry warrior.

The elder of the two Mexicans spoke of the blond captain that led Mangas in chains to General West. He could not recite the general's words, but he spoke poorly of the White Eyes' Chief. He told Nana of the cries that woke them in the night and the chief's fearsome last words before the gunshots. Lastly, he described the horror of the blond captain hoisting the severed head like a trophy.

Nana gasped, and Geronimo howled in sorrowful rage. Chewawa and Fun, struck with disbelief, stared in disgust.

"The White Eyes have no honor!" Geronimo raged.

Nana wept. He wept for the loss of his friend and chief but more for the damnation of Mangas' afterlife. He would be doomed to walk forever headless in the place of happiness. Such cruelty was unimaginable.

The brothers held hands and closed their eyes.

"Open your eyes!" said Nana. "We do not kill those who surrender to us, we are not like the White Eyes!"

Geronimo remained silent.

They opened their eyes, but their hands remained locked together.

"He must be returned to us," said Nana. "You will speak to the soldiers."

"They will not return the body, and they will kill anyone that asks who is not white. The general has hatred for the Apache, nor does he care for Mexicans."

"I do not care for Mexicans!" said Geronimo.

"I give you the gift of life. To honor that gift, you will do this for us," said Nana.

"Of course," said Pedro. His compliance was not optional.

Nana spoke quietly to Fun, who disappeared over the trail's

embankment. They stood in silence for several moments. Geronimo stared with murderous curiosity as if he were straining for an excuse to defy Nana.

Fun returned along the trail leading a bay roan stallion, powerfully built and outfitted with a Mexican Cavalry saddle. He gave the reins to Nana.

"This horse belonged to Mangas Coloradas. He will ride one last time." Nana handed the reins to Pedro. "Return with him, and your debt is paid."

Geronimo raised his rifle and pointed down the trail, and the brothers turned around and walked back the way they came. The horse followed obediently behind.

The scale in Pedro's mind now held his soul on one side and a swirling nothingness on the other. They walked in silence until the trail widened. They reached the place where the creek and the trail met. While the horse took water from the stream, the brothers collected their wits.

"See, Brother, things are looking up! We have a horse!" said Andres.

Pedro did not find it funny. He felt watched, threatened, and frustrated. Neither spoke fluent English, yet they were to be the Apache ambassadors to the white men. They had likely traded one death for another.

"Shit! This is all shit!" Pedro kicked a small rock that tumbled into the creek with a splash.

"Let's just take the horse, who's to stop us?" Andres smiled.

"You're a fool," Pedro said and grabbed the reins. "Let's get this over with."

The high clouds cleared over the afternoon, urged on by a steady breeze out of the west. Blue returned to the sky, and the sun was warm on their shoulders. The horse drifted along beside them, softly stretching at the reins.

They reached the western edge of the Skids and found it much the same as when they left that morning. Some had moved on, while others had arrived. The small adobe structure by the fortification appeared abandoned. Soldiers lingered around the barracks and near the compound. A fire smoked by the livery where a small pig was being roasted, tended by a soldier with a greasy white apron.

The brothers led the horse across the terrace toward the camp where they last saw Mangas. Near the ash-caked fire pit, a cast iron kettle lay overturned. Frothy gray slime clung to it, punctuated by what seemed like fleshy bits of tallow. Larger pieces, caked with matted black hair, lay in a dried river where the kettle had been dumped. Dark patches of clotted blood clumped with dirt under living balls of flies and a sprawling swamp of muddied blood indicated where Mangas fell.

"I don't see him," Pedro said.

"There," Andres pointed.

Protruding from a mound of loose dirt and sod, they saw a massive hand. Pedro began uncovering the body. Sand and dirt clung to the tacky blood of the stiff corpse. A broken spade lay near the failed burial site, and Andres used it to help uncover the body. When they cleared the dirt and sand, the head was not found.

"What do we do?" Andres asked.

"They probably took it for a trophy. There's nothing we can do about that."

The weight of the body was daunting. Together they dragged it, but the awkward bulk was impossible for them to heft. After several failed attempts to lift the body up on the horse, Andres had an idea. Taking the horse to the lower terrace, they dragged the body over and lowered it onto the horse from above. The body lay with its midsection on the saddle, his legs on one side, arms and torso on the other. They secured it as best they could with twine and a leather belt.

Pedro made the sign of the cross and said a prayer for the dead.

When they reached the creek and started down the trail for the second time, Pedro crossed himself again and thanked the Lord. They kept an eye out for pursuers, but none came. If there were witnesses, none bothered to state a grievance.

It was dusk when they reached the spot where they met the Apache. The hateful one was the first to appear. He came walking up the trail behind them with two other warriors. One of them whistled, and the older Apache with the crooked foot stepped out onto the path ahead of them. Three more came from behind the rise.

It took three of them to lift Mangas from his horse. No one spoke.

The hateful one approached them and took the reins. A long scar on his face gave the impression of a scowl. He handed the reins to Pedro.

"Take the horse and go."

Pedro nodded and put his foot in the stirrup. After he was mounted, he helped his brother up. They rode into the growing darkness and didn't look back.

"I told you, Brother!" Andres said after they rode a distance. "Things are looking up!"

THREE

February 1863
Hembrillo Basin, New Mexico Territory

V ictorio was dreaming again. It was the same dream that had haunted him for years, the same that had tormented Mangas. Now, with his death, it came with increasing frequency.

It was hot and dark. The air was thick with smoke, and the earth rumbled. A faraway light grew larger and trailed fire through the sky. He stood at the peak of the tiny mountain, but everything around him was different. The fire in the sky grew as it approached, illuminating the heaving landscape. It hissed and screamed as it came closer, filling the sky with its terrible sound. The flaming object became clear, it was a man as large as the mountain, with skin of yellow metal. It impacted the earth with a sound too loud to hear, and the world was filled with fire.

"It's time," said Lozen, shaking his arm.

The dream faded, and the details evaporated, leaving only the residue of dread. He stepped out of his wikiup and inhaled the cool night air. Dozens of fires, representing the assembled tribes of the Chiricahua, stretched across the basin. Juh had come from his stronghold in the Blue Mountains and, with him, the warriors of the Nednhi. With Juh rode Geronimo, medicine man and warrior. Loco led a band from Ojo Caliente, joined by others from Santa Rita del Cobre and Pinos Altos. Cochise brought a formidable band from his stronghold in the Dragoons. He came prepared for war to avenge his father-in-law, Mangas Coloradas. Victorio, who had chosen the site for the council, and his sister Lozen arrived the day before, accompanied by nearly every Mimbreno warrior.

One fire burned larger and brighter than all the others at the base of a rocky outcropping that formed a small peak. It was a cursed place, the Chiricahua called it the Tiny Mountain. Its distinct shape rose alone from the basin like a child separated from its parents. Around this fire, the war council gathered. Victorio and Lozen crossed the basin and joined the assembled leaders of the Chiricahua.

Among the Chiricahua, Lozen was known for her Power. This gift of Ussen enabled her to detect the presence of their enemies. As the council sat quietly around the crackling fire, she began to sing, slowly dancing a circle around the flames.

Upon this earth on which we live, Ussen
has power, this power is mine
I Search for my enemy, which only Ussen can show to me

Victorio watched his sister turning. Clearly, she did not feel the tingling in her palms in any of the four directions. There was no enemy near, and there was no danger.

Lozen sat by his side, and Nana stood. While all had heard of Mangas Coloradas' death at the hands of the soldiers, Nana shared his firsthand account of the story. He spoke of the pale captain named Sheldon, who rode to Janos delivering words of peace and told how that man led Mangas away in chains. Nana spoke of how this captain took his head so that none of his ancestors may see his face when he went to the happy lands beyond.

The warriors of the council were moved by Nana's heavy words. Nana had ridden with Mangas and the great Cuchillo Negro when they took sacred retribution against the Mexicans in Chihuahua and Sonora after the evil of Santa Rita. This was no different, their responsibility was to avenge.

Loco was also moved by Nana's speech, though he disagreed

that they should take the warpath.

"This enemy is too powerful," he said. "We must seek peace with the White Eyes."

Cochise calmly stood, his face grim with resolve.

"No, there can be no peace with the White Eyes."

"Look at this fire." Loco gestured to the flames. "This fire is our gathered tribes. Look at all the fires in this valley..." He waved his arm in a sweeping arc. "These are all the tribes of the Indeh." He tilted his head back and looked upward. "Now look at the stars, those are the armies of the White Eyes, they are too numerous to count. We can no more kill them all as we can remove sand from the desert!"

"With Mangas, I killed more than I can count. We have chased them from their forts, running into the east. It must be war," said Cochise.

"Did you not run from their cannons when Mangas was wounded deep in his chest? It was not we who sent the soldiers to the east, it is their war with the Gray Riders."

The lines of Cochise's face drew into a scowl.

"I will not make peace!" he said.

"Enjuh!" Nana said.

"Enjuh!" echoed the assembled warriors.

There were no further dissenters, and the council was decided.

With the death of Mangas, Victorio was now Chief of the Mimbreno. He knew Loco was right, but war was inevitable. The council looked to him to lead them and direct their vengeance. In his prayers, he asked Ussen for a sign. The only answer came in dimly recalled dreams of the mountain.

"There is truth in Loco's words. The White Eyes come in countless numbers. If we killed ten for every warrior, it would not be enough. If we fight in this way, we cannot win."

Victorio turned and pointed toward the negative space in the sky where the Tiny Mountain blocked out the stars.

"A vision has filled my dreams," he said. "In it, I see this place alone in the unmade world. The sky is burning with a strange falling star. From the mountain peak, I see it is not a star but a man. Then all the land is fire."

The eyes of the council fixed upon him. None doubted his words. In grim silence, they awaited Victorio's interpretation.

"This mountain is cursed," he said. "Evil lives inside."

Victorio picked up a torch made of calico and pitch and lit it in the fire. Then, holding it before him, he set out from the fire to the trailhead at the base of the peak.

"Come," he said, and the council followed.

Among the Chiricahua, only Mangas and Victorio carried the burden of the mountain's secret. The knowledge passed down from their fathers and their fathers before them. Now, Victorio would share that secret with the assembled chiefs of the Chiricahua.

The path wound around the mountain with several sharp switchbacks. When they reached the top, they stood on the north side, facing away from the basin and the campfires. The star-filled sky ripped like a piece of paper in jagged lines where mountains rose to the east and west with the flat expanse of the Jornada to the north.

"White Eyes believe there is nothing that cannot be owned," said Victorio. "Ussen made the world and everything in it. White Eyes tell its price in yellow metal. Without it, there is nothing for them. The miners will not come, the soldiers will not fight. This is how they can be defeated. Not by death, but by the metal that gives their lives meaning."

Victorio stood near a tall, vertical rock. The reflections of tiny fires danced in his eyes. His torch flickered, spitting off hissing pieces of burning pitch.

"Yellow metal cannot be destroyed, it is sacred to Ussen and not for us to use," said Cochise.

"This is true, no fire can burn it, no rust may harm it, no hammer will break it," said Victorio. "It can only be returned to Ussen, so that he may keep and protect it."

Victorio stepped behind the tall rock and bid the others wait.

The rock concealed a small alcove, not tall enough to stand in without hunching over. He knelt by a large, flat rock which he pulled aside and brushed the dirt away, uncovering a wooden hatch made of ancient planks. Lifting it revealed a lightless portal, just big enough for a man. He then stepped out to the others, handing the torch to Lozen and inviting them to enter.

Lozen held the torch over the pit, and Victorio fished around until he found the edges of an old wooden ladder. He pulled it up to the portal's edge and put a cautious foot on one of the rungs. Finding it stable, he descended into the darkness. Lozen passed the torch down to her brother and climbed into the abyss. Cautiously, the others followed.

The torch flickered in the humid darkness, carving a tiny circle out of the gloom. Crude picks, shovels, chisels, and other broken tools lay strewn about the ladder's base, mixed with a collection of dry and blackened bones. A shattered wheelbarrow lay near a pile of rotting timbers and human skulls.

Exploring further, the cavern walls showed evidence of tool marks where the natural passage had been widened. Several drifts could be seen, branching off to indeterminable depths.

"This way," said Victorio, ducking through one of the portals.

The narrow passage opened into a larger room with a stoped ceiling, the peak of which was an unknown distance above them. The air was still and dead. More tools and rusted refuse lay scattered about, and everywhere, something was glittering.

Stacks of dusty ingots, too numerous to count, lined the chamber walls. The unmistakable luster of gold latched onto the torchlight and pushed away the darkness. The stacks were as tall as a man and continued as far as the torch could reveal. Chests, crates, and barrels proliferated throughout the cavern, each overflowing with coins and other precious objects.

"In the days of my grandfather's grandfather, the Spanish

came and took the yellow metal from the mountain," said Lozen. "They called it Soledad, this is the mine they made."

"They killed or enslaved our people for many years while they dug," said Victorio. "Others brought more metal from the south, hiding it in the mountain. They also brought sickness with them, many died. Our ancestors fought and killed them and sealed their bones in the mountain with their precious yellow metal."

Their eyes adjusted to the light, and the scope of the hoard became clear. Additional tunnels meandered out of the main chamber into others filled with bones and gold. Centuries of dust settled like snow on quiet graves, untouched by living hands.

"This place has filled my dreams for many days. Now I understand what my visions mean to say. We cannot defeat the White Eyes by force, but we can remove the curse that compels them."

"How will you fight a curse?" Asked Cochise.

"The yellow metal is the source of the White Eyes power, without it, they will not fight."

"We cannot destroy the yellow metal," said Loco.

"No, instead, we will take it, bury it in the mountain, where it will have no power over them. When they bring the metal for their soldiers, we will kill them and take it. Everything they value that moves across the land will find its grave here!"

"Enjuh!" said Cochise.

"Enjuh!" echoed the others.

Nana walked beside Geronimo as they descended the winding path of the tiny mountain. When they had fallen out of earshot of the others, Nana spoke.

"I fear we have brought this curse upon our people."

"I have no fear of the White Eyes, let there be war," said Geronimo.

"The yellow metal was not for us to take," said Nana.

"It has no power over me."

"You must stop taking the metal from the mountain."

"We need guns and bullets. For that, I would take it all."

"You must stop."

"I keep none for myself. What of Nana?"

"It has power of life and death, it serves me," said Nana.

"It has power over you," said Geronimo.

"Give me your word."

"So be it. You have the word of Geronimo, I will not take the yellow metal from the mountain."

"Then it is done," said Nana.

FOUR

February 14, 1863
Fishkill, New York

Samuel Sheldon took the road from Poughkeepsie toward Fishkill Landing. His imagination drifted with the falling snow, mesmerized by the meter of his horse's hooves crunching through the late winter ice. The canvas sack fixed to his saddle horn slapped in gentle polyrhythm against the horse's flank, from which Mangas Coloradas sang his death song.

It was a song he was not meant to hear, a prayer between the old chief and his maker. A lot of things happened that weren't meant to. General Joseph west happened. Two dim soldiers with a rifle happened. Sam did not kill Mangas, but he took his head with a hatchet and boiled it down to a skull; that happened too.

The skull was not a trophy. Rather it was a request from Danfort Collins, who was as concerned as Sheldon regarding Edwin Stanton's mysterious orders at Fort McLane. Sheldon was uncertain what Collins intended to do with the Apache's skull, but it was not his place to question.

Danfort Collins was a great man. Behind closed doors at hidden tables, where men decided the fates of nations, Collins was there, orchestrating secrets and speaking in whispers. He was a charter member of the Skull and Bones, along with its founders, William Huntington Russell and Alphonso Taft. Together they formed The Trust, the hidden table where Sheldon hoped to earn a seat. First, he needed only to prove his worth. Sheldon believed he had proved it in the New Mexico Territory, the proof swinging mournfully from his saddle horn.

He reached a fork in the road and came out of his trance. A small wooden sign poked out of the snow that read 322. He had arrived. The road was marked with heavy traffic, pummeling the snow to slush. Sheldon turned his horse down the road, and the song's cadence changed to a hiss as the horse's hooves slurped through the muddied mess of dirty snow.

The Octagon House rose out of a clearing in the tall pines at the end of the road. Conceived, designed, and constructed by noted phrenologist and lifestyle pundit Doctor Orson Squire Fowler, the house was as fascinating as it was massive. Fowler claimed the eight-sided design maximized light and usable living space. He suspected ulterior motives, likely rooted in the doctor's obsession with the occult and the spiritualist movement.

The house had four levels, the first three ringed in verandas. Symmetrically placed windows covered the entire structure like the facets of a jewel, oozing with brilliant light that refracted in the falling snow. A dark brick turret rose from the center of the roof, its dome formed from queer, milky green glass.

Sheldon dismounted at the gate, greeted by one of Fowler's odd septuplets. The man was skeletal thin with wispy white hair. He had the ambiguous look of a man that could be either fifty or a hundred years old.

His father, Jay Sheldon, often had business with Fowler over the years. As a child, he had once accompanied him on one of his deliveries to the Octagon House. The sight of four identical men in matching clothing assisting with the freight disturbed him greatly, and he shuddered to think of the picture of all seven together. Beyond their physical peculiarity, he had long suspected that they belonged to that unsettling phylum of humanity that produced the men of the Guild.

"Allow me to take your horse, sir. You are expected," said the timeless servant. His blue eyes reflected the house lights.

"Thank you." He removed the sack and handed the man the reins. "See that he's fed, it's been a long ride."

Sheldon followed the path toward the house, where laughter and singing poured out from every window. Danfort Collins reclined in a rocking chair, smoking his pipe in the only piece of shadow to be found on the veranda. Every button of his coat was fastened against the cold, his bushy grey beard fenced between his upturned collar. The curious lenses of his gold-framed glasses caught the light and reflected like golden mirrors.

"You've arrived, Sheldon."

"I have."

"Let's go inside," said Collins.

"Did you throw me a party?"

"Have you forgotten? It's the Bonesmen's Ball."

"Ah, I've been gone a long time."

He followed Collins through the double doors into the primary level of the house. While the outside appeared simple in its geometry, the interior was confounding. Rooms inexplicably opened into other rooms, while others were inaccessible unless entered from the veranda. Every space teemed with costumed guests, many wearing masks. The scene reminded him of a Hieronymus Bosch landscape. Oddly placed stairways confused their movement between floors, seemingly necessitating their passage through every room. Guests in all stages of dress and undress moved through the rooms like spawning salmon, reaching increasingly lofty heights of intoxication and debauchery.

He was grateful when their route required stepping out to the veranda to reach the fourth floor. Already his clothes were damp from spilled drinks and the humidity of Fowler's lascivious guests. Sheldon stared curiously up the stairs, the only apparent access to their destination.

One of Fowler's septuplets waited at the top of the staircase, ushering them to the fourth-floor entrance. Past the servant, another staircase led to the upper deck with its strange turret. Sheldon craned his neck for a view of the odd, glass-domed tower. Though the sky was dark and blanketed by snow clouds, the glass was luminous, as if filled with moonlight. Collins cleared his throat, indicating that he should follow. Sheldon turned back to the wispy-haired servant who now held open the door.

The fourth floor was dedicated entirely to the ballroom. A perfect circle of hardwood spread across the diameter of the space, edged by an octagon of black and gold carpet. Thick black drapes covered the eight floor-to-ceiling windows, so no light shone through. Velvet chairs and chaise lounges were placed symmetrically around the room, sitting between the eight dark wood columns.

Doctor Fowler sat almost invisible, reclining on a chaise lounge and sipping absinthe. He resembled a scarecrow dressed for the opera, his fine clothes ill-fitting his slender build. His thin gray hair clung firmly to his skull with pomade, and his triangular beard was so perfectly manicured that it could have been a wire brush. Upon noticing them, his eyes sharpened like a bird that caught sight of a worm.

"Welcome, friends!" Fowler said.

"Doctor Fowler," said Sheldon

Danfort Collins nodded.

"Captain Sheldon! Back from your expedition in the savage lands, very good!"

Doctor Fowler counted among the many men to visit his father at their home in Conway and was perhaps the most eccentric client of Jay Sheldon's shipping company. As a child, young Samuel would play in his father's warehouse, crawling among crates with labels written in strange languages, cryptic like hieroglyphs. The items came from exotic places he could only imagine, borne on his father's ship, the Albatross. They were always delivered by the dim and blank-faced guildsmen, Jay's silent and tireless laborers. Then men like Fowler would come, excited as children on Christmas morning, and haul the crates away. The business did well, making Jay Sheldon a wealthy man.

"Don't you think it's rude, Doctor, to keep this lovely ballroom all to yourself?" asked Sheldon. "Your guests are going feral from their confinement!"

"Such is the nature of the Order, stone of skin but wild of heart. A little chaos is all in good fun. Would you care for a refreshment, you must be exhausted from your travels?"

A door opened directly across the room from the main entrance. A thick black curtain concealed what lay beyond. One of the septuplets emerged from the dark void carrying a pair of petite glasses filled with absinthe and delivered them to Collins and Sheldon.

"No bourbon?" Collins asked.

"I'll not befoul my lips with it!" Fowler was indignant.

"Suit yourself," said Collins. "We have business, gentlemen. Shall we get to it?"

"Yes, of course," said Fowler. "Let us meet the scourge of Apacheria!"

Sheldon handed the sack to Fowler, who removed the skull. He held it up to the candlelight, noting the bullet hole with intense dissatisfaction.

"This is not good, not at all!"

He ran his fingers over the skull to the point above its right eye. The eye socket was not complete, and there was evident damage to the inside of the skull and a hole at the base where the bullet had exited.

"I told you, I need an intact specimen! What happened to him?"

"There were... problems."

"Is there anything you can do?" Collins asked.

"I will try," said Fowler. "Divination is my science, science requires precision."

"Do what you can," said Collins.

Fowler nodded and exited through the veranda door,

carefully clutching the skull. Sheldon noticed him turn toward the stairs that led to the rooftop tower.

"What is he going to do with it?"

"Do you believe it's possible to speak to the dead?"

"No." Sheldon furrowed his brow in confusion.

"You will."

A chill went down Sheldon's spine with Collins' unsettling assertation. He went to the window and drew back the curtain, watching the snow drift past the panes.

"Who is Morya?" he asked.

"How do you know that name?" Collins sat up.

"He came to me in the desert before I found Mangas."

"And you are just now mentioning this?"

"I didn't think it prudent to wire about it."

"I suppose not," said Collins, pacing the dance floor.

"He told me that Mangas was chosen, as I was chosen. Do you know what that means?"

"I'm not certain, but it is a troubling thought."

"Why is that?"

"Sam, you were chosen for the Trust, not by myself or the others, but by a much higher authority. The gold coin you carry is the evidence of that choice."

"What, like a badge or maker's mark?"

"No, nothing like that. Your coin is a seed from which a bond will grow."

"A bond, with who or what?"

"It's more than I would care to discuss right now, Sam. However, I never take Morya's words lightly, and if he says Mangas is 'chosen,' the implications are troubling."

"How so?"

"There are no accidents, not in our business. If Morya says he was chosen, there is a reason."

"It seems that Stanton certainly chose for him to die," said Sheldon.

"Another curious turn of the screw, though I will certainly get to the bottom of that mystery. Hopefully, Fowler can pry out his connection to the castle, and we can finally complete La Rue's work."

"I thought I was looking for a trove of gold, not a castle?"

"It's not an actual castle, you fool," Collins shook his head. "I realize there is a lot I haven't told you, but get used to it, that is the nature of our work."

"If you expect me to find something, don't you think I should know what it is?"

Collins paced from one end of the ballroom to the other, measuring his words, then returning to his seat on the chase, he drained his glass and thought some more.

"Sam, I once asked you of what use is gold."

"Yes, and I still don't know what you meant by it."

"Gold is more than a commodity. In fact, therein lies the irony of it all. Our Trust is dedicated to preserving and collecting it. The castles represent the culmination of our work."

"And ours is lost?"

"Unfortunately, it has been for generations."

"How does Mangas figure into all of this?"

"I wish I knew," Collins relit his pipe.

"What about this castle? How was it lost?"

"It has always been lost, really. It was only briefly discovered by a man named Padre LaRue. He oversaw one of the most significant accumulations of gold ever amassed in the western hemisphere. You see, our order goes back thousands of years and stretches to every corner of the world. The Trust is only our collective. Each generation chooses its own face, and this is ours. One constant is the papacy. One of our order has always sat upon the Chair of Saint Peter and worn the Ring of the Fisherman.

"In the time of Clement VIII, LaRue was an agent of the Pope. He sailed from Spain to the New World, ensconcing himself with the Jesuits in Mexico. There, he began a campaign of carnage, piracy, and subjugation. He and his brothers built a secret network across Mexico and the southwest. They plundered Spanish treasure ships loaded with Aztec gold, raided settlements, and developed rich gold mines.

"His last known location was a place called Santa Rosalia. The territorial governor received reports that something was very wrong at the mission. LaRue had enslaved the indigenous population and put them to work in the mine there. Worse, he did not pay his taxes to the governor. These accusations came in tandem with evidence tying him to piracy in the gulf and other crimes against the crown. When the Receptor arrived at Santa Rosalia to arrest LaRue, he found it and the nearby settlements razed to ash and corpses. Wagon tracks heading north were all that remained of the padre. Clement declared it an apostasy to save face with Spain but did little to assist in his arrest. I suppose he believed LaRue would turn up someday to fill the Vatican vaults with gold. He never did."

"We believe LaRue ended up somewhere in the New Mexico Territory. This hypothesis was bolstered when some warriors from Mangas' band turned up at a trading post with Aztec gold."

The door opened, and Fowler blew in with a draft of wet snow. He walked stiffly toward them, frowning and shaking his head.

"I failed," he said. "There's nothing I can do."

"Damn it," said Collins.

"Of course not!" said Sheldon. "You can't speak to the dead!"

"Sheldon!" Collins scolded. "What is the problem, Fowler?"

"He resisted mightily. He is beyond my skill to conjure."

"That is disappointing, Doctor, though we still may have an opportunity."

"Ah, yes, I'm sure Robert could be of service here if he

were to take our friend to Deer Island."

"Bobby Fucking Crow? The pariah of New Haven! Tell me, he's not part of this?"

"I thought you might know Mr. Black." Collins sipped his absinthe.

"Of course, I know of him. He and his dead girl are legendary at Yale," said Sheldon.

Robert Black was a Bonesman like himself. Before Collins' sponsorship of him, much of what he understood about the Trust came through the enigmatic whispers about Robert Black. Whenever a powerful banking executive turned up missing, a young real estate magnate died in his sleep, or when an incumbent congressman quietly chose not to seek re-election, it was said that Bobby Crow was flying somewhere nearby.

"I'm intrigued to hear what you know of the matter," said Collins

"I'm surprised it didn't intrigue the hangman."

"Now, Sam, you shouldn't spread such foul and nefarious rumors!" Fowler objected.

"I admit, my curiosity is piqued by these rumors," said Collins.

"As I understand it," said Sheldon. "Black was having a relationship with the daughter of one of his professors. Of course, this was frowned upon. Fearing her father would find out, she called it off with him. A few days later, her naked body turned up on a patch of grass near Connecticut Hall. Crows had been feasting on her corpse."

"Ghastly," said Collins.

"Complete hearsay, utter nonsense," Fowler said. "Robert was my ward. I raised him from the time he was a small boy, he would never commit a crime so heinous!"

"A dubious endorsement from a man that practices necromancy," said Sheldon.

"He loved Elizabeth, he would never kill her!"

"The world may never know," said Sheldon.

"Enough, gentlemen, we're all on the same side here," Collins raised his voice. "Robert Black will take the skull to Deer Island. Sam, you've had a long journey, it's time you get some rest. Perhaps you can bed in one of Fowler's guest rooms. Tomorrow I've got another task for you."

"I doubt I'd find one not being employed as a brothel! I'd be better off in the stable!"

"Suit yourself, just be ready in the morning."

FIVE

February 14, 1863
Smith Island, Maryland

The Albatross sailed west from Crisfield as the sun sank like a tarnished coin behind a veil of clouds. A frigid wind filled their sails from the northeast, where dark skies reached threateningly toward them. Thomas Rogers kept a wary eye on the approaching storm, though the captain of the vessel, Jay Sheldon, showed no concern.

He hated the Albatross and its cursed crew of Guildsmen. He found the way they moped about the dank timbers, silently laboring at their tasks, unsettling. His feelings toward Jay Sheldon, however, were warmer. In some ways, the Sheldons were a second family to him since attending William Russell's military academy with Sam. Russell adopted and gave him a home, but it was never a family. Terressa Sheldon did her best to offer kindness, including him in their holidays and family events.

"Gripping a bit tight, don't you think?" Virgil Price asked, waddling out from the warmth of the cabin.

"I don't sail," said Thomas.

"You ain't soft like those Yale boys, you'll do just fine."

In fact, Thomas Tadodaho Rogers had almost nothing in common with his white colleagues. Yale, or West Point, would undoubtedly be on the table for a man of Thomas's intelligence, resources, and connections if not for the color of his skin.

His father was a freeman from Vermont, a farrier by trade.

His mother was Haudenosaunee from the Onondaga tribe. Since Thomas could walk, he had few illusions of where he fit into the world of whites. Such lofty towers as Yale never entered his mind. Instead, he was raised on his grandmother's tales of the Six Nations, which was said to be his birthright to lead as Sachem. She was clan mother once but had lived in exile long before he was born. She promised to return someday, and he would be Sachem, bearing the title of his namesake, Tadodaho. Such a time would never come. His grandmother, mother, and father all perished before his ninth birthday.

The icy mist blew over the bow, and stalactites formed in the rigging.

"How's the General holding up these days? I haven't seen him since we laid Old Kinderhook low. He say anything about me?"

"Nothing," said Thomas.

"I see," said Price, the conversation dying with him.

Virgil Price was a loathsome creature, fat and squat, with lips like sausage links and eyes that would look more natural on stalks than a human face. Price was a necessary evil in the world of the Trust, a conduit through which their more unsavory transactions occurred. Presently he was their principal contact in Richmond and liaison to their southern interests, cut off by the war.

The pitch of the waves increased, and the dark clouds progressed from the east. Marshall steered ahead, oblivious. To the west, the daylight faded to a thin slate line, barely discernable on the horizon. Mist blew over the bow, stinging their faces, and the wind went on like some great asthmatic beast, circling the boat in the darkness.

"Port side," said Jay.

"That's the Fog Point Light," said Price. "It won't be long now."

"Good," said Thomas, squinting his eyes against the biting frost. "You're familiar with this place?"

"I've had some dealings here. Let's just say, my welcome has worn thin."

"That inspires confidence."

"Remember, you're John Dolly's man, that's your ticket. You're just there to trade this for that."

"Who is this John Dolly anyway?"

"A dead man," said Price

"Anything I ought to know?"

"Such as?"

"I don't know, that's why I'm asking," said Thomas. "What does he look like? Who's in his crew? What kind of nefarious bullshit are these cocksuckers familiar in?"

"John Dolly don't deal with the likes of the Tyler clan, at least not on a personal basis," said Price

. "In fact, sending a negro is just the kind of insult they would expect from old John. It's perfect."

"Yes, perfect."

They sailed south around the dim beam of the Fog Point Light, and the coastline began to materialize out of the darkness. Snow was swirling with the freezing mist, and the black clouds now seethed overhead. Jay kept his distance from the frozen marsh of Smith Island's shores. Plates of ice drifted sluggishly in the frozen surf, fading into the darkness of what Thomas assumed would eventually be solid land.

"Full of dead heads, rocks, and God knows what," said Price. "Whole place is sinking. On a clear day, you can see down to the chimneys of the houses that used to be."

The Albatross cut toward the center of the blackness into a narrow inlet, where the ice thinned but did not cease. There they dropped anchor, and several guildsmen lowered a dinghy over the rail. Jay pointed to a destroyed pier on the southern shore where jagged pilings rose out of the ice like frozen fangs.

"You'll want to land there," said Jay.

"Watch your step," said Price as Thomas climbed over the icy rail. "Follow the shore east. If you see lights, that'll be Ewell, and you've gone too far."

"Understood," he said, checking his pistol.

"One more thing, there ain't no silver this time."

Price reached over and handed Thomas a small leather pouch.

"Make sure they're counted, direct from Morya," said Price.

"You've seen Morya?"

"No, it was his minion, the poet, though the message was clear."

"And Virgil Price makes a profit," said Thomas.

"Just do your work, son, don't think too hard about it," said Price.

Thomas emptied the pouch into his palm, four rubies, each the size of a small grape, shone blood red in the moonlight. He carefully returned them to the bag, placed it in his pocket, and sat down at the oars.

When he reached the broken pilings, he hopped over the side into the frozen mud. His boots were sucked in by the sludge, and snow began falling in earnest. He went east, finding his path over a frozen mudflat. A skeletal stand of trees cut in toward the shoreline, inviting him to deviate for a more concealed approach.

He quickly spotted their lookout, a boy of maybe fifteen, shuffling back and forth for warmth near a crumbling stone wall. Thomas smelled smoke. Undoubtedly, the shack was near, concealed in the darkness beyond the young sentry. He circled quietly around the shivering watchman until the structure came into sight, a modest collection of planks leaning seaward in leisurely decay. Outside, several dozen crab pots were stacked tall and recklessly near a sad skiff sitting low in the water, moored at the tiny dock there. He heard the voices of three other men squabbling incoherently within. Thomas observed the site for a moment before doubling back toward the sentry.

"You Tyler's man?" Thomas asked when he was a few paces behind the young man.

"Jaaysus!"

"I could hear your teeth chattering from around the point."

"Yah, I'm Aaron Tyler. You'll want not to be frightening folks, it gets you shot!" scolded the boy, thick in the peculiar dialect of the watermen.

"I am not concerned."

The boy frowned. Thick wedges of brown hair jutted out of his wool cap, where traces of snow settled on the folded edges. He brushed the offending hair back with his mitten-encased hand, rendering his trigger finger helpless to follow through on his threat.

"Dolly's man then, are ya?"

"That's right."

"Cam' on then. This way."

They trudged together on an established route along the shore. Thomas took mind of the tracks and their age in the snow. He saw no evidence to suggest a larger presence at the shack. The winds picked up, and the driving snow stung their eyes like cold sand.

Reaching the shack, the boy swung the door inward with a hard, sweeping blow from his fist and forearm. The walls shook with the force of it.

"I fond 'em!"

Three men turned from the hearth in unison, regarding the youngster with exasperated glares. Their beards were steel gray and wild, faces worn like they had been eroded from sandstone. The men shared a semblance of features; protruding brows, thick mouths, and deep-set eyes common among the Tyler clan.

"So ya ded," said the oldest of the three. "Naw shut tha dam daar!"

"You Tyler?" asked Thomas, standing fully in the shack so the boy could close the door.

"Cheston Tyler, I am. These are my brothers, and that's my boy, Aaron." said the grizzled waterman. "You ain't John Dolly, for sure you ain't!"

"My name is Thomas Rogers. Is that a problem?"

"No," said the elder Tyler. "Odd lookin' for a negro, you are."

"My mother is of the Six Nations," he said, looking around the single-room dwelling. Neglected crab pots lay heaped in piles, creating nearly unnavigable clutter. One lay in the process of repair on a rickety table, the room's only piece of furniture.

"Six what?"

"Iroquois, you'd call them."

"Ahh, gawdless heathens, ya mean!"

"With respect, gentlemen," said Thomas. "I'm here to execute a transaction, nothing more. If it pleases you, I would like to proceed."

"Wood ya then, ha, pra-ceed!"

"Produce the notes, please."

"Oblige em' boy," said Cheston, gesturing toward a stack of bedding in the corner.

The young Tyler reached the bottom of the bedding and withdrew two heavy, fat leather satchels. Reaching in, Aaron produced a bundle of neatly stacked, hundred-dollar CSA notes. He repeated the process with the other satchel, confirming that both bags were indeed filled with counterfeit bills.

"Sha me yars, Mr. Nations!"

Thomas reached into his jacket, withdrew the tiny leather sack, and emptied the contents into the palm of his hand. The gems shone translucent red in the firelight.

"Blood must be paid," said Thomas.

"Blood, is it?" said Cheston, drifting between Thomas and the door.

The other two Tyler brothers drew their pistols. Outside, the wind howled, and the snow mindlessly obeyed. The boy backed slowly away into the collection of pots.

Thomas smiled, a broad and open smile, like a snake unhinging its jaw. From the back of his mouth, four golden molars caught the dim light of the hearth fire. The other awakened within him.

"Who sent ya?" Cheston asked. His pistol had migrated to

his hand.

Thomas began cutting.

Old Cheston stared dumbfounded at his dangling digits, unaware that his intestines were pooling in his woolen shirt like a lumpy pot belly. Thomas dashed away as the two Tylers unloaded their pistols, perforating Cheston with their errant shots. He fell back against the door, gray and pink innards sliding out of his shirt.

With two quick slashes, he sliced the throats of the two remaining brothers. Frothy blood bubbled around the wounds as they gurgled in rage, fingers pulling desperately at their triggers. The hammers fell on empty chambers as the two tangled in an awkward waltz and fell into the clutter of broken crab pots. A steady carpet of blood stretched out toward the hearth.

Thomas turned his gaze to the boy, recoiling in the corner of the shack. Picking up a hatchet from the pile of broken crab traps, he tested its balance as he crossed the bloody planks. A tiny stream of urine ran down the boy's leg and puddled at his feet.

"Take this," he said, tossing it at Aaron Tyler's feet. "Get to chopping up these bodies, small enough to fit in the crab traps."

"What," he whimpered.

"I'm told your family has been slurping down crab guts for generations, it's time to return the favor."

"Please, mister," the boy begged.

Tiring of the boy's hesitance, Thomas raised his blade. Something stayed his hand, an undefinable urge to spare the boy. It came from the hollow place within the golden cage of his bones. Was it pity? Or perhaps a deeper directive from the other, some whispered warning. Thomas could not say.

"You ain't made for this work," he said. "Find another life if you can."

The boy stared at him with empty brown eyes.

"Go on!" he said.

The boy ran past his father's corpse and pushed through the door, vanishing into the swirling snow.

Thomas retrieved the two heavy satchels of counterfeit notes and set them outside the cabin, then spread lamp oil around the room. He made a pyre of Cheston Tyler's shack using the damaged pots as kindling. He took the bags and hastily made his way west to the boat. Undoubtedly the fire, if not the boy, would bring attention to the carnage.

When he reached the dinghy, he removed the pouch from his pocket and emptied it into his palm. There were three common gray stones and one blood-red ruby. Thomas tossed the three rocks into the icy water, then held the remaining ruby up to the moon, examining it curiously. He tucked it back into his pocket and pushed the boat offshore.

"You get my money?" Price called down from the Albatross as Thomas rowed near.

"I got it, you fucking vulture," Thomas tossed the satchels over the rail and onto the deck.

"My services don't come free, young man," said Price. "Did you keep the count?"

"I did," Thomas lied.

"Good," said Price. "That was Morya's end, not mine."

February 15, 1863
Near Norfolk, Virginia

The confederate ironclad was making its second pass, Jay could wait no longer. He had seen his share of broken deals in his decades of service to the Trust and the Russell family. From his humble beginnings smuggling opium out of China for Sam Russell, Samuel Sheldon's namesake, to even more illicit freight from Jamaica and

Bavaria for William Russell, Jay had seen some queer things. However, never had one of their own failed to deliver when gold was on the charter.

Yet, Price had done just that. If there were an inkling of hope, Jay would know it. It would announce its coming in the strange heat of the dead wind. There was no hint of it here, only a curious ironclad in hostile waters.

Jay gave the order to lift anchor, and the sails were raised. The ghostly helmsman caught the wind and guided the Albatross from the murky shores. They sailed north toward the Union blockade, content to not be further harassed by the rebel warship.

Jay could not imagine what kind of fool would betray the Trust in such a profound way, even Price, filled with venom as he was, valued his head more than that. Whatever ill plot was afoot, he was confident of one thing; the General, William Russell, would not be pleased.

February 17, 1863
New Haven, Connecticut

William Russell stood in review. These were fine boys, tough and disciplined. Of the twelve boys that had started the exercise, nine had finished, one had retired to the infirmary kicked by his horse, and two were cinching the girth on their mounts almost simultaneously. It was unlikely that a circumstance would arise that required the blind saddling of a horse, but that was not the point. Russell forged his cadets to excel over any obstacle, regardless of any disadvantages inflicted by fate.

The two boys fumbled with their cinches, feeling for slack. It wasn't a race, but neither wanted to be last. When the eleventh pulled his blindfold, he was relieved yet not pleased at his place in the order. The twelfth slipped his blindfold off a second later, radiating disappointment.

"Fine work, all of you! Now stable those beasts and get some grub!" said Russell.

The boys gave a rigid salute, then led their horses toward the stable.

He was known as the General and always had been, earning the moniker decades before his appointment to the State Militia or founding his military academy for boys. War was in his blood, though not the wars of squabbling nations. His battles were fought on strange shores, in forsaken places overlooked by righteous sovereignties. There were not, nor would there ever be, any statues or plaques to mark his victories. Nevertheless, the ramifications of his conquests quietly reverberated across the globe.

"Thomas, you're like the voice of the leaves."

Thomas Rogers stepped out of the shade of the tree line and stood in the gray-lavender light of the Connecticut sunset. His black pants and jacket seemed to absorb sunlight, concealing his thin limbs and knotty muscles. Standing on the parade grounds, his shadow stretched out like the bony hand of a winter tree. Only his eyes betrayed life, perched in his skull like black globes of marble.

"Only when I choose to speak."

Thomas pulled the hood of his jacket up over his smooth-shaved head, and his face retreated into the shade of it like some murderous monk. Only his chin was visible, pocked with a crescent scar below the thin slit that was his mouth.

Russell's academy graduated some of the nation's finest soldiers and future leaders. To date, neither West Point nor Yale had refused a single student, with the notable exception of his most talented pupil and protege, Thomas Tadodaho Rogers. If West Point accepted black or mix raced cadets,

Russell had little doubt that Thomas would be at the top of his class.

"Walk with me, Thomas."

Russell pulled his collar up to where it met the coarse hair of his beard. The winter chill ran deep, and only days ago, it snowed. He led Thomas across the compound toward the headmaster's house. He felt more comfortable in this two-room cabin than with his wife and family in their sprawling property on Miller's Hill.

The cabin's front room was sparsely furnished, occupied only by an oak desk, a small cabinet, and a solitary chair. Hewn in the wall above his desk, a single window allowed entry to the last light of the day. He lit a lamp sitting on the otherwise clean desktop, then sat behind it.

"I've just received a distressing wire from Jay Sheldon," said Russell. "Price did not deliver the Richmond gold."

"What? Was he intercepted?"

"No, according to Van Lew and other sources, there has been no significant activity at the banks nor near the harbor. Price has just vanished."

"How are we to extract the bullion now? He had the only access!"

"How indeed," said Russell. "Did Price say or do anything out of character on Smith? Act in such a way as to arouse your suspicion?"

"Everything about Virgil Price is suspicious," said Thomas. "He's been running unfettered since Van Burren passed."

"So, nothing unusual?"

"No, plenty unusual. Instead of silver, he brought rubies from Morya."

"What!? You're just now telling me this?"

"I thought you knew. Rubies do not come lightly."

"I haven't spoken to Morya since the funeral at Kinderhook, yet he chooses Virgil Price, of all people, to be his voice? Why should Morya want the Tylers dead with such prejudice to invoke rubies in the matter? This is extremely unsettling,

Thomas."

"It is not my place to question, sir. I thought you were abreast of the situation."

"You're right, Thomas, I don't blame you."

"He also asked about you personally, if you had mentioned him at all."

"Certainly fishing for information, perhaps to test how close I was monitoring him. There is no doubt now that Virgil Price has betrayed us. I hate to admit it when I'm wrong, but Collins has had doubts about Price for some time now. All of this couldn't have come at a worse time. We're on the cusp of a significant step forward in finding La Rue's gold. We don't need these distractions!"

"General, a question..."

"Certainly, Tom. What is it?"

"About Deer Island, does Mr. Collins still intend on sending Robert Black?"

"Yes, Thomas." Russell examined his student. "You think it should have been you?"

"Yes."

"We all have our talents. Robert Black's happen to lean toward the esoteric."

"Mine is killing, is that it?"

"Thomas, there is much more to it than that. You're different, you always have been."

The flickering lantern cast Thomas' shadow like a wicked undulating tree against the naked pine logs, though he stood perfectly still.

"Only the clan mother decides who hears the voices. My grandmother was clan mother, and I was to be Sachem, that place is my birthright."

"I've given you a new birthright, lest you forget. I wish I could. The memory haunts my dreams to this day."

Thomas opened his mouth wide to argue, the lamplight finding the gold in his mouth, reflecting like the sun on a dark lake.

"You gave me this! While others are so blessed to receive a coin, buckle, or some other innocent bauble. You could not be satisfied with such gifts. No, you lashed me to a chair, ripped out my teeth, and poured molten gold in the bleeding holes!"

"Watch your tongue, Thomas. You don't know what you speak of."

"I speak to the changes in my body and soul of the voiceless whisperer you put inside me."

Russell stood and reached into his pocket, removing a slender rectangular piece of gold the size of a playing card. He held the tiny plaque to the lamp, revealing strange engravings, part hieroglyph, part writing. The symbols reflected in reverse on the desk, they changed and moved with the flames. Thomas stared transfixed at the shifting landscape of golden words.

"We all bond with Him in our own fashion. You may not see it, but you were lucky, you had me."

"It feels like misfortune."

"I had no such guidance, I was confronted by a dead man who offered me greatness or death. I sailed halfway across the globe before I realized I had even made that choice. It took the prattling of a broken old hierophant to explain that I was not alone, nor would I be ever again. Be grateful, Thomas. Your path is clear. I've made it for you."

"I made no choice."

"Didn't you?"

Thomas did not answer.

"Your grandmother, the witch, had her secrets. We have ours. Count yourself privileged that I give you mine freely, where she took hers to the grave." Russell's tone softened as he spoke, and he ended his words with a hint of a smile.

"Yes, sir. Is that all?"

"Probably not." The smile faded. "For now, head to Fishkill. I'll meet you there."

Thomas Rogers exited wordlessly, slipping into the cold Connecticut night as quietly as he had come.

SIX

February 16, 1863
Kinderhook, New York

Winter clung to the gravestones in the pine-lined clearing, and the wind blew with cold malice. The stones here reflected meager means. Locals called it a slave cemetery, but gold, or the lack of it, determined its residents. Sheldon found the privacy he required among these neglected and unvisited graves. The dead in attendance paid no mind to his pick and shovel.

Some things are better done at night. Samuel Sheldon qualified graverobbing among them. With such a distasteful task, waiting was the easy part. He needed an hour so lonely and dark that not even the moon would be watching. An intimate hour fit for wretched work. That time had not come.

It was his mother's birthday, and he wondered if she had received the letter he sent. Jay Sheldon gave her the silver key on her birthday, the year Sam was born. It opened no lock, but she treasured it and kept it on a chain around her neck. When he joined the Army after Yale, presumably bound for the war, she passed the heirloom on to him. Unlike her husband, Teressa was a creature of sentiment. He wondered if his father even remembered her birthday; those weren't the types of milestones Jay Sheldon tended to observe of late. He wished he could be home with her now, celebrating. Instead, he sat on a cold rock in a potter's field, waiting for an exceptionally dark hour.

As he sat, he held his hands out like scales, the silver key in one, the gold coin in the other. It was a familiar meditation he liked to believe kept him balanced and focused. As he sat, his hand tipped lower on the side of the coin, that was duty. For some time now, the coin seemed to be gaining weight and importance, not only in the figurative sense of his exercise but in an objective, literal sense. The key now seemed like a feather.

He never fully understood the gift of the Caligula coin. It was brought to him by Danfort Collins, who insisted it was anything but a coin. Its significance was both profound and hidden. Like a father constantly procrastinating to explain life's mysteries, Collins promised to reveal its secrets in time. His own father, Jay Sheldon, seemed to understand its importance but shunned from acknowledging the thing altogether.

Sam knew nothing of necromancy, not even whether he believed in it. However, he believed in Danfort Collins, and Danfort Collins was a great man. One day, Sheldon wanted to be, like Collins, a man of fate and consequence who decided things, whose whims charted the courses of nations. He wanted to stroll through the halls of Congress and write laws with his raised eyebrows and subtle nods. When presidents gave inaugural speeches, he wanted them to feel him standing in the throng and to know who allowed that moment to be. When kings sent their fleets to sea, he would be the wind in the sails. The ink of every declaration of war or peace treaty would come from his well and be written on his stock. No one would speak his name, save in hallowed places of prayer when they petitioned not for God's mercy but for his. Danfort Collins was such a man. If Collins sent him to Kinderhook, deep in the icy hold of winter, his reasoning would not be questioned. He would complete his task and prove worthy of his trust. If that task involved exhumation, so then was the price of greatness.

When the hour came, the air grew colder, and clouds rolled over the moon like hands, mercifully covering its sight. Sheldon slung the pick and shovel over his shoulder with the empty canvas sack and made toward the pines and the graveyard that sprawled beyond.

A short distance through the pines, the rest of the necropolis stretched out on a snow-crusted carpet of Kentucky bluegrass. The living flaunted their wealth in handsome mansions and pretentious social stratification, a habit carried into the afterlife. The ornate monuments and mausoleums at Kinderhook distinguished the financially elite from those fiscally unworthy of proper remembrance. He had no problem finding the one he was looking for. It was grand, fit for a president.

His boots slurped and crunched through the virgin snow in a rhythm that invoked thoughts of Mangas and his death song. The monuments tapered upward in size as he neared his destination. These men and women were not great; no memorial can mark greatness. They merely reveal the vanity of the dead.

He reached the spot. A tall stone obelisk stood out against the gray clouds. Sheldon paced out his dig in the snow, each boot-fall a syllable in a song he was never meant to hear. He broke earth and the song continued as his pick carved its way through the soil. It continued as he shoveled out the loose dirt; old Mangas would never cease singing.

The raw, pungent-smelling dirt began accumulating in a wet, icy mud pile beside the grave. A morbid vigor fueled him to a remarkable pace. He did not tire, nor did the cold creep through his gloves, and blisters did not trouble his hands. The earth moved with ease and speed that Sheldon did not question.

His shovel struck something hard, and he bent down to brush away the dirt, revealing the oval top of a rosewood casket. As if by design, the clouds pulled away from the moon and provided just enough light for Sheldon to read the inscription on the silver plaque:

MARTIN VAN BUREN
DIED JULY 24, 1862

AGED 79 YEARS, 7 MONTHS, AND 19 DAYS

The lid came open with relative ease, requiring only minimal prying. Rot stench escaped the casket, causing Sheldon to gag and nearly retch. The body was well preserved, probably embalmed. The eyelids closed over sunken craters, and the skin receded over the skull like wet leather dried in the sun. Wispy tufts of thin white hair puffed out the sides of his head in delicate, ash-like tendrils. He had the impression that the whole head might cave in with the ease of a rotten egg.

Sheldon reached into the canvas sack, removed a bone saw, then straddled the corpse in its coffin.

"Hello, Mr. President," he said. "I'm very sorry about this..."

The ease of labor continued as he put the saw to work. He fought off the urge to vomit as the blade took purchase on the neck vertebrae. Fortunately, the head did not collapse, even under the considerable force of his hand on its forehead, keeping it stable. Undefinable fluids leaked out and soaked the President's collar, and bits of loose flesh flaked off, adhering to the silk-lined walls. Finally, the whole head tore free, and he placed it in the canvas sack with the saw.

The air cooled even more as he filled the grave and the moon retreated to the clouds again. Snow began to fall as Sheldon replaced the section of grassy sod under the obelisk. First in crystal-shaped flakes, then in lighter and more numerous offerings.

His boots sang Mangas' song through the new snow as he walked back through the field of gravestones. He looked over his shoulder before stepping into the pines. Everything was white, and not a blade of Kentucky bluegrass could be seen.

SEVEN

February 1863
Superstition Mountains, Arizona Territory

Summer was monsoon season in the Sonoran. When the rains came, they did so with sudden and biblical strength. Water rushed down the washes and arroyos with enough force to carry a man away. Typically, July spawned the fiercest storms. At noon, a traveler might be gasping for water only to be drowned and washed away by twelve-fifteen. Everything in the desert had killing on its mind. Why should the rain be any different?

February was the perfect time to adventure into the Superstitions, if such a thing could be said. This thought did not occur to Pedro as he and Andres sheltered from the unseasonal storm under a rocky shelf. Water came down the hillside in torrents, threatening to wash their camp into the river. The storm came on so swiftly that they only had enough time to hitch the animals to the nearby ironwood trees. It kept them out of the wash but provided little shelter from the rain.

The storm broke a string of fortuitous days the Gonzales brothers had been enjoying. After the affair with the Apache, they followed the old Butterfield trail east. Luck smiled on them in a mining camp called Lordsburg. A skilled assay was in residence and proved willing to purchase the brother's ore. The price was fair enough that they could outfit themselves with another horse and two burros and the equipment and provisions they required for their expedition. Andres was so consumed with optimism that Pedro could not help but become infected with it himself, going so far as to rename Mangas' horse Fortune.

The journey to the Rio Salado was largely uneventful. There was plenty of grass for the animals, and potable water was plentiful. Though they encountered no one along the way, Pedro could not help feeling they were being watched. For all his time in Apacheria, that usually meant that he was.

They had just arrived at Pedro's former campsite and gotten a fire going when the rains came.

The storm intensified. Lightning devoured the sky, illuminating the rain with an unnatural silver color as it roared against the rocks. Pedro sat helpless as the engorged river splashed over their firepit and absconded with their coffee pot. Two tin cups, Andres' hat, and a handful of oranges went bobbing downstream after it.

A lightning strike whited out the sky, followed by an earth-rending cacophony, and the ironwood securing Fortune split in flames. The horse screamed and bolted from the wreckage of the tree. Andres caught sight of him galloping back down the trail they came in on. He rose to give pursuit, but Pedro grabbed him by the belt and pulled him back to their shelter. In morbid silence, they watched the river consume their firepit, claiming more of their gear.

The rain lasted till nightfall. Then, as abruptly as it came, the storm vanished into a multitude of stars. They gathered what they could find of the gear and laid it out on flat rocks to dry when the sun rose. The pack mules and remaining horse were spooked but otherwise unharmed by the ordeal. When they accomplished all that could be done, they found a soft bit of earth between two boulders and huddled together for warmth. The night passed in a dreamless instant, replaced by the welcome warmth of the sun.

Cold and wet, they picked themselves off the ground and surveyed the consequences of the storm. Pedro had never wanted a cup of hot coffee more than he did at that moment.

The river had receded and returned to its original state. A hefty branch of the lightning-struck tree formed an eddy in the river where it fell. To Andres's delight, he found his sombrero caught in its tangled branches.

"Hey, a tiny miracle!" Andres said. He fished the hat out of the bramble and brushed off the sand.

"Now, if the river would only return our coffee pot, I could make a cup of miracle," said Pedro.

"Not to worry, soon we will make our pots out of gold!"

"Perhaps," said Pedro. He reached into the breast pocket of his jacket and removed the Bible he carried with him. He undid the leather strap and opened it to the page where the folded map was secured. "Ah! Dry as a bone!"

"You see," said Andres. "More good news!"

Pedro unfolded the map and laid it on one of the rocks near their soaked bedding.

"Here, look."

Andres squatted down next to him.

"Where are we?"

"We are here." Pedro pointed at a spot on the map. "Here is the cache that I recovered. It is right below the mine that produced the ore."

"That's not far from here," said Andres. "How long do you think?"

"Maybe a day? Perhaps a bit longer. The terrain is very rough. The way is not always good for horses."

"Do you know where it happened?"

"Where what happened?"

Andres donned his saturated sombrero, steam rising from his head like a halo.

"The battle where the Indians caught them."

"I don't know, it isn't marked on the map," said Pedro. "But if I had to guess, it would be over here," he pointed.

"That's where many of our kin fell. I would like to find the place. If we can raise a marker or pay our respects, we should.

Pedro folded the map and secured it in his Bible.

"Yes, Don Miguel would be grateful if we did. But now, I should track down Fortune. Hopefully, he is still near."

"Good idea. I can get a fire going and see what I can do about breakfast.

Steam began to rise from the blankets stretched out on the rocks. The sun climbed in the sky with the promise of a warm day. Pedro retrieved his saddle from the rock and saddled Andres's horse.

"I will leave the rifle with you. I have my pistol," Pedro said. "I won't be long."

"Good luck, Brother. Maybe bring home some breakfast while you're at it!"

Pedro followed the path the horse had taken the night before. The trail would rise and give him a decent vantage of the river and the surrounding terrain. Previously, they passed a clearing with easy river access where they debated camping, a logical place for a horse to graze and take water.

Life proliferated along the river. Lizards sunned themselves, small birds lingered in multitudes, and rattlesnakes shook their greetings from grassy beds. One large rock near the trail formed a natural basin where a cluster of yellow butterflies gathered to drink or breed, possibly both.

Pedro reached the clearing, relieved to find Fortune there, grazing on a creosote bush. He dismounted and approached the stray. Fortune remained docile and gave no resistance as Pedro looped a rope around his neck to make a crude leash. Having secured the runaway, he led both horses to the river to drink.

Something caught his eye as he bent down to fill his water skin; a glint of metal shone from a tiny inlet made by a sand bar. There, half-submerged and bobbing in the river was his coffee pot. He grabbed a stick and stretched out to catch the pot's handle, which floated just out of reach. In Pedro's opinion, a man could overcome almost any trouble if he had a strong cup of coffee. Hope swelled as he anticipated getting a pot over the fire.

A gunshot shattered the serenity, sending a rooster tail splashing upwards as it ricocheted off the submerged rocks at Pedro's feet. Startled, he lost his balance and fell into the river with his coffee pot. Leaping up in a panic, he put himself behind the horses and looked for his attacker. Several more shots rang out, pinging off the rocks at his feet and echoing across the river. Andres's horse broke free and charged back up the trail toward camp.

Pedro leaped up on Fortune's bare back and dug his heels into the horse's flank, commanding him to the trail. Blood splashed on his cheek, followed swiftly by pain. It was like a bullwhip slashed across his shoulder, leaving a wake of torn flesh and ripped cloth. Instinctively, he looked at his shoulder and then back at his attacker. The shot had only grazed him, but the mounted man behind him was leveling his pistol for another try.

The stranger spurred his horse and charged forward in pursuit. His hat came loose and dangled behind him by the chin strap, causing his aim to be distracted. Pedro tried to count how many shots his attacker had fired. It seemed like long division amid his frenzied flight. The answer bounced against his thigh. Pedro had six shots regardless of what his pursuer may still have chambered.

Fortune carried him over a rise in the trail, and Pedro pulled back hard on his mane. When his horse reared, he leaped from its back and rolled to the side. The stranger was directly behind him, and his horse spun wildly in a circle to avoid a collision, spoiling his aim. Pedro drew his Colt Navy revolver and took aim at his attacker.

Click. Click. Click... the cylinder spun with no report. Either the rains or the river had got at his powder. Click. The attacker now caught sight of Pedro and leveled his pistol. The Anglo stared down the barrel bearing the countenance of a man poised to dispatch a rat or some other bothersome pest.

Click.

The man eyed Pedro's gun and settled his hand as his horse

fought the reins.

Pedro's final chamber came alive and sent its load careening through his enemy's chest. The man was thrown from his horse, falling awkwardly with one foot stuck in the stirrup. The horse bucked the corpse, sending it to the rocky trail crackling with shattered bones.

He stood over the dead white man while his now calm horse began to graze. Pedro pondered the origin of the contorted corpse. Rancher, scalper, settler, or generic killer? He did not know. The man sprawled across the trail with a blood-soaked crater of flannel sunk into his chest; Pedro counted himself fortunate it was not his body lying there. This was the first man he ever killed.

"Sorry!" he said. "I'm sorry, but you were shooting and-"

Gunshots in the distance interrupted his apology.

Pedro saw a shotgun sheathed on the dead man's horse. He snatched it up, hopped on Fortune's back, and sped up the trail toward camp.

The gunfire ceased just before he reached the camp. As he rounded the bend in the trail, it came into view. Four white faces turned as Pedro rode up on them. Their shocked expressions indicated that he was not who they were expecting. Laying between the white men, bloody and lifeless, lay the body of Andres.

Pedro emptied both barrels into the cluster of men. The closest collapsed in a cloud of red mist, taking the brunt of the blast. Another fell to the ground grabbing his knee, blood oozing between his fingers. One of the men raised a rifle to defend himself.

He tossed the empty shotgun and dug his heels into his horse's flank; Fortune responded and accelerated down the trail. Several rifle shots thundered, followed by a wet thud as a bullet found his thigh. Fire raged through him and blurred his vision. Fortune screamed and raced faster, defying all attempts to guide him. Pedro held on in primal fear as the horse chose their path.

They deviated from the river trail at the first opportunity, charging up a narrow canyon with the ghost of a creek running through the center. They crossed the creek and went up the canyon, where the terrain was less rocky. There were no more shots. Behind him, he could see only the dust kicked up by Fortune's hooves and none from pursuit.

Pedro's pants leg was soaked in blood, some his own, some Fortune's. The bullet passed through his leg and into the flank of his horse. He was becoming dizzy as blood poured out of his thigh. Finally, he forced his horse to stop in the shade of a rocky bluff. He slid off the saddle and tried to stand but found it impossible. He looked out at the saguaros, trying to focus his vision. Pedro realized he knew where he was. He was sure that if he went back to the mouth of the canyon, the first saguaro would have the image of a knife carved in it. He had been here before.

The sun was rising high in the sky, and its heat felt oppressive. He had to keep moving. He pulled himself up and stood on his good leg, using his horse for balance. Fortune's flank was wet with blood. The saguaros blurred into monstrous shapes with wild and malicious arms reaching for him.

"Come on, Fortune. We can't stay here."

Pedro took a step forward, and the world went black.

The throbbing in Pedro's leg alerted him that he was not dead. His body felt like bread in a brick oven. Flies buzzed mercilessly around his head and crawled around the cracks of his eyes, only slightly deterred by his fluttering eyelashes. Thirst was the only thing greater than the surging fire in his leg. He tried to rise, but the world grayed around him, and he fell, the inches feeling like miles.

"Take this, don't drink too fast."

The words were in Spanish.

Something hit the dirt in front of his face, heavy with the faint sloshing of water within. The flies scattered from his face and buzzed around in a cloud. The voice was familiar. It was not friendly, but not hostile either.

Pedro opened his eyes. Andres' water skin was inches from his face. Beyond that, he perceived legs rising to a height he could not bring his head to see. Again, he summoned his muscles into service and tried to push himself up on his side. Again, he failed.

"Here," the voice said.

His focus returned, aided by recognition of the stranger, the scar-faced Apache called Geronimo. He stooped down and offered the water skin. The water soaked into his dry cheeks and tongue like a sponge, then slowly into his throat. It seemed like none of it made its way to his stomach. Geronimo rationed the sips into three conservative draughts. The water was hot, like soup, causing him to gag when it finally started to fill his belly.

"You did not die, good for you," Geronimo said. "But you still might."

"How long?" Pedro gasped.

"We found you yesterday. We killed the whites."

"Andres..."

Pedro pushed himself to his knees but could go no further. The pain in his leg seared, and his eyes twitched and burned. He wept, but his body was too dry to provide tears. Even his lips proved too dry and broken to pray.

"You carried Mangas from our enemies. You are not like the whites or other Mexicans. We carried you from your enemies."

Pedro took the skin from Geronimo and took a long pull. His composure began to return, and he examined his surroundings. They were in a wide, shallow cave. The white light of the sun streamed in at its mouth. Three others sat by a small fire, drying meat on flat rocks. He recognized Fun and Chewawa from the business with Mangas, but the other he did not.

Chewawa gathered a few pieces of dried meat and passed them to Geronimo, who, in turn, gave them to Pedro. It was dark and brown and completely unidentifiable. Pedro put it in his mouth and began to chew it with water.

"I know why you have come here," Geronimo said.

"How's that?" Pedro replied.

Geronimo tossed a small metal ingot that splashed with a dense thud in the powdery dust at Pedro's knees. It was crudely forged, dull, pitted, and clinging with slag. Unmistakably, though, it was gold. Then he held up Pedro's map.

"It was you that followed us," said Pedro.

"You will die seeking the yellow metal. It's not for you. Long ago, my people killed the Mexicans who made their mines here. They will do so again."

"I traveled so far, lost so much," Pedro whispered. "My brother..."

"You have been given much," said Geronimo. "You have been given life... again!"

Pedro did not answer. The scales in his mind swayed in the breeze of indecision. Live with failure and loss or die in anonymity with his bleached bones marking the precipice just below achievement.

"I choose life," he said, and the scales came into balance.

"One more gift, a name. I call you Na'hi'da; he lives again."

The corners of Geronimo's mouth tilted in the suggestion of a smile.

Pedro held the ingot in his hand and let the heft of his dreams slip from his fingers. There was pain, enough to make him forget his leg for a moment, followed by peace.

"Take that. If you are strong enough to make it out of the mountains, maybe it will help you yet," Geronimo said.

"Thank you," said Pedro.

Chewawa brought him another hunk of dried meat, and he

drank again from the skin. His leg had been bandaged and packed with dried moss. The pain was severe, but it showed no sign of infection. After a time, he forced himself to stand and put some weight on it. Geronimo was right; it was no certainty that he would escape the mountains.

"There is a stone corral down the slope and to the east. Your horse is there," Chewawa said as he kicked dirt into the fire and smothered the flames.

"Goodbye, Na'hi'da. Do not return to the Thunder God's Mountain. No Indeh will see you as friend," Geronimo said, his features turning to shadow against the bright white sunlight in the mouth of the cave.

"Are we friends?" Pedro asked.

"We are not enemies," said Geronimo.

"If you find yourself as far south as Chihuahua, look for me north of Parral. I own a rancheria there."

Geronimo paused, then disappeared into the white, and Pedro was alone, baking in the afternoon heat.

"What a fool I am, inviting an Apache home for dinner!"

Pedro limped to the cave mouth and stepped into the sunlight. He stood on a narrow ledge above a rocky slope and the canyon floor. To the east, as promised, was a natural rock corral with his horse hitched inside. Pedro slid down the rock slope on his butt, careful not to agitate his wound. Near the corral, he found Andres' pack and a few other supplies from the camp. Fortune's wound had been treated like his own, plugged with the dry moss and herb mixture. The horse would live, but he would not be ridden.

He fixed as much on Fortune as he thought the horse might carry and slung the rest over his shoulder in the pack. Noting the sun's position in the sky, he took Fortune by the reins and started walking.

EIGHT

February 20, 1863
Mount Auburn
Cincinnati, Ohio

Alphonso Taft did not feel like himself. In fact, decades had passed since he had. Still, he kept a portrait of himself, cloistered in the vault of his mind, in hopes that he would somehow return to that unburdened self. In his heart, he knew it could never be. Even if he could pluck the festering cancer of the other from his soul, too many years had passed.

Another package arrived that evening, and, like the others, it bore no postmark. It was an unsettling correspondence, always timely and always relevant. Though Taft had managed to seal away the gnawing mind of the other in yet another vault of his compartmentalized soul, it did not prevent the external communications from the nebulous powers beyond the Trust. To that end, these packages had been arriving for years, ignorant of his internal treason to the secret master.

Taft considered the package on his desk, wrapped in plain brown paper, a smooth and perfect rectangle, lying conspicuously among the other unopened mail. It oozed with dread and insisted urgency, though he could barely put his eyes on it. He chose to ignore it for now. Instead, he opened his desk drawer and retrieved a bottle of Scotch, poured himself a glass, and drifted into his thoughts.

A small chest, hardly big enough for a suit, occupied the bottom shelf of his oak bookcase. It was painted green, and its latch was bent so severely that it barely locked. He lifted it from the shelf and placed it in front of the package. It opened crookedly on bent hinges, revealing a collection of Taft's most intimate joys and tragedies.

Inside was a bundle of letters, bound with a silk ribbon, all of which he had written to his first wife, Franny, now deceased. Another stack of letters was fastened to a sketchbook of charcoal drawings. The drawings detailed the growth of a boy from infancy to about four years. Tucked into the notebook was a folded piece of vellum with a portrait of himself. The image showed him at his current age, rendered in loving detail, emphasizing his large nose and sad, tired eyes. The picture was dated 1827 and labeled "Alfie."

"Just like a mirror," he said, refolding the drawing.

It was just another piece of himself, locked in the many cells of his soul. Taft did not distinguish whether these facets were good or bad, only that they required containment, less the swirling chaos of the other consume them. In this sense, he was a jailor, a keeper of locks and keys. And as the arbiter of this prison of ego, he was keenly aware of the fragility of his judgment and the delicate balance that, if upset, could compromise it all.

Usually, the Scotch helped, allowing him to believe that he was merely insane. The Scotch wasn't helping tonight. The outside world clawed at the doors, and the jailer was too sober to refuse. He replaced the chest on the shelf and latched it as best he could. His other self was calling.

The door to his study slowly creaked open as if by ghostly influence.

"Father?" asked a timid voice. Tiny fingers stretched through the dark and gripped the door's edge.

"Don't lurk, child, come in," Taft smiled.

William Taft stepped quietly into the room, dressed in his nightclothes.

"I can't sleep," said William.

"It's late," Alphonso said. "What troubles you?"

"The tree by the guest house is talking to me, he wants to

take me."

"Nonsense," Alphonso laughed and lifted William up to his knee. The boy's blue eyes were glassy with tears. "Now, where do you think a tree will take you? Hmmm? They're rooted to the ground! So you tell that old tree you've got an axe, and you want him to come with *you* to the woodstove!"

"He waits till I'm asleep, then he taps on the window! He told me that you would let him take me."

"I shall do no such thing," said Alphonso, setting the boy on the floor. "You run along to bed, and I will come and check on you when I finish this deposition."

"What's a dez...position?"

"A deposition is a legal term for a statement, like a story."

"Will you read me a deposition?"

"I promise, now get to bed." Alphonso nudged the six-year-old gently toward the door. The door closed, and his footsteps creaked down the hall toward the stairs.

When William had returned to his bed, Taft put on his slippers and crept quietly from his office, down the hall, and to the front door. Walking out into his lawn, he stood gazing at his house like a stranger. The severe geometry of the Greek Revival style, with its perfect rectangles, seemed obscene against the gentle grass slope that it perched on. To Taft, it invoked connotations of being condemned by a high court or an altar of sacrifice to pagan gods. Both options felt entirely plausible.

"Father, is everything all right?"

Robert Black stepped from the shadows of the trees. He wore his captain's uniform, his dark hair coifed just above the pressed collar. The buckle of his belt, the only item deviating from his military attire, was a gold relief of a crow pecking sinew from a human heart. His face commanded a handsome countenance, defined by rigid lines, dark eyes, and pale skin. He carried a small nap sack slung over his shoulder.

"Call me Mr. Taft, we never know who may be listening."

"Apologies."

"You called to the wrong window, William believes the tree is speaking to him."

"I've only just arrived, I haven't called to any window."

"Strange," said Taft. "Regardless, come inside, please."

Robert followed him into the house and quietly made their way to his office. Taft through another log on the fire and poured two glasses of Scotch.

"Hello, Mr. Black," said a tiny voice.

Taft turned to see William's tiny face poking up over the back of his leather chair.

"William, why aren't you in your bed?" asked Taft.

"The tree was scaring me again."

Robert scooped the boy up in his arms and smiled. He clutched a small, blue blanket in his arms and snuggled in against Black's chest.

"You know that trees can't talk," scolded Taft. "What did I tell you about making up stories?"

"But he can talk!" William insisted. "He whispers to me from under my pillow!"

"That sounds terrifying!" said Robert.

"It is! It is!"

Taft shook his head and turned back to the fireplace, stacking wood splits on kindling. In a short moment, he had a small fire burning. Robert bounced the child slightly in his arms, and the boy's eyes began to get heavy. William's head nuzzled in against Black's as he paced slowly around the study. A slight smile forced its way onto Alphonso's face.

"Why don't you go back to bed, William? Mr. Black and I have important business to discuss."

"But..."

"Now, William."

Robert set the child on the floor. With sad eyes, William made one last appeal to his father for asylum. Taft was unpersuaded. He opened the door for the boy and waited for him to shuffle off with his blanket in tow like a bride's train.

"You're hard on the boy."

"He's got to learn that there are no monsters under his bed."

"But there are monsters."

"Not for him."

Robert sat in the leather chair and sipped at his Scotch while Taft stood with his back to the fire. Neither spoke for some time.

"Tell me about Mangas, let's start there," said Taft.

"Fowler was unable to reach him; beyond his skill, it would seem."

"Skill? That fool with his skulls and sacred numbers has no idea that the glass alone makes it even possible."

"Collins has requested that I take the skull to Deer Island. He wants me to enter the cavern."

"What did you tell him?" Taft asked.

"I haven't replied, it's been several days now. I felt it prudent to discuss it with you first."

"Yes, I appreciate that."

"What should I do?"

"Oblige him."

"Are you sure?"

"I think we can predict the outcome; Mangas Coloradas knows nothing about a mountain filled with gold."

"I understand," said Robert.

"Soon, it won't matter, the situation in Richmond will ensure that."

"Yes, Price has gone into hiding. Collins and Russell are already panicking," said Robert.

"When you speak with Collins, ask him what he intends to do about it."

"No doubt he will send Thomas, possibly even Sheldon. Though he is still rather green."

"Don't hesitate to offer your services,"

"Of course."

Taft finished his glass and poured himself another, staring at the golden liquid as if it were something other than alcohol.

"You seem weary, how have things been?"

"I'm shattered, Robert. I feel like a collection of parts and pieces that no longer fit together. I don't know how much longer I can continue like this. Moreover, I think He knows. I hear Him calling in dreams. It's becoming more intense with every day."

"Is there anything I can do?"

"When the time comes, you already know what needs to be done."

"Let's hope it doesn't come to that," said Robert.

"If only I could remove it from this place, far away, where I could be free of its mockery."

"I want to see it."

"That is not wise," said Taft.

"Show me the monster."

"Very well, follow me."

They set their glasses down on the desk and quietly left the office.

"A malaise is growing in me, a festering I can't describe," Taft said as they made their way through the kitchen and out the rear of the house.

"That sounds awful," said Robert.

Taft started down the path to the guest house. The old maple tree next to the structure was just beginning to get its leaves. But, naked against the sky, its long, twisted arms did seem to stretch menacingly toward the house and William's bedroom window.

Taft shut and locked the door behind them as they entered.

"I know that what's inside me, that creature I've locked away, is part of Him, a piece of his loathsome soul."

Taft kicked up the edge of the rug and pulled it away from

the trapdoor. He undid the latch and lifted it open.

"Physically, it's changing, it's hideous," he said, standing at the edge of the darkened portal.

He stepped on the ladder and descended into the gloom.

A hot, dead wind emanated from the absence of light below. Taft struck a match for the lamp, and its flame did not move in the breeze. He held the light high for Robert to follow, then proceeded down the hall to a staircase. The temperature increased as they went down the twenty-four steps to the brick-lined cellar. At the bottom, they reached a reinforced iron door. Taft unlocked it with a long bronze key. Darkness spilled out with the strange wind.

"Go ahead." Taft held the door wide.

Robert stepped through. The room was alight with gold. Stacks of ingots rose from the floor in tightly spaced, rectangular columns. These stacks seemed to fill the entire room, save for a narrow path from the door down the center of the cellar.

The gold had come from California, and it had come from Mexico. It was plundered by the English and swindled by the French. Some had come from American banks or in a steady stream from an eternally compromised U.S. Treasury. Still more was pried from the thrifty coffers of Dutch traders and all manner of European transgressors of commerce. All purified in fire and converted to the pleasant geometry of identical twenty-five-pound bars.

The light streaked across the columns as they passed, so tightly stacked that they looked more like walls. The light became glaring, over-shining its nature, casting strange shadows that looked like faces. Taft looked over his shoulder. Robert was stoic, his face illuminated in the garish shimmer. Alphonso understood that the faces were for him and the voices meant only for his ears; all the same, all Helena.

The columns abruptly ended, breaking Taft from his trance. There was a vacancy in the darkness, a space replaced by something massive. The dull brick terminus of the room was thirty feet away, barely recognizable in the negative space of the gold. Standing before the wall was a tiered dais occupied by a grotesque and enormous hand made of solid gold. It was both human and inhuman, possessing the proper digits, yet disproportionate and monstrous. The perfection of detail, from the elongated and sharpened nails to the organic texture of its skin, revealed the true horror of the thing.

Robert gasped, unable to produce words.

"He knows, Robert. He knows everything," said Taft.

NINE

February 20, 1863
The Octagon House
Fishkill, New York

The skull of Martin Van Buren did not sing, nor did it swing with any rhythm on the Poughkeepsie Road. It hung like a sad, useless anchor, sucking up the freezing rain. For the second time in a month, Sheldon turned past the sign numbered 322 to the unconventional home of Doctor Orson Squire Fowler, delivering a human skull in a canvas sack.

Only a smattering of lights shone in the now dim facets of Fowler's jewel-like house. No septuplet was there to greet him. Sheldon hitched his horse and stepped up to the darkened porch. He found the lights inside only lit along the route required to ascend the house's four levels; otherwise, the home was dark and empty. He followed the lights and sconces to the fourth-floor ballroom, now well-lit with open curtains.

Sheldon entered to find Fowler, General Russell, and Collins sitting on the chaises, talking quietly. A bar cart sat near them, amply stocked with absinthe. A fourth man stared out the window, arms crossed behind his back and fingers interlocked. He turned when Sheldon opened the door.

"Thomas!"

"Hello, Sam."

"It's been so long."

"Well, some of us aren't cut out for Yale," said Thomas, with a half grin.

The two met in the hardwood circle. Thomas' sardonic smile

quickly melted into one of genuine happiness. Thomas pulled him in for a hug and clapped him on his back.

"You look well. What have you been doing with yourself?"

"Mostly doing unto others." The dark smile returned.

"Are we going to be working together?"

"Someone's got to keep you in line."

"Sheldon, glad you're here," said Collins, joining them. "Everything go well in Kinderhook?"

"Yes, no issues," he said, offering the dripping sack to Collins.

"Hold on to that."

"No sign of Robert Black?" Thomas asked. "And what of Mr. Taft?"

"Mr. Taft will not be joining us this evening, regretfully, he has pressing personal matters to attend to," said Collins.

"Though what could possibly be more important than this, I certainly couldn't say," said Russell, joining them on the hardwood.

"What of our dear friend, Bobby Crow? It was my understanding that he would be defiling my birthright today?"Collins exhaled an exhaustive sigh, "Thomas, save your lamentations, I have neither the time nor patience for your grievances. Robert is on task, that's all you need know."

"What do we expect to learn from Van Ruin?" Sheldon asked, breaking the awkward silence that followed Collins' rebuke. He held the sack as if he were Perseus presenting Medusa.

"I'll take that." Fowler snatched the sack. He dropped a kerchief on the puddle that had formed underneath it and mopped it around with his foot.

"As I'm sure by now you're aware, we've had some unexpected interruptions in our Richmond operations," Collins said, stepping back from the spreading pool of skull water. "Van Buren was instrumental in setting the groundwork there before the war. I have some questions for the man."

"You're going to question his skull?"

"Sheldon," said Fowler. "Understand, this is not the hollow rituals and parlor magic you practiced at the Tomb."

"Of course."

"Shall we get started?" Fowler asked, holding the sack out ahead of him like it were some leaking sack of garbage.

They followed Fowler to the veranda, where the rain came down mixed with snow. He led them up the narrow staircase to the dark rooftop deck and its enigmatic turret. The structure was made of fat, dark bricks, rising to twelve feet. The roof curved into a gentle dome, with the apex being a flat green disc of translucent glass about four feet in diameter. An ironbound, wood door stood waiting for them at the end of a short brick-tiled path. Fowler unlocked it with a slender key and pushed the door in.

Stepping inside, Sheldon found that the turret's interior reflected the ballroom's design but inverted. The center of the room was a black-tiled octagon surrounded by a circle of white tiles. A large, eight-sided table of stone sat on the black tiles so that its points offset those of the octagon. Set in the ceiling was a smooth, flat disc of green glass. A smaller disc of glass was inset in the stone table, with peculiar symbols radiating in measured intervals outward like a spider's web.

The milky light of the turret descended like a thing of volume and mass. It looked like pure, clear water, frozen in perfect and un-refracted stasis. The circumference of the room, covered by the white tiles, was untouched by the perfect column of luminance. Sheldon passed his hand through the air before him; it passed through the light, causing no disturbance and casting no shadow.

Fowler removed the skull from the dripping sack and laid it on the central disk of the table. He lifted a small satchel of implements from a short, curved bench opposite the door.

"Don't stand in the light!" he said. "And please endeavor to keep your silence! Not you, Danfort, you will want to stand near me."

Collins took his position near Fowler, immersed in the spectral light. Fowler nudged him a few feet further away, seemingly aligning him with some invisible tangent line. Collins' brow furrowed with the transgression of Fowler's touch, though he did not complain.

Sheldon observed as the doctor executed an extensive series of meticulous and inexplicable measurements, employing an array of baffling instruments. Occasionally, he would pull or push at the skull at gentle degrees, aligning it with unknown points of reference. Finally, he reached a state of satisfaction and ceased all movement, staring deep into the column of light like he was looking through a window.

The quality of the light changed, waving and vibrating as if some invisible thing was churning inside it. Collins' eyes widened, witness to something Sheldon could not see. Thomas pointed to the skull. It was slowly rotating on its own and rising.

"Stay out of the light," Fowler whispered.

Sheldon and Thomas backed up to the dark brick walls. Russell leaned against the bricks with his arms folded across his chest.

When he appeared, it was as if he had always been there. The faint outlines of his living image projected over the floating skull like it was drawn in smoke. The image sharpened and wrapped around the skull, ceasing its rotations. A violent silence exuded from the light, muting all sound so that Sheldon could not even hear his own breathing. The spectral head spoke, though it made no sound. All doubts about Collins' preternatural claims evaporated in the undeniable presence of the Eighth President of the United States, Martin Van Buren.

Collins began speaking to him, though the silence persisted. Perceiving only the emoting of his face, Sheldon speculated that Collins was not receiving good news. He seemed angry and pushed past the limits of his patience, while Van Buren exhibited the stoicism one would expect from the dead. The exchange seemed to last for hours, though, in fact, it was only moments.

As the visitation ended, Collins turned to Fowler and spoke. Sheldon read his lips, believing him to say, "Make him suffer."

The light calmed, and the skull appeared on the disk like it had never moved.

"Excuse me, gentlemen, I am exhausted," Fowler said, pushing past Thomas to reach the door and exiting without further comment.

Collins ignored him, wringing the remaining rainwater from the sack and returning Van Buren's skull to its confines.

"Is it the news you wanted?" asked Thomas.

"It was the news I expected," said Collins. "We're done here, let's return to the ballroom."

The frozen rain stabbed at them from the darkness, and the wind howled through the trees. They descended the stairs quickly and dashed into the ballroom. The candles and sconces remained lit, but Fowler was not present.

"I can't drink any more of this noxious green piss!" said Collins, riffling through the bar cart. Finding nothing to his liking, he took a flask from his jacket pocket and unscrewed the top. He emptied the golden-brown contents into a fresh glass and sat on the chaise.

"What did the spirit say?" asked Thomas.

"We have been betrayed," said Collins.

"Price," Russell spat.

Collins nodded, "Price made his final trip north last June to visit Van Buren in Kinderhook. Apparently, he put something in the old man's tea that exasperated his asthma. He died shortly after."

"Bastard!" said Sheldon.

"Price has been Van Buren's man from the beginning, has he not?" asked Thomas.

"He has," said Collins.

"Curious that he should choose now to strike against

us," said Sheldon.

"Gold can be a powerful motivator," said Russell.

"So what does this mean for Richmond? How much of our gold is there?" asked Sheldon.

"How much is left would be the better question."

"Van Buren claims that Price brought him an offer from a man named Stallworth, operating out of Mexico. The deal was lucrative: silver for gold, two to one on the dollar."

"That's absurd, who would make such a deal?" said Thomas.

"Van Buren refused," said Collins.

"And it would seem that Price did not," said Russell.

"Do we know..." Sheldon began.

"No, we don't. We know nothing of Stallworth beyond his name, and we have no indication of how much gold has already transacted between them. Only that they have had a year to accomplish it."

"Why was our gold in Richmond in the first place?" asked Sheldon.

Collins tipped his flask into his glass, coaxing the last drops of bourbon, marking its meagerness with a mournful scowl. He paced silently for a moment before swilling it down, then answered.

"Van Buren was one of the first politicians in our fold, we guided him from a meddling idealist to the highest office. Our intent then, as it is today, was to turn our nation toward the gold standard, represented by federal fiat. Obviously, this has been a struggle, though we did accomplice the Specie Circular act, requiring the sale of federal land to be paid for in gold. Under Jackson's administration, vast swaths of land were sold, and gold flowed like a river."

"Land that was not the government's to sell," said Thomas.

"Since when have you become so sensitive," Russell chided.

"This gold was diverted from the treasury and funneled through a community of southern banks, all orchestrated by Virgile Price. It was perfect until the war," said Collins.

"What's important now is retrieving it," said Russell.

"How do you intend to proceed?" Asked Sheldon.

"You and Thomas are going to Richmond," said Collins.

"We have a safe house already secured, it is the home of one of our operatives, Elizabeth Van Lew. Thomas will go there straight away and establish himself in her household," said Russell.

"What would you have me do?" Asked Sam.

"Sam, I need you to meet one of Robert's contacts that may have information on Price's location and activities. Then you will rendezvous with Thomas at the Van Lew house."

"Very well," said Thomas. "I'll leave immediately."

"Jay will see that you two make it over enemy lines swiftly and discretely," said Russell.

"Any more questions before I send you on your way?" Collins asked as he took a second pass through Fowler's bar cart.

"What do you intend to do with the President's skull?"

"I intend for him to learn that not even death will excuse him from his responsibilities. He can think about that while his skull gathers dust on my mantle!"

TEN

February 23, 1863
Deer Island, New York

D anfort Collins reclined on a comfortable leather couch, sipping bourbon by the fire in the Overlook House. Outside the multi-paned window, frozen rain fell into the Saint Lawrence River. He stared through his gold, wire-framed glasses at a rare, original edition of Shakespeare's First Folio, randomly thumbing its pages in boredom. Somewhere, in the subterranean recesses below the house, Robert Black communed with the dead.

Collins was restless. He set the book on an end table and walked the room in the fire's flickering light. His hands clenched and unclenched behind his back as he paced the floor.

The room was a monument to the Revolution. Collins designed it that way. On the mantle sat a sword once owned by George Washington, displayed with a copy of the Declaration written in Jefferson's own hand. Opposite the framed document, a scorched flintlock pistol perched on a gnarled stand of deer antler. The pistol had belonged to his father, Daniel Collins. Lieutenant Commander Daniel Collins served in the War of Revolution and again in the War of 1812.

He tapped his fingers on the mantel and gazed out the window where the sleet tried hard to be snow. He wandered back to the opposite side of the room for the countless time. He kicked against the rolled-up oriental rug and peered down into the blackness of the open trapdoor, wondering if Robert was making any progress. He detected no light or sound below.

It was called the Place of Voices by the Onondaga, where the dead may be called and commanded to speak the truth. This had long been the claim of Thomas Rogers since his earliest days at General Russell's academy, though it took an unsettling tragedy for Russell and the men of the Trust to validate the neophyte's wild tales.

Ten years previous, Thomas sought out the cavern in the company of George Miller, the son of the former property owner, Samuel Miller. Though none but Thomas can attest, George refused to heed all warnings and immersed himself in the icy waters. When he emerged, he was very much not himself. The boy had become possessed by the vindictive spirit of his grandfather, Samuel Senior. George was so shattered there was nothing to be done but institutionalize him where he currently remained.

Collins covered the incident up, buying both Samuels Silence and Deer Island itself. The secret of life and death, pondered over since man's creation, was purchased by the Trust for the sum of $175 and concealed in the crawlspace of a stately lake house.

The cuckoo clock flung open its doors and began to chime. According to the yellow bird, Robert Black had been in the cave for an hour and seventeen minutes. Perhaps he wasn't coming back. That would make for an inconvenient design, Collins decided, but not surprising. He clenched and unclenched his hands behind his back and paced the floor.

If the bird appeared again, Black was dead, or worse... The hands crept around the dial. In the shadow of the dark, hardwood leaf and deer motif, a family of wooden bears waited for the bird in perpetual anticipation. At ten minutes to the hour, Robert climbed out of the square-shaped void in the floor.

He flopped awkwardly to the hardwood, naked, wet, and so pale he appeared bloodless. Beads of water formed a puddle around him. Robert crawled to the fire where he had left his clothes and golden belt buckle, stiffly forcing himself to sit cross-legged in front of the fire. He set the skull of Mangas Coloradas on the bricks of the hearth before him.

"Well?"

"Rage," he said, his words vibrating through his shivering. "Their anger is terrible."

"You made contact?"

"Yes."

"And?"

"Unbelievable," he chattered. "The entrance is so small... I had to squeeze through..."

"Here," Collins said. He handed him a small blanket from the back of the leather chair and draped it over Black's shoulders.

"Then the way opens... to an immense sphere, smooth and perfectly round. Most of it is underwater... where the light is."

Collins filled another glass with bourbon and handed it to Robert. The tremor of his hands caused tiny waves to splash toward the rim as he sipped at the whiskey.

"So cold, colder than the river... impossibly cold... should be solid ice."

"Yes, but did you learn anything?" Collins held a distaste for Black's theatrics. By order of the Trust, Robert once pushed a state senator into a stamp mill; his blood was already ice water. Collins did not want a weather report. "Did you find him?"

"It's not what you think. Not like finding... more... like being found," Robert took a gulp from the glass and coughed. "So many voices... all shouting... Elizabeth was there."

"Who?"

"I focused... I called... He came!"

Robert scooted closer to the fire, pushing aside the skull. He wrapped the blanket tighter around himself, but the tremors continued. He pushed the grate back and began rocking, his knees almost touching the flames.

"Robert, are you ok?"

"So much anger. He came, and we fought. He tried to smash my mind, but he was bound to the skull. I told you he would be." Robert handed the empty glass back to Collins. "More, please."

Collins emptied the decanter into the glass and gave it to the shivering man. He stirred the coals with the poker and threw on a couple small, dry logs. The fire crackled and popped, accepting the offering.

"I tore open his mind, and I went inside."

"What did he show you? Did you see the mountain?"

"No gold, only fury."

"What? Do you believe him?"

"He doesn't know about the gold."

"How? How is this possible?" Collins growled. "What about the gold idol his warrior traded?"

"He knows nothing about it."

"That goes against everything he admitted to Sam," said Collins.

"Sam is certainly eager, but he's green. Can we really trust his judgment here?" Robert asked.

Robert Black fell into a violent fit of shivering.

"What a waste," he muttered and bent down to pick up the skull of Mangas. Collins stared thoughtfully through the bullet hole to the hollow interior. "Is he still there?"

"I can't tell... I don't think so."

Collins placed the skull on the mantel beside his father's burned pistol.

"Send it back to Fowler, I suppose," he said.

Outside, on the Saint Lawrence River, snow was falling steadily.

ELLEVEN

February 1863
Sulphur Hills
Sulphur Springs Valley, Arizona Territory

The Chiricahua had Power. Some feared it and called it witchcraft. To those with Ussen's gift, it was a blessing. Lozen was a shield to her people, and she had Power.

It began with her eyes closed, standing quietly. Then, with her hands outstretched, she began to move. Her feet lifted and fell, moving her in the four sacred directions.

The Power came, and she began to sing:

> *Upon this earth, Ussen has Power*
> *This Power he gives to me*
> *With this gift, I find my enemy*

Lozen opened her eyes, extended her arm, and pointed to the north.

"There! Indah!"

There were the Indeh and the Indah. The people and all the other people, us and them, and sometimes friend or enemy. Lozen was never wrong. The shadow of her slender finger stretched long like a spear toward the northern end of a small, deep valley below them. Its floor was narrow, wide enough for a wagon but little more, and its curves would limit the enemy's vision. Near its head was a natural spring representing the only reliable water source in the thirsty, forty miles between Apache Pass to the east and Dragoon Springs to the west.

Victorio planted his foot into the front quarter of his horse and leaped on its back in one fluid motion. He raised his rifle overhead and rode down the hill. Lozen and forty-five Mimbreno warriors fell in behind him.

The soft gray haze of sky stretched above, marked by a white coal sun. Their unshod horses moved quietly over the baked earth as they secured them in a natural corral. They stripped to breechcloths and prepared their weapons, speaking few words. Words were unnecessary. The battle was scripted and would be told by the terrain. Like raindrops being swallowed by the desert, they vanished, concealing themselves among the rocks and shrubs high above the valley floor, and they waited.

A useless, weak breeze crept through the air, carrying the smell of sweat and tobacco. The sound got lost between the canyon walls. Voices, horses, and the dry squeal of wagon wheels distorted and warped like reflections in a curved and uneven mirror. The White Eyes were near.

Thirty-seven mounted California volunteers, and six wagons stretched along the valley's north end. Another seventeen rode the wagons, mainly carrying rifles. Their dust-up clung mercilessly to everything. Some covered their faces with kerchiefs, and some were gap mouthed with darkened teeth. The horses sensed the water and pushed forward eagerly. They began to cluster and jam toward the front of the column and congest the narrow path.

Victorio witnessed their misery without pity. Their pink faces disgusted him, sun boiled and starved of water. The company carried the marks of violence. Many riders bore dark blood stains on their blue coats, blending seamlessly into the patches of sweat-drenched fabric. The teams strained, and the wheels of the overloaded wagons squealed under the crushing weight of the cargo. Most showed damage and improvised repairs. Some bore the wounded and dead on top of the covered loads. The entire column increased its pace as they approached the spring.

With the soft mimic of a bird whistle, dozens of arrows

sailed toward the beleaguered soldiers. The breeze ended. A strange, dead wind manifested in its place, leaving the flags limp and the air still. Its hot, rank smell filled Victorio. Time slowed, and the arrows hung like bees in the breath of a sick beast. The gulch swallowed the soldiers' death cries, muting their wavering and warbled screams. A second volley of arrows was loosed. The Apache reached for their rifles to continue the fight, but it had already ended. They descended from the rocks and moved among the dead and dying.

Lozen looked to her brother, her face filled with awe and fear. Words struggled to form behind her eyes to describe this impossible thing.

His sister did not do this. The wind came from another Power, a Power that would pretend to come from Ussen but was more like Ussen's shadow. They walked in the dream world, but not as the dreamer.

"Guided by a dead wind," said Victorio.

Not one arrow missed its mark; all had struck true and fatal. Death bubbled out of the mouths of the soldiers, still clinging to the world in shallow gasps of blood and spittle. One clung to his Springfield with wild and bulging eyes. Impotent to raise the weapon, the effort toppled him from the wagon to where he fell still in the dust. Two men lay in the back of the wagon among the cargo, arrows protruding from them as if their hearts had grown feathered shafts. The dead wind passed, vanishing with the souls of every White Eye in the valley.

Victorio pried open a crate on the back of one of the wagons. He expected to find weapons, bullets, or some other ordinance; he saw none. Instead, it was stacked neatly to the top with brilliant gold coins. He opened another crate with an identical result, then another and another.

The warriors looted weapons and useful items from the fallen and returned to Victorio. He could see the spell in their eyes as well. He could not determine whether it was for good or evil, only that it was powerful and favored them.

"Take it all!" Victorio said.

February 1863
Janos
State Of Chihuahua, Mexico

"I'm sorry," said Ignacio. "All the gold in the world is no use, I have no guns!"

"Liar!" Geronimo struck the door frame with his fist.

"Easy, friend, all I need do is raise my little finger, and you'll find more than enough guns bearing down on you."

"When will you have more?" asked Fun.

"It could be a very long time. The Juaristas snatch them all up before they ever reach me. The same is true for horses, blankets, food, and medicine."

"Have I not been fair with you, Ignacio?" asked Geronimo.

"Of course you have," said Ignacio.

"Then why do you continue to lie to me?"

"Have you noticed there is a war going on! If you want weapons, you're going to have to get them from the soldiers! There is nothing I can do."

"Bah!" Geronimo waved his hand dismissively and slammed the door of Ignacio's shop behind him as he stomped away.

Fun slung the sack of gold ore they had brought with them over his shoulder and followed Geronimo into the dusty street.

"Shall I gather warriors for a raid?" asked Fun.

"Not yet," said Geronimo. "I have one more idea."

TWELVE

March 2, 1863
Baltimore, Maryland

The Gabby Saloon and Mercantile stood on Thames Street, near the intersection of Broadway in the waterfront district of Fell's Point. The establishment had been in constant operation for well over a hundred years. Danfort Collins tasted his first whiskey there and maintained a fondness for the place ever since. When he found occasion to visit, he would sit at the same table by the window where he last met face-to-face with his mother. That was in August of 1828. She had died the following spring, soon after he arrived at Yale.

Forgoing his morning coffee for bourbon, he spread the newspaper before him and began perusing the headlines. On page seven, nearly lost among the numerous war reports, was a curious story that immediately commanded his attention.

The Baltimore Daily Gazette
February 26, 1863
"Murder and Desecration"

NEW HAVEN, CONNECTICUT - The Associated Press wire reports that, on Friday morning, officials from Grove Street Cemetery and representatives of Yale College made a grisly discovery at the home of Professor Cyrus Allen Goodrich. The body of Professor Goodrich was discovered in the study of his Chapel District home, brutally slain in what investigators are calling a "crime of passion." There are currently no suspects. Police continue to question Professor Goodrich's personal and professional acquaintances.

In a related occurrence, during the small hours of the same morning, vandals exhumed the grave of Elizabeth Goodrich, daughter of the Yale professor. Mr. Roger Adams, caretaker of the Grove Street Cemetery, called upon the Goodrich home to inform the professor of damages to his family plot. Investigators are not commenting on whether the two incidents are connected.

Ms. Goodrich's remains were reinterred by the vandals, seemingly intact. What, if anything, was the object of exhumation remains a mystery.

Yale faculty members arrived at the home at approximately 10 a.m. to inquire about the wellbeing of Mr. Goodrich, who was absent without notice Friday morning. Receiving no answer to repeated knocking, the party, including Mr. Adams, entered the home through the unlocked front door and made the ghastly discovery.

"I am bewildered and mortified!" said one colleague of Mr. Goodrich, who preferred to remain anonymous. "I can't imagine who would do such a thing!"

The investigation is ongoing, and officials appeal to the public for information.

Professor Goodrich, a widower, leaves behind no known family. Funeral services are pending.

Collins cut the article out with his pocketknife and tucked it into his jacket pocket. Outside, the sun was beginning to peek through the clouds, finding its way through the window and into his bourbon.

"What's gotten into you these days, Robert? What are you working at?" He muttered before draining his glass and setting out for the telegraph office.

February 26, 1863
Deer Island, New York

Robert Black could not be bothered to seek out a boat. He stripped nude on the shores of the St Louis River and left his clothes in a pile before plunging into the icy water. The only item he did not remove was the curious necklace he wore, a leather cord strung with three human teeth. The teeth once belonged to his dead lover, Elizabeth.

His skin was nearly blue as he clambered onto the boat dock of the Overlook House. Shivering and dripping wet, he kicked in the front door with his bare foot and entered the darkened house. Briefly, he considered starting a fire in the hearth of the study but instead sought out a small oil lamp. After struggling with quaking hands and wet fingers, he finally struck a match, lit the lamp, and opened the trap door to the cavern below.

By the lamp's light, he felt his way down the narrow, damp passage to where it narrowed like the passage to a womb. Beyond the stone slit, an unnatural light manifested, greenish blue and undulating in its intensity. Robert squeezed through the opening and into the Place of Voices.

The chamber was a perfect sphere of polished granite, perhaps thirty feet in diameter, the only flaw being the breach he entered by. A smooth mirror of icy blue water filled the space up to the equator. Robert slid down the smooth stone wall and submerged himself in its depths. Beneath the surface, all light failed, and he found himself in a perfect void of sight and sound. Then the screams came.

It was as if all the world's anguish had been consolidated

in the ocean's roar, an undefinable cacophony of voices directed upon him. They were a sea of minds, raging with despair and calling out to the single point of salvation, Robert Black. He clenched the teeth of his necklace in his fist and listened through the storm. The frigid water numbed his body, and his lungs begged for air. Still, he remained calm and waited for her to come. The ocean's roar subsided until it held but a single voice.

"Robert, you came," she said.

He held the necklace out into the void.

"Take me from this place, my love."

The teeth began to quiver and shake in his palm.

"It is done," she said. "Now breathe!"

Robert swam through the darkness, praying he knew up from down. Slowly the voices returned, blathering madness from the maelstrom. When he broke the surface, he emerged in cool green silence, the necklace of teeth burning warm in his hand. He looped the cord around his neck and climbed out of the frozen water.

February 26, 1863
Richmond, Virginia

Sheldon sat on a muddy stump beneath the north end of the Mayo bridge. The James sloshed mindlessly along as he waited patiently for Robert's contact to make himself known.

He was no stranger to Richmond, though Richmond had become a very strange place since his last visit five years previous. He and his father had often come for business, making the quick trip down the coast in the Albatross. Now the place seemed as far away as the moon and equally alien. It was a grey city now, a town of ash and iron. There was a grim resolve to the place that death and destruction were certainties, and the only thing yet undecided was when.

As time passed and his mind drifted, the coin and the key found their way into his hands. And, as he had done so many times before, he held his hands out like ballasts and considered the objects, each in their weight and balance. The silver key invoked memories of family, what it used to be before Yale, Skull, and Bones, or any knowledge of the Trust. It was an idealistic, half-remembered thing, filled with choices he had not made. The coin was his equally unrealized, yet tangible, future. A world to be taken, amorphous and vast, yet somehow non-inclusive of his silver past. As he held them in the ashy moon glare by the James, the coin was heavy and dense, the key light and frail, as if the former were growing and the latter fading from the world.

"Well, by my word, paint me shocked and amazed! If it isn't a neophyte of the Trust, living like a troll under my favorite bridge!"

Sheldon had ignored the horses, believing them to be just another patrol. Instead, several riders were making their way down the muddy embankment, led by the fat man, Virgil Price. He was mounted on a white pony, fitting for his height but painfully inundated by his girth.

Sheldon came to his feet and started off downriver, quickly discovering he was surrounded on both sides. He considered diving into the James, but even the most challenged marksman would find him a generous target as he fought through the mud to the deep water. There was no escape. Without thinking, he slid the gold coin into his mouth and swallowed, and somehow, it slid down his throat like an oyster.

"Hand's where I can see them now, boy. I don't mean to kill you, but then again, I can't say as I'm overly concerned not to!"

Sheldon raised his hands, the silver key hanging from his

fist by its chain as he turned to face Price. Two of the men dismounted and met him at the bank. One snatched the key, gun, and coin purse, while the other fixed manacles to his wrists and locked them behind his back.

"Very nice, good dog," Price laughed.

Sheldon glared back at the obese man with his greasy lips and beady eyes as the soldier handed him his silver key.

"Oh, now what's this? Silver? Hardly seems the right style!" Price pocketed the heirloom and turned his pony up the hill. "Take him to the toybox," he said with a wave of his hand.   Sheldon watched as the beast bent under strain, hooves struggling for purchase on the muddy slope. Though the thought crossed his mind to inform Virgil Price of his intent to disembowel him, Sheldon prudently remained silent and followed the instructions given to him by the men holding guns.

PART TWO
THE AMBIGUITY OF SELF-PRESERVATION

war springs from my flesh
gathering tranquility
till I am complete

-Matsuo Sogi

THIRTEEN

April 1, 1865
Baltimore, Maryland

Sunlight dappled through the trees on Thames Street and streaked through the window of the Gabby Saloon and Mercantile. The shadows of leaves danced across the ancient table, carved with the epitaphs of generations of patrons. There was a mark placed by his father, a relic of his parent's love, and a heart with the initials D&A inside. He ran his fingers over the scar while he looked down Thames Street, waiting for his guest.

A man appeared, turning the corner from the shaded end of the street. He was oddly overdressed for the pleasant spring day, the collar of his heavy coat turned up against the phantom cold. His tentative steps down the cobblestone suggested doubt and trepidation. Collins could smell the guilt and fear radiating from the man like it had been sprayed from the gland of a skunk.

Collins smiled as the sharply dressed young man sat down across from him. His dark hair was naturally coiffed in wavy locks, and his features were distinct and handsome. There was a subtle but resolute rage contained in his dark brown eyes, and his body seemed coiled in tension.

"You failed," said Collins.

"We should have had him after the hospital. We waited by the Soldier's Home. He never left Washington," said the young man.

"How is this my problem? I told you in Montreal I am removed from this."

"It was a missed opportunity. It won't happen again," he said as he fidgeted with his mustache.

"Yes, I understand. Our mutual friend told me of your troubles."

"Can you help, sir, or have I come in vain?"

"Let me be blunt with you, your plan is flawed. Kidnapping will accomplish nothing, you must cut off the head of the snake. Death to those waiting in succession as well. That is, if you mean to realize your goal. The war is almost over, soon, it won't matter what you do."

"Kill him?"

"Don't be coy! Is your heart true or merely filled with rhetoric?"

"What about you? What do you stand to gain, sir?"

"What does it matter? Such knowledge would be an unnecessary burden to you."

"Trust, sir, simple trust. You have no southern sympathies, why should you want this man dead?"

"My world requires balance. Evil should never rule, nor should good triumph over evil. It is the struggle to obtain one or the other, the commerce of conflict, that suits me."

"Where do I stand in your eye, among the forces of Heaven or Hell?"

"Would you prefer an answer or a sack of silver?"

"You lack honor, sir."

"Good, take this." Collins passed over a small satchel heavy with silver coins.

The young man checked the contents nervously and acknowledged him with a nod. The barman approached, prompting him to close the satchel quickly and place it on the bench by his side.

"Can I bring something for the gentleman?"

"No, he won't be staying."

Collins observed the man through the curious gold lenses of

his glasses as he squirmed in his seat, clutching the satchel.

"These coins will cover your services and expenses. My agent will reach out to you soon. Look for a letter to arrive at the theater in your sister's name. You have what you need."

The young man knew that their meeting was complete. He collected the satchel and stood from the table, extending his hand to Collins. Collins regarded it with a blank stare. Awkwardly, the man shuffled toward the door, unsure whether to walk or run.

"Oh, Mister Booth," said Collins.

The young man turned.

"Don't fuck it up."

Mister Booth nodded and continued down Thames Street.

"I think I'll enjoy another bourbon, Barkeep."

The barkeep smiled and reached for a bottle under the counter, a bottle he was well-paid to keep private. Bourbon, real bourbon, was difficult to come by these days, particularly so far north. Collins had no taste for the common rotgut that passed for whiskey.

"Do you think the owner would sell?" Collins asked the barman as he set down two fingers of contraband liquor in a fresh glass.

"Couldn't say, mayhap."

"I'd want to change the name, never liked the sound of Gabby or mercantile for that matter. What mercantile? It's all saloon!"

The trees on Thames Street swayed, and the sunlight wove its way through the leaves to the cobblestone below. Another man was making his way toward the establishment at a vigorous but waddling pace. The new arrival was short and husky with a suit that seemed one size too large. His beard was long and wild, and his eyes were hidden behind the glare of his tiny white spectacles, giving the impression that his eyes were silver coins.

"Thank you for being punctual, Mr. Stanton," said Collins. "My itinerary is very taxing these days."

"Your itinerary! Christ's sake, man, I'm orchestrating a war! To come to Baltimore, of all places, half-full of Rebels and spies? To think I should be seen here, cavorting and conspiring when paying a visit to my office would be infinitely less conspicuous!"

"Because my time is more valuable than yours."

"Would the gentleman care for anything from the bar?" asked the barkeep, materializing alongside the table.

"I'm parched-" started Stanton.

"No, thank you, he won't be staying long," Collins said, and the barman retreated behind the dark oak of the ancient bar.

Stanton frowned.

"Did you bring what I requested, Edwin?"

"Yes, take them," he passed over a stack of envelopes and folded documents loosely wrapped together with string.

"Thank you. What of our mutual friend?"

"Captain Sheldon? Dead, I should think. Not that I even knew the man. You insert a man under my agency as if I possessed any authority over him, send him on a fool's errand, then complain to me when he turns up missing? Your man Rogers, however, has been exceptionally active."

"Captain Sheldon is not dead, and mind your tone in that regard, or I may give him authority over your funeral arrangements."

"Threats, Collins?"

"You know very well, Mr. Stanton, I have no need of threats."

"Of course, forgive my temperament. I'm under great strain."

Collins thumbed through the documents, his brow furrowing. He took a sip from his glass and appreciated the bourbon's quality.

"What am I looking at here, Edwin?"

"My agents are efficient accountants, if nothing else. These documents represent the extent of Robert Black's use of military and federal resources. Black has utilized safe houses, commandeered horses, and contacted several network assets, though he has sent back no actionable information. To my purposes, utterly useless. To yours? Of course, it's not for me to say."

"Are you certain of the date on this?"

"Quite sure."

"And the recipient?"

Stanton examined the document, "General Joseph West, yes, I'm sure."

"Very disconcerting," he said.

"What, that your lot would order someone's death? You surpassed 'disconcerting' long ago."

Collins referenced the dates a second time, muttering to himself, then tucked them into his satchel. The wind blew through the trees, rustling through the new spring leaves. His brow unfurled, and his expression softened.

"What do you think of a saloon or tavern?"

"What?"

"As a business enterprise, that is."

"Mr. Collins, I desperately need to be in Washington."

Collins shrugged and produced a leather bag filled with silver coins. He passed it over the tabletop, where it was received with sweaty palms.

"Well, be off then," he said, turning his focus to the shifting patterns of light between the shadows of leaves on the sidewalk.

Stanton tucked the bag inside his oversized jacket and quickly ambled down Thames Street. Collins had never seen a penguin, though he imagined they would walk like Edwin Stanton.

April 1, 1865
Richmond, Virginia

Thomas' father, Isiah, had a phrase he used when results differed from their planned intents, "Sometimes shit don't go right." A lot of shit had failed to go right in Thomas' two years in Richmond. In fact, shit continued to go wrong at an alarming rate.

Thomas began correcting wrongs at an early age. At nine, he killed his first man, a white grocer that murdered his father over an alleged theft. That night, he found his father's neglected pistol, cleaned it, oiled the moving parts, and measured out the powder. Loading the gun was hard but pulling the trigger was easy. It became a metaphor for his life; proper results required preparation and rigorous attention to detail.

Richmond was a city that afforded Thomas infinite opportunity for such corrections. With the underground connections of Elizabeth Van Lew and her mother, Liza, he could spend a lifetime there doing just that. Though expansive, his personal scorecard was secondary to that of the Trust. The chief items of that agenda being the locations of Samuel Sheldon and millions of dollars in missing gold. There was only one man who could answer these questions, Virgil Price.

It was Robert Black who found Price. Freshly returned from a two-year absence of his own. Black claimed to have spent the time incarcerated, locked within the wretched confines of Libby prison. He and another prisoner, James Reavis, recently escaped and turned up on Elizabeth's doorstep. The news had come as quite a shock to the Van Lews, who frequently visited the prison to deliver food and medical supplies to the prisoners. Libby was deeply connected to their spy network, and they had repeatedly inquired there for the missing Black.

Robert came with a fantastic story that his new friend Reavis had provided, not only the location of Virgil Price but also Samuel Sheldon. After a brief discussion, it was agreed that Robert would retrieve Sheldon and Thomas would go after Price. None of it sat well with Thomas; it didn't feel right, though he was at a loss for any reason to argue.

Just off Broad Street, on Church Hill, near the Egyptian building, Virgil Price was hiding in plain sight. He cloistered himself in a comfortable home, casually growing fat on cream and bacon while Richmond starved. According to Black, Price was preparing to leave for Mexico; thus, it was paramount to act immediately.

It was after midnight when Price put a match to his bedside lantern and found Thomas standing above him with his forefinger perched over his lips in the sign of silence.

"Hello, Virgil," said Thomas.

The light from the lamp dimly lit the room. With his dark skin and black clothing, Thomas was little more than a silhouette with ghost-white eyes. The tiny light reflected faintly on his hunting knife. Virgil kept his silence.

"Remember me?"

"You think you're clever, but you have no clue."

Thomas flicked his wrist and cut a bloody swath across his cheek.

"You made a deal, Mr. Price. We both understand the consequences of reneging. Before I assess that penalty, let's discuss a few things."

"There's nothing to discuss, the gold is gone, beyond your reach."

Thomas ran the blade along Price's cheek in a quick upstroke, lobbing off the majority of his ear. The man recoiled across the bed and rolled onto the floor, reaching for the drawer in his nightstand. To Virgil's horror, his pistol was not there.

"Aggghhhh! Murder! Murder!" he screamed.

Typically, Virgil's servant Mr. Casey would have come running, shotgun in hand, at such an alarm. This was not to be, as Mr. Casey had quietly bled out in his only moments before.

Thomas hopped across the bed and pinned Virgil to the floor, straddling his flabby chest. He held the knife point so close to Virgil's eye that his lashes scrapped the blade when he blinked.

"This will be the last opportunity to make things right, Virgil. You understand my meaning?"

Virgil Price spit blood on the floor.

"Where is the gold, Mr. Price?"

Virgil's body was slack, with his head resting on the hardwood floor, resigned to his fate like a blubbery possum. Blood seeped from his voided ear and began matting his hair.

"Gone," he sighed. "What little remains will be gone soon too."

"Come on, Virgil, don't draw this out." Thomas traced around his eye socket with the blade, gently carving into the soft flesh.

"What do you think I've been doing the last two years, polishing it?"

"Why do you have to make it ugly?"

Thomas let the blade fall point down into Virgil's eye. It sunk in nearly an inch before the curve of the blade caught the orbital socket and lodged there. Blood and fluid flowed down his cheek in violent tears.

"Mexico!" Virgil howled.

"Yes, Mexico, we know. Tell me about Stallworth, and where do we find him?" Thomas twisted the knife.

"You think Stallworth is your problem!?" Virgil thrashed, laughing hysterically, fighting vainly to throw Thomas off his chest.

Thomas carelessly drew the knife across his face, cutting his nose and lip.

Virgil gurgled in his blood and rolled his head back and forth. Even in the dim light of the lamp, the blood was coming bright and crimson. It splashed on his cheeks as he turned side to side.

"Veracruz! Davis took what was left! A lot of good it will do you, though! You fucking idiots have been undone!" Virgil drooled blood and fixed his remaining eye on Thomas. "You gonna end up worse than me, you know that, right boy? Just wait, you'll see!"

"Undone, how?"

"It was the Poet, Sogi, that set it up and your own man that helped make it possible!" Price screamed in pain.

"Matsuo Sogi orchestrated this theft?"

"Yes, you idiot!"

"What man helped him?"

"Mercy," he whimpered, quivering in shock and blood loss.

"Tell me!" Thomas shook him by his silk pajamas.

Virgil Price gurgled, choked, and died in a trembling heap.

"Fuck!" he said, burying his blade in Price's chest.

Thomas reached into his pocket, retrieved the single blood ruby, and held it to the lantern light. As Virgil Price lay dead in an expanding lake of blood, he watched the ruby. Several minutes passed, and the gem remained perfect. He had expected it to turn gray as granite, like the others that had passed through his hands.

"Then who is it for?" He wondered.

FOURTEEN

April 1, 1865
Belle Isle Prison
Richmond, Virginia

T ad Taffy was dead. Despite Sheldon's best efforts, there
was no saving him. In the quiet that came after, there
was nothing left to do but wait.

Ironically, it was Taffy who taught him the waiting game.
The rules were simple; be still and listen very carefully. "Ears
are your eyes in the dark," Taffy said. "Every noise has its own
shape and color." The steady James River, the distant rumble
of artillery, and the raspy breath of dying men; each could
be isolated by focus. Once focused, the tiny feet of scurrying
rats were like boots stomping down the stairs. Patience was
the secret to the game. Wait for the tell-tale sound of rustling
clothes; let them get in deep. Once they get a taste of flesh and
feel secure, that's the time to pounce. Strike fast and hard, and
don't be distracted by the scatter. Pick one and kill it good. If
you're lucky, that rat will be enough to keep you wheezing and
choking for another day.

He heard them clearly when they came, bold as wolves,
squeaking to each other in the dark. He heard the rustling
of Tad's shirt and the gnawing of tiny teeth. Still, he waited,
crouched in the scalding darkness. The tiny claws of rodents
tickled his bare feet as they scurried over them to feast on his
friend.

As the rats became emboldened and frenzied, he lashed out with both arms, pummeling the writhing chest of Tad Taffy. Squeals of rage and pain filled the darkness. When it was finished, and the survivors retreated to the crevices from which they came, he held the limp and greasy bodies of two rodents bloated on Tad's dead flesh. The waiting was over. He did not hesitate and devoured them immediately.

Two years had passed since that night at the Mayo Bridge. Every rat, every worm, and every crawling insect that Sheldon consumed in that time, he did so to sustain his vengeance. Sleep, when it came, brought dreams of the fat, greasy folds of Virgil Price's neck flesh squeezing through his fingers like a sausage bursting from its skin. Not a day passed that he didn't have the dream as he withered in Price's "Toybox" on Belle Isle.

The prison camp on Belle Isle was an open-air enclosure festering in the shadow of a defunct iron foundry. Just outside the walls of its general population was the former slag pit, now an open grave for prisoners. A rotting tangle of libs and fleshy skulls congealed at its nucleus like some necrotic meteor. Arranged in a semicircle around this hellish crater was a row of small metal huts, one of which Virgil Price employed exclusively for his collection of toys.

As Sheldon languished in the sunless void, the war lingered in ambiguity with nothing but the contents of the slag pit to gauge its progress. Every morning, a detail of guards hauled the dead from the camp and fed them to the pit. "Hut, hut, heave!" was the only eulogy afforded them. On some occasions, this ritual seemed to last for hours. The horrid stench defied description, and the air vibrated with the buzzing of flies.

Tad Taffy was there from the beginning, a man Sheldon would only ever know by his voice. His smooth country drawl and optimism remained undiluted by the misery of their condition. Lieutenant Alden, a tight-lipped cavalry officer, also counted among the original occupants, as did a nameless and silent man consumed with dysentery. The silent man had died the first night.

That night, Taffy taught him the waiting game. It happened when the flies ceased their buzzing, and the sun retired from fueling the oven of their metal cell. The wheezing and coughing became pained and labored breathing, then stopped entirely. Lieutenant Alden cursed Taffy as inhuman as he lurked near the corpse and waited. When it was over, Taffy held two dead rats for his efforts. He gave one to Sheldon and kept the other, offering none to Alden.

"You a spy?" Taffy asked, with his mouth full of rat.

Sheldon did not speak.

"I'm a spy," said Taffy. "That's what they tell me. I don't know if it's all that, though."

Sheldon sat indifferently.

"Spy or not, I'm no stranger to incarceration. I spent a year in a cell in Mexico with no windows or doors. Hole in the ground, really, sort of a big latrine. Sometimes they would piss down on me just for laughs. I can tell you, this place is paradise in comparison! You ever been to Mexico?"

"No," said Sheldon.

"You ain't missing much," he slurped. "So, how is it? You a spy?"

"Who the fuck wants to know?" The tail of Sheldon's rat was still warm and twitching in his hand.

"Name's Tad Taffy," he said. "But you can call me Tad Taffy."

"Do I look like a spy?"

"Ha! That's a good one, I like you! Price put you here?"

"How do you know him?"

"You gonna eat that or pet it like a puppy?"

Sheldon tossed the rat to Taffy, and it hit the packed dirt floor with an audible thud. The sound of crunching bones and ripping flesh followed shortly after.

"We all know Price," Taffy belched. "This here's his private toy box, and we're his discarded toys!"

"You're a filthy bandit and smuggler!" said Alden. "Don't conflate my lot with yours!"

"Ha!" Taffy snorted. "And you're a treasonous snake! If you weren't here, Jeff D would have shot you, so don't you go waving fingers!"

"Keep talking, sir. It will be you the rats come to eat!" Alden's threat tapered into a fit of coughing.

"You're just lucky I don't fancy human flesh, Lieutenant," Taffy taunted as he sucked the eyes out of the rat's skull.

Three days later, Alden died. He passed quietly, without the typical wheezing and gasping that marked most departures. In those three days, hunger allowed Sheldon to overcome his scruples. He trapped a girthy rat in the shirt sleeve of the dead lieutenant and beat the beast to death. He and Taffy feasted on rat flesh for the next five days until the guards finally came and hauled Alden's corpse the short distance to the slag pit.

On the rare occasion the door to their hut opened, it was like the sun itself walked in. Black turned to white, replacing one blindness with another. Meals were served in a careless splattering of moldy bread or fleshless soup bones, invariably deposited in or around the overflowing pails they used as latrines. Water was distributed in the same buckets, drawn from the James, gritty and tasting of piss. Typically, these rations were more detrimental to one's health than fasting.

Six more prisoners came after Alden, and the door opened six more times to remove their rat-chewed corpses. Sheldon and Taffy played the waiting game, and they survived. Those who did not play did not live long. In that time, their alliance bloomed into a friendship fueled by their mutual hatred for Virgil Price.

Tad Taffy talked a lot. Sheldon surmised this trait to be the likely cause of his incarceration. Originally from Illinois, Taffy was the eleventh out of twelve siblings; an uneven dozen, he called them. Early in life, he wandered, sometimes for days at a time. No one seemed to notice, so one day, Tad opted to never return. He worked the roads, robbing and stealing his way south years before. After a few months on a cargo frigate, he tried his hand at piracy, a rougher go than he would have liked. Eventually, he fell into smuggling, and by the time the war broke out, Taffy had become a master at his craft.

Taffy made some extraordinary claims in their time together, the most fantastic account being of his time in the employ of Virgil Price. He claimed to have transported over twelve tons of gold ingots to Mexico. He ran it out of Jacksonville to Havana, where it was transferred to Cuban ships and sent to Veracruz. There it would be taken by a "Bonafide witch" in Stallworth's employ. He bragged that he knew every crooked captain in every port from the eastern coast to the Gulf of Mexico. By his admission, his downfall came from sharing those nefarious connections with Virgil Price, eventually nullifying his necessity. The story was truly remarkable, at times stretching credulity. Considering the cargo and what he knew of Price, Sheldon believed every word.

The daily chants of "hut, hut, heave!" slowed and stopped altogether, replaced by the ever-encroaching artillery fire. Even the buzzing of flies had decreased, and the smell of the pit subsided somewhat. He guessed Richmond was besieged, and the other prisoners had either died or been relocated. How long Taffy's final gift would last was a mystery, but it was inevitable that, unless he escaped soon, Sheldon would be the rats' final feast, leaving no one to wait over his corpse.

It was not the rats alone that gave Sheldon sustenance. Something was changing within him. At the Mayo bridge, he was forced to choose between the silver key and the golden coin. Thomas said the coin was like a seed, a statement that proved eerily accurate. While the world around him steamed and reeked, inside his soul's fertile soil, a golden sapling sprouted. Nourished by some invisible sun, its branches were weaving through his arms, and its roots dug deep into his core. It was a thing of power, separate from himself, yet connected and willing to share its strength. Sheldon imagined that the tree spoke to him, though the rustling of its golden leaves was of a language just outside of his comprehension.

Still, he had not forgotten the silver key. Teresa Sheldon did not give gifts without meaning. The key had come from before Jay Sheldon's inundation with the Trust. He could not help but think that the key was also a seed in some way, a rooted connection to a life and world clean and protected from that of the Trust. And, as the golden sapling grew, he could only ask himself if the refusal of that key had sealed his choice in permanence.

As he sat with Tad's bloodied boots in his lap, sucking the meat from the rodent's bones, he contemplated tunneling out. Taffy said it was a fool's errand, that the metal walls were reinforced with spikes, too small for a man to squeeze through but easy for a rat. Besides that, the guards were always watching. Then there would be the river to contend with and, of course, a city full of soldiers. Despite such obstacles, Sheldon would make an attempt. Perhaps the golden tree might bless his efforts and fortify his resolve.

Sheldon's meditations were interrupted by voices and the metal friction of the cell's lock. Blinding light filled the hole, piercing his eyes and staining his vision with red and white splotches. He shielded his face with hands still slick with the guts of his kill and scurried back into the corner of the cell. Cool air filled his lungs; conversely, his filthy wind inspired the guards to gag as it escaped.

"Is that the one you're looking for?" The guard fought to keep from vomiting.

"Yessir," said a familiar voice. "That's the wretch."

"Well, go on and take him then! And good riddance, he's the last one here!"

"Last one?"

"Why they keep us here for one fucking man, I can't say. This one must have made some powerful enemies!"

"He'll hang soon enough," said the voice. "Take comfort there."

The voice was so familiar, but he couldn't place it. He let his fingers separate just a crack and tried to adjust his eyes. Their forms were black cutouts on a white field at first, then slowly, the details began to fill in.

"Prisoner, can you stand?" the voice asked him.

Sheldon groaned and rose to his haunches, then it came to him.

Bobby. Fucking. Crow.

FIFTEEN

April 1865
Hidalgo Del Parral
State Of Chihuahua, Mexico

T he gate was shut at the fort on top of Cerro de la Cruz. The mostly Belgian garrison lingered in the shady places of the ramparts and out of direct view of the passing column of killers. Colonel Basalt stood alone in the late afternoon sun, observing the procession. The riders advanced slowly, but the brown fog of their dust-up carried them like an unnatural tide, lazily assaulting the road under their feet. They rode in ones and twos, having no set order save that of the leading rider, their indisputable leader, Maria Bonita.

She rode a freshly gelded roan of exceptional size and strength. In any sensible encounter, the beast would border on majestic. However, amongst its present entourage, it presented an image of abject horror, invoking primal revulsion in those unfortunate enough to witness it. Two long strings of black scalps, caked with matted blood and seething with buzzing flies, stretched from the roan's nose skirting to its cantle. The stinking, fleshy mass of them descending from the roan's head gave the impression of gills from some abominable sea creature. Abstract patterns of dry, rust-colored blood dappled the horse's shoulders, flanks, and hindquarters like a painting on a murderous canvas. The saddle was nearly black with the seasoned staining of human blood, the accumulation of which implied a veritable submersion. Bits of paste jewels ornamented the horn and ridges of the saddle, the faux rubies and emeralds glittering like beacons in the sun.

Maria Bonita rode naked to the waist, as was her way. A light, billowy scarf of yellowed silk was wrapped around her neck, loosely falling over her shoulders. She would pull it over her mouth and nose in a gallop, though she preferred to display her mutilations. A wide, jagged triangle of scar tissue descended from below her left clavicle to the tip of her sternum, occupying the space where a breast should be. The pale and pink furrowed landscape of scars contrasted dramatically with the totality of her otherwise smooth, dark skin. Her remaining breast rivaled any sculptor's work in perfection. It haunted her chest in an erotic mockery of her heinous defilement. A matrix of tiny scar mounds, raised by heated blades, cigarillos, and campfire embers, filled her right arm from the elbow to the shoulder, one for every soul she'd extinguished. Thick locks of straight, dark hair fell down her back and trailed between her naked shoulder blades like a black bridal train. Behind her ear, a golden poppy was woven into her hair, the brilliant flower dipping low to her earlobe.

Central to her visage was the broken symmetry of her facial features, marked by the near complete removal, by blade, of her upper lip. The swath of voided flesh started just past the corner of her mouth, crossed under her nose, then cut upwards into her cheek. Tiny black dirt clods clung to the exposed teeth and gums, and her tongue was occasionally visible between the gaps like some caged, pink beast. Maria's eyes were hateful black siphons that sucked the life out of everything that met her gaze.

Behind the heathen witch trailed a collection of motherless filth assembled by the merits of their atrocities. They were a host of devils, set upon the land to wreak the arbitrations of a mad god's vengeance and to inflict a reckoning upon all things foolish enough to exist. They were the excommunicated wretches, banished from humanity, to whom all doors were shut. They had brown skin, white skin, and black skin. They spoke with different tongues, but in their hearts, they carried the solidarity of hate. On a cloud of filth and dust, they rode, virulent, behind their queen, past Stallworth's impotent Belgian soldiers and toward the town of Parral.

Maria turned her head to the ramparts as she passed and fixed her eyes upon the colonel. She slid one hand down between her legs and lifted her single breast with the other. Then, parting her teeth slightly, she slid her tongue across the trail, grit on her teeth, and leaned back in the saddle.

"Dime que soy hermosa!" she called, blowing him a kiss from her destroyed lips.

Colonel Basalt knew better than to acknowledge her gesture. Involuntarily, he shivered at the sight of her.

Maria laughed and rode on.

Cerro de la Cruz overlooked the southern road into Parral, which wound between low and barren hills down into the merchant district. Typically, carts lined the road manned by merchants not fortunate enough to occupy market stalls. Only a few dawdlers remained, rolling up their blankets and packing their wares before falling under the long shadow of Maria's company. The men at the livery shut and barred their doors, and children were dragged off the streets by frantic mothers. Frightened whispers carried through the plaza and marketplace, alarming all those who heard and driving them like rabbits from wolves.

Padre Allende stood alone on the steps of the Santuario del la Virgen del Rayo, running prayer beads through his fingers and muttering his petitions toward Heaven. The riders passed with only token jeers and insults for the old priest. His prayers were apparently granted. The company passed through the plaza and took the wide road west toward the river, crossing Rio Parral via an ancient stone bridge into the town center. Here the buildings were the oldest, with bricks laid by arrogant Spanish architects and paid for with silver and blood.

Iron shod hooves clacked out their terrible warning against the ancient brick road, warnings heeded by the gentry, hidden behind the rich curtains that were all that stood between them and Hell's soldiers. The river flowed, unconcerned, beside them as they followed the bricks to their destination, Casa Stallworth.

Casa Stallworth was a neo-gothic monstrosity, built with its back to the river and standing alone at the end of the brick road. It was a new construction, and the scars of its birth marked the freshly cleared land. The estate was surrounded by the obliterated foundations of buildings, razed so that gardens could be built with unobstructed views. It was as if a massive hand descended from the clouds and swept clear the land, ordained by the master of the estate, Fredrick Stallworth.

The two story building was broad, with high ceilings. A central staircase led to the main door, topped by a balcony with floor-to-ceiling French doors. Banks of evenly spaced, arched windows wrapped around the structure, each ornamented with carvings and statues of Nordic mythology. The main wall and gate sat in a state of perpetual construction; the sizeable wrought iron bars piled neatly alongside the brick path that led to the front door. A large half-circle of bricks formed a courtyard in front of the house. A cherub-lined fountain occupied the courtyard's zenith, which met with the path.

Maria Bonita crossed through the unmade gate onto the path and approached the house. Her men lingered behind, some watching, some watering their horses. One filthy Anglo dropped his trousers and squatted in the freshly dug garden at the gate, loudly ejecting runny excrement.

"Stallworth, my love!" she yelled up to the balcony.

A moment passed, and the large double doors swung open. Stallworth stepped out into the late afternoon sun, dressed in an elegant black suit with a wide silk tie, pearl in color. His mustache was trimmed, and his hair was coifed to perfection. He placed both palms on the rail, looked down with calm blue eyes, and smiled warmly.

"You look positively radiant," he said. "Truly, I am humbled."

"Well, you look like shit!"

"Deepest regrets, my dear."

Maria reached for the Bowie knife strapped to her thigh and

used it to cut a string of scalps from her rigging. She reeled them into a fleshy mass of blood-matted hair and tossed them into the fountain. Clouds of blood spread through the water until it was uniformly tainted.

"Twenty-three," she said, cutting the second string loose and tossing it after the first. As they began to float freely, they took on the appearance of bloody anemones, gently undulating in the polluted water. "I'll have payment today."

"Just the savages? You've come a long way to sully my fountain."

Maria wiped the blade on her pant leg and sheathed the knife. Her nose twitched in a manner that would have produced a sneer if she possessed enough of her lip to articulate it. She regarded him with gun-bore eyes as muddy saliva flowed freely from the damaged corner of her mouth.

"No, of course not," he said. "What is it then?"

"You owe."

"What do I owe?" asked Stallworth, his German accent becoming more pronounced.

"More. You owe me more!"

"I see."

"I have expenses. I need guns and horses."

"Yes, I suppose murder is an exhausting business. A moment, please, while I examine my available resources."

Stallworth returned to the house, leaving the doors open while Maria sat upon the roan, watching the flies land on the floating islands of hair in the fountain. Having taken great amusement in the Anglo's defecation, some in her company replicated the act themselves. The men tried to outdo each other in the locations where they squatted, the contest culminating with a nimble Pima who perched on a bird bath and shat in it.

The front doors opened, and two Mexican servants emerged carrying a small chest. Meekly, they set it on the bricks before her and opened the lid. Four canvas sacks sat inside it. One of the servants retrieved one and held it open for Maria. The sack was filled with loose silver coins. He replaced it and stood away on the front step of the house.

"Will that be enough to satisfy the extra expenses?" asked Stallworth, returning to the balcony.

Maria waved her hand, and two riders moved forward to join her. She pointed at the chest, and they spirited the bags away. Stallworth looked on, smiling.

"Enough for now," she said. "Next time, try harder, asshole."

Maria snapped the reigns, and the roan carried her back the way she came, casually taking her place at the head of the column. When she had passed the pile of iron gate posts, one of the servants fetched a broom from the house and began to fish the scalps out of the fountain.

SIXTEEN

April 1, 1865
Richmond, Virginia

The James choked slowly by, gray with ash and pushing all manner of debris in its current. A restless wind shifted aimlessly, blowing new foulness at each turn. The early evening sky was the color of milk strained through charcoal. It blanketed Richmond in a sick haze, fed from unkept fires burning in all quarters of the city.

Sheldon leaned against a smooth rock, half-submerged in the river, his chin pinned to his chest as he stared at the swirling water between his legs. A greasy film emanated from where the water touched his rags of clothing, slicking past his feet and joining the gray waters. His right fist clenched something tight, with his otherwise limp arm resting on the rocky river bottom.

"He don't look good," said Reavis.

James Reavis was in his early twenties, slender, and of average height with sharply cut sideburns that tapered down toward his pointy goatee. His thin mustache sat atop lips that, in conjunction with his beard, attempted to project a mature countenance on his youthful face. His eyes, dark like a baby crow's, seemed ready to fly at any moment. He wore a Confederate cavalry uniform with lieutenant's bars, his weathered hat impregnated with dust and ash.

"He'll come around, no doubt," said Robert Black.

"You sure he ain't dead and just don't know it?"

"Help me get these rags off him."

Reavis held him up while Robert pulled his shirt over his head and tossed it in the river. The shirt left an oily wake as it trailed down the James. Reavis pulled Sheldon's pants off while Robert held him under his arms, then sent them after the shirt among the flotsam. Pulling a ditty kit out of the haversack, Robert found a straight razor and started hacking off Sheldon's lice-infested matted hair. The trauma solicited only a murmur of disapproval and feeble resistance.

"Trust me, you don't want this hair, Sam."

When it was too short to grip, he lathered it with soap and shaved it to the skin as Sheldon gasped for air, naked and shivering in the filmy water.

"Fuck you, Crow!" Sam managed.

"Lean down, let's rinse." Robert baptized him in the stream.

"How did you manage to keep that?" Reavis asked, noting the gold coin in Sheldon's fist.

"Fuck you," Sheldon sputtered through chattering teeth.

Robert produced a bottle of coal oil from the haversack, soaked a rag in it, then proceeded to wipe Sheldon from his nicked and bleeding scalp down to his gnarled feet. His skin lit up in a violent rash, and the shivers became convulsions.

"It's to your better health. Believe me, I take no pleasure in washing your filthy cock!" Robert said as Sheldon tried to slip from their grasp.

When it was done, they helped him into a dingy set of long underwear and covered him in a horse blanket.

"War's almost over, Sam," said Black.

"Well, huzzah."

"We shouldn't linger," said Reavis. "My ink is good, but you never know when one of these cousin-fuckers might get it in their mind to seek verification."

"Who the fuck is he?"

"This is James Reavis, he forged your release. He's right, though, we'd not be wise to stay. Can you walk?"

"I'll flap my arms and fly if I need to."

Reavis lent a shoulder to Sam, who struggled to keep his balance. The long underwear sagged in unusual places on Sheldon's body; his legs had withered to bone, and his chest sank inward. His freshly shaved head completed the skeletal image. Robert put his jacket over Sam's shoulders and lent his support. It almost appeared like he was dragging a dead man, not an uncommon sight in Richmond.

It didn't take long to reach the James' southern shore and the rail bridge crossing back to Richmond proper. The bridge, not meant for foot traffic, was the only crossing still standing. A steady volume of freight and men rode the line in a southern exodus toward Danville and beyond.

The heavy, iron clatter of a train thumped from the far side, followed by the singing of the wheels screeching across the rails. They stepped off the tracks and waited for the train to pass; thirteen cars filled with passengers, soldiers, and all imaginable objects, stretching away from the encroaching reach of the Union army. Bloodied and depleted of soul, a dozen soldiers clung to crates and boxes strapped to the flat car at the rear. They held on to the freight like shipwrecked castaways floating to an uncertain fate.

With the tracks clear, they hastily dragged Sheldon to the opposite side, narrowly evading another empty train that rolled in behind them to be filled.

"Water." Sheldon's legs quivered as they stood aside from the tracks.

Robert offered his canteen, holding it up to Sheldon's lips. The water vanished into his mouth like it was absorbed into dust.

"The house is not far, on Sugar Bottom," said Black.

Wagon teams were at work hauling the contents of warehouses toward the railyard. When one pulled out, a new one swiftly replaced it. They gave the wagons a wide birth and kept to the far side of the road. Robert led them up a broad and mostly deserted street that intersected at a place that looked well-suited to commerce if the shops had not all been shuttered. This street put them a stone's throw from the Capitol, where several fine-suited men moped about on the steps. They turned southwest from there, up a narrow street with a slight incline, stopping for Sheldon to retch several times.

They arrived at a broad two-story building with a hitching post set off to the side. It was offset from its neighboring houses by two narrow gaps, both fenced off. A wide veranda extended from each floor, the upper segmented into private boxes with rose trellises separating them and private doors leading out from the house. The lower patio was a simple porch of wood planking. A red-painted door stood central, with no windows. The three of them turned up the walk and made for the door.

The Sugar Bottom Parlor, or the Parlor, as it was commonly known to its patrons, was a well-established and delicately sanctioned bordello. Josephine "Josie" DeMerrit, the proprietor and madam, catered to the elite of Richmond society. However, the war caused her to extend her services to the military officer class as well. In the shadow of Richmond's impending fall, her standards had sunk even lower to accept nearly anyone with a semblance of civility and silver or gold in their pockets.

She greeted them as the red door swung in, and the smoke-choked daylight was repelled by the cool, sweet darkness of the Parlor.

"Good evening, gentlemen!"

The sultry quality of Josephine DeMerrit's voice suggested seduction with every syllable. She wore a forest green silk gown with cream-colored lace around the neck and cuffs. A cameo pendant hung from a thin, gold chain just above the curves of her bosom. Constellations of emeralds burned in the lamplight, accentuating her earrings, broach, and silver hairpin. Her auburn hair was in a loose wrap, as she was fond of letting it fall free to punctuate her lascivious innuendos. While it was generally accepted that she had reached her fortieth year, her smooth skin and youthful eyes gave the impression of a much younger woman.

They walked into a large, open room segmented into smaller areas by couches, tables, and lace curtains. A long mahogany bar stretched across one end of the room, its dozen or so stools sparsely occupied by a few quiet men looking straight down into the pits of their whiskey glasses. The room was dimly lit by a pair of Tiffany glass chandeliers and supplemented with votive candles on the bar and tabletops. A one-handed piano player with captain's bars played the left hand of a nocturne on the piano at the far end of the room. His right arm hung loosely at his side, truncated in a stump wrapped in a yellowing bandage tinged by blood. Opposite the piano was a veiled doorway leading to a staircase. They chose an empty table near the fireplace.

"Josie, you're the picture of radiance!" said Black.

"I see my handsome captain has returned with a friend. By the looks of it, I'd say he'd tell a sorrowful tale."

"Indeed, he would, though such mortal tortures ought not to be spoken of in such fine company and pleasant hospitality."

"Of course, I would never imagine to pry!"

Robert produced five twenty-dollar gold pieces and laid them between himself and Josie. A thin smile creased her lips as she spirited them away to a hidden place on her person.

"We will need another room, otherwise another bed in mine. Also, draw a bath, and we'll enjoy whatever fare you see fit to serve us."

"I'll bring another bed, it's the best I can do. We'll heat a bath for you right away. Would you like to dine in your room as well?" Her glance at Sheldon's unhealthy appearance made this seem more like a suggestion than a question. Then, turning to Reavis, she said, "Regretfully, Rose left us last night and evacuated with the others, so your choice of company is... limited."

Black answered for them both. "I'm certain my spry companion here would be delighted and entertained by whatever company is at hand, though, as usual, I would prefer to share my time with a bottle of bourbon, if possible."

"The Captain is in luck. My house is immune to the Mayor's imposed abstinence, and I still have several fine bottles at hand," she laughed. "I'll be just a moment!"

Josephine disappeared behind the bar and returned with an opaque, brown bottle bearing no label or identifying marks. She set the bottle down with three glasses, smiling sweetly.

"Your bath is being drawn. Would you like to eat while you wait or take repast in your rooms?"

Robert, again, took her meaning to prefer the latter. He lifted a finger and pointed to the curtain that veiled the stairway to the second floor.

"Thank you, Josie."

"If not Rosie, I would be grateful to receive whoever remains on staff. If that's ok with you, sir?" Reavis waited for Black's approving nod.

Robert shrugged and passed him a small gold coin.

"That would be Edna or Cora Eve. Though, in fairness, Edna has a wandering eye if such things unnerve you."

"I'm sure Cora Eve will be delightful," said Reavis.

Josie nodded and vanished behind a discrete curtain that led to the kitchen behind the bar. The muffled sounds of pans clattering could soon be heard against the one-handed lullaby played by the doleful amputee at the piano.

Reavis poured himself a thick cut of bourbon from the bottle.

"Thank you, sir. If you need anything, you know where to find me," he said, tipping his dusty hat and walking toward the staircase.

"Who is that man?" Sheldon croaked.

"A friend. After Price fucked us, he helped me break out of Libby. How do you feel?"

"What kind of question is that?"

"Can you make it up the fucking stairs is my meaning!"

"Yes."

Robert scooped up the bottle and the remaining glasses

before heading toward the stairs behind the curtain. Sheldon followed, weak but stable. They ascended and entered the second room on the right, where the bath was already being drawn and the second bed had yet to be installed. To that score, a boy of about eight years reported that no additional bed could be provided, but he would supply them with extra bedding to outfit the room's sofa.

Sheldon sat on the bed and fell backward, closing his eyes. The boy returned quickly with a tray of fried fish and cornbread and laid it on the low sitting table next to the wobbly couch.

"Catfish, freshly caught this mornin'!" he said.

Robert tipped the boy with a silver coin and waved him out the door. Sheldon rose from his stasis like a cat stalking the scent of its prey. He descended on the feast before the kid crossed the threshold. Robert took a piece of cornbread and a small piece of fish.

"Eat what you will, but pace yourself," he said.

"Ugh," Sheldon groaned, chewing a piece of fish. "Is this rat? Tastes like rat. Everything tastes like rat."

"I doubt it."

Edna, the cross-eyed woman, finished drawing the bath as Sheldon mopped the last of the juices and butter with cornbread. Water had splashed on her blouse, rendering a slightly translucent view of her breasts. She smiled amiably at Robert as she exited but did not make eye contact.

"You paid in gold. No silver?" asked Sheldon.

"A little, not enough."

"We collect, not distribute."

"Most of the gold is gone, but we can still get what's left. That's why I'm here."

"It was that fat fuck Price. I'll cut that craven shit bird into jerky and feed him his own rank flesh!" Sheldon's last words trailed as the effort winded him.

"If Thomas has not already dispatched him."

Sheldon abandoned the discussion and set to undressing.

Strength was returning to his appendages, though his control of them was shaky. His hands trembled at his shirt buttons as if undoing them in a snowstorm. Robert helped him step into the bath, shocked that he didn't float like a twig.

"Don't fall asleep and drown. I'm going to take this bottle down to the bar and find something more pleasing to stare at than your withered corpse!"

"Get on then," Sheldon said, sinking into warm oblivion.

Robert left him in the steaming water and descended the stairs. The faint creaking of beds and dusty grunts haunted the hall. He found the bar deserted, with only the barkeep holding vigil over a formation of well-polished glasses. He took a seat with his back to the piano and poured himself a glass of bourbon.

Edna emerged from behind the kitchen like a spider whose web Robert had just disturbed. She walked slowly past with her head turned away, brushing his shoulders delicately with her fingertips. Robert stared straight ahead, declining her invitation. She sat at the piano and began awkwardly making her way through Beautiful Dreamer. The stuttering pace of her playing encouraged Robert to drink faster.

Her voice mumbled through a few lyrics until finally coming to an accord with the melody and finding confidence:

Beautiful dreamer, out on the sea
Mermaids are chanting the wild lorelei
Over the streamlet vapors are borne,
Waiting to fade at the bright coming morn

It started with electricity, the raising of hair on his neck and forearm, then a pressure came as Elizabeth's three teeth, on their leather cord, slowly dug into his neck.

Beautiful dreamer, beam on my heart
Even as the morn on the streamlet and sea
Then will all clouds of sorrow depart.

The movement was undeniable beneath his collar, the teeth shifted and thrashed until finally pushing their way out of his shirt like pupa from a cocoon.

Beautiful dreamer, awake unto me
Beautiful dreamer, awake unto me
Awake unto me, awake unto me, awake, awake...

The music of Steven Foster modulated smoothly to Mozart, a lullaby drifting at the edge of familiarity as the words "awake unto me" floated into the new key. He turned his head in the direction of the new melody and found Edna's eyes, now straightened, waiting for him, her face away from the piano while her hands played on flawlessly. The brown of her eyes began to cool and fade, settling to pale blue, her lips rising into a smile poised to speak his name.

"Elizabeth," he said. "I've missed you, my love."

"Do you like this flesh? I could have chosen the barman," said Elizabeth, rising from the piano in the vessel of Edna's body.

"I would not love you less."

She sat at the table across from him and reached out to hold his hand. The barkeep took brief notice, then returned to sentry over his glassware.

"Lies," she smiled.

"Seeing you is like rain on a sunny day. I could reach out and touch you, perhaps kiss your lips, but it would not be you."

"The world is an illusion, why should love be any different?" She leaned in and kissed his neck.

Robert sighed and closed his eyes, imagining another face. When he opened them, the barman was staring at him again.

"That was almost real," Robert sighed.

"You freed the Sheldon boy," Elizabeth whispered into his ear.

"Yes, on my father's orders."

"Your father gives me cause to worry."

"Do you know something I don't?"

"Almost everything," she smiled. "This world holds few secrets from me."

Robert sipped his bourbon and looked into the clear blue of her eyes. Her smile faded as she continued.

"Your father runs a risky gambit, sending you here."

"Risk that he also shares

"Wouldn't it be more prudent to run?"

"He can't outrun that which resides within him."

"Yes, I know. But you can."

The distant clatter of pans from the kitchen interrupted her words. Robert looked toward the curtain behind the bar and saw the shape of Josie fussing about. Voices were raised, though he couldn't make out the words.

Josie appeared through the curtain with a plate of cobbler and a fork. She whispered something to the barkeep, who nodded, then turned toward Robert's table.

The vessel of Edna twitched slightly, and her face became slack.

"My handsome captain had second thoughts on the company?" Josie asked. "Such a fetching creature such as yourself might even inspire me to come out of retirement. I don't mean to impose, but you must try my peach cobbler, made fresh this morning. It rarely lasts this long, I put a bit away. Special for you."

She set the plate down in front of Robert.

"On further thought, such turbulent times as ours give occasion for exception. I'm certain Edna wouldn't mind, providing the good captain was also inclined to perhaps increase the party by one?"

The madame leaned over the table, her chest displayed inches from Robert's nose.

A guttural growl belched from Edna's lips as she took the fork from the cobbler plate and thrust it down with inhuman force into Josie's hand, pinning it to the table. Before the scream escaped the madam's lips, Edna pounced upon the bar, kicking over the meticulously polished glassware, and fell upon the barkeep, tearing and biting at his face.

"They've betrayed you," Elizabeth spat. "He sent a messenger to the garrison, you haven't much time."

Robert turned his back to the fray and ascended the stairs, three at a time, yelling for Reavis. The door to Reavis' room opened before he could lay his fist to it.

"We're leaving now!" Behind Reavis, Cora Eve clutched the sheets to her chest. Black added, "Kill her if she tries to stop you."

Reavis looked back at the girl. She shot past the two of them from the bed and down the stairs. He collected his clothes in the filtered moonlight while Robert crossed the hall.

Sheldon had bathed, dressed, and donned his boots before falling asleep, sitting upright on the couch. His eyes rolled open when Robert rushed in. Snapping alert, he looked to Black for direction.

"Get up, now!" Robert ordered.

Sheldon lurched to his feet, and they met Reavis in the hall. Together they descended the stairs, Reavis leading with his Dragoon in his fist, arm extended. The barkeep slumped over his rail, bleeding on the oak, a broken bottle neck protruding from his throat. Josie stood there, screaming obscenities, her hand firmly nailed to the table. A trail of blood led through the kitchen curtain toward the sound of violence and death.

They dashed for the door and hit the cobblestone street running. Sheldon limped along behind, trying to keep pace. They turned into a narrow alley and ran on in the dark.

"We've no choice but to make for the Van Lew house," said Robert.

"I'm right behind you," Reavis answered.

An invisible rush of force laid against Robert's chest. Briefly, it felt as if a person's weight hung from his necklace, then it was gone.

Their flight from Sugar Bottom was a short but maddening trip Sheldon would only remember in blurred and fragmented images. Below them, the fires of the warehouse district reflected in the James while drunken looters moved like devils through the streets.

A fat constable poured whiskey barrels into the streets as depraved and desperate men lapped it from the ground like dogs, with blue flames crawling the gutters and chasing their lips as the officer set it alight.

The river slowed like honey, choked with fleeing horses, blood, and burning ships. Gaunt soldiers in sorrowful firing squads aimed at the sinking beasts swimming through the blood-frothed fire. They wept as they reloaded, over and over.

Lines of Rebels stretched across the horizon toward the rail line. They lurched and hunched and slithered like snails, burdened with packs, rifles, and flour sacks stuffed with anything that would fit.

Sometime in the dirty light before dawn, a thunderous explosion shook buildings and shattered windows. Sheldon plausibly identified it as the end of times, though in fact, it was the Richmond Armory disintegrating in advance of the impending Federal occupation.

SEVENTEEN

April 1, 1865
New Haven, Connecticut

The Goodrich estate stood out defiantly against the spring, its paths, and gardens waging a war of attrition with the weeds and wildflowers. The house sat shuttered, its roof covered in moss and swaths of shingles missing from its walls. The long-unchecked trees leaned in with bony arms, embracing it as if it were an ancient abandoned bird's nest. No one lived in the house of Cyrus Goodrich.

William Russell met Alphonso Taft at the gate and stood a moment before passing through. A group of children watched from across the lane, marveling at their bravery, for the house was surely haunted. Ominously, a single ray of sun broke through the clouds to shine upon the roof.

"Curious purchase," said Taft.

"Real estate speculation has always been a hobby of mine."

"Considering the history, it seems in poor taste."

"Are you offended?" asked Russell. "At such a bargain price, I could hardly resist."

Taft did not answer, instead gazing up at a beehive fixed in the eaves.

"Did you know a gruesome murder took place here?"

"Is there a point to all of this?"

"One that was never solved," said Russell. "Largely because of my efforts; you see, the police chief is a former student of mine. Had I informed him that Saint Peter had committed that heinous crime, no doubt he would have stormed Heaven to get his man. Of course, the name of Robert Black was never mentioned in such conversation."

"Nor should it be now, William! You're trying my patience!"

Russell chuckled, "Very well, I'm just having a laugh. No need to become unhinged."

They stepped around to the back of the house, and Russell fumbled through his pockets for the keys. A dozen or so crows cawed at them from the surrounding trees.

"After you," Russell opened the door.

Razors of light permeated the darkness through the cracks in the shutters, illuminating walls of swirling dust. Russell carefully navigated his way to a window, opening it for the first time in nearly two years. They stood in a dining room, looking over a fine mahogany table, gray with dust. He ran his finger across to test the depth and shook his head in disapproval. He opened the remaining two windows and flooded the room with light. Outside, the clouds dispersed, and a light breeze found its way into the long-dormant house.

"Thank you for traveling early, I understand that your practice in Ohio is hard to put down," Russell said.

"Don't you think it's morbid?" asked Taft.

"What?"

"Planning to attend the funeral of a man you intend to murder."

"You're just as culpable as I in the matter," said Russell. "Since when did you develop scruples?"

"I'm not so jaded that the absurdity escapes me."

"Good News out of Richmond," Russell changed the subject.

"Oh?"

"Collins tells me that Robert Black has resurfaced," Russell Continued.

"Really?"

"You don't seem surprised," Russell said, casually scrutinizing his partner.

"Yes, well…"

Russell ignored his muttering and moved through the

rooms on the first floor, unshuttering windows and opening the house to the encroaching spring air. He took note of the furnishings as he went, nodding approvingly at some while grimacing at others as if saying, "that will have to go" or "that might do."

"I do have my concerns about Mr. Black," Russell said while pondering a painting of Cyrus's young daughter, Elizabeth.

"How so?"

"Robert claims to have been incarcerated at Libby Prison for the last two years, betrayed by Virgil Price."

"That would account for his absence," said Taft.

"Except, it doesn't," said Russell, brushing cobwebs from a doorframe.

"Explain."

"It seems Collins has acquired several invoices, requisitions, and orders, made by Robert, all of which occurred while he claims to have been imprisoned in Richmond."

"Curious," said Taft.

"What's even more curious is that he has managed to locate both Virgil Price and Samuel Sheldon. According to the Van Lews, he and Thomas are currently retrieving them."

"That's fantastic news!"

"So it would seem."

Several honeybees joined them in the parlor, buzzing erratically around their heads. Russell stuck his head out the window and observed a cluster of them around the hive in the eaves. He shut the window, and they retreated into the dining room.

"Perhaps we could sit?" Russell gestured to the dusty table.

"If it pleases you."

The two men pulled chairs from the table and sat across from each other. An intrepid honeybee trailed tracks through the dust between them. The sunlight streaking in lit up the dust like a layer of frost, with tiny golden storms kicking up every time one put their hand down on the wood or shifted in their chairs.

"You haven't seemed yourself these days," said Russell. "In fact, you haven't for some time. Is there something you should tell me?"

"How ironic," Taft mused, eyeing the bee.

The bee between them shook the dust from its wings and took flight. It bounced off the window glass, drawn to the futility of light. After several attempts, it rested on the invisible barrier, defeated.

"What is?"

"That you should say I'm not myself when none of us are. It's the nature of our existence now, is it not? To never be alone. I haven't been myself since Bavaria, and I defy you to say anything different of yourself."

Russell traced his finger through the dust, mindlessly creating abstract doodles.

"You know that that was not my meaning."

"What then?" Taft looked sternly across the table.

"I want to know that it is not your hand that works against us," said Russell, meeting Taft's stare.

"Are you mad?"

"That is not a denial."

"Of course not, you fool!"

A resounding thud interrupted their conversation and shook the floorboards. A pair of gruff voices argued on the porch, muffled behind the door; three sharp knocks followed.

"Very well, I'll take your word," said Russell.

"Are you expecting someone?"

"Indeed," Russell rose to answer the door.

Standing on the stoop was the tall and stoic Jay Sheldon, flanked by two Guildsmen in workman's overalls. Their faces were dim and expressionless, with eyes nearly void of iris. Between them spanned a massive crate, effortlessly hefted as if it were filled with straw.

"Russell," Jay nodded as he entered.

"Sheldon," Russell extended his hand.

Jay Sheldon shook his hand and stepped into the parlor. He looked around the room and swiped at the squadron of bees buzzing around the room.

"What do you want to do with it?"

"Unbox it. Place it against that wall."

"What of the furniture?"

Russell stroked his beard in thought.

"Take it all. Sell it if you want, or burn it. I don't care."

Jay turned to the guildsmen lurking at the threshold.

"You heard him, get to it!"

Without further invitation, Jay moved deeper into the house and found Taft still seated at the dining room table. He nodded to the man, then turned back to Russell.

"Well?" Jay asked.

"Your son lives," said Russell.

"Tell him he needs to come home, his mother is gravely ill."

In the front parlor, the guildsmen effortlessly maneuvered the crate, the mass of it shaking the house every time they flipped it over. Russell added to the din, removing paintings from the wall and tossing them into the debris from the discarded crate.

"Teressa is not well?" Russell's tone shifted to one that was as close to compassion as he was capable of.

"She is not. We've engaged an army of specialists whose unanimous appraisal indicates she will not survive the year."

"I'm sorry, Jay. I don't have the words."

"You never have."

They were interrupted by a series of heavy thuds and crashes carrying the timbre of a polyphonic gong or a chorus of iron bells smashing on wooden planks.

"Easy!" Russell shouted.

Taft stood and joined them in the parlor. Russell knelt beside an ancient harpsichord, attaching one of the disassembled legs. The lid was ajar, the underside revealing an ornate design, the theme of which was carried out across the casing. The enamel was cracked over the black and gold paint, and the ivory keyboard was of advanced age.

"Is that?"

"Yes," answered Russell

"I haven't seen that thing since Ingolstadt! How did you acquire it?" Asked Taft.

"I retrieved it," said Jay.

"At my request," said Russell. "This instrument brings back memories."

"Indeed, it does," Russell agreed.

The guildsmen began hauling out the boxing and discarded paintings. Russell busied himself assembling the harpsichord's legs and supports. When all four legs were attached and the supports secured, he enlisted the workers to help him lift and place it where a small couch had existed moments before.

"Lee intends to surrender soon," said Russell. "It won't be long now."

"Murdering Lincoln will ensure that this war will outlive our generation if it ends at all," said Taft.

"Conflict begets motion," said Russell.

"So we are told."

EIGHTEEN

April 1865
Hidalgo Del Parral
State Of Chihuahua, Mexico

T he stone thoroughfare ended, and the wheels went quiet save the squeaking of the axles. Fortune plodded along, pulling Pedro's wagon on the dirt road toward the livery, the last building of note on the way out of Parral. Esteban waited for him near the road. Pedro wouldn't need to step down from the wagon to conduct their transaction. Sick dread baked in his stomach. It was the last opportunity he would have to turn back. He pulled up on the reins and contemplated having the horse reshod, lingering until it was too late to proceed. The thought passed as the farrier, Esteban, walked out to meet him.

"You are late today, Pedro! You may find yourself still on the road when the sun goes down," Esteban said.

"Troubles all day, my friend. Haggling and arguments have been the sum of my existence!" Pedro lied. In fact, he was perfectly on schedule.

"Ah, sorry to hear it, take care my friend!"

"Thank you," he said and continued up the road.

The time was upon him, and he could not turn back. He rode into a narrow canyon filled with scrub oak, mesquite, and many large boulders. A dry creek ran through the middle, running parallel to the road, his landmark. He stopped the cart where the little gully came closest to the road. Sweat soaked the rim of his sombrero. He nervously shifted it on his head and scratched at his scalp. The sun dipped low as he waited for a sign.

Two Apache had climbed into the back of his wagon before Pedro noticed. He turned only in time to catch a third hopping in and hiding under some blankets. Pedro recognized the fourth, Delgadito, as having been with Geronimo when they found him shot near the Rio Salado. Once hidden in the canvas-covered wagon bed, Pedro snapped the reins, and the wagon moved on.

Pedro was well known at the fort on Cerro del la Cruz. Most merchants and vendors refused to deal with the soldiers, as they were in the pocket of Frederick Stallworth. This trepidation was in no small part due to Stallworth's private army and its mistress, Maria Bonita.

Colonel Basalt had no illusions about his place in the land. Mexico was a savage place of feudal corruption where loyalties shifted with the sand. While the Stallworths of this world would come and go, the only true masters were gold, silver, and of course, lead. He took his stipend and kept his post, never interfering and practicing silence. It took some time, but France was made to understand this, even if Maximillian did not. The troop ships left daily from Veracruz. Soon Colonel Basalt would be on one as well, bringing his men back home to their families. He had been fortunate, only one man in his charge had perished, which occurred during a drunken brawl over a prostitute. He made his regular patrols, filed his reports, and made no effort to interfere with Stallworth or the loathsome doings of Maria Bonita and her degenerate horde.

Pedro knew of Basalt's faux patrols through the wastelands, avoiding any possible hostility or conflict. He planned his visit that day, knowing the colonel and the bulk of his men would be away from the post on what the colonel often referred to as a fishing trip. Pedro whispered a warning to his passengers as he turned the wagon off the main road and up the slight incline of the rutted path to the fort. He scanned the rocks and hillside and wondered where Geronimo and his warriors could be hiding in such a barren landscape. Not so much as a lizard moved.

He stopped the wagon in front of the ancient wood gate. The fort had outlived its Spanish builders by nearly a hundred and fifty years. Generations of repairs and improvements marked the efforts of its many occupants. Endless mortar patches and discolored stones pocked the walls while a reinforced gate of scrap iron smiled from the demented face of it. The walls sank low and uneven with jagged ramparts, resembling something a child would draw rather than a practical fortification. No army of consequence would be daunted by the crumbling assemblage of stone and adobe, and surely, no serious army would reside within. It was a sad and futile outpost.

"Bonjour!" Pedro yelled up at the gate.

It swung in without a response. Two soldiers waved him through. Pedro snapped the reins, and the wagon rolled forward. The entire garrison lived within the enclosure. A series of crude bunkhouses leaned along the walls, and a two-level commissary building sat centrally. A blasted chapel, with a partial roof and a missing wall, was converted into a commode. The chapel's bell lay half-buried in the dirt outside, cracked and the color of dead moss. Pedro brought his wagon to a halt outside the commissary and hitched Fortune to the post there.

"Pedro!" Ricard called out. His tendency to roll his r's gave his speech a musical, if not comedic, quality.

Ricard was one of the few Frenchmen in the troop, though Pedro couldn't tell him from the Belgians. Ricard assured him that the difference was profound. He served as the quartermaster and chef of the company, transacting most of the fort's business with Pedro and the few other merchants willing to trade. Ricard was thick but not fat and below average in height. He wore an apron that covered him from chest to kneecap, every inch of fabric covered in a millennium of stains, obliterating any record of the garment's original color.

"Ricard, good to see you!"

The Frenchman waved him into the empty mess area. He was in the process of cleaning up from the dinner service. The number of plates indicated that service had been light, as most of the company had ridden out with Basalt.

"Have you brought me any butter or sweet cream today, my friend? There is very little to be had in town, at least that anyone will part with."

"Not as much as you would want, but I did bring some. Also, I have more salted beef and some smoked goat jerky."

"That sounds amazing! I still dream of the smoked trout you brought me a few months back. You are very talented, my friend, are you sure you aren't French?"

"I imagine you will want all my butter and cream, but what of the beef? I have about forty pounds, you want the whole load?"

"Yes, of course," he said. "You always have the finest quality. I think the other farmers piss in everything they sell me! Savages, I swear!"

"Ha! Good then. I'll be right back."

Pedro went to the wagon and carefully looked inside before removing his goods. The Apache were gone. The two soldiers at the gate could not be seen, but the gate stood open. Certainly, they were already dead. Something moved in his periphery, though he turned too late to see. Something like a muffled yelp sounded, then silence. Pedro lifted the burlap-wrapped side of beef over his shoulder and returned to the commissary.

"Listen, Ricard, I was wondering if we could make a different trade today?"

"How so?"

"I dropped my rifle chasing a deer this week," explained Pedro. "It fell down a hillside, completely smashed the breach, and bent the barrel. I think it struck every rock... twice! Any chance you can sell me a new one?"

"Colonel would have my hide if he found out, but if you keep it between us, I think I can help you. Let me grab my key. Go ahead and bring in the rest of the order."

Pedro returned to the wagon to find Geronimo standing calmly beside it. Before he could ask, the Apache nodded his head. Everyone in the compound had been slain. A sliver of moon looked down from the darkening sky; nothing moved in the twilight. He saw no bodies nor signs of struggle. A shiver went down his spine as Pedro returned the nod to Geronimo and went back into the commissary with another load.

"Just so we understand each other, I cannot give you one of the repeating rifles. It has to be one of the older ones, or it would be missed."

Ricard waved the heavy iron key at him to emphasize his point and then walked out the swinging doors to the compound. The armory sat on the opposite side of the commissary building, an independent room accessed only from the outside. Ricard disappeared around the corner; Pedro stood a few paces back. His stomach turned at the gurgling and slosh of blood that followed.

"I'm sorry, Ricard."

Pedro turned the corner and plucked the iron key from Ricard's hand as the dirt greedily sucked up the blood where he lay. He put the key in the lock of the fort's only formidable door and released the sturdy latch. Racks of pistols and rifles lay before them amid cases of ammunition. The weapons looked clean. Pedro had little doubt that they had never been fired. Delgadito stepped forward with two warriors as if the shadow itself was a door. Several others manifested like spirits around them. Then, wordlessly, they loaded the weapons into Pedro's wagon.

Geronimo put a hand on Pedro's shoulder, heavy and dense as stone.

"It's time," he said, his mouth a slit in his broad face that barely seemed to move.

"Wait," said Pedro, holding his hand up. He stepped over to Fortune, who remained hitched to the wagon. "Goodbye, boy. You are a fine friend!"

He caressed the horse's muzzle and patted him on the flank.

Fortune neighed.

Delgadito stepped behind him and held Pedro's arms back. Geronimo drew his blade. He carefully sank the tip into Pedro's chest and drug the edge through his flesh. Before the scream had totally escaped Pedro's lips, Geronimo brought the pommel down hard on the back of his skull. Pedro fell to the blood-muddied ground near the body of Ricard.

It was dawn when Pedro came shuddering back into consciousness. The sky was nearly the same darkened color as when he fell, confusing dusk with morning in his mind. Two soldiers hauled him by his arms and legs toward a row of bodies laid out in the center of the compound. Startled by his reanimation, the soldiers dropped him to the ground. Pain streaked across his chest, and his head throbbed. His clothes were drenched in blood, and he felt weakened and sick by the loss of it. The soldiers cried out for Colonel Basalt, staring at him with shocked faces as if beholding a Mexican Lazarus.

"Pedro, you live!" cried Basalt. "Who did this?"

"Juárez," Pedro croaked. The effort nearly caused him to lose consciousness again.

"Pig fuckers! You're certain?"

Pedro's eyes focused on the commissary wall, past the fuming Basalt. Written in blood, now darkened and coagulated, were the words, "Viva Mexico! Viva Juárez!"

"Juáristas," said Pedro, laying his head in the dust.

April 1865
State Of Chihuahua, Mexico

Geronimo held the flat rock between his fingers, the edges jagged where it had been intentionally chipped away. He took a few steps forward and dropped the stone tool, picking up another rock. Turning it over in his hand, he sniffed the soot.

There was a scattering of such stones not far from a slight depression in the earth, which he kicked at with his moccasin.

"Mescal."

Delgadito nodded, "Days old."

No other traces of the camp existed. Geronimo speculated it had been a small group, perhaps a family or hunting party. They must have felt comfortable, he thought, to stay long enough to roast mescal. He sat on a flat rock, took a few pinon seeds from his pouch, and chewed them. The rest of the party filed into the clearing and laid down their heavy bundles of rifles and packs of ammunition. Once unburdened, they took up places of rest in the shade of the rocks.

An arrow struck the dirt at Geronimo's feet with a dry thud, startling him from his thoughts. He came to his feet, shouldering his rifle and looking for cover. Laughter echoed down from the rocks above, mixed with whoops and hollers. Chatto stepped up on a boulder holding his bow over his head triumphantly.

"Ha! I could have crept down under your boot if I wished!" Chatto shouted between bursts of laughter.

Geronimo scowled, the scar on his face becoming cavernous. He looked to Chatto, not yet unshouldering his weapon. Geronimo's aggressive stance caused Chatto to laugh harder, doubling him in a full belly convulsion.

"Next time, come from downwind, I could smell you long before your shot," said Geronimo.

Chatto just laughed harder.

Geronimo grunted in frustration. Six other Apache rose out of the rocks and scrub oak, laughing. He recognized them as warriors from Juh's band.

"Enough of your child's play! Come down, help carry the load! We have many guns!"

Chatto joined Geronimo in the clearing, his small band quick to follow. His mirth lingered, nearly renewed to laughter with every scowl from Geronimo.

"There is a wagon filled with guns and powder. We had to

leave it and hide many weapons. Perhaps a half-day from here. Chewawa can take you there."

"Geronimo decides for us now? I did not know this!"

"Do what you will," Geronimo growled. He waved his hand, and the Apache in his party took up their burdens and fell in. Chewawa went to Chatto and spoke in muted tones, his hands enunciating his disapproval, eventually convincing him to retrieve the guns. Geronimo did not look back.

By mid-afternoon, they had come to a place where water issued directly from the rising cliff face. It trickled noiselessly through a narrow wash and pooled in a sandy rock bowl in the mountain's shadow. One of Chatto's band had taken Chewawa's place, a malnourished-looking youth barely as tall as the rifles he carried. He struggled to keep the blanket secured around the bundle. Some skewed forward, others back. When they reached the water, he fell to his knees before all others and slurped straight from the pool.

Only one path led up the rock face to the stronghold of Juh. The initial ascent was narrow and full of switchbacks that could only be taken single file. Those who did not possess the Chiricahua's attributes for climbing might consider the path impassible entirely. Any that attempted the climb would find themselves vulnerable to all manner of attack from above. Even undefended, the foremost in a group could inadvertently assail those who followed with a rain of tumbling rocks larger than a man's skull. Horses would find the way impossible altogether. The upper ascent followed a gash in the mountain hidden by tall pines and withered black trees that sprung out from cracks in the rocks. The canyon walls shot up steeply to the tree-lined ledges, naturally suited for defenders to dispense death on the uninvited. It opened to an expansive mesa top at the crest, forested and bountiful with fresh springs and game. This was Juh's land and the land of his people.

Geronimo stopped to drink, then took to the path. He had yet to rise far on the trail before being met by several of Juh's warriors, led by Lozen and Nana. They divided the guns among the larger group, and the path was joyfully taken. Nana climbed with Geronimo as he told the story of their raid on the fort on Cerro de la Cruz. He recited the account of Pedro's deception, the slow crawl of the wagon as they fled upon the soldier's road, and the caching of the rifles. Geronimo did not speak of the meeting with Chatto other than to say that he had gone for the guns.

It was another country on the mesa. The tall pines and cool springs existed in a merciful and unlikely respite to an otherwise blasted landscape of scorching rocks governed by the hostile sun. Deer infested the pine stands and loitered in the grassy stretches of meadows. Rabbits, thick as roaches, ran through the grass with impunity in the absence of wolves and coyotes. Only the occasional shadow of raptor wings gave them any pause. Cook fires gave up their smoke from camps scattered throughout the shallow, mesa-top valley. Wickiups, richly covered in pelts and painted deer skins, clustered around the fires around which women and children made moccasins or cut arrowheads from iron barrel bands. Yet, for all the abundance, they lacked contentedness as the entire encampment prepared for war.

Nana led Geronimo through a sun-dappled wood of soft, dry earth, reddish in color. They came to a charred and desolate clearing. The blackened bones of a longhouse lay like a fossil turned to charcoal in the ashen waste of blackened earth. The vaguely circular ghosts of wickiups spotted the field around the central house. A withered string of flowers, partially burned, lay fluttering in the wind on a rocky piece of earth. Geronimo sighed deeply and looked at Nana.

"Ekta," said Nana

Geronimo knew of the girl; the ashes spoke to her loss.

"Mexicans?"

"The wicked one whose face is scarred. We found their bodies below the mountain. Her men took their scalps and destroyed their bodies. They will not walk peacefully in the Happy Place that is after."

Many years before, Geronimo had set fire to his own wickiup, where his wife and child once slept. He had also set fire to his mother's. The memories were renewed in the ashes of the longhouse, where Ekta would never dance and never take the path of the White Painted Woman. Like his Alope, Ekta and her memory now belonged to the flames and violence they would visit upon the enemy.

They left the burnt place and passed through another stand of trees, thicker and shadier than before. The clearing beyond it was wide and shallow, butting up against the mesa's edge and the blue and cloudless sky. The shelters here were larger and more permanent than the others they passed. Well-fed fires blazed while the Apache prepared for war.

They found Juh, central in the operations, naked to his breechcloth and barefoot in the dried grass. His hair was pulled back with a beaded leather cord, exposing his square jaw and broad forehead. Juh stood slightly taller than average but presented an imposing presence. He compensated for what he lacked in height with massive shoulders and powerful limbs. His features carved an expressionless mask in which only the black orbs of his eyes seemed to move. When Geronimo stepped into the clearing, he noticed immediately and moved directly toward him.

"I brought guns, enough for all."

"Good," said Juh. "Soon."

Juh spoke with forced effort, his words were often stuttered or spaced with unnatural timing. Thus, his communications were often truncated and formed with an economy of words. He led them to his fire, where he had tobacco. They rolled cigarillos from a tin painted with a maritime scene of a ship sailing upon rough seas, and Juh listened to Geronimo's story of the guns. When he finished, they ate roasted rabbits and drank a small amount of tizwin.

"I saw a camp below the mesa," said Geronimo.

"Ekta went with her sisters to prepare for the Sunrise Ceremony," said Nana.

"The scarred woman... was gone," Juh said.

"But she returned," said Nana.

"Lozen, could she not detect the enemy?" asked Geronimo.

"Lozen... was away... watching... the Mexicans' camp," said Juh.

They spoke no more about it and sat quietly by the fire, smoking tobacco. The sun fell away, and the fire turned to coals. Only a thin, jagged line of sky held back the army of stars from falling on the mesa top. They slept safely in their glow.

Geronimo woke before dawn and before Nana and Juh. Voices carried from a distant camp on the other side of the valley. He strained his ears to hear. The voices seemed to be in celebration. Juh and Nana woke as the voices became louder and grew in number. The sun came up, peaking through the tall pines.

Many in the camp joined them as they traveled across the valley to investigate the disturbance. In the largest clearing, near the trail down the mesa, dozens of Apache had gathered. They encircled a central figure, not readily visible in the glaring dawn. As Geronimo drew closer, he did not need to see the man to know who it was.

Chatto and his band had returned with the remainder of the guns from the cache. In a flamboyant display, he began to hand them out to the eager warriors, the air thick with shouts and war cries. The warriors praised the name of Chatto; Geronimo's name was not spoken.

Geronimo shook his head in disgust and returned to the still, shaded pines, walking back the way he came.

That morning they met in council to talk of war. Juh, Nana, Lozen, and Geronimo were present, as were Delgadito, Chewawa, and Chatto. Nana spoke for Juh, though his words were few. It was Juh's wish that they make their fire away from the others amidst the ruins of Ekta's clearing.

"In time, the grass will grow through these ashes, and it will be as it was," said Nana. "Again, we will make the longhouse and build our wickiups here. Girls will dance and become women. Children will be born. But first, Ussen's will must be done. First, we must destroy our enemies completely. These are the words of Juh."

Juh nodded.

"I have been to the camp where the Mexicans have their mine," Lozen said. "If we attack from the cliffs, we will easily destroy them."

"What of the Scarred woman?" asked Nana

"She was gone. If she returns, we will defeat her and her soldiers if we attack with surprise."

Juh sat a moment in silence, the eyes of the council upon him.

"We go... now... with... Lozen before us," said Juh.

The matter was decided.

NINETEEN

April 4, 1865
Richmond, Virginia

Thomas watched as the man in the stovepipe hat stepped out of the rowboat and onto the muddy bank of the James. The bloated corpses of horses floated amid the charred wreckage of the Mayo Bridge. Unused ordinance, discarded cannons, and the gaping hulls of scuttled ships choked the waterway. Groups of freed slaves began to gather as he clambered up to the road. His twelve-member entourage scrambled for position like awkward disciples. The gathering throng cheered for him when he crested the bank, some bold enough to shake his hand while others, struck with awe, stood and wept.

The sun was incapable of piercing the dense haze of smoke. Thick columns of it, too innumerable to count, curled skyward in every direction. The very air tasted burnt. He panned about with uncertainty as to which direction to take. Finally, a young naval officer in his company pointed north, and they began to walk.

They traveled among the defeated masses of Richmond, a sorrowful populace ambling about the destructed city like it was their first day in Purgatory. Those who recognized him stared at him contemptuously, like an uninvited guest at a funeral. He did not ignore them, and he did not gloat upon their misfortune. Instead, he regarded them with a hollowness emptied of tears. He looked at them with a tenuous hope that they, too, had taken their fill of sorrow, that maybe they also embraced the end of it.

Thomas walked behind the entourage until his path diverged, and he turned toward the Van Lew house. It was the first time he had seen the man in person and his conflicted emotions made it difficult to form an opinion. Mostly, he felt pity for the man.

Thomas entered the house without knocking. Elizabeth was sitting on a sofa by the window, reading her bible. At her feet, several cats lapped cream from a saucer. He thought to tell her about the spectacle he had just witnessed, then decided against it.

"Hello, Thomas. Do you have a moment?" she asked.

"Afternoon, Ma'am," he said. "Certainly, let me check on Sam, and I'll be back directly."

"Very well."

He walked through the pantry and lifted a loose board in the larder, revealing the handle for the trapdoor. He pulled it open and descended the ladder into the darkness. The space had been used for hiding fugitives, escaping slaves, and the occasional meeting, but the need for secrecy had been moot for nearly two days. Samuel Sheldon had been sleeping, utterly oblivious to the fall of Richmond.

Sheldon was sitting on the end of the cot taking stock of his faculties, when Thomas struck a match and lit the lamp on the shelf.

"You're awake."

"Yeah. I think I pissed myself."

"You look well, considering."

"I feel like I'm dead," Sheldon groaned.

"You make a lovely corpse."

"If you say so, Thomas. Where's Robert gone to?"

"Gone. Miss Van Lew said he went scouting for intelligence. That's all he told her."

"Fucking Crow," he sighed. "Ugh! I need fresh trousers."

"There's fresh linen and clothes in the trunk, water in the

basin. I'll find you something to eat."

"Thank you, Thomas."

Thomas nodded and left Sheldon to collect himself. He found Elizabeth in the kitchen, stoking the fire in the wood stove. A cast iron pot sat atop the burner. She was reheating the stew from the night before.

"I heard a rumor today from one of the sergeants of the occupational police force," said Elizabeth.

"Anything useful about Davis?"

"No, nothing like that, I'm afraid." She refilled the cat's saucer with cream. "Something entirely different."

A rare beam of sunlight fell through the charcoal clouds and filtered through the kitchen window, framing Elizabeth where she stood. It illuminated the silver streaks in her carefully pinned hair. Her white dress turned gold, but her hands somehow refused the light and remained as pale as the cream in the saucer.

"The sergeant spoke of some ghastly business in Sugar Bottom, something horrible in one of the public houses."

"Oh?"

"Like a scene from hell, he described it," she laid the saucer on the floor. Cats descended upon it from all vantages. "The women of the house, guests, soldiers, and the barman, all dead. Torn to shreds with knives, teeth, shards of windows... whatever was at hand. He said they were possessed by demons, tearing each other apart for no earthly reason. Only one soul survived, he said."

"That's awful! What do you mean they tore each other apart?"

"The madam survived the ordeal, though she was quite mad and utterly incapable of clarifying the matter. Her hand was skewered to a tabletop with a fork, of all things! When questioned, she just repeated herself, sobbing, 'Their eyes were blue, their eyes were blue!'"

"What a bizarre tale."

"Isn't it?" Elizabeth retrieved the dish and again filled it with cream. The mewing at her ankles reached a feverish pitch as she set it on the polished oak floor. "Mr. Black took his lodging at one of the houses on Sugar Bottom, did he not?"

"He did, until the night of the evacuation."

"Exactly the night in question." The full bore of her gray eyes was upon him, one hand rooted to her hip. She was poised to receive his explanation.

"You think Robert had something to do with this?"

"Don't you? I don't trust him! He comes and goes mysteriously, always on some mission, though he is not connected to the network in any way that I'm aware of. I've spoken to Grant's men, and they have no knowledge of him. What of that mousy little man following him around like he's under some spell of obedience? Have you seen the queer necklace he wears? It's made of human teeth! Who would wear such a thing? Furthermore, what kind of man associates with a man like that, Thomas? I don't want him in my house, do you understand?"

"I don't like him either, Elizabeth. He's no friend to me, but I have my orders like anyone else, and I must tolerate him for now."

"You will send him away, or you can all go together, am I understood?"

"Yes, ma'am. I understand perfectly."

"Thank you. Now go out of my kitchen, I'll call you at dinner."

"I'll make sure he never darkens your door again."

"Thank you, Thomas." The saucer was empty again, and the cats ringed around her like tiny hyenas prowling for more.

After Sheldon had eaten and rested, Thomas roused him from the basement. They sat under an awning at the back of the house. The lawn was wide and lush with grass, sloping gently down to a symmetrical stand of fruit trees, a rose garden, and a tiny gazebo. The air was getting cool, and the light was fading in the west. Thomas puffed gently on a cigar and looked out across the lawn. Sheldon's eyes were focused out of space and time.

"See that gazebo?" asked Thomas. "About four or five times a week, in the middle of the night, Elizabeth sneaks down to it in her nightgown."

"To what purpose?"

"She's got a book buried under one of the stones, I think. She sits out in the moonlit hours and puts ink to it."

"What does she write?"

"Couldn't say. Secrets, I suspect."

"If I had such a ledger," said Sheldon, "it would be filled with horror."

"You're past that now, Sam, and you're stronger for it." Thomas blew a smoke ring and watched it expand into the twilight. "I should have been there when Price took you. I'm sorry, Sam."

"I don't blame you, that sonofabitch was ready for us. He knew our movements like he was listening."

"Or someone told him", said Thomas.

"You mean like Robert?"

"Maybe, it's an unsettling thought," he said.

"Then why break me out of Belle Isle? Why not let me die there? Why deliver Price?"

"Cover his tracks, I don't know, really. Something just ain't right."

"He's got an eye on Jeff D and the rest of the Trust gold," said Sheldon.

"And you mean to go after it with him?"

"I do."

"Don't you think we should consult the Trust? Russell and Collins might have something to say about all of this?"

"There's just no time, every minute, that gold is getting further out of reach," said Sheldon.

"I'm coming with you," said Thomas.

"I wish you could, but you would look mighty suspicious in a Rebel officer's uniform."

"I would do it just to see the looks on their faces!"

Thomas laughed and passed the cigar to Sheldon. He took a puff and blew his own smoke ring, which floated up toward the orange-streaked clouds.

"He's not like us, Sam. You understand that, right?"

"How do you mean?"

"You've been fortified, as have I, endowed with a hollow place, empty now, but one day it will be occupied."

"By what?"

"By *Him*, Sam, by the Other. It's preparing you. When Collins goes, He will be with you."

"When Collins goes?"

"Danfort hasn't told you, has he? Well, it doesn't matter, it chose you, and it doesn't make mistakes." Rogers took the cigar back and puffed. "You're changing, Sam, how do you feel?"

"I feel... indestructible. Like metal roots growing through every imaginable obstruction as I grow..."

"Into a golden tree," said Thomas. "Yes, I see it, and at the core of the tree is a place reserved where something will sit one day."

"Yes, like that."

"Robert is not like us. He is something else. If there was a seed, it did not grow. He is with us, sent by the Trust, but something is wrong. Taft has done something I don't understand. It's not our place to question, so I do not. Watch him, that's as much as I can say."

Sheldon nodded, and another of Thomas's smoke rings reached for Heaven.

"Did you suffer like I did?"

"Not like you, but I suffered, and I still suffer." He ran his tongue over the smooth gold teeth and remembered when molten metal burned through his bones, casting them like golden fossils.

"Was it by design? Did they mean for me to rot in prison eating rats and drinking my own piss?"

"Perhaps, but it was no design conceived by any earthly mind of that much, I'm certain."

The sun went red on the horizon, its golden rays ended. Pink turned to blue and darkened backward across the sky from west to east. Frogs, crickets, and screech owls made their opening speeches to the night. It was a peacefulness abruptly interrupted by the creaking of the porch door.

"Evening, gentlemen!" Robert called to them, stepping out of the house behind them.

"Evening," Sheldon said.

"It would seem I overstayed my welcome!"

"It would seem so," said Thomas.

"It's of no consequence. Now we need to act. I have information and the required outfitting. The time's come to put Richmond at our hind."

Thomas crushed out the cigar.

"No consequence to the great Bobby Crow, who breathes in good fortune and exhales destruction," he said. "Some of us have to live in this fucking world and don't have the privilege of walking in and out of it according to our whims!"

"Easy, friend," said Robert.

"Next time, shit your own bed. Friend."

"You have viable intelligence?" Sheldon asked.

"It's good," Reavis affirmed. "Time is crucial, however. Every blue jacket in the Union has been set on a fox hunt to catch that Rebel cocksucker, just pouring south with nothing to stand in their way. We need to move now."

"Agreed," said Sheldon.

"What's your stake in this, Reavis?" Thomas asked. "Ours is a short list. Your name ain't on it."

"You can take that up with Captain Black," Reavis said.

"I'll add it to the list of things I intend to take up with the captain."

"Enough, Thomas! I vouch for him," Robert said. "I'd still be locked up in that piss trench if not for him! Our interests intertwine, that's all you need know."

"If you say so," said Thomas.

"You look remarkably well rested, if you don't mind me

saying," Robert gestured toward Sheldon. "You were just a couple broomsticks wrapped together with string when I found you, now look at you!"

"Chalk it up to my natural resilience. When do we leave?"

"Morning makes the most sense if Miss Van Lew will allow the delay. We could use the time to study the rail maps and plot out our route. Reavis needs a little time to finalize our papers, but I managed to secure some fresh uniforms."

"Shall I be your loyal slave or perhaps your colored squire? I think I see windmills! I best grab your lance, sir!" Thomas sneered. "I don't need an officer's uniform to get where I'm going. Besides, Russell wants me in Richmond for a while longer."

"I'm sorry, Thomas," Robert said. "I wish you could come..."

"Do you?"

Robert shrugged and returned to the house. Reavis followed, and the door closed quietly behind them.

"We'll continue this conversation at another time, Thomas."

"Yes, we will. But, remember what I said, Sam. His seed didn't grow."

"I will." Sheldon stepped on the porch and entered the house.

Thomas stretched out on the stairs and puffed the cigar as frogs called out to each other and the moon prepared to take her place in the night sky.

TWENTY

April 1865
State Of Chihuahua, Mexico

T he Apache war party was formed into four groups, totaling one hundred eleven warriors. Juh led the largest band of more than fifty warriors. Geronimo and Nana each led a group of about twenty each, and Chatto took charge of the smallest group of fifteen. Lozen went with Nana, they would be the vanguard. She would use her Power to find the enemy and guide them undetected.

Clouds, like gray ink, soaked into the afternoon sky and a golden corona pulsed around the bloody heart of the sun. Geronimo took the redness as an omen, auspicious for killing. Lozen, at the head of the Apache host, descended the mountain like water, splashing over stones in the swiftest and most direct path. They moved effortlessly like floating ash in the dead heat of a kiln, silently flowing behind her.

They moved north from the base of the stronghold, Nana and Lozen ranging ahead of the larger force. She moved in a trance, pausing with her hands extended, feeling for the heat of an invisible fire. Sometimes she would chant and sing to Ussen, petitioning for the sight with which to see her enemy.

The mining camp existed among the ruins of a centuries-old Spanish mission, nestled into the shelter of a tall box canyon. The canyon cut into an arm of the Blue Mountains in the Sierra Madre Occidental range, protruding through the surrounding hills and pointing directly into an empty expanse of the Sonoran Desert.

The camp fortifications were formidable. Adobe bricks were salvaged from the mission and cobbled into two reinforced bunkers at either side of the narrow canyon mouth. They commanded a protected line of fire over the entire canyon. When fully manned, the camp was as defensible from frontal assault as any presidio in Mexico.

The Apache did not intend a frontal assault, nor was the outpost at full defensive strength. As Geronimo had predicted, they arrived under auspicious circumstances. The scarred woman and her horde of killers were not present. Only a handful of defenders manned the fortifications. Sickness had come over the camp, overwhelming almost the entire population with a crippling fever. Mining operations had stopped entirely, along with virtually every other activity. Those few unafflicted paced nervously around dim fires or slept in bedrolls away from the sick tents.

Few matched the Chiricahua in their climbing ability, even other Apache. The mountain did not hinder their movement or present an obstacle to their assault, rather, it provided a distinct advantage. Lozen and Nana led their group up the east walls of the canyon while Geronimo took his to the west.

Lozen extended her hands, chanting softly. She turned to Nana and began pointing out locations in the canyon below.

The strategy was simple. Nana and his group would climb down behind the barricades and dispatch the guards there, allowing Juh to bring his warriors up the canyon unmolested. Geronimo would provide support, cutting down anything that moved against them with their repeating rifles.

Nana reached into his medicine pouch and removed the gold watch, cool and smooth. Lozen watched him open the case with his thumb and run his finger over the engraving inside the lid, words he would never decipher. He gazed through the crystal to the bone-white enamel dial, the hands pointing indifferently at the arcane symbols that circled its face. He nodded. It was time. They sent runners to Juh and

Geronimo, and the attack began.

In the black before dawn, the warriors descended, deliberate as spiders, down the sheer rock face of the canyon walls. Lozen led seven warriors to the east, and Nana took eight to the west. The strange wind followed them through the canyon but moved no sand. It swept through and filled them, lifting their limbs, driving them forward, and fortifying their killing directive.

Lozen found her gifts enhanced by the effects of the strange, dead wind. The quivering souls of the enemy flickered like dim candles in the dark. Her warriors were drawn to them, pulled like magnets. They found sick men at their posts, weakly holding their rifles against the nothingness of the desert, all in the sway of some terrible fever that brought blisters to their lips and caused the whites of their eyes to go red.

The Chiricahua cut them down where they found them, opening their throats without resistance. Their blood came thick and black in noiseless torrents, pooling like mercury and pushing back the sand. They bled out without a struggle, their eyes the milky color of the moon, staring into the empty desert.

Lozen could hear the bodies drop, she counted them as she went down the throat of the canyon. The dissolving souls flickered and extinguished like candles in the heat of the wind. All had perished when she reached the central line of defense at the bottom of the canyon. She pushed on, unchecked, through the fresh reek of death, into the camp. The Chiricahua fell in behind her. They kept to the shadow of the canyon walls, like frost avoiding the creeping dawn.

Ahead, the shell of the great mission lay like a wrecked ship, half submerged in the dirt and sand. Its walls were burnt black by some ancient misfortune, crumbling and leaning everywhere. Pale wounds shone through where the burnt brick and adobe had been gouged by time or violence. Its collapsed sat wrecked as if bitten off by some hungry god. The tower's bell lay skewed and buried in the hardened clay.

She reached the bell, corroded in cracked shades of green and black, hopelessly devoid of function. Lozen took her club and struck the bell hard with the back of the cudgel. It rang with an earthy resonance that quickly faded into the clay that encased it. The uncanny call to prayer was answered by the voices of many rifles, eagerly singing a hymn of death. Tiny clouds of gun smoke appeared in the gray morning, floating in formation from the ridge above. The clouds became a haze over the canyon, precipitating deadly rain on the men of the camp.

Lozen observed the fleeting souls of the sick, fluttering like fireflies behind the canvas of the trembling tents. The dead wind blew, dense, burnt, and vicious. The rifles went silent, and the haze of smoke hung low in the valley.

She heard the faint scraping of the mission's door against the flagstone threshold; emerging from the structure came a man of unusual height, lean and fit, with eyes and lips contorted in hatred. His beard bristled from his face as he cried out with rage and exploded into the dawn like a man-turned-bear. He wore only a thin pair of cotton trousers. His naked chest was thick with hair and matted with sweat. Clenched in his fist was a Colt Dragoon, like a toy in the leviathan's mighty grasp.

The Dragoon vomited fire and smoke. Lead ripped through the air.

Whether by chance, intent, or divine intervention, each shot struck the bell. Later, Nana would say the hairy man killed the ghost of the bell. It rang as it would have, before centuries of decay, when it hung like a crown above the mission. It rang clear like it spoke to the long-vanished faithful, gone to the place where dead things go. It sang out bright and clear and cracked, from peak to earth, and would ring no more.

Lozen brought her club across the temple of the giant, and the fire went from his eyes. In a drunken pirouette, he stumbled past her and fell to earth near the bell. The Dragoon tumbled across the dusty ground, oozing smoke.

The Apache went cautiously from body to body through the tents, prodding with their rifles or lances at the lifeless miners. Juh did not let his warriors loot the bodies and ordered them to stay upwind near the mine and a giant stamp press.

"This place is cursed," he said. "It must be destroyed."

Nana and Lozen went to the mission door and peered into the darkness. He kept his rifle ready and stepped into the stagnant mouth of the burnt chapel. Lozen followed close behind. The wind did not blow there. When the first rays of sunlight dissolved the ash-gray sky and filtered through holes in the ruined ceiling, she understood.

The room was an empty furnace. What pews may have been had long turned to ash and blown away. No furniture existed, nor any object of human use. Standing on a simple dais encased within the ruin stood a stack of golden ingots taller than Lozen and equally wide. She lifted one, and it came easily to her hand. Though of proper density and significant size, she hefted it like a block of dried wood. It glimmered benignly, innocent as the sunshine shedding its light upon the morning's carnage. This was the source of the dead wind, and by its design, they had arrived there.

TWENTY-ONE

May 1865
Parral River Valley
Chihuahua, Mexico

In the darkest hours of the morning, long before dawn, the door shook with pounding knocks. Pedro's hands fumbled for his pistol as Claribel went to the bassinet to retrieve their crying infant. He crossed from his bed to the door and pressed himself against the wall, taking as much shelter as possible. Many voices were shouting and moving all around the rancheria. The wound in his chest throbbed with the sudden movement.

"Who's there?" he shouted.

"In the name of Emperor Ferdinand Maximillian of Mexico, I command that you open this door!"

"What have you done?" Claribel whispered, clenching the child close to her chest.

The voice was not familiar, though Pedro did not doubt its authority. He did as the voice commanded, revealing a company of Rurales standing at his doorstep. Terror replaced the pain in his chest. Only men of flexible moral bearing rode with the Rurales, men with unlimited potential for violence and curious conceptions of justice. Benito Juárez called them into existence, but the Rurales were loyal only to coin.

Men poured into his home. One stayed by the door, holding a lantern; another plucked the pistol from Pedro's grasp and pushed him back down onto his bed, while another pried

Donna Sophia from Claribel's arms, causing mother and child to scream in terror. Pedro shot up to intervene and was immediately struck on the head with a rifle butt. Claribel's screams intensified as she lashed out at her attackers, gouging the cheek of one. The wounded man struck back, sending her careening into the wall.

"You filth! You Pigs!" Claribel lunged back.

The Rurales' commander drew his pistol and fired. The deafening report silenced all other sounds. The bullet struck Claribel above her right eye, driving her back a final time. In the dark shadows of the room, Pedro could see little and hear only silence. Then, slowly, the cries of Donna Sophia began to permeate the ringing in his ears.

"Claribel! Claribel!" Pedro screamed.

"Are you Pedro Gonzales?"

The commander was a short, rigid man with an immaculate mustache and a well-pressed uniform. He unrolled a short, vellum scroll.

"Claribel!"

"I am Colonel Miguel Lopez," said the man. "You are accused of treason. You will come with me!"

"Claribel!" Donna Sophia's cries were the only answer.

Pedro scrambled across the bed, stretching for a view of his wife. His progress was immediately halted by the Rurales, who pulled him forward to his feet.

"Silence the child," said the colonel.

"Wait! No! I can pay you; I have gold!"

"Get him up!"

"Please, listen!" Pedro pleaded. "I have gold hidden... I can tell you where to dig! If you kill me, you will never find it. All I ask is that you let my child live. Please, I'm begging!"

"Why should I play nanny for a dead man?"

Two Rurales dragged him toward the door, and another pulled a burlap sack over his head as he strained for a view of Claribel. Pedro screamed and thrashed against his captors, breaking free, only to be struck again with a rifle butt. He fell to his knees but did not lose consciousness, howling against the burlap.

"Please... Please! Take my map! I can show you where there is more! Don't hurt my Sophie, please don't hurt her..."

"Jefe?" said one of the men.

"Light! Bring me light!" said the colonel.

The room brightened through the loose fibers of the sack, the terrified screams of his daughter the only sound.

"Be still, Sophie, I'm here. Papa's here, don't fear..."

The sack was ripped from his head, the face of Colonel Lopez only inches away from his own. A pungent smell of cologne surrounded him, failing to mask the stench of liquor and tobacco. His face was pale, almost European, contrasted by the pits of eyes so dark that no color could be detected. His thin hair was slicked back with some fragrant grease that he also employed on his mustache and goatee, crafting them to flamboyantly flared points. His finely tailored uniform did not appear to crease with his movements, laying perfectly as if painted upon his body.

"Where did you find this?"

The lantern's light danced in the quartz and shone brightly in the golden blaze of the ore in the colonel's hand.

"North, over the border near the Rio Salado, I can take you..."

"There's more of this here?"

"Yes, not far. I'll tell you where, you can take it all!"

"Perhaps you may purchase a nanny yet," said Colonel Lopez. "Tell me where it is. Then, if it pleases me, I might let the child live."

"Follow the fencing along the river. You will come to a hill that I use as drift fence, it's very rocky and barren of growth. On top, there is a throne-shaped rock, you won't miss it. Look for a patch of bare earth behind it, maybe ten or twenty paces, just before a stand of pines. That's where I buried it."

"Too much trouble."

The colonel drew his pistol.

"I'll take your soldiers! Please! I promise it is twice Sophia's weight in gold!" Pedro wept and struggled to remain standing.

Colonel Lopez tucked the pistol into his belt, reached into his breast pocket, and removed a silver case. He flipped the latch with his thumb to reveal several finely rolled cigarillos. He removed one and lit it. The smoke swirled around his perfumed head as he inhaled.

"You have until I finish."

The two Rurales holding Pedro dragged him toward the door, and four more followed them. He craned his neck to see Sophia writhing in the filthy arms of a random soldier, her screams not lessened. The cruelty in the man's eyes, looking at the child with loathsome contempt and profound irritation, terrified Pedro. Beyond the man, a slowly spreading pool of blood crept across the floor like an overturned inkwell. It was all that was visible of Claribel.

Pedro moved swiftly under the escort of the Rurales, stopping only at the barn to retrieve a pick and shovel. The sky was infested with stars, presided over by half a moon that looked like a thumb partially covering a gun bore. They made their way through the field of disinterested cattle toward the hill, cut out black against the sky.

"You see, there on the hill? That rock is where we are going," Pedro said and jogged forward.

One of the men reached out immediately and grabbed his shoulder, "Walk!"

Their pace caused him great anxiety. The Rurales seemed to slow their steps, intentionally agonizing him. Finally, they crested the hill, and Pedro threw the entirety of his strength behind each pick strike. The pick struck the hard wood of the buried crate, and his efforts doubled.

"Here! Here it is! See!" He dragged the crate out of the hole and lifted the lid. "Look, gold!" He handed one of the ingots to the stoic gunman standing above him.

"Keep digging," the Rurale said, tossing the ingot back in the crate with a clank.

"What?"

"I said keep digging, you piece of shit! I'm not going to make your grave for you!"

"No... No... No!"

The Rio Parral babbled its condolences, and the cattle mingled silently. He had never noticed how beautiful the hill was at night, the rocks almost glowed silver in the moonlight. Pedro turned back to the hole, barely knee-deep. He took the pick in hand, his shoulder sinking with the dismal weight of it.

He was sure of one. Even if they unloaded every shot into his heart and brain, he could get one of them. Pedro set his feet and took his grip, then poised the pick. Tears ran down his dirty cheeks. He imagined those, too, would be silver in such beautiful light. He raised the pick.

"Ha! I'm only joking!" the man laughed. "Pitiful bastard! Did you think I would defy the colonel? Not for ten times this gold! Now pick up that crate and get moving!"

Pedro dropped the pick and lifted the crate. As he turned to descend the hill, he observed another light, a single smear of yellow on the black and silver landscape.

"Oh no!" mocked another soldier. "You were not quick enough!"

Pedro dropped the crate and ran. The soldier's pistol puked fire, thundering across the sleeping valley. The bullet whizzed by his head, and he stopped in his tracks, watching his home burn through blurry tears.

"Pick it up and walk." The gunman was no longer laughing.

They walked through the tall grass, past the hulking shapes of cows. The rancheria was in flames, including the feed shed and all the outbuildings. The black silhouettes of horsemen danced about like mute demons. The wind rushed through the grass, sucked toward the inferno, whistling as it went. He listened for Sophie's cries but heard only the crackle of flame and the curious whistling wind. His mouth moved, but words would not emerge. In his mind, the words were clear, formed with hate and sorrow.

"I curse it... I curse it... I curse it," he repeated.

The fence blazed by the time they reached the compound. One of the men kicked a burning split rail, which collapsed on itself, already more ember than fence. The horses trotted nervously in place, pulling away from the flames and the nauseating heat. The soldier moved to kick down the next rail when a rider approached, jumping what remained of the fence.

"What did you bring me?" said Colonel Lopez.

Pedro set the crate down and removed one of the ingots, it betrayed its unmistakable luster to the light of the flames. A thin and terrible smile stretched across the colonel's lips.

"You are a lucky man, Pedro Gonzales. You find me merciful this day. It so happens that I am charged to deliver you to justice in the city of Parral. In my infinite graciousness, I have decided to spare this child. I'm sure I can find a church stoop or some other suitable waste bin to deposit the wretch."

Pedro barely understood the colonel's words. Beyond him, through the shifting flames, he heard the frightened screams of his daughter. He crossed himself in gratitude, and part of his grief dissolved.

"I have only ever been a faithful servant of his Imperial Majesty. What crimes am I accused of? I swear my innocence!"

The colonel laughed heartily with genuine mirth, "Innocent? It wouldn't matter, either way, you understand?" He laughed again; the mirth replaced with something more menacing. "However, we both know you are not innocent. I came from Cerro de la Cruz, where I met a remarkable man. A man who, like yourself, is very lucky to be alive. Speech is still difficult for him, understandable considering the slashing his throat endured. Fortunately, he is a capable writer and penned a terrifying account of what happened there. Your name is mentioned prominently in this document. I believe you are familiar with the author. His name is Ricard."

Pedro's heart sank.

TWENTY-TWO

April 1865
Naica
State Of Chihuahua, Mexico

The whole village sloped into the hillside as if, at one time, it had all melted and then once again became firm. Adobe huts slouched in senseless clusters, linked and divided by crumbling walls and meandering clay streets. The remnants of an ancient wall surrounded the town in a broken semicircle of crumbled brick and timber, like a destroyed smile full of broken teeth. The pitted dirt thoroughfare wagged out from the wall like a vulgar tongue past the suggestion of what may have once been a gate. Nothing living showed itself. The homes were shut, and the streets were silent.

The company of killers hung back beyond the grotesque mouth of the gate like an army preparing for a siege. They spread their mounts across the bleak expanse of the town's approach. A single rider carried on through the dust-up like a solitary locust of immense proportion. As if some invisible barricade blocked the path, the rider dismounted at the voided gate and lashed their horse to a piece of timber protruding from the rubble.

Maria Bonita stood on the hard-packed clay and shed her clothes to the dust. She kept only her bowie knife strapped to her naked thigh. She retrieved a leather sack tied to the bejeweled horn of her saddle and fixed its cord to her ankle. The sun streaked through the dust like the earth was burning; it went through the town like a plague visiting every window and door. She prostrated herself, naked, on the caked dirt and crawled like some terrible and fearsome worm, scraping through the center of the place on her belly.

The filth clung like pale ash to her flesh, then turned to mud as her flesh surrendered blood. The gash of her mouth filled with it and blackened her teeth. A tiny river of sludge flowed unchecked down her chin. She went at a measured pace and spared herself no discomfort. The warped shadows of the looming mud hovels crept into the thoroughfare as the sun drifted west like a sullen vulture. The pale dust soon clung to all parts of her naked body, forming a carapace over her sweat. Her hair was filled with it, and she looked like something fresh from the grave, faded and choked with dirt.

Near its terminus, the road narrowed and became less traveled, dipping in ruts and pits. Her strange trail slithered behind her, slimed in places with sweat and blood, and wiped smooth in others by the dragging leather sack. Maria was close enough to hear the whimpering of terrified children cloistered behind the mud walls. The manic baying of a goat bleated from one of the houses, and horses neighed from some distant place. She grinned, and dirt fell from her mouth.

They were right to hide their animals.

A stagnant pool of brown water filled a pitted, low place in the road. It gave off a horrid stench of rancid piss or aging carrion. She neither diverted her course nor sought to skirt it. She fully immersed herself in it and smeared the gray crust encasing her enough to reveal her smooth flesh beneath.

Beyond the fetid pool, the road opened to a small, hidden courtyard and the object of her prostration. The road ended at the blasted facade of a church, with no visible trace or suggestion of what once stood there. A small circle of colored glass still existed at the apex, glowing red in the failing sun. The stoop was a simple mud dais made into an altar populated with bizarre offerings.

Dried flowers, aged beyond identification, sprung like straw from every conceivable crack. Tin cups, wooden bowls, pieces of China, empty bottles, water skins, and myriad other vessels littered every possible surface. Tobacco, in all its forms and trappings, thrived among the gifts. Small baubles, scrawled notes, a glass eye, mescal bottles, coins of every type, a whale-bone effigy, a pair of children's shoes... All these things swam in the sea of candlewax surrounding the Lady of Bone.

The great lady was adorned with finely tailored robes, immaculately cared for, and carefully placed. The assemblage of her bones revealed no artificial connections, allowing her body a curiously life-like posture. She stood, palms out and at her sides, welcoming and reverent. Her age was a matter of speculation, the slight amber hue to the skeletal matron suggested decades, possibly centuries, of service. White polished teeth gleamed from the immaculate skull, shining from the shaded darkness of the carefully draped hood. Closer examination revealed them coated with enamel and detailed with delicate gold leaf.

Beside the pedestal, kneeling in the dust, was the priest of this place. He was a boy, naked save a wrapping of unbleached cotton covering his midsection. He held a cord tethered to a hairless dog in his hand, covered in sores and ravaged with parasites. The animal squirmed and cried, contorting and straining to escape. The beast looked like a dead thing whose skeleton somehow came alive and now clambered to escape its loose and sickly flesh.

The boy's name was Pascal, his surname unknown even to himself. His limbs were bony and underdeveloped. His chest sucked straight into the thin, curved rails of his ribs. One eye was blue, and the other was brown, both large and looming in the sunken round orbitals of his skull. He appeared to be perhaps eleven or twelve years of age. His appearance had not changed during the five years that Maria had been making this pilgrimage.

She knelt at the altar and placed the leather sack between her thighs. First, she produced tobacco in the form of a finely rolled cigar. She lit it and puffed slowly till clouds rose between herself and the Lady of Bone. She placed the burning cigar on the altar before her and delved again into the sack. This time she removed a small bottle of mescal. She sipped a little, causing the mud to resume its flow down her chin. Pouring a tiny amount into a crucible, she set it next to the cigar. She began to pray. She quietly uttered her petition in words made of blood and dirt. She bowed her head and swayed with the rhythm of her secret utterings, sometimes striking herself to emphasize her arcane proposal.

As her cadence peaked, she reached back with her left hand, and Pascal deftly placed the dog's cord in her possession. With her right hand, she drew the long blade from her side. When she brought her arms together, the mongrel yipped and snarled, baring its rotted teeth as it lashed at her face. She made no notice of the animal's objection and drew the blade across its throat, becoming washed in its blood.

Pascal began to convulse in laughter and shake with the raging mirth of it. Then, as quickly as the laughter came, it turned to sobs of profound despair, then swung like a pendulum back into hysterical cackling. The polarity of his outbursts merged until he was both wailing and laughing simultaneously, like a sunbeam piercing through a thundercloud. His bones shook violently, rebelling against his skin, the whole of him enslaved by the spasm. Bits of blood rained down from the pulsing, arterial spray of the dying animal and fell with audible impacts on the maelstrom of his skin.

Maria turned to Pascal to reckon the will of the Saint. One brown eye and one blue eye focused on hers. They stared, steady as stars, while Pascal's flesh raged in a tempest of twitching pain and pleasure. The stinking heap of the dog lay with its head between Maria's naked thighs. Its body lay lifeless, half on the altar. Its back legs still kicked, propelling it toward whatever place death set aside for dogs.

"THIEVES!" Pascal croaked.

Her lower lip descended in an inverted sneer, exposing the

entirety of her blackened teeth.

"They are dead. Not you! Safe in my arms!"

The boy's head cocked to the side, but the eyes did not break their gaze.

"Revenge?" His tongue hung out as if in mockery of the dead and hairless creature in her lap.

Maria's face darkened, the blood streaking down in rusty tears. It was not why she came, it was not her prayer nor query, yet these were the priest's words.

"The gold is gone, the thieves fly away." His head moved in a slow orbit, eyes fixed but unseeing.

"Bring your child to the Tres Castillos, you will find them there."

"I have no child," she said.

Pascal laughed in spasms, gasping and choking until it seemed that he would lose consciousness, then he spoke again.

"Seek the father among your enemies, you will know him by his eyes!" A final convulsion took him, "Blue and dead like the pools of Naica!"

Pascal collapsed to his knees and was silent.

Maria stood and sheathed the knife. Pascal's eyes clouded over, and he fell to his side in the blood-soaked dirt, making no effort to catch himself. A moment later, he rose timidly to his feet, a child again.

"Ours is a violent God," he said.

Maria turned back down the path, retracing it in long strides. The sun was setting, and bats leaked out of the mountain in streams over the town. By the time she reached her clothes, she was running, ejecting herself from the town like its bloody spawn. She dressed in swift, violent movements and leaped upon the roan. The army of killers sat on the plain, their shadows mingling with the saguaro. She set off at a full gallop, and the killers fell in behind.

They rode south through the night, through a bowl of darkness with blooming agave striking out against the starlight. They rode through a narrow and treacherous canyon where lean wolves chortled in cabal, waiting for a fatal slip or some unfortunate opportunity to ply their teeth. They crossed a river strewn with boulders and hidden pits where one rider fell, and they left him screaming in the darkness. At dawn, they came riding through the Allende Valley and saw the smoke rising from the hills at the foot of the mountains. They rode east, past the ruins of a town rising like gravestones through the dust of their wake. In the full light of the angry sun, they came to the mouth of the narrow canyon and the carnage of Santa Rosalia.

Swarms of turkey vultures moved among the bodies, removing strips of flesh and absconding away in short hops before consuming it and returning for more. Maria ordered the column to halt and dismount to not further disturb the ground. She continued on foot, absorbing the scene as she went deeper down the canyon's throat. She repressed her rage as she passed more bodies and focused on reading the signs.

There were fresh prints, faint on the hard earth, fifty men or more... Their tracks were not made by boots. Moccasins, perhaps? The wounds were caused by blades at an intimate distance. The bodies were not molested, many still had their weapons. Observing the blisters and pustules, she pulled her scarf over her mouth. She went on, watching the ground; the attackers ran in but walked out. Then she noticed what she had missed before, wheel tracks heavy enough to break the clay. She didn't need to look in the blasted mission to know it was empty.

Shadows of the burned tents scarred the ground where charred arms and legs rose from the crumbled shapes of human things, now made into coals. The greatest smoke came from the stamp mill, which almost entirely collapsed. The iron shafts and stamp shoes glowed a dull and angry red, half covered in coals and white ash, the mass of them skewed and crooked. One wooden beam survived, only partially consumed in the inferno. It remained by intent, executed with cruel design. Lashed and nailed to the beam was the inverted body of a massive man, crucified like an antichrist before what must have been a hellish blaze.

Maria recognized the blackened thing as Tomas Ulric, the foreman and Stallworth's principal assay. A black pool of tarred flesh hardened below his enormous skull, where his fat rendered like a roasted hog. When the wind blew, it was sick with the smell of him. The rage overcame her, and her screams echoed through the canyon.

When her voice failed, Maria returned to the wagon tracks and examined them further, following them out of the canyon. Curiously, the tracks did not appear deep enough to suggest the amount of gold stacked in the mission. The tracks led north through the silent assembly of her heathen horde. They looked down from their mounts in curiosity as she followed the tracks toward the empty northern horizon.

No horses. Only the missing mules and wagons from the camp passed that way. Her rage turned to anguish as she realized that she could not follow. There was no dust on the horizon, they had past far out of the reach of her spent horses. By the time her company could be made ready, it would be hopeless.

"Three castles? A child? Blue and dead eyes..." Maria whispered as she stared north into the wasteland.

April 1865
Hembrillo Basin, New Mexico Territory

The dead wind swept them across the salt pans and desiccated wastes of volcanic rock and formations of crumbling shale. Like fleshy ghosts, they moved without strain through a dream, carrying an increasingly terrifying freight. An invisible shade kept the vampiric sun at bay, and they knew no thirst nor suffered hunger. They traveled without rest through the nights, following the stars across the moonless sky. Not even the horses faltered in their pace, despite meager rations of feed and the absence of water. No one spoke of these things. Only the quiet rumble of wagon wheels and the cyclic squeak of dry axles interrupted the silence in the wind.

The Tiny Mountain appeared the way morning appears after strange dreams, a slow release at waking, defying remembrance. Like a column of ants carrying lumps of golden sugar, they wound around the peak, working as a single mind to complete their task. When the load had been secreted into the depths, they broke their company. Juh and his warriors returned to their fortress in the Blue Mountains. Chatto and his band disappeared without words. If he had a destination, it was known only to him. Nana, Lozen, Victorio, and the remaining Chiricahua made camp in the valley and were joined by Loco and a few of his band from Ojo Caliente.

◆ ◆ ◆

The dust was visible on the horizon for over an hour before the column began to take form. At the far reaches of vision, the hills and ridges of the landscape faded into the blue sky, creating the illusion of a distant sea. Victorio observed the approaching cloud shifting through the mirage lines rising from the flat of the basin, lending life and movement to the fraudulent waters. Soon, the cloud was filled with dark shapes and many legs. A long shadow rode out front. Cochise had returned.

Only a day after Nana returned, riding on a mountain of gold, Cochise now matched his spoils. He tried to count the horses but lost the number. Too many horses returned, easily double the number Cochise rode out with. They all bore soldier's saddles, heavily laden with packs and bulging saddle bags. Those without riders, doubly so. An advance rider raced out past Cochise and galloped toward the camp below. Cheers and hollers rose from the camp as the Apache greeted the returning warriors.

Loco rose from his shaded seat and stood next to Victorio near the peak of the Tiny Mountain. His eyes squinted to slits, his face broad and round.

The two chiefs stood together like trees rooted to the rock. One slight frame, prematurely bent by the burden of wisdom, the other tall, proud, and brutally handsome. Loco, the diplomat and peacemaker, and Victorio, the warrior and tactician. The Warm Springs and Copper Mine people were united behind them, but there was a growing divide between them.

"This is a mistake," said Loco.

Victorio did not answer.

"A blind man could follow their trail!"

Victorio continued to look out across the basin. Sixty-eight riders had followed Cochise and sixty-eight returned with over two hundred horses. Rifles protruded like branches, or the bones of wings, from nearly every mount. He began to smile.

"They will come for vengeance, and they will keep coming until they are satisfied," said Loco. "Yet you would fill the mountain with yellow metal and invite death among our people."

"Cochise rides in victory, and you speak of defeat. I do not see defeat."

"The yellow metal bends the minds of white men, calling to them from the cracks of the earth. There is no distance too great to follow. They will come, and there will be no hiding.

The very sight of it is a curse to us! We take by blood their most precious thing? This is not victory, it is a great mistake."

"The council has decided. I don't fear death, none here do. Stay or go as it pleases you!"

They stood in silence and watched the column approach. The camp stirred and churned with excitement below. Women rushed to stoke cookfires, and children ran out to meet the riders. A unified cheer went up as the advance rider reached the camp and was surrounded by a group of women. None would be made widows today, the rider reported, all the warriors had returned.

"I will go to Ojo Caliente with any that choose to follow. I will not make war with the whites."

"It is your choice. I will not judge you."

"Take this." Loco handed him a long object wrapped in deer skin. "This belonged to Mangas Coloradas and, before him, Cuchillo Negro. I had thought to bury it, but I think now that you should have it."

Victorio unfolded the skin, revealing a long knife with a black-stained bone handle. The blade was pitted and ancient, but the edge was still keen.

"I will keep it," he said, sliding the knife into his belt.

Below, the riders were reaching the camp, and the shouting and celebration increased. One warrior threw a handful of gold coins up in the air for the children, who loved the whirring sound they made when launched from their slings, and they shimmered down among the little ones like rain in the sun.

TWENTY-THREE

April 5, 1865
The Octagon House
Fishkill, New York

Something was amiss at the strange octagon house of Doctor Fowler. Nothing remained of the sun beyond a pale blue line clinging to the treetops in the west, yet the windows of the house were dark. The front door gaped open, and the yard lay in disarray, scattered with abandoned tools and household implements. Horses, visible through the open stable door, paced nervously in their stalls. Suspiciously absent were the strange septuplets employed by the doctor. The ominous silence did not bode well for Jay Sheldon.

He pulled the wagon up along the railed fence of the stable and secured the team. Typically, his deliveries were met with attentive and eager hands. Considering the importance of the cargo, he expected Fowler's men to be doting over the delicate delivery of the rare and mysterious moon glass.

He set off for the main house and its carelessly open door.

"Hello?" he called out to the darkness.

No reply followed.

One of Jay's early partners in his shipping company, old Horace Fowler, adopted the Aldrich Septuplets sixty-four years ago when their mother died in childbirth. The headmaster of the orphanage provided little information regarding the father of the Aldrich boys, only that he was of cruel disposition and overly fond of spirits. The elder Aldrich vanished from public knowledge after depositing the boys in the care of the orphanage, claiming, "These boys ain't right with God." His meaning was a matter of speculation at the time, though Horace Fowler treated them kindly and loved them as his own. He educated the boys and brought them up in the Christian tradition. Then came Orson Squire.

By the time Orson reached his sixteenth year, the Aldrich boys were largely withdrawn from the public, resigned to a reclusive existence on the Fowler estate. They never married, though their bond with each other remained undeniable. Outsiders speculated on the nature of their subjugation, often with fantastic theories spun from their unusual septuple birth. None suspected the Fowler family's association with Jay Sheldon and his peculiar Guild, though all would agree that, by the time of Old Horace's passing, the Aldrich brothers existed as no more than servants, minions to Horace's only heir.

When Jay stepped into the darkened Octagon House and felt his feet slip in the sickly blood pooled across the foyer, he was at a loss to identify which of the Aldrich brothers it belonged to. Even if he were capable of discerning the individual identities of the brothers, the complete obliteration of this one's face by an axe left the features unrecognizable. In a savage postmortem desecration, the killer severed and distributed the septuplet's limbs around the room, the final stroke, leaving his axe deeply embedded in his victim's chest.

Jay drew his pistol and backed out of the room slowly, tracking bloody prints across the whitewashed deck of the veranda. Night set on the yard, and the cat claw moon offered little light. After pausing to allow his feelings of trepidation to pass, he returned to the wagon to retrieve a lantern before circling around the house.

Near the well, he encountered another dark pool soaking into the earth. Drag marks led from the pool's center to the well's mouth. Blood streaked over the smooth river stones and stained the mortar that held them. Jay did not doubt that a second Aldrich would be found below, bobbing in the cool, dark water. Bloody footprints faded away toward the stables. With morbid curiosity, he followed.

The source of the horses' agitation became apparent when he entered the stable. A third corpse hung there, a hay hook thrust through his neck, under his jaw, and out the side of his face, its handle stretched across two large spikes in a heavy beam. Judging by the broad arcs of the blood splatter, the septuplet struggled to free himself before he died. In the closest stall, a white palomino bore the splatter of the arterial spray. Jay ran his finger through a long, red splash on the stall's gate and held it to light, noting little coagulation in the fresh blood. The practitioner of the savagery was still near.

He approached the back of the house, with its gardens and gazebo, holding the lantern high in one hand and his pistol ready in the other. It did not take long to discover the fourth Aldrich brother crumpled like a wispy-haired spider, his body splayed on the stone walk between the house and rose gardens. Fractured bones poked through his limbs, and his face was frozen in a contortion of horror. Sheldon looked up at the sinister tower and its strangely luminous moon glass.

At the back of the house, the door to the kitchen and servants' quarters stood open, and the firelight could be seen flickering behind the window. Sheldon quietly ascended the stairs and peeked inside. Another sprawling pool of blood spread across the wooden planks of the kitchen, emanating from a headless body. An iron kettle bubbled on the wood stove, bloody tuffs of gray hair roiling within.

Shattering glass crashed from an upper floor. Jay navigated the illogical rooms and narrow corridors toward the sound of the disturbance. He discovered the sixth brother leaning out of a broken window in a third-floor guest room, his entrails stretching down the finely papered wall. Jay reached through the broken portal and lifted the man's still-warm head, observing his face fixed in a visage of surprise and terror, dead no more than a minute or two.

A quiet chanting began from the room at the end of the

hall. The deep and otherworldly voice sang in a language unknown to him. Jay's feet creaked across the floorboards as he approached, his pistol trained on the open doorway. When the circle of light stretched into the room, the seventh brother was revealed. Jefferson Aldrich, the oldest of the septuplets by three minutes, sat cross-legged on the floor of Fowler's study. His eyes were a strange brown color, like dark tree bark, utterly alien to his countenance. Blood saturated every piece of his clothing; it painted his limbs and face completely. Between his legs sat a package, about the size of a human head, wrapped in brown paper and covered in bloody handprints. From Jefferson's bloody lips came the Apache death song.

He smiled at Jay and drew a bloody kitchen knife across his own throat. Blood bubbled from the wound, hissing as he laughed and choked. The dark brown eyes faded to blue as life drained from the final Aldrich.

Jay Sheldon had witnessed many unsettling things during his tenure with the Trust, but none of them inspired the dread of what he saw in Fowler's misshapen manor. His thoughts turned to his son, adrift in their mad world, serving the whims of monsters. His excuses to Teressa's incessant inquiries were now exhausted. It was time to bring his son home, even if only to say goodbye.

◆ ◆ ◆

Hours later, when Orson Squire Fowler returned to the Octagon House, horrific carnage awaited him. Paralyzed with the knowledge that Mangas could still be present, he rushed through his preparations. With trembling fingers, he cleaned and repackaged the skull under the curious light of the moon glass turret. Then, muttering prayers, chants, and incantations from every imaginable source, he vowed to forsake any further acts of necromancy.

He addressed the package to the Smithsonian Museum of Natural History. Jay Sheldon refused to ship the package, nor did he ever return to the Octagon House.

TWENTY-FOUR

April 6, 1865
Baltimore, Maryland

"**I**t doesn't resonate," said Russell. "The Golden Dragon sounds more like an English pub. Fuck the English."

"I suppose you're right," said Collins. "I haven't the time to run a saloon, anyway."

"I should think so," Russell agreed. "Besides, why would you want to invest in this God-forsaken shit hole?"

"It has its charms."

"Yes, the wharf rats are delightful."

"They bring more cheer than that depressing murder house you're so fond of!"

"What dreary hobbyists we make," said Russell.

"Huzzah," said Collins, lifting his glass of bourbon.

Thames Street was green and gold, with the sun hanging low in the trees. A pair of dock workers looked in the glass and grinned at their reflections as they passed. One stooped and ancient, the other bright-eyed and incapable of whiskers. They passed on, not tempted by the wares of the Gabby Saloon and Mercantile.

Collins refilled his glass from the bottle the barman had left before retiring to his sweeping of distant corners. No other customers were present.

"Do you know when it will happen?" asked Russell.

"Soon, I imagine."

"Seems such a tragedy, he's a good man."

"There are no good men," said Collins. "Least of all, us."

"Do you believe his assassination will accelerate the divide, increase the conflict, and so on?"

"Morya does," said Collins. "Or, he did. Who knows where that devil has gotten off to."

"I find it unsettling that not even the Poet has surfaced at such a critical phase in our endeavors."

"Perhaps he recognizes that our endeavors are on target. He cannot hold our hands through every mundane and menial motion."

"Yes, these are very mundane times, " Russell said.

Collins shrugged and turned his gaze to the trees outside. A breeze sifted through the branches making a rustling sound through the new spring growth. Patches of sunlight danced across their table.

"The leaves are really moving. Or rather the wind.

"Neither," said Russell. "Only the movement of your mind."

"Touché." He lifted his glass.

The barman swept, the wind blew, and the two men sipped their drinks as the shadows crept across the room.

"Do you trust Robert Black?" asked Collins.

"I'd say we haven't much choice, he's beyond our reach," said Russell.

"It happened so fast, I never had the chance to speak with them before they set off after Davis and the remaining gold. I can tell you, Elizabeth Van Lew has no lost love for Robert."

"I spoke at length with Taft on the matter," said Russell.

"And what was your impression?"

"I found him elusive."

Collins took off his glasses and held the lenses to the dusty sunlight swirling at their table. Two orbs of golden light burned like dying suns against the scarred oak surface.

"It would be inconceivable for one of us to defy the other. The length and nature of our bond prohibit even the thought of it. Even if it were possible, it would be tantamount to suicide and would require a titanic effort of self-loathing just to imagine it."

"From the beginning, our Trust was built upon faith. Like men falling from a great height, we can no more turn our minds from Him than we can stop falling. I agree, we have no instinct but to have trust in him. Ours is an impenetrable brotherhood."

"Well said," Collins agreed.

"I do have a thought," said Russell.

"What is it?"

"It is no easy thing to stand in His presence. I have always felt deeply unsettled when standing in the vault beneath his house. I cannot explain it other than to say I felt naked, ripped open like a lab animal, and exposed to His thoughts. Essentially, Taft lives directly above the vault. I can only imagine the accrued dread of such a habitation."

"That is a remarkable observation, William," said Collins. "If that were indeed the case, that he was somehow affected by Him, it would assuage all my doubts."

"And illicit my deepest sympathies," said Russell.

"Agreed."

Collins picked up the bottle of bourbon and swirled it around, holding the brown glass up in the sunlight to gauge its level.

"This war is making it very hard to get quality bourbon," he said.

"We all have our burdens."

"Yes, on another topic," said Collins. "As present circumstances are out of our immediate control, I've reached out to the European Order."

"Probably wise."

"If there is a player such as Stallworth gathering vast quantities of gold in the middle of his war, he should probably know about it."

"Or, be responsible for it," said Russell.

"Wouldn't that be a conundrum!"

"It would deviate wildly from everything Morya has

designed and everything we have worked for."

"Exactly," said Collins.

"What if the American Castle has already been recovered, and Napoleon III is reuniting it with the others. He could be shipping it out of Veracruz as we speak!"

"Then our work is done, is it not?"

"I don't like it," said Russell.

"I don't like not knowing," said Collins.

"What of that puppet prince? What's his name, Maximillian?"

"Drawn from the inbred legions of Hapsburg spawn, beyond that, I don't know anything of the man."

"That seems to be the theme of our conversation," said Russell.

"What's that?"

"That we don't know anything!"

"Ironic, isn't it? That for all the secret chess pieces we move, for all our machinations, that knowledge of the most critical aspects of our life's work should be withheld from us!" Said Collins.

"I am unamused," said Russell.

"We can only do what we can do, unfortunately."

"What if you're right about Napoleon III? What if he's uniting the castles?" Russell asked.

"Does a pot of honey lament the bee?" Said Collins.

"I suppose not."

Russell picked up his ignored glass of bourbon, sipped, then contemplated the golden brown liquor as the last rays of the sun slipped away from the table.

"I'm going to Richmond," said Russell.

"To coordinate with Thomas?"

"Yes, and I may need your help."

"Of course, what can I do?"

"If they capture Davis' caravan, we'll need to ensure it ends up in proper hands. I've already arranged a cavalry commission for Thomas, but I need help diverting union forces."

"I can certainly assist," said Collins.

"I appreciate it."

Collins put his glasses back on. Despite the failing son, the lenses shone brilliant gold. He ran his fingers over the engraved graffiti and drifted into thought.

"So many memories at this table," said Collins.

"Any regrets?"

"Only one," he said, sipping at his glass.

"And what's that?"

"That this bottle is empty."

PART THREE
MOVING FORWARD, LOOKING BACK

I was ejected
from within a churning star
I was not alone

-Matsuo Sogi

TWENTY-FIVE

April 19, 1865
The White House
Washington D. C.

T here are many chambers in the house of the human heart. Some of us go from room to room, displaying their pride in brightly lit rooms, while others restrain their sins in forgotten cellars. Only in moments of great intimacy the windows to these mansions are un-shuttered, and the heart is bare. In the black silk-draped East Room, where Abraham Lincoln lay in state, all those in attendance collectively shared a chamber of paralyzing grief.

General Grant sat at the head of the black-draped catafalque, tears falling unchecked into his beard. Before him, under a cross of white lilies, Abraham Lincoln lay in a black metal coffin. His sons, Robert and Tad, sat at the foot of the coffin with Mary Todd's relatives. Their eyes were dark stains on blank faces.

Johnson stood below, newly cloaked in the dead man's mantle. A cabal of black-suited cabinet members lamented behind him. Each breath was painfully extracted from the air, steeped in the humid tears of senators, congressmen, military officers, and dignitaries. Pressed to the shoulders, they spilled a sea of human sorrow into the hall.

Taft's eyes wandered among the grief-stricken cabinet members and settled on a man shifting and squirming from some unknown angst. Occasionally the man's gaze turned in their direction, casting a hateful glare on Danfort Collins. For his part, Collins seemed oblivious.

"1861," said Russell.

"What?"

"The last time the three of us were together in a room."

"Ah, the inauguration, how ironic." Collins discretely pulled a flask from his jacket. "It's painfully muggy in here." He sipped from the flask and offered it to Russell, who declined.

"I have my own," said Taft, producing a flask from his inside breast pocket. "Who is that mournful-looking wretch who has you fixed in his baleful sight?"

"That would be Mr. Edwin Stanton," said Collins. "Likely, he views me as having some culpability in this sad gathering."

"What could have inspired such a fever dream?" said Russell.

A grim-looking minister knelt before Robert and Tad, muttering labored prayers and clutching a small wooden cross as the catalyst of his spell. The children looked through the man and past the black walls to some imaginary vista far from the oppressive throng. The reverend's words were lost in the murmuring of the mourners, no more articulate than the bleating of goats.

"This feels wrong." Taft took another long pull, but the liquor did nothing to expel his anxiety.

"Strange," said Russell. "I feel nothing."

Taft tilted his flask to find it empty, sighed, and returned it to his jacket.

"Regardless, that's not why we're here," said Collins.

Collins removed his gold-framed glasses and wiped the lenses on the silk of his tie as they had begun to fog from the humidity in the room.

"Have you made contact with Napoleon III?"

"I have," said Collins. "He claims that neither Stallworth nor Maximillian are connected to the European Order. Likewise, I've received word from Victoria, disowning any authorship of our tribulations."

"What of the Pope?" Asked Russell.

"No reply."

"Curious," said Taft.

"It's not as if he has anything else to occupy his time," said Russell.

"Where does that leave us?" Asked Taft, ignoring the sarcasm.

"Without a clue, without Morya, and helpless to the currents of fate, it would seem," chuckled Collins. "Sam and Robert are after the Confederate Treasury, and we can only wait."

"A fool's errand," said Taft.

"Should they succeed or fail, Thomas is riding south for support," said Russell.

"Still, I can't help but feel something is amiss in our own house," said Collins.

"Do you suspect one of the Neophytes?" Asked Russell.

"Perhaps, what are your thoughts on Thomas," asked Collins.

"He is upset with me," said Russell. "He feels I'm holding him back. The business with Deer Island was of particular consequence; it injured his pride when Robert was chosen to enter the cavern."

"Do you feel that he would lash out against you because of it? He was very recently with Price during that business with the Tyler clan. Perhaps they conspired together?"

"No, that is not his style, he is much more direct. If he were truly disgruntled, he would simply cut my throat."

"Agreed," said Collins.

"What about Sam?" asked Collins.

"Well, I doubt he threw himself in Prison, and before that, he had no real interaction with Price, Richmond, or had any knowledge of the Gold," said Collins.

"There was that unfortunate circumstance regarding the Apache," said Russell.

"Sam didn't kill him, it was General West. Interestingly, by Robert Black's orders. Can you think of any reason why Robert would do that?" Asked Collins.

"No, I cannot," said Taft. "We've been over this, Danfort! Shall we put it at our hind and move on to more fertile fields of discussion? You both know the nature of our bonds, it is unthinkable that one of us should defy Him. He chose us, as he chose our Neophytes. We shouldn't waste another moment in doubt of our Trust."

"Very well, Alphonso, I suppose you're right," said Collins.

"It was, after all, one of Brother Spartacus' first lessons. You choose this covenant, or you choose death," said Russell.

"And death does not break our covenant," added Collins.

Taft shifted uncomfortably where he stood and unbuttoned his jacket, seemingly affected by the rising warmth and humidity in the room. Bodies were still pushing their way into the overcrowded East Room. An Episcopalian priest stood on the catafalque, looking out serenely across the wriggling congregation as if conducting a symphony of quiet babble.

"I came to Ingolstadt in twenty-nine," Russell said. "A dead man sent me."

Collins swirled his flask in a semicircle, gauging its volume. "I arrived in the summer of twenty-eight. I received a gift and an invitation, both bequeathed by Joseph Balsamo, a man said to be dead for decades."

Taft reached in his pocket for something he knew he would not find. His hand clutched the emptiness around the phantom object, guilty of its loss. He felt the compulsion to run, to put time and distance between them. Something stirred in the magma at the core of him. It would always be there, seeking its way toward the light, like a moth thrusting itself at the moon, relentless and eternal. His mind repeated a prayer, taught him to suppress the thing. The eyes of his companions stared back at him, anticipating, compelling him to speak.

"I tutored students to earn extra money," began Taft.

His words droned over the murmur of the mourners. He soon found himself lost in the memory, almost forgetting that he spoke.

"At the time, I had not yet considered Yale. In the winter of 1826, I agreed to take on the ward of a curious European nobleman. He gave his name as Leopold George, the son of Prince Francis Rákóczi of Hungary.

"He interviewed me several times over December and January. He never gave details about my tutelage, though he was immensely interested in my credentials and personal life. Each time he would visit, the interview ended with his affirmation that I had won the job and he would soon deliver the student, though it was never the case...

"Time passed, and he returned with further queries on ethics and spiritual abstracts. I began to think him mad. Nearly a month passed before his final visit. He explained that his charge would not be arriving, but he nonetheless wanted to retain my services. He would require me to travel instead.

"I thought the whole affair must be some elaborate joke or that the man was indeed mad. However, he produced a generous advance of silver, more than sufficient to secure passage to Europe and nearly double the negotiated compensation, along with an address in Eckernförde, a port on the Baltic Sea. Leopold also gave me a costly and beautiful gift as a token of his appreciation and told me to come when able; he placed no urgency on the date.

"My father thought it prudent that I decline the invitation, and it took some time to convince him otherwise. This significantly delayed my departure. I did not arrive in Eckernförde until August.

"I traveled to the estate described by the man to find it occupied by a hospital where none present had ever heard of Leopold George. I spoke to a nurse of advanced age who told me the property had once belonged to the Comte de Saint Germain, but he had died years previously. She directed me down the lane to an ancient church, the site of the man's internment. "Having no further direction, I visited the decaying churchyard. The place was lonely and unvisited, nearly every grave in disrepair, with one noteworthy exception. One monument stood clean and kept, adorned with fresh flowers and a note bearing only an address.

"None in that place wished to discuss the dead man. The innkeeper, a man named Vinther, threatened to toss me on the street if I uttered the name, Leopold George. Having only the address from the note to guide me, I left the next morning for Ingolstadt."

The murmuring ceased as a pastor coughed and began the service. The three men surrendered their conversation to the words of the sermon.

"I have said that the people confided in the late lamented President with a full and loving confidence. Probably no man since the days of Washington was ever so deeply and firmly embedded and enshrined in the very hearts of the people as Abraham Lincoln."

He went on to give an emotionally stirring eulogy. Upon finishing his prepared words, he began reciting the Lord's Prayer. Nearly the entire congregation recited with him, speaking in one voice. The effect was powerful and brought tears to nearly all in attendance.

Danfort Collins remained silent and did not weep.

TWENTY-SIX

August 1827
Eckernförde
Duchy Of Holstein, German Confederation

T he way ahead was dark, lined with thick elms and beech trees that arched over the road like the interlocking arms of titanic nymphs. A road cleaved the center, stretching beyond sight and rutted with centuries of wagon tracks and iron clod hooves. The forest stood menacingly before him with its claustrophobic invitation. He had the irrational thought that if he lost the sky here, it would be gone forever, like a coin dropped in a well. Unconsciously, his fingers fidgeted in his pocket over the case of the gold watch. He removed it and flipped it open with his thumb, and read the inscription:

Alphonso Taft, December 3, 1826

The watch had stopped, further fueling his trepidation.

"Take care to wind the watch, 'tis more than time will be lost," was the curious warning that Leopold gave him with the gift.

An ominous omen.

The hands were frozen at twenty-two after three, though he couldn't remember if it had been running when last he checked. He wound the watch and the hands ticked to life, albeit with compromised accuracy. Perhaps it was a good sign, maybe it wasn't the right time to leave. He slid the timepiece back into his pocket and contemplated returning to town to set it and have a hot meal. Surely, one more day would only better prepare him for his journey.

"That is a magnificent device! The owner of such an exquisite treasure must truly be a great man!"

Alphonso jumped back, startled by the sudden voice. Its origin eluded him until his eyes focused on an old Romani woman who appeared to have stepped out of the forest. Layers of colored fabric wound about her in a dust devil of skirts, scarves, and shawls. The pointy tips of her black boots protruded slightly from the bottom of the array, and one gray and gnarled hand stretched out with crooked digits. Her other arm was wrapped in an elaborate sling to carry an infant. Only a tiny bulbous lump and a flash of pale white peaked from under the protective layering to suggest the form of a child. The woman's face was textured like tree bark, with sucked-in lips and a knuckle of a jaw, her eyes dull black, like living orbs of tar.

"Yes, you must be a powerful chief!" She spoke English, but her accent suggested a Slavic or Russian origin. "Crossed the sea, did you?"

"I'm just a traveler, madam. I'm no one special."

"This road was old when Charlemagne was king." She gestured more to the forest than the path. "But you don't go lightly. No, you do not!"

The woman encroached slowly, gesticulating in lazy circles with her bony hand. Her head slighted to the side, and she turned to engage his eyes with hers. Her lipless mouth stretched into a tiny crevice of a smile, and her boots scuffled forward.

"A mighty fortune seeker, that's what you are! My eyes are old, and the world is dimmer, but you are adrift with fate, I can see that."

The woman came closer, turning the bundled child as if she intended to present it to Alphonso.

"Perhaps I could see more? I suppose that I could. Mayhap a

tiny token, an offering, let's say, may clear the fog from my eyes and reveal a glimpse of what waits ahead?"

"I take no part in divinations, nor do I give credence to the words of seers."

"Is that so?" The woman exhaled a coughing giggle. "Then you've certainly taken the wrong road!"

She pressed the child against him, her hip against his, staring at him with shapeless eyes.

"What?" Alphonso backed slowly away, the crone matching his pace and pressing herself up against him.

"A tiny mercy might serve, such a man as you can surely afford a single coin? Please, sir, a coin for the child, an innocent babe in need of human kindness." Her last words trailed into a hissing whisper.

Alphonso felt something subtle touch his thigh, like spider legs brushing against him from inside his pocket. He looked down to see the woman's gambit. Her arm, which initially appeared to support the child, was a ruse. Hidden behind the baby sling, her free arm worked to pick his pocket. The twisted gray twigs of her fingers wrapped around the golden watch and gently lifted.

"Away, witch!" he screamed and rapped his knuckle hard on her gray, bony wrist.

Her hand jerked back like an eel into its den within her layered fabrics. She gasped and pulled back, the infant jostled and shifted in her arms. An errant scarf fell away from the child's face and revealed it for what it was, a white kerchief with two black buttons pinned for eyes around a flour sack stuffed with loose and lumpy objects.

Alphonso backed away from the wretch, patting down his pockets to confirm that his belongings remained. The woman stared at him with her seething black eyes and chuckled, her other hand still outstretched and churning slowly. Satisfied with his inventory, he took off down the ancient road in a dead run. His pack bounced on his shoulders and slapped against his back as he went.

When fatigue overtook him, he stopped and looked back the way he had come, expecting to see the crone hobbling behind. He saw only the empty road. Alphonso caught his breath and set forward again. His nerves calmed, and he resigned himself to the long walk to Hamburg and beyond.

If only he had a horse, such encounters could be mitigated. However, in the inhospitable town of Eckernforde, none were available for sale or hire. Alphonso attributed this to his open questioning after the mysterious Leopold George. The name invoked darkness and dread from his lips to every corner of the town. Only the innkeeper, Vinther, offered him any services, and even he seemed to do so under some duress.

No direct sunlight filtered through the tree canopy, instead, it diffused through the thick forest leaves casting a pleasant but surreal luminance over the landscape. Birds proliferated and called to each other from the trees while red squirrels roamed the forest floor. Occasionally, deer wandered near, regarding him with lazy curiosity before eventually returning to the depths of the woods, all quiet and peaceful in the absence of humanity.

At dusk, he made camp near a creek with clear, clean water. He followed it to a flat place with a stretch of soft earth, out of direct sight of the road. He took stones from the creek, made a small firepit, and soon had it stoked with dry tinder. He sipped on schnapps while the fire crackled, ejecting embers of glowing stars, transient and swiftly dimming. The world retracted into a modest ring of flickering light; somehow, Vermont didn't seem so far away. He leaned back into the crook of an old elm and closed his eyes.

Sleep took him, and he dreamed of dogs. He woke to the howling of wolves. Only dull coals remained of the fire, and darkness encompassed the forest. Time and distance distorted in the absence of perspective. The snarling jabber of the creatures was urgent and violent, sounding at once miles away, then suddenly within arms reach. He counted the seconds between cries as if they were some mindless thunderstorm whose distance and trajectory could be anticipated. Filling his hand with a smooth round stone of decent heft, he waited, his ears perked for the sound of their breath or the pads of their feet rushing across the soft earth.

Another sound, deceptively distant but decidedly familiar, interjected at intervals, the unmistakable voices of men. No words could be deciphered and the speech overlapped with that of the wolves. The howls and voices seemed to occupy the same place at times, sounding simultaneous, suggestive of some singular entity. Whatever their intent, it had no wholesome end.

He quickly packed his meager items into his pack and struck out toward the road and away from the subtle traces of his campfire, from which vague traces of smoke still lingered. The sounds followed him, growing louder. He considered the possibility of men and wolves working in tandem or even something more terrifying such as the dog-headed men known as the Cynocephali. According to the mutterings of Vinther, this was indeed a land of monsters. He scrambled through the forest, tripping and careening as if the vomited hordes of Hades lapped at his heels.

He crossed the path and kept going until a fallen tree sent him flailing to the earth. Alphonso calmed himself and sheltered beneath a slightly raised portion of the tree, further concealing himself under loose leaves and dirt. He heard them shouting in the distance and wondered if they had found his camp. The lupine wailing, however, faded and disappeared. He cowered in the composting waste for a small eternity. Though not confident, he believed he saw torches drifting around the road.

Eventually, the black submitted to gray, and tiny spears of sunlight streaked through the leaves above, ushering the return of birds and wholesome creatures. He was alone again with no evidence of ever being otherwise. No tracks, marks, or other signs of wolf or man remained to validate his fears. Alphonso set out immediately at a brisk pace.

After about a mile, he saw a light at the end of the road where the forest ended. A less conservative pace the day before may have avoided the night's terrors. In contrast to the land beyond, the forest road glommed into the darkness like a train tunnel. He increased his stride with relief and enthusiasm.

Something moved in the trees ahead of him. The first sight caused him to panic, dodging off the path. It looked human but was moving, turning in slow, uniform circles, swaying slightly back and forth. He approached cautiously. It was human, drained of life, and swinging with the breeze.

The old crone hung by one of her long scarves from the low-hanging branch of alder. The pointy tips of her black boots protruded from her skirts as they did before, only now they dangled just above the forest floor. Both her arms hung limp, though one of them swung curiously in an oblong pendulum independent of the body, the hand frozen in an arthritic claw. The sling gaped open with the mock infant hanging from a loose piece of fabric like a noose. A rip in its sack body revealed a disturbing menagerie of stuffing. Scraps of paper, locks of hair, buttons, and tiny pouches of unknown content, all swimming in feathers, dirt, and unidentifiable miasma, spilled out of the thing.

The crone's eyes were open but static and glazed like the bulbous eyes of a dead fish. The mouth gaped, revealing a few decayed fragments of teeth visible against her swollen purple tongue. Flies, busy in their visitations, crawled tentatively about her face searching for a suitable place to conduct their trade. The whole scene squeaked with the flexing of the branch, mesmerizing in its horror. Alphonso could not look away.

A cluster of objects started leaking out of the doll's head, falling beneath the haunting orbit of her hand. One of the objects continued rolling to his feet, shiny and flashing gold. Without a thought, he retrieved it, discovering it to be an ancient coin of Roman origin bearing the face of Emperor Caligula.

A coin for the child...

Alphonso put the coin in his pocket and jogged the remainder of the way to the forest's edge toward the sunlight and the open country. His pack slapped against his shoulders as he ran, eclipsing the creaking of the tree and washing it from his memory. Finally, he burst out of the forest, birthed into the warm blaze of the sun. Greeting him was a landscape of small, grassy hills and open spaces where trees existed in sensible congregations, and the sky stretched above, blue and infinite.

The road took a meandering southward course, as Vinther said it would. Hamburg waited, still more than a day away, though surely he might acquire a mount providing he kept the name of Leopold George off his lips. He checked his watch, giving it a wind, and, with the forest at his back, he carried on under the sun.

TWENTY-SEVEN

April 28, 1865
Richmond, Virginia

Lieutenant Aristotle Johnson held the battle flag of Company E high above his head as he slowly rode the line of his assembled cavalrymen. It was stained with earth and blood, perforated by bullets, and frayed at every edge. The men of the 6th USCC sat silently in their saddles, watching as the wind rippled their banner; forty-six men and horses holding still enough to hear the fabric flutter.

"Bertram Augustus carried this flag out of Ohio, he was the first. Bertram Augustus fell in Kentucky, shot in the chest, and pierced with bayonets," said Lieutenant Johnson. "Where is he now?"

"He rides with us!" the men shouted.

"Benjamin King took up that flag and carried it to Tennessee. Benjamin King died with this flag in his hands in some nameless field. Abel Adams took up our flag and carried the charge until he, too, met his mortal end. Robert Garland did not let the flag touch the earth! He carried it, and we carried the day. Robert Garland never left that field in Tennessee, but he did not let our banner fall. I ask you now, where are these men?"

"They ride with us!"

"We came to Virginia, and Sam Anderson held this flag high as we made charge after charge at Chaffins Farm. Sam

Anderson died of his wounds in a surgeon's tent with this flag in his hands! Where is he now?"

"He rides with us!"

"We came to a place called Fair Oaks and met those graybacks head-on! Elijah Jackson was the first of four to carry our standard that day. Jordy Brooks, Ambrose Rooney, and Sims Conner carried this flag and died for the privilege. Their names will not be forgotten because..."

"They ride with us!"

"Now, Lee might have made his X on a line, treaties made, and these hostilities could be said to have ended, but it is not over. Not for us. Our work is not complete, this war has use for us yet. Today we have been reassigned from the 6th to a new command, with a new commanding officer..."

The men murmured and groaned their discontent with the news, interrupting Lieutenant Johnson with boos and moans. E Company had six previous commanders, all white men. Aristotle Johnson took command in Virginia with a brevet promotion when there was no white man willing to do so. The company excelled under Johnson's command, and all dreaded what replacing him might bring.

"Easy boys, go easy!" said Johnson, holding up one hand to calm the men. "I consider my time with you the single greatest honor in my life, and I would gladly give my mortal soul for any man in this company! I've seen you this far, and I won't quit you now!"

"Amen!" someone bellowed.

"Our assignment will certainly meet your approval. Company E is riding south to catch ol' Jeff himself and bring the sonofabitch to justice! Now, who will ride with me?"

"We ride with you!"

"Who rides with me?"

"We ride with you!"

"Huzzah!" Johnson turned his horse down the Loblolly Grove Road with his company in formation behind.

Fire had swept through the area, consuming the grass and young pines along the road. Further along, the pines gave way to oaks that lined the road closer to the manor house. Several of these oaks were scarred by flame, their blackened and leafless branches frozen in a charred winter. Household items and clothing littered the road the closer they got to Jansen House. Clothing, broken dishes, loose documents, cooking utensils, and other looted jetsam. A derelict wagon with a broken axle lay to the side of the road just beyond the grounds, its contents scattered and thoroughly rifled.

Johnson led his men into the debris-filled yard, where they reformed their lines. He called to a corporal, who rode beside him and received the battle flag. The man saluted and then returned to the ranks. The door to the Jansen House was missing entirely, and the obliterated windows at either side of the egress gaped with jagged shards. A black void waited beyond the apertures of the white manor house, giving the impression of a crude skull imposed on the otherwise pristine structure.

A figure appeared in the doorway as Johnson stepped down from his horse. The man's head was shorn smooth, and his eyes and skin were dark like ash. His mouth was a severe slit above a crescent-shaped scar bisecting the cleft of his chin. The man carried his hat in his hand and wore captain's bars on his lapel. He was thin but muscular, with knotty joints and shoulders that looked like they should end in wings. His boots rang out on the wooden porch of the Jansen House as he descended the stairs and approached the lieutenant.

"Lieutenant Aristotle Johnson, I presume?" he said.

"Yes, sir!"

"Well met, lieutenant. My name is Captain Thomas Rogers."

May 2, 1865
Wilkes County, Georgia

"Don't shoot, I surrender!" Reavis shouted to the Confederate soldier standing in the road.

"John, is that you?" The soldier asked.

"No, I'm a deserter," he said.

"I'm tired, John, very tired. If you wanted to leave, you should have gone with the others."

"My name is James Reavis..." he said.

"I can see you plain as the day, John Reagan, now get to camp and stop this foolishness," the soldier pointed to a sparse grove of trees where quiet voices could be heard.

Reavis followed the soldier's direction, intent on surrendering to the first officer he encountered. As he passed through the trees and into the clearing beyond, he was shocked to find Jefferson Davis, his entourage, and remaining cabinet members sullenly consuming their suppers around several small campfires.

"Reagan," President Davis beckoned with a wave. "A word, sir."

A strange malaise hung over the camp, an unnatural dread reaching from somewhere beyond the tangible world. It was as if a malignant thought had manifested into some unseen but amorphous cloud, enveloping the camp and infesting the minds of the men. In fleeing Robert Black and his perverse communes with the dead, Reavis had stumbled into a greater power, one with unknown but terrifying intent.

"Yes, sir," said Reavis, accepting their perception of him and abandoning hope for reality.

"I fought for years to prevent this war, now, in a moment, it threatens to swallow us all. I'm weary, John, but there is much work to be done. I would ask for your help if you are willing."

"What can I do, sir?"

"I have little use for a postmaster here on the eve of destruction. I do, however, desperately require a treasurer. With Trenholm's departure, I would prefer to elevate you to that office. What say you?"

"Certainly, sir, I would be honored," said Reavis.

"Good, I knew I could count on you," said Davis. "I'd like you to start immediately. You'll find Treeholm's records in the lead wagon. Review them and complete a thorough audit of all gold, silver, and bonds. Report to me when you've accomplished this."

Davis pointed to a line of wagons, lined up along the rutted path through the wood, then turned back to his meal.

"Of course, sir," said Reavis

He stood there for a moment, ignored and confused, before ambling toward the wagons. As promised, he found Treeholm's records neatly organized in a portable army desk, packed into the foremost wagon. Lighting a lantern, he went down the line. A strange heat emanated from that direction, oozing like a formless and malevolent breeze. He pulled aside the canvass covering the bed of the first wagon and revealed it to be stacked with large barrels. Jarring loose the lid of one, he peaked inside to discover it filled to capacity with gold coins.

There was no escaping, he understood that now. He was guided, propelled by hidden powers. His flight from Robert Black had only succeeded in achieving Black's desires. Whatever the identity of this sick wind, he was sure it would not allow him to leave without obeying its commands.

Reavis, who had never been to church, slid down onto his haunches and wondered how and to whom to pray.

May 4, 1865
Wilkes County, Georgia

Uncertainty descended on the world like a new and previously unknown season. They traveled roads swollen like rivers with men, vagrants untethered from hope drifting toward the idea of home with no promise of what they might find there. They traveled among the displaced and unwashed who went from ruin to ruin, seeking places untouched by grief, while rumors moved like a tainted wind bringing messages of a fierce reckoning. Lincoln was murdered, and every southern soul was culpable by the simple fact of their birth.

Davis was not difficult to find. The desperation was palpable, paving a wretched and hopeless path south. They followed through the Carolinas and into Georgia, waiting for an opportunity. Sheldon witnessed soldiers queuing up like a bread line for silver coins at the Abbeville courthouse, a sight that became common over the weeks. A final, futile effort took them east as Davis attempted to connect with General Johnston and the last standing army of the Confederacy, only to find him surrendered to Sherman. The war was over, but Davis went on, and they followed.

"Where do you think he's got to?" Asked Sheldon. "I would have thought he might have picked a more northerly location to abandon ship."

"He's a dead man if I find him," Robert broke off tiny pieces from a hard biscuit and tossed them in the direction of a skeptical crow. The bird nervously hopped forward to take it.

"That's a waste of food," Sheldon said, sitting on the trunk of a fallen pine tree, absently carving a saddle-like depression with his belt knife.

"You call this food?" said Black, throwing another piece of the biscuit to the crow.

"If there were any meat on it, I'd have the feathers off that thing already."

"I'm sure he's thinking the same of you!" Said, Robert.

Sheldon's uniform still hung loose, but his bones no longer shook like a winter tree when he coughed or laughed, and his health had improved dramatically since Richmond. He snapped a small, rotten branch off the fallen tree and set at removing the knob with his blade. A pile of bark and woodchips lay about him like fresh snowfall.

Satisfied with its meal, the crow took flight and disappeared through the canopy of trees. Robert tossed the rest of the biscuit onto his bedroll, lying near their fire. He returned to pacing the tree line of the tiny clearing where they made camp. The woods were quiet, save for the occasional pop of the fire and the steady chipping of Sheldon's knife.

"What if he's found out?" said Sheldon.

"He won't give us up."

"How can you be certain?"

"He understands the consequences. He values his soul."

"You collect souls now?"

Robert did not answer.

The crow reappeared, gliding down to claim the remainder of the biscuit.

"We have to find Thomas," said Sheldon. "We have no hope of seizing the treasury without him.

"Patience," said Robert.

"We are extended far beyond our means as is. If you have a plan, I'd love to hear it."

Again, Robert did not answer.

Sheldon took up the blade and resumed his hacking.

More crows appeared in the clearing, cawing at Robert as he paced in the pines.

"Why did you kill that girl at Yale?" Sheldon asked.

"Would you believe I'm innocent?"

"Honestly? No."

Robert walked to where Sheldon sat and knelt among the bark and wood chips, scooping up a hand full. He looked

Sheldon in the eye as he stood again.

"I did not kill Elizabeth," he said. "I was in love."

Three more crows entered the clearing, hopping around the perimeter of their camp. They cawed expectantly, though no further biscuits existed. Robert stood next to the fire and tossed woodchips on the coals. Little spirals of smoke rose as the fire consumed them.

"We were betrothed, and I had her father's blessing until I was tapped for Skull and Bones. He forbade her to see me again, which she ignored. The lawn near Connecticut hall was our meeting place, I would see her there most mornings. One day, I came late, and she was dead. You've heard the story. Not long after, I received this," Robert uncovered his gold buckle with its morbid crow motif.

"Who killed her then?"

"For years, that was between her and her killer."

"And then?" asked Sheldon.

"And then I killed the man who murdered her."

"How did you find him?"

"She told me."

"Who?"

"Elizabeth."

"I would say that you are insane, but it would be an insult to lunatics."

Robert let the remaining chips fall from his clenched fist into the fire like an hourglass.

"Believe what you please."

Sheldon cut another knot from the tree and consigned it to the fire. He hacked a few more pieces of bark and brushed them to the dirt with his hand. Thoughtfully examining his work, he slid over and sat in the smooth depression he had carved.

"Perfect," he said.

They sat in silence, listening to the demands of the crows as they danced about searching for crumbs. Then, a moment later, James Reavis appeared on a horse outfitted with cavalry tact, ducking branches and weaving his way to camp.

Reavis was changed. Physically, he had altered his appearance, cutting his hair and shaving his beard. He wore spectacles, a new suit, and a beaver pelt hat. Aside from his attire, he looked weary and aged.

"I don't know which was bolder, you running off or returning," said Robert.

"I'm certain that you will forgive me," said Reavis.

"Bolder still," Robert's pistol was in his hand.

"I am prepared to deliver the entire Confederate treasury into your custody."

"Oh, in that case," Robert pulled the hammer back.

"It's true, the gold is there, waiting for you. I have the proper documents. I have your new commissions, and I've even arranged for a detail to assist you. Though I admit, these claims seem born in fantasy, I assure you, they are genuine and true of fact."

"Commissions?"

"You'll find it all in my pack, as well as a change in uniform. Captain Sheldon, you've been given a star. Henceforth, you will be Brigadier General Basil Duke of Kentucky. Your charge is the safe transport of bullion, specie, and precious objects to a location where they may be suitably stored and secreted from Union confiscation. This location is to be selected at your discretion, and you are to act upon these orders immediately."

"Who is Basil Duke?" Sheldon asked.

"A man halfway to Jackson by now, according to the orders I delivered to him."

"Perhaps, you should start from the beginning," said Sheldon.

"It's true, I meant to run, and I did, straight into the arms of Jeff D's outfit. Somehow, they mistook me for one of their own, though I directly denied it. It was like they were under some kind of spell."

"So, they just let you right in?" Asked Robert.

"I wasn't there five minutes before he offered me the Treasury post, I swear it's true. I cannot account for the location of the actual John Reagan, I can only report that I became accepted as this man, even as I tried to deny it. Their belief was so complete that any insistence I made to the contrary only agitated all those concerned. An apt and quick study, I took to the identity and became privy to the council of Davis and the rest of the cabinet, such as it was. Immediately, I was immersed in a collective dread, both melancholy and terrifying. They were rife with it. Of their intents and objectives, I can only report the desperate and irrational state guiding their actions. They talked of Savannah, sailing to France, and setting up a government in exile. None acknowledged that Savannah had fallen. Apparently, the wisest among them defected the party for unknown fates before my arrival. I suspect this may account for Mr. Reagan's absence. "

"Beyond the delusion, the bickering, and the ambiguous destination, something even more terrible permeated the caravan. A curious heat lingered, though it did not radiate from the sun but rather from the air itself. Some tangible dread, humid and dead, clung and pulled on everything like gravity. The wheels of the wagons labored on smooth, dry roads. Every step was made in fatigue. The heaviness of that cargo was incalculable and multiplied by their hatred of it. With every passing minute, it grew to be nearly unbearable."

Reavis took a deep breath and stretched, seeming to gather himself in the pause. He returned to his horse and retrieved a large package wrapped in a yellowed bed sheet and a small leather satchel. He tossed the package to Sheldon.

"Put these on, we don't have much time. Robert can retain his alias, but your alterations are imperative."

"Unbelievable," said Sheldon, unwrapping the package and revealing a new uniform.

"We came to a town called Washington this morning,

and the cabinet was dissolved. The fate of the treasury was largely left to my council, the terms of which I previously defined. At this moment, the treasure is under the watchful but weary eye of Captain Parker and his men at the Washington Bank, who eagerly awaits the arrival of General Duke."

"Let's hear the factual account now if you please," said Robert, aiming his pistol at Reavis' face.

"Do it. It would be a mercy, sir," said Reavis.

"Walk with me, James."

The two of them walked out of the clearing and into the pines. Sheldon picked up the satchel and began reviewing the documents. They were detailed, official, and plausibly legitimate. The voices of Reavis and Black conversed behind a dense growth of pine. Robert asked questions, and Reavis answered in ever-softening tones. After a moment, the voice of Reavis seemed to change and become more feminine, almost entirely different, until Sheldon was convinced that he heard a woman's voice. Alarmed, he again cocked his pistol and moved to investigate. Robert and Reavis returned before he reached the edge of the clearing.

"It's true, Sam, all of it," said Robert. "There's much to do and little time."

Reavis' hands shook violently, and his face had lost all color. A peculiar fogginess or lack of definition affected the iris of his eyes. He walked with uncertain footing as if he doubted the ground to be solid.

"He looks like Lazarus, fresh from the tomb. I believe it would be a mercy to end him."

"Sam, this is why we've come, this is the time," said Robert.

"Why can't you feel it?" Reavis muttered. "It put me there, and it will put you there too, right, where it wants you to be."

"Quiet," Robert instructed.

Sheldon closed his eyes and felt the sunlight warm his face and the golden tree inside him stretched out with blooming vines. Reavis was right, except it was he who was exactly where he wanted to be.

TWENTY-EIGHT

August 1827
Ingolstadt
Kingdom Of Bavaria, German Confederation

The entire campus of the University of Ingolstadt lay derelict and uninhabited. Ruined gardens lined the grassy path, now the kingdom of sparrows and finches. Dividing the path sat a massive fountain of cracked stone, ages dry, standing like an epitaph to the idea of water. The institution faced the east with wings extending north and south, both terminating in L-shaped arms as if it were reaching out to embrace the gardens. Now, with the sun late in its arc, the vast shadow of the place spread ominously toward him. Standing at the outer wall and looking in, Alphonso reckoned it was a fitting address for a dead man.

At the end of the path, a semicircle of arches formed a gazebo of sorts, beyond which stood the entrance, a simple door with flaking red paint. The arches supported a veranda set in an arc serving a wide central turret fixed with tall, narrow windows. A curious weathervane of metal orbs and crescents extended from the spire, drawn into sculpture from some forgotten alchemical text.

Alphonso set down the path, assailed by the high-toned protests of sparrows. He knocked on the door and waited. No response came, so he tried again. As he prepared to try the handle, the door creaked and scraped across the threshold, and a sliver of darkness slowly expanded. He could see nothing inside, the sunlight seeming reluctant to intrude.

"I am Alphonso Taft. I come at the request of Leopold George," he shouted into the darkness.

Four tiny fingertips, pale like tallow, stretched out along the edge of the door as it continued to swing inward. The round face of a girl, perhaps seventeen years of age, appeared in the gap, called from the ether like a reluctant moon drawn into the daylight. Her hair was cropped short, like a soft helmet, defining the borders of her sprite-like face.

"We have no Leopolds, go away!" Her accent was Russian or, possibly, of Ukraine.

"I will not." An awkward silence followed where he had intended to speak further, but Alphonso could find no other words to describe his intention. "I am meant to be here!"

"Are you sure? I was meant to be napping, yet I am not."

"I have a note."

He fished through his pocket.

"With a proper quill and ample stock, I would draft you many notes. Perhaps you are *meant* to be in Egypt?" She mocked. "Let me fetch my ink."

Somewhere beyond the young doorkeeper, thin, drifting notes of music echoed from a far-away hall. Hollow, like a music box, the notes were barely audible.

"What is that noise?"

"Do they not have music in Egypt?"

"What?"

The door closed, leaving him staring into a curled, red landscape of lifting paint.

Alphonso stood at the threshold and waited. No sound betrayed the intentions of the occupant. Nervously, he fiddled with the gold watch, winding it before returning it to his pocket. Its microscopic heartbeat tapped out against his fingertips and brought him comfort.

The door swung in deeply, and the wary light entered. Standing just inside was a frail old man in a long silk jacket drawn at the waist. His finely tailored blouse and trousers hung on his bones like an undersized mannequin form. His feet were engulfed in eloquently designed beaver pelt slippers with soft leather soles. If his body seemed withered, his demeanor directly opposed the image. His glacial eyes glittered between arrogance and genius, conveying a confidence generally reserved for knights-errant or mad kings.

"Why are you standing on the stoop?" asked the man.

"I was not invited in."

"I thought that you were. I was told you had a note."

The man laughed and stepped back into the interior shadows. His bony hand extended in a beckoning gesture, and he disappeared into the darkness of the institution.

Alphonso stepped through the doorway. The girl stood just beyond the threshold. She closed the door and set the bolt as his eyes adjusted to the gloom. She was barefoot, wearing only a cream-colored dress of plain cloth draping just past her knees, tied with a faded black ribbon below her breasts. The old man moved down the hall, the leather soles of his slippers scuffing gently on the faded tiles. The girl rolled her eyes in the old man's direction, and Alphonso hurried to catch up.

"Helena, would you bring tea to the library?"

"Of course," said the girl.

"And biscuits, please, dear."

They took the west hall, deeper into the school. This was the darkest of the halls, having no windows along or above the path. The stairways to the second floor were at the mouth of it, rising at either side. Passing between them was like being swallowed by the place. The ceramic tiling of the hallway was darkened by a century of dirt, the designs of which rose through the grime like abstract arcanum. Several sealed, wooden doors marked the tombs of classrooms where now only mice conducted lectures over their dusty droppings.

The library was at the end of this hall on the northern side. The open, double doors shone like a light to the afterlife in contrast to the gloom of the west hall. Upon entering it, Alphonso was struck by the absolute absence of books. The empty shelves spread like the ribs of man's collected wisdom, murdered and left bare to display. Here the sunlight enthusiastically illuminated the barren shelves and voided spaces. The severity of the place was unsettling. He felt witness to some crime, though he was at a loss to describe what it could be.

The old man sat in a small wooden chair, around which sat an arc of other poorly crafted furnishings. Alphonso chose a footstool that resembled a tiny church pew. As he settled, a sparrow drifted from a hidden corner and took roost on a short stool next to him. The bird regarded him with tiny black eyes and peeped.

"Biscuits," explained the old man.

Alphonso shrugged.

"You've come a very long distance, why?"

"An elaborate and cruel joke, I suspect," said Alphonso.

"True, only the joke is not meant to be at your expense, young Master Taft."

"Who are you?"

"A fair question," he said. "You may call me Brother Spartacus."

"What is this, Mr. Spartacus?"

"*Brother* Spartacus."

"Who is Leopold George, and why have I crossed sea and continent against my own better sense and judgment?"

"Your sense and judgment are flawed, that's central to the case. As to the why let us enjoy our tea and fortify our nerves for the coming discourse. There is much to discuss, and I must make certain that you understand."

Presently, Helena entered with a tarnished silver tray occupied by a mismatched tea set and oddly shaped lumps of biscuit. She set the tray down on a stool with a missing leg. The cups and spoons rattled and then were quiet as the tray settled. Then she vanished without a word, her cream dress dissolving into the darkness of the west hall.

Brother Spartacus broke off a piece of the malformed biscuit and tossed it to the bird's stool. The sparrow took it in its beak and fluttered to the higher regions of the library, where the tops of titanic shelves gave way to peeling yellow walls of pitted plaster and latticed windows. He took a cup and stirred a brown lump of sugar into his steaming tea with a large spoon, clearly not designed for the purpose.

Alphonso took his cup, poured his tea, and added no sugar. As he sipped, the bird appeared, descending from the sun-cursed rafters and landing on the tray, causing only the slightest disturbance of balance. It pecked another, larger piece of biscuit, then absconded with it to its lair near the ceiling.

"Peter! Such a greedy beast!"

Alphonso's tea was tepid and flavorless. He set the cup back on the tray between them.

"I was a friend to Leopold. I knew him when I was much younger."

"Would it sadden you to know that he is dead? I stood at his grave less than a week ago," said Alphonso.

"Would it surprise you to know that I killed him?"

"What?"

"I jest, of course... I did no such thing! But for that moment, you believed that I had."

"Can you provide answers or not?"

"In terms of how a dead man might convince you to leave your home, journey to foreign shores, and further employ his gambit to direct you to my door?"

"Precisely."

"Best not to reason too long on that subject, those answers are mired in even darker questions. Considering the *why,* rather than the how, might yield more productive results."

The old man slurped at his tea, then rooted through the cup with his index finger, pressing at the bottom. It emerged damp with sugar crystals clinging to it. He sucked the digit clean and renewed his efforts at stirring the cup with his oversized spoon.

"Well? Why am I here?"

"Ha, if it were that simple! It's late into that opera, and

your summary of the plot will not be derived from simple equations. It's like asking why the Roman Empire fell. There is a short answer, but it explains very little."

"So, what is the short answer?"

"Because Alaric kicked in the gates and took all their heads!"

"This is a mistake," Alphonso stood.

"It has been a mistake since the day you put that golden bauble in your pocket. Walking out that door before you understand the consequences would be another. With that understanding, perhaps you might still choose to leave, or perhaps you'll stay a little longer."

"The consequences of a long walk back to Hamburg?"

"Death. Likely before you see your home again."

"Are you threatening me, Mr. Spartacus?"

"*Brother* Spartacus, and no. I have no use for threats, though death may be your preference after you hear me out."

Alphonso slid the chair under himself and sat down, rigidly facing the old man. His fists balled on either side of his thighs as his attention focused entirely on the quizzical elder.

"Proceed then."

"Man has long inundated all levels of academia with his childish queries, intrepidly finding answers in the vanity of science. Nature is not meant to be made naked like some grave-robbed cadaver, cut, dissected, and sketched by the butcher's hand. The truth is more eloquent and less rigid than the arrogant proboscis of human intelligence. Secrets are secrets because they are meant to be that way. They are not a set of obstructions aligned for subjugation. Simply put, our world is not a puzzle put here to be solved.

"I belong to an exclusive association to whom many such secrets and mysteries have been revealed. Revealed with purpose, to an end. This is our great work, labored since the cradle of human existence. The piece of gold pressed against your thigh is an invitation to take up this labor, to join our work. It is also a poison arrow that has already reached its mark. It is not a thing to walk away from. This work cannot be refused. Should you decline, and there are legitimate reasons to consider refusal, it will simply choose another, and you will die."

The sun dimmed like an ember gone to ash, and the brightly exposed bones of the library faded in the late afternoon light. Brother Spartacus spoke with conviction, breathing reason into his bizarre collection of statements. The dichotomy precluded only two possible conclusions. Either Brother Spartacus told the earnest truth, or he was mad. Alphonso found that his hand had slipped into his pocket, his fingertips falling over the smooth curves of the gold watch.

"I don't believe you," said Alphonso. "You tell no secrets nor produce a possible danger. I believe that you are quite insane."

"No, you don't. You knew what you would find here because you have not been alone since you left your home in Vermont. That's what it means to be part of our work, to never be alone. You've been joined by a fellow traveler who's been traveling since this world was made. You followed this traveler's compass to arrive here. You could not have found it otherwise.

"Now, at this place, this is your pledge of free will. You will be with us and all we are, or you will not. Accept and step beyond the veil, operating in the transcendence of natural law. Decline and retain the favor of whatever gods you serve, free of moral complexities and depredations of the soul. Do you understand?"

"I suppose I do," said Alphonso.

"Would you like Helena to show you to your room? Or will you be taking to the road before the light fails?"

Peter, the sparrow, brazenly perched himself on the lip of the sugar bowl and pecked at a biscuit with impunity. Flakey bits of the bread fell from his beak with gluttonous disregard.

Alphonso sipped his tea and watched the sun as it seemed to fall from the highest shelf and into the night. Brother Spartacus sat attentively, waiting for his response.

The dark blue rectangles of the north hall's high windows glowed down on Helena's dress as if it were sewn from stars. Alphonso followed eyes on the hem where her pale calves swam under the tent of moonlight. The sound of his rucksack shifting on his shoulder, his deep and resigned breaths, the heaviness of his shuffling feet, and even the nervous contractions of his dry throat all played in concert with the empty hall. He was compelled to speak, to fill it with something more than silence, to stave off the vacuous rush of his evaporating soul as it escaped, like mist, through the cracks in the walls.

"Are there more here? More besides you and I and Brother Spartacus? I mean, are we alone here?"

Helena smiled, her face rising like a moon over the smooth contour of her shoulder.

"We are never alone."

TWENTY-NINE

May 5, 1865
Washington, Georgia

J ames Reavis was true to his word, and his ink was good. Robert found his man in a clearing outside Washington, orders in hand. Sergeant Wallace Reed could not have been more suited for the task. His regiment, the 1st Georgia Cavalry, had already laid down their arms in South Carolina. The war would not be so quickly resolved for Reed and his men.

They were the hard cases, the bitter enders, those who had nothing left but the fight. Reed's family had been murdered in Atlanta, and his land and property razed. Every man in his outfit shared a similar story. At first, there were only a few, chosen by Reed from the remnants of 1st Cavalry, but as they rode, their numbers grew to almost one hundred. Now, in the collapsing moments of the Confederacy, they found themselves desperate for purpose.

Robert Black was happy to give it to them.

"Sergeant Reed?"

"Yes, sir," said Reed. "Captain Black?"

"I am."

Without further discussion, Reed mustered his men and broke camp. They were armed with superior weapons and well-supplied with abundant ammunition and provisions. Their mounts were fresh, and their kits were clean and complete. Reed had commandeered these items from the thousands of soldiers eager to lay their weapons down and quit the war.

The road into Washington darkened with the shadows of swaying beech and chestnut trees. Abandoned farms and homesteads, bathed in late afternoon sunlight, sat like eerie monuments to the unplowed fields barren of crops. The land was quiet save for the rustling of wind in the trees and the sound of horses.

"Captain, is there anything further you can tell me about our orders?" Reed asked.

"Ours is the most urgent of tasks, Sergeant. To that end, we will be escorting a precious cargo."

"What cargo, sir?"

"The artifacts of our heritage. The sum of everything integral to our sovereignty."

Reed stared ahead, waiting for some further word. None came, and Black rode on in silence.

"Thank you, Captain. My men and I are grateful and enthusiastic for the opportunity."

"I am happy to hear it, Sergeant."

As they approached the town and the first buildings appeared out of the open country, a queer melancholy manifested itself. The wind died, and the trees became still. Robert felt a heaviness over everything and a strange heat that moved through him like a wind with no recognizable source. His movement became lighter, less affected by gravity. More than this, there existed a compulsion to move forward, drawn to a specific destination. He looked to Reed and found the man calm and subdued, almost happy. As if he were taking a casual ride in the country.

They rode on.

"Captain William Parker, this is General Basil Duke," said Reavis.

The three men stood at the steps of the Washington Bank amidst a throng of Navy Midshipmen, feverishly at the task of loading wagons and readying their teams. Captain Parker, a man of about forty, stood like a ghost in his uniform. His eyes were sunken and dark, his skin ash gray, and his movements were labored as if he were walking underwater.

"Well met, General Duke," Parker saluted.

"At ease, Captain," said Sheldon.

"I've been properly apprised by Secretary Reagan, and I am fully prepared to remit custody of the treasury and archives. Mr. Reagan can provide you with a detailed inventory, as for myself, I can only offer some advice. That is if you will hear it, sir."

"Of course, Captain," said Sheldon.

"I am not a superstitious man, sir, so forgive me if I sound deranged. That is no natural load, it is like nothing I have ever known. I'd say it was cursed if I believed in such things. I have protected and carried this freight for thirty-three days, and it is no hyperbole to say it feels like thirty-three years. There is a madness about it, a debilitating grief that clouds all judgment. More than that, it seems to drain the very life out of a body. I am not sorry to see it go, though I am a Christian, sir, and I would not wish this burden on any other. Know that I pray for your souls, sir."

"I'll take that under advisement, Captain," said Sheldon.

The thirteen wagon teams were assembled in the shadow of the old brick bank. All were typical supply wagons, possessing arched canvas covers. The men preparing them lingered with a curious mixture of dread and relief on their faces.

"I understand you will provide drivers and teamsters," said Parker.

"That is correct, and it looks as if they have just arrived,"

JASON ROBERTS

said Sheldon, looking down Main Street, where Robert and his company were approaching.

"Very good, sir," said Parker.

Sheldon imagined the look on Parker's face to be the same as a man who had just stepped out of Sing Sing after twenty year's incarceration.

"You're dismissed, Captain," said Sheldon, taking the inventory list from Reavis.

"Thank you, sir, and God's speed to you."

A moment later, they were joined by Robert and Reed, who dismounted and tethered their mounts to the bank's hitching post. The rest of the troop kept formation on the road.

"General Duke, sir," said Robert. "This is Sergeant Wallace Reed."

"General Duke," Reed saluted.

"At ease, Sergeant," said Sheldon. "Sergeant, I want to be on the road in less than half an hour. I need thirteen drivers for these wagons, volunteer your most qualified. Also, canvass the town for whatever ammunition and provisions you find, understood?"

"Yes, sir!" Reed returned to his and began dispatching orders.

"Just like that?" Asked Robert, looking at the line of wagons.

Several of Parker's men still ambled about the bank, delirious in the relief of their duties. One young sailor sat on the steps and openly wept, none attempted to console him.

"So it seems," said Sheldon.

"I'm not sure if now is the most appropriate time, but I can think of none better," said Reavis. "As I have delivered on my end, I would certainly appreciate it if I could be dismissed. I really want to go home and...."

"No," said Robert.

Sheldon looked up from the inventory, his brow slightly furling at the interaction.

"Robert, there is an impressive discrepancy between the

amount of gold you claimed would be present and what is actually hear. That is if Mr. Reagan's inventory is correct."

"It is," said Reavis.

"How so?" Asked Robert.

"Well, there is more than quadruple the amount of bullion you said there was, and though it's difficult to measure barrels of coins, safe to say, much more specie as well."

"Consider my sources; scoundrels and spies," he said.

"There is only one source that concerns me," said Sheldon, walking toward the wagons.

"I consider that an insult," said Robert.

As Sheldon checked the inventory against the wagon loads, he noticed Captain Parker gathering his men in a tiny lot behind the back. Though he couldn't hear what was said, it appeared he was dismissing his company. The assembled lot of them, unwashed and ragged, took to their knees and prayed.

"You haven't been with these men," said Reavis joining him. "Unnatural, dreamlike it is! They go about as if everything is right and proper in the world, but from my perspective, it's like something from an opium pit! I fear for our souls if we carry on with this load."

"What is Robert's hold on you? Why did you run?" Asked Sheldon.

Reavis began to speak, then paused as if weighing some great decision.

"Whatever tide of horror this gold rides upon is nothing compared to the evil of that man," he said.

"Impressive, isn't it," said Robert, interrupting them.

"My impression is that we need to get this train on the road and find Thomas quickly," said Sheldon.

"Agreed," said Robert. "I think you'll find Reed's men well enough stocked and aptly prepared for that journey. If all is in order here, let's get moving."

"Excellent; get those men mounted up, and let's see if we can put up twenty miles before sunset."

"Sam, don't let that star go to your head, remember who's in charge here."

"By your tone, I assume you think that's you?"

"Has all that rat meat you've been eating affected your mental acuity? Of course, I'm in charge!"

"All right, Crow, for now. But the moment I get the hint that something ain't right...."

"You'll what? Put a bullet in me? You wouldn't be the first."

Robert strode off to find Sergeant Reed.

"It will take more than a bullet, Mr. Sheldon," said Reavis. "I'm sure of that much."

Thirteen wagons took the southern road out of Washington, extended past capacity with gold and silver, gliding smoothly as they went. A strange silence cloaked them in the settling evening haze. No wheel strained or squeaked as the wagons eased along the path. Only the muted sound of hooves clopping across the dry dirt road interrupted the quiet. If any in the company had taken the care to mind their tracks, they would have noted the wheels left barely a mark, despite the cargo exceeding all rational limits.

Sheldon rode at the head of the column like some triumphant Caesar. Behind him, Robert and Reavis parallel each other. The curse that Captain Parker spoke of was no horror at all, it was a blessing. It was more than a wind, it was a second sun shining upon him and the golden tree within. Two years after that night in the Octagon House, the end of his mission was finally within reach. He imagined Danfort Collins' face when he returned victoriously. He felt pure, he felt mighty.

The road was silent but for the rhythmic trotting of his horse and his own gentle humming as he sang old Mangas' song.

THIRTY

A lphonso awoke on the artist's block as squares of morning sun stole through the windows and filled the room. His dreams slid into oblivion, and he stretched out on the block like a model for some long-departed artist. The room was more desolate in the light of day than it had appeared the night before. Gouges, scrapes, and blemishes covered the walls where art installations or decorative ornamentations once hung. A solitary sconce existed on one wall, apparently overlooked by whoever plundered the studio.

The notes of a distant harpsichord drifted in from the north hall and assembled themselves in a fugue. Alphonso craned his stiff neck to listen, the musician responsible was skilled. He folded up his makeshift bedding and wandered to the hall to locate the source of the music.

Standing in the hall brought him no closer to its origin, the melody seemed to be extruding from the flaking walls and dirt-caked tiles like it were conjured from memory. He moved south through dust-filled ladders, floating between the sunlight and shadows descending from the slatted windows. Ahead in the gloom, Helena sat in her cream-colored dress. She rested on the bottom step in the shadows of the northern staircase, looking like a dejected apparition tired of the haunt. The music was clearer there, and Alphonso now recognized it as Bach.

"We wait," she said. Her elbows propped on her knees with her chin resting in her cupped palms. A dusty scythe of light was stretching out from under the massive front door of the university, slashing toward her bare toes at glacial speed.

"What about breakfast? Is there food here?"

"You can kill a chicken, maybe. You don't look very fast, though."

"Oh." He was unsure if he should be insulted.

Helena did not speak again. He took a seat opposite from her on the southern staircase. The fugue played on while a spider spun his web between the broken spokes of the banister.

When the music ended, the invading silence was startling. Helena calmly stood and ascended the stairs, leaving behind the tiny pool of sunlight that had finally reached her feet. Alphonso climbed his staircase, and the two met on the second floor's landing.

Brother Spartacus made his residence in the eastern-facing turret. Like Alphonso's room, the bare wood floors and stripped walls bore the scars of previous installations. Otherwise, the furnishings were spartan, dominated by a massive, circular wood table with chairs in the center of the room. On opposite sides of the French doors leading to the veranda stood a harpsichord, a small cot, and a primitive armoire. Besides these items, only a few incidentals existed. Oil lamps, a smattering of books, and several empty wine bottles offered a full account of the quality of Brother Spartacus' existence.

"Mr. Taft, I'm pleased you've decided to join us."

"The alternative is less preferable. That is if your wild tales are to be believed."

The summer sun was escalating its assault on the university's eastern facade. Entire universes of swirling dust drifted through the brilliant shafts of light. Peter the Sparrow, or some identical kin, peeped from an upper window ledge, occasionally fluttering into the sunlight before returning to his perch.

"Sit."

Helena and Alphonso chose one of the decrepit wood chairs and sat at the table. Sunlight revealed the tragic state of the pitted and splintered wood, illuminating centuries of wine stains and meal services.

"To think that the world's fate will be conceived and directed right here at this humble table. You doubt?"

"I doubt everything," said Alphonso.

"Did you know that I'm not even allowed within the borders of Bavaria? True, I'm an exile. However, here I am. An amusing irony, really, sitting here with new students, nestled in the walls of the university that shamed and deported me. I was a professor here once," he smiled. "And now I reprise my role."

Alphonso ran his fingers nervously through the valleys of jagged wood on the tabletop and absorbed the old man's words. An indefinable anxiety haunted him, born from the possibility that what the elder fugitive claimed was actually true.

"When last I befouled a lectern, things were much different than they are now. The rabble of inbred kings under Francis II still clung to the Empire, albeit on borrowed time. I lived to see it all undone to the satisfaction of our design."

"Francis abdicated after being defeated by Napoleon," said Alphonso.

"Power is a tenuous thing. Napoleon himself would agree."

"Yet, you suggest that we have the power to direct the course of history?"

"No, Mr. Taft, we are only the conduit, the hands by which the clay is shaped. So consider this your first lesson: we are not kings."

"Of course not, what does that even mean?" asked Alphonso.

"In the course of our work, you may wield terrifying power. Nations may crumble, and the earth may yawn with the graves of legions. Though this is done by your hand, it is not your will that makes it so, nor should it be for your benefit. We are not kings."

"What possible kingdom would tremble at my might?"

"One that will never know your face nor hear your name, yet they will fear you nonetheless. They will feel the tremors of your actions rising like dreams and premonitions. They will wonder over the mystery and strain over your intangible nature like you were an angry and whimsical god. Where they look, you will not be, though you pass them in their own halls and sit at their tables."

"You're mad."

Brother Spartacus rapped his knuckles on the table.

"Helena would be wise to pay attention!"

Helena snapped back into focus, withdrawing her eyes from the billowy white clouds soaring above the university. Peter chirped from the windowsill, scolding her for her lack of attention.

"There is no single divine agency, in this world or any other, by which man is granted regency over any kingdom. When you step behind the veil and witness the multitude and depths of powers in the universe, you will understand that man's attempt at order is a pale mockery of a balance he is too dim to fully perceive. Men are like children at play in their parents' clothes, mimicking nature's orchestrations with grotesque vulgarity. We are privileged to see these powers for what they are and, to an extent, to share in their glory. To taste this fruit, you must remember: you are not the source, nor do you own or sit in authority over this power. We are not kings."

Brother Spartacus examined the faces of his two students as if gauging their comprehension of his words. Then, settling on Alphonso, he continued.

"The golden watch you carry keeps more than time. Do you understand what I mean?"

"I do not."

"It is the binding link in a lineage not carried by blood. It is the door by which *He* will come, the house in which *He* will live, and the window from which *He* will see. With *Him*, you will never be alone."

"Who is he?" Alphonso asked.

"You will know Him. Gold is his flesh."

The old man turned and looked through the window at the ruined gardens.

Alphonso sat in mute consideration of the cryptic words of Brother Spartacus. Internally, he debated whether they should be interpreted literally or as a metaphor. Either definition inspired an exhilarating kind of dread.

"He always says stuff like that," whispered Helena.

"Yet, you still don't understand," said the old man, watching the tall grass blow.

Helena rolled her eyes.

"Sir, I am very hungry," said Alphonso.

"I suppose that you are. Go then, maybe you can catch a chicken."

Helena reacting to the cadence of his voice stood immediately, and Alphonso followed her out of the turret room.

"Come on, follow me."

She descended the staircase and turned down the dark, west hallway. Alphonso followed, his stomach groaning as he went.

At the end of the hall, they passed through double doors into the bright sunlight of the university's overgrown campus. Walls of stone and mortar circumnavigated the grounds, and overgrown paths snaked through the neglected gardens. A tiny amphitheater lay in ruins near a reed-choked pond where waterfowl plucked insects from the muck. An infestation of capons strutted throughout the campus. The feathered eunuchs pecked about in the dry grass and kept a wide berth from the intruding humans.

"Where did all these chickens come from? Did you burgle a farm?"

"I can't say. I've only been here a few days longer than you. They are tasty, though. Nice and plump!"

Helena strode down a particularly overgrown path past a cluster of apple trees. Nestled in the overgrowth was a small greenhouse where tomatoes and beans vined around crude lattices, sticks, and posts. She retrieved a broken piece of a broomstick from where it leaned against the discolored glass and brandished it like a sword. The end of the stick was darkened by an unsettling rust-colored stain.

"We are not kings. We are chicken slayers!"

The stick arced through the air with a swoosh.

Alphonso watched as she stalked an unfortunate congress of birds debating over fallen sunflower seeds. They noticed their peril too late, and Helena struck, deftly braining one of the creatures. It flopped and flapped, propelling itself in circles before finally falling in a heap among the weeds.

"This is how it's done!"

She handed Alphonso the stick.

Blood dripped from the end of the weapon. He brushed it clean in the grass. Helena looked at him expectantly, and he raised the stick. The previous action startled the chickens to the far end of the yard, their nervous clucks rising like crickets' voices concealed in the yellow grass. Alphonso chose a direct assault and charged into the waist-high grass, swinging wildly.

"Alphie the Terrible!" laughed Helena.

After minutes of frenzied slashing, Alphonso paused, hands on his knees, breathing heavily. Collecting himself, he reinvested in the hunt and singled out a pair of birds partially corralled in the corner of the stone wall. With a triumphant downward stroke, he came down on the back of one and broke its spine. He immediately followed it with a barrage of blows until it ceased to move.

"Pretty sloppy work, but not bad for your first time. Come, I'll show you how to clean them."

Helena led him to a small brick courtyard near the well. She laid the chickens on a broken and blood-stained sundial. The surviving chickens sensed that danger had passed and dispersed throughout the yard, returning to their mindless pecking.

"What do you think, so far?" asked Helena. She took up

a bird and demonstrated her plucking technique. Clumps of feathers blew across the mossy bricks.

"It's overwhelming. The more I think about Leopold, how odd he was, and just the absurdity of everything, the more I think the old man is right. That I did know. I wouldn't have come here otherwise. Still, it is difficult to absorb."

"It was different for me."

The wind picked up, and the fallen feathers gathered in small dust devils at their feet.

"How? Explain."

"I see things." She scanned the ground for some lost object. "Ah!" she said, finding a rusty cleaver near a stone bench.

"See things?"

His skill in plucking did not match Helena's. His capon was a mangled thing with wings and neck swinging loose and horrible.

"Yes, see. Things that have happened, things that will. I know things about people too. I think that's why they chose me."

She chopped down hard, separating the chicken's head from its body. The metal chinked against the stone of the sundial, and blood sprayed in a line where time was once told.

"What do you know about me?"

"Your heart is good, it doesn't belong here."

"Well, that inspires confidence!"

"Take it however you may," she said.

"Can you see *Him*?"

"No, not yet," she said. "But I have only just arrived. For all his words, Brother Spartacus can't see, at least not me."

"Are you afraid?"

"Of course, aren't you?"

Helena scooped out the innards from the chicken's open cavity, tossed them into the grass, and shook the blood off her hand.

She finished cleaning her chicken and assisted Alphonso with his. She then guided him to a room near the library that had served as a dining hall in the days of the university. The wood stove there still worked, and they put the birds to roast in a blackened, cast-iron pot. Helena threw in a few beans and tomatoes, then sprinkled it all with clumps of salt from a jar in the pantry.

"Alphie, would you believe me if I told you I knew you were coming?"

"No, I would definitely not believe that! Why would you have behaved so rudely to someone you were expecting?"

"Come to my room, I can prove it."

She set off down the gloomy hall toward the eastern wings of the building.

"Fine," he followed. "And my name is Alphonso!"

Helena's room was in another classroom, down the southern spur. A solitary desk of enormous size occupied one end of the room, on it were a few pillows and a patchwork quilt. The room was void of any other clue pointing to its previous use. She pulled a leather-bound ledger from the desk drawer and brushed the blankets back to clear space on top.

"Here," she said, opening the book to the desired page.

He looked down on the sun-washed page at his own unmistakable likeness, but decades older, rendered in charcoal, with his large nose and thick brows exaggerated in detail.

"You are quite skilled, but you could have drawn that after I arrived."

"I saw you, frightened in a forest," she said. "I knew you were coming."

Alphonso flipped through the pages and examined the other images. Almost every image depicted a person, the flourish of detail applied to specific facial or physical characteristics gave each work a personal feeling. The unsettling image of a dark, gnarled tree was repeated several times, shown from varying distances. The final image in that series showed a distorted and haunted face in the scaly knot of the tree. It was contorted as if screaming in pain or rage, he could not tell which.

"You saw all these people?"

She nodded her head.

The gentle hammering of the harpsichord once again resonated through the halls. Helena snatched up her book and returned it to the drawer. The music triggered some internal clock, causing her to move with a new purpose.

"I'll meet you for supper," she said and ushered him out of the room.

Confused by his sudden dismissal, he wandered back toward the kitchen and smelled the cooking meat. His hunger was so great he contemplated eating the half-cooked chicken right then. Eventually, the greenhouse returned to his thoughts, and he went in search of vegetables, a venture that produced a suitable supply of green tomatoes, string beans, and young peas. He spent the remainder of the morning and early afternoon lingering in the shade of the amphitheater, where he fell asleep on one of the stone benches.

THIRTY-ONE

June 5, 1864
Cold Harbor, Virginia

B lood turned to steam in the brutal heat. It rose from the void between the two entrenched armies like a fog of souls forced to witness their own mutilations. For those still living on that field, misery was evolving. Days of screaming had faded to dry-mouthed petitions of salvation as hope dissolved. Trapped between worlds, they languished, begging for death. Only the occasional burst of sharpshooters interrupted the death throes, felling would-be saviors foolish enough to brave the carrion fields. Still, no flag of truce had been raised to sort the living and dead.

James Reavis was astounded at the sudden manifestation of flies. They formed from nothing, like dew, moving in clouds that blocked the sun, and the spasm of their wings was the sound of death's reaping. He could hardly believe the world could possess so many of them. Today, he decided, was his last day in the Army of Northern Virginia.

That afternoon, he lingered in the shade of the Bethesda Church, forging his new papers from items lifted from the corpses of dead Federal soldiers. Forging signatures and creating fraudulent documents had served him well so far. He had never fired his rifle in anger or worked an honest day in his Army career. However, as the stalemate progressed, that streak of luck seemed doomed to break.

The buzzing faded with the setting sun, leaving only the tortured groans drifting through the stench of the field.

Reavis stood where the creek met the swamp and looked in from the periphery of carnage. He had brokered a deal with a man named Clemens to take his watch, a bargain which netted him a small amount of tobacco and unwitnessed access to the no man's land. While his comrades snored in their entrenchments, he crossed the creek, carefully avoiding the slurping pits of muck that threatened to pull him down into the blood-sopped sludge.

He crouched low over the bodies, guided by the light of icy stars. He pawed at the corpses, prodded them, and pulled at their clothes. Then, like a demented necrophiliac, he removed their uniforms and compared them to his own form, keeping plausible garments in an old flour sack and discarding those too damaged or washed in gore. He collected wallets, personal items, papers and photographs, and anything he found useful to his cause. Then, satisfied that he could cobble together a complete outfit, he slid into a corpse-filled depression and made himself naked among the dead.

The trousers fit perfectly, as well as the accompanying belt. He kept his boots as they bore no markings of allegiance. The undershirt he chose was tainted with blood along the hem, a reasonable compromise under the circumstances. The first jacket was too small and too blood-soaked to make use of. He discarded it among the bodies. As he investigated the second offering from the sack, he was startled by a curious gasping just over the rise of his crater of death.

It was separate from the constant moaning, rising from the ones death had neglected. This was monstrous, like the salutations of some lonesome demon. Worse, it spoke human words.

"I'm here, my love," it said.

Reavis slid into the jacket and fumbled to fasten it with trembling hands. The heat and humidity were replaced by a frosty blanket of terror that covered his skin in gooseflesh. His eyes scanned the landscape for a path away from the unknown horror, but he could find no clear egress. Slowly, he edged around the pit and attempted to crawl over the edge at the point furthest from the voice.

"Will he work?" said another voice, closer and clearly human.

The original voice responded this time with defined clarity and the unmistakable timbre of a woman.

"Yes, but he's fading fast."

"I will be happy with whatever time we have," said the male voice.

"Robert, I am capable and willing to inhabit more virile hosts."

"Yes, I know. But then I have to kill them, lest we leave a curious wake of witnesses."

"I admire your morality, but lurking in such morbid places is equally distasteful."

The stars above him darkened as Reavis found himself at the feet of a shambling shadow draped in human form. The limbs hung loosely, the head dangling from an uncooperative neck. The legs propelled it like an infant taking its first steps, lumbering toward him. Technically a man, it hardly seemed human in its movements, more like animated flesh controlled by invisible marionette strings. Blood flooded from gapping perforations in its midsection, its hands and arms covered with it as, until recently, it had been holding the wound closed. Gold leaves caked with mud, blood ornamented its shoulders, and a sword swung from its hip in a scabbard. Then, in a sudden flash of movement, its arm lashed out, grabbed Reavis by his shaggy hair, and lifted him to his feet.

"A spy!" it said, identifying itself as the origin of the female voice.

James Reavis made water in his newly acquired trousers.

"Set him down! Let's not make a target for sharpshooters," said the man. He wore only trousers, boots, and an undershirt. A strange necklace of human teeth hung from his neck. Blood and earth splotched his clothes and matted his wild, dark hair.

The animated major fell to his knees and thrust Reavis into

the piled corpses, holding him in place by his throat.

The man crept over the edge from which Reavis had come and investigated the area. Satisfied they were alone, he returned with Reavis' flour sack and discarded uniform. He tossed the clothing down at his feet.

"Disenchanted with your present company?"

"It was a mistake!" Reavis choked. "I should have never taken up with the Rebs. I should have come north, I should have..."

"Robbing corpses to facilitate desertion? That's bold! Perhaps you should take him before you go? He may have information," he said to the bleeding major.

"This one is fading, and this place is foul. I should go. Just kill him," the officer gurgled.

The blood ceased flowing from its wounds, and the flesh of the major fell like a tower of meat onto James Reavis. It did not move, nor did it speak again.

Reavis scrambled to escape the weight of the bloody corpse. Rising to his haunches, he backed away in terror from the advancing man, now armed with the major's saber.

"I know things, lots of things, I'll tell you everything!" he pleaded. "I know all about..."

The teeth began to twitch and dance on their cord, pulling forward from the man's neck and the air quivered with curious energy. Reavis' complaints ended abruptly as he crouched, gap mouthed in paralysis. He drifted above himself, expelled yet trapped by his own flesh. Despite the dim starlight, he could see his eyes shift and lighten from brown to blue.

The shard of the moon cut deep into the landscape of corpses, defining their mutilated features with cruel clarity. A strange symmetrical motion swept over their destructed forms as their eyes collectively blinked open at once. All of them were the same soft and feminine blue as the eyes haunting his own face. He saw his lips moving below him, yet he could only feel the cold permanence of death settling in.

"I'm here, Robert."

It was the woman's voice again, announcing her agency

over the body of Reavis.

"Is there value?"

"Oh, yes, this one is very useful! Seldom will you find such a scoundrel. He's perfect! Can we keep him?"

He was gone, only Elizabeth remained, moving through the shell of his mind like black ice. Her voice resonated in his empty husk, shredding his memories and obliterating the last vestiges of self. There was darkness, quiet, and still. He drifted toward it, abandoning any claim to whatever remained of James Addison Reavis. Yet, whenever it seemed he would be swallowed by the darkness, her voice pulled him back into the seething sea of blue eyes, peering from the eviscerated corpses piled under the jagged moon. Reavis surrendered to the voice.

"I've spoken with him," the woman communicated through him. "He will assist you in any way you require. I have made him intimately familiar with the alternative."

"I love you, Elizabeth."

"Of course you do."

July 6, 1864
Harlan County, Kentucky

They were lost on Black Mountain. Vague charts, dead-end trails, and endless bramble confounded them at every step. For three days, they circled the peak, climbing as high as they could and descending into every holler, yet Black Ash Hollow remained elusive despite Robert's persistence.

On the fourth day, they followed a rise through a narrow gulch, thick with witch-hobble and white ash, to a place they had been before. When they crested the rise, they did not find the familiar vantage, instead, they found a wide, well-kept road large enough for a wagon. Robert and Reavis stood mystified. It was unimaginable that they could not have seen it earlier if not crossed it several times.

"I suppose we go this way," said Robert.

As they followed it, the road gained elevation dramatically, leading them deeper into the range. In the early afternoon, the road left the trees and followed a vertical cliff face, overlooking a deep valley of lush hardwood before descending again in a series of sharp switchbacks.

They sank into a green abyss of maples and ash carved between two fang-like peaks. A thick white mist hung over the holler like a seething blanket from which only the treetops escaped. Following the final switchback, the road straightened before plunging into the forest. A clear-cut piece of blasted earth lay before the stand. Nothing grew there, and the birds were silent. Two immense pine trees, utterly alien among the hardwoods, stood like sentinels on either side of the road. Robert smiled. He had found Ash Hollow.

"What do you expect to find here?" Reavis asked, breaking his day-long silence.

"Him," said Robert.

Ivy proliferated under the canopy of hardwood. A sea of it covered the forest floor and sent tendrils up the trees like an angry, green Kraken. Spongey moss completed what the ivy was negligent in covering, so hardly any trunk showed bark. The effect was a madman's temple of warped columns with the heads of lush deciduous trees.

Silence drew them down the road, swallowing the sound of their boots and muting their breath. No living thing disturbed the stillness. The path was shunned by the birds and squirrels that otherwise infested the mountains, leaving only the white mist swirling through the empty spaces.

"This place is unsettling," said Reavis.

"It is."

An hour passed, then two, until finally, they came to a place where the trees had been cleared from one side of the road. Something dark loomed in the white mist where the trees had been. Robert approached hopefully as the shape became more defined and the mist revealed its secret. It was not what he had expected to find.

Perched on raised posts was a Japanese-style Minka house with a thatched A-frame roof. The singular oddity of the structure distracted Robert from the man standing in the road.

"Hello!" he said, startled by the alien-looking figure in a black and red silk robe.

The man did not answer, remaining still in the center of the path clutching a staff made of bamboo. His long black hair was streaked with generous coifs of white and neatly kept back with a tie. Robert waved, but the man made no effort to reciprocate, his ageless features fixed in a forward stare.

"Is that him?" whispered Reavis.

"That's Sogi. I know this man, stay vigilant."

Matsuo Sogi, bathed in madness, observed the intruders.

"I've come for Morya. I have no quarrel with you, Sogi." Robert showed his open palms.

Sogi lifted the bamboo staff and brought it down next to his wooden sandaled foot. He called out to them:

Robert Black has come
deceived by a falling star
he took the wrong road

Robert took a few steps forward, holding his hands out empty before him.

"I'm going to Black Ash Manor. Morya is waiting."

As Matsuo lunged forward, the staff arced through the air in a whirling frenzy. Robert fell back, upended by the sweeping bamboo attack. Reavis fumbled for his pistol, then he, too, was deposited on the road by a swift strike to his knee. Sogi evaporated into the mist, leaving the two men to collect themselves from the dust.

consider two paths
put this forest to your hind

only death awaits

Robert drew his pistol and stood in the road. The mist swirled through the forest, waiting for an answer. He took a step forward, and Reavis followed tentatively. They had not yet reached the Minka when the man stepped out of the mist brandishing his bamboo staff.

Reavis drew and fired but the man had vanished. Reflexively, he unloaded his pistol into the space where Matsuo used to be, the muted reports sinking harmlessly into the quiet holler. Robert looked back over his shoulder in disgust as Reavis hastily reloaded.

none will remember
lonely grave under ivy
too late for regret

Like a bamboo dervish, the staff whirled out of the mist. Reavis was struck unconscious, falling just off the path with a soft thud, his spent shells scattered around him. Robert dove out of the reach of the man's attack, swinging his Colt pistol around but failing to secure a shot.

As he scanned for his target, he felt the staff come down on his head, sending him sprawling into the road. He looked up at Matsuo through blurry eyes, poised to deliver a death blow. He felt the sudden heat as the teeth around his neck jumped on their cord. One of the man's eyes faded to blue while the other remained brown. The staff quivered in his hands, and the scraggly facial hair on his chin and lips vibrated with his facial twitching.

Robert he is mad
control is an illusion
I cannot escape!

Elizabeth's voice was warped, merging somehow with Sogi's. A series of grunts and failed enunciations drooled from his lips as he struck the road repeatedly with the staff.

"I will not speak that way!" she said, and Matsuo went twirling into the ivy-choked forest, swinging wildly with his staff.

"Get moving!" Black ordered, pulling Reavis up by his collar.

Reavis achieved a standing position and wobbled forward on the path. The two pressed on, leaving Elizabeth grappling with the mind of Matsuo Sogi. Pained howls echoed through the mist with the dull thwack of the bamboo strikes. Reavis shuddered as he went.

They stumbled on for another mile, slowly regaining their faculties. The screams subsided into the oppressive silence. Gradually the ivy began to lessen, and the mist dissipated as the sunlight penetrated the canopy through the thinning trees. Tiny sprouts of white pines, the size of Christmas trees, populated the open spaces in the hardwood until, abruptly, the deciduous trees ended, yielding evenly spaced and uniformly sized white pines. Rows of them stretched out across the holler in unnerving symmetry, like some massive army waiting for orders to march.

The road suddenly ended in an enormous field of Kentucky bluegrass, lush, green, and immaculately manicured. In the center of the perfectly square clearing sat a two-story plantation house supported by six grand columns. The structure mainly consisted of bricks, save for the verandas, columns, and trim. The most striking feature of the house was that it was entirely black. Every brick, every accent, down to the curtains in the black-paned windows, was jet black.

"Black Ash Manor. Morya is here."

Robert stepped onto the perfect lawn and strode across the grass toward the black house. Reavis followed with reluctant steps. Crows, previously concealed by the black roof tiles, took to the sky in a murder, screaming down their warnings. The sun shone down with cosmic indifference.

They found the approach unguarded and the doors unlocked. Ignoring the persistent objections of the crows, they entered the house. Sunlight failed to penetrate the curtained windows with any meaningful luminance, casting a solemn murkiness in the open expanse of the interior. Dark oak floors stretched across the empty foyer and into the adjoining rooms. The walls were clad in rich maroon wallpaper, highlighted by black leaf designs, and framed by carved black moldings. A massive staircase curved down from the second floor, bordered by a mahogany banister with black oak stairs.

As Robert's eyes adjusted to the light, dark fingers appeared on the banister, followed by the shadowy form of their owner stepping onto the landing halfway between the two floors.

"Robert Black, what a pleasure!"

"Morya."

Morya descended the oak stairs, his heels clicking loudly against the wood. His skin was dark, at times barely distinguishable from his finely tailored black suit. His eyes had no discernable whites, and his features baffled any ethnic categorization. The lack of any hair or eyebrows further added to his unsettling appearance. A billowy tie of bright red silk and a jade ring with a golden orb set in it struck out brilliantly as the only color opposing the darkness of his presence.

"You haven't aged since the day you murdered Elizabeth," said Black.

"Kind of you to notice. Your companion is terrified. Does he have a name?"

"That's not important."

"Why have you come? To kill me, I assume, but what are you hoping to accomplish?"

Robert's hand rested on the handle of his pistol, and his heart accelerated. The crow buckle caught the light and refracted wavering gold lines on the pommel of his weapon.

Morya smiled with large and immaculately white teeth.

"You die today," said Robert.

"Is that a joke?" Morya's black skin raised where his eyebrows should have been, stretching his eyes in an unsettling visage.

Robert drew his pistol and leveled it at Morya, who paced

slowly as he spoke. The man in black expressed no concern. Reavis drew his weapon as well, holding it with shaking hands.

"Robert, you are so much like your father, gallantly persisting under the illusion of free will... The two of you have done so much to change the course of things, never ceding that the end remains the same."

"You took my father from me like you took Elizabeth!"

"The philosopher in me would argue that if it can be taken, it is not truly yours!"

"Forgive me if I don't subscribe to your wisdom."

"You've gone through a great deal of trouble to find me, and it gives me no pleasure to inform you that your efforts are in vain. You have a fundamental misunderstanding of what *this* is."

"I know that you are the mind behind the Trust, you are the orchestrator of all this madness, this ridiculous obsession with gold that has plagued our lives. I took exceptional measures to find you. Samuel Sheldon sits in prison... Price took him as payment for selling you out. I won't let it be in vain."

"Robert, your entire existence is in vain, as is your cause, and killing me will solve nothing."

"You are the enemy, Morya."

"Ah, perhaps I can bring light to that. There is no *enemy*, at least not from my perspective. That is an entirely human construct. You might see Price and his associates in Mexico as adversaries, though this is not true. They are working toward the same goal."

"What goal is that?"

"The accumulation of gold, of course," Morya laughed. "Simply think of it like gravity. If you throw a ball in the air, it will fall to earth. If someone comes along and puts the ball in the tree, eventually, the tree will fall along with the ball. It's an inevitable force. Whether the Trust, Price, Stallworth, or any other agent, the result is the same. One day all the gold will be together, and *he will be whole*."

"He?"

Morya stopped pacing and fixed his gaze on Robert, the red tie reflecting like flames in his eyes. The smile widened.

"You think that I am the antagonist of your sad tale? Ah, now we arrive at the nexus of your errors."

"Who is he?" Robert demanded.

"*He* is the fallen star, and gold is his flesh," Morya smiled, his black and purple gums clutching the pearls of his teeth.

Robert discharged all six shots into Morya's chest, as did James Reavis. The bullets pierced the fine cotton frock coat, leaving smoking holes in their wake. The man in black did not flinch.

A change came over the man, he stood taller, and his clothes seemed to melt into vapor. Robert and Reavis stood with their arms extended, clenching their empty pistols. Black swirling smoke around pulsing lines of red, magma-like contours assembled themselves into a facsimile of human form. It sparked and danced in the gray light of the shaded mansion, then, in a blink, Morya returned.

Something heavy sounded, dragging up the front steps, accompanied by hard-soled feet. The door opened behind them, and the sunlight poured in, illuminating the foyer but refusing to touch Morya. Heavy iron chains clanked across the dark oak floor as Matsuo Sogi stumbled into view.

"Thank you, Matsuo, though I don't think the restraints will be necessary. Perhaps a pick and shovel would be more useful."

Matsuo lifted a length of chain and held it up to the light, seeming to admire the pitted lengths of it. Then, with a flurry of motion, he lashed out at Morya with the chain, striking him in the head and dashing beside him. In a whirling blur, the silk-robed man entwined Morya in the heavy chain and fastened the ends tight with heavy locks.

"Sogi!" Morya screamed in his wrath.

Roses are red, violets are blue.
I'm not Matsuo, and the chains are for you!

Elizabeth's mad laughter poured out of the Japanese man's mouth, her blue eyes shining in bright contrast to his dark brows and beard.

"Do you remember me now, you son of a bitch?"

Robert and Reavis were released from their stasis, stretching their limbs awkwardly like they had been held by invisible hands. Morya fought against the chains and hissed curses in an unknown language. Matsuo kicked him in the face, courtesy of Elizabeth's direction.

"I do not die, Robert," said Morya. "You're making a grievous error!"

"I suppose I will see about that," he said. "Take him to the cellar."

Matsuo dragged him to the cellar door and kicked him down the stairs. Morya did not cry out. With a cruel giggle, she descended the stairs after him.

"Find oil, anything flammable!" Robert ordered.

They ransacked the house, Reavis searching for oil while Robert searched for clues and information that might be germane to the workings of the Trust. Very little furniture was present, expediting their search dramatically. Besides a small wooden cot and a locked sea chest in the upstairs master bedroom, almost nothing existed to show that the house was occupied.

Robert drew his pistol and shot the lock off the chest, discovering only a leather-bound journal sealed with a golden latch. Breaking it open, he found pages of neatly inked text written in a language he could neither read nor identify. Judging by the fragility and color of the velum pages, the book was ancient. Placing it in his jacket pocket, he continued his search.

When he returned to the main level, Reavis was there with a collection of lanterns and several glass jars of paraffin oil. Hammer strokes on metal rose from the cellar among Morya's threats and curses.

"Prime it to burn," Robert said, then took a jar of oil and went downstairs.

Matsuo found a collection of iron fence posts and tools in the cellar. In a sadistic effort to restrain Morya, Robert pounded several spikes through his legs and a large fence post through his midsection and into the hard, clay floor below. Despite the savage nature of his staking, no blood flowed from the body.

Robert smiled and applied the entire contents of the oil jar.

"It ends here," he said.

"It continues unrestrained," said Morya.

Robert struck a wooden match, and Morya was consumed by flames.

As the fire rose up around him, taking his flesh, Morya's voice rose, calm and deliberate, from the rushing flames.

"I will strive to ensure that your death exceeds this in every detail."

Robert turned his back and ascended the stairs, Matsuo close behind. Upstairs, they found Reavis busy stacking, kindling, and spreading oil.

"Burn it," said Robert, stepping out of the gloom and into the sunshine.

Reavis lit his fires.

Matsuo's eyes were swirling, shifting between blue and brown, and his body convulsed with fits and spasms.

"Go," said Elizabeth. "I'll catch up."

With tortured steps, Sogi entered the inferno.

Robert and Reavis ran across the green lawn, only stopping when they reached the rows of evenly placed white pines. Black Ash Manor was consumed in flames, sending dark coils of smoke into the clear sky. They turned their back on the sunlit lawn and faced the darkness of the forest road. The shrill cries of crows called down to them from the pines, speaking threats that only Morya could understand.

THIRTY-TWO

August 1827
Ingolstadt
Kingdom Of Bavaria, German Confederation

"**A**lphie!"

Helena's voice awakened him from his sleep on the amphitheater benches. The last rays of the sun played upon the tall grass as Helena's cream-colored dress appeared in the kitchen doorway long enough to wave at him before retreating back inside.

"Food!" she called again from the darkness. He jogged to the door.

The simple table was set in Brother Spartacus' chamber with three plates, knives, and mismatched tin cups. The pot of chicken, several bottles of wine, and a bowl filled with hard, lumpy biscuits completed the fare. Helena sat across from him while the old man stood at the window, watching the shadows creep over the gardens.

"Eat," said Brother Spartacus. "Don't wait on my account."

Helena and Alphonso began carving the roasted birds and filling their plates with meat and vegetables. The tender, greasy chunks of chicken slid down his throat, rivaling any feast in memory. The old man came to the table, uncorked a bottle of wine, and then filled each of their cups.

"Of what use is gold?" Brother Spartacus asked, taking his seat. "What good is it? Why is it valued over all things? It has no practical purpose, is worthless for weapons, utterly inedible, and yet it is the lifeblood of nations. By its merits, wars are won or lost, people prosper or perish, and the value of all things is described. But why? Because it shines with a luster that never fades? Surely, it is for more than its immortal beauty. What do you think, Mr. Taft?"

"There are also gems and silver, even copper has value."

"Yes, that's true," said the old man. "I would argue that their value is an imitation, borrowed from the qualities of gold. I'm asking you, do you understand what those qualities are?"

"Are you going to tell me?"

"No." He skewered a chicken thigh with his knife, then sipped his wine and smiled, gently drumming his fingers on the battered tin cup.

"Why taunt me then?"

"There are so many things you do not understand because you refuse to believe they are possible. You asked me how a dead man brought you to this place. Would you still like to know?"

"Yes," said Alphonso.

Brother Spartacus stood and went to his lectern, then reached into its cabinet to retrieve what looked to be a small vanity mirror. However, instead of a mirror, a strange disc of jade-colored glass was mounted in it. He set it on top of the window ledge, where the light of the moon immediately found the glass. A pale green cone of viscous light emanated from it, shining down on the floor.

"Please, stay where you are, and by all means, do not touch the light!"

Alphonso and Helena looked on, transfixed by their curiosity.

Brother Spartacus then retrieved an urn from beneath the lectern, from which he pinched a small bit of ash. He sprinkled the ash into the light, where it seemed trapped, floating in the eerie green luminance. A moment later, a man's face appeared alive and silently screaming in the light.

"Oh, hush yourself," said Brother Spartacus.

"That's him! That's Leopold George!" Alphonso said,

jumping to his feet.

"So it is," said Brother Spartacus, closing the curtain and dispelling the light.

"How?! Is it a trick? He was screaming, but I couldn't hear him," said Alphonso.

Helena sat morbidly silent.

"No tricks, just another secret, waiting beyond the veil."

The old man returned to his seat, cut a wedge of flesh from the bone, and slid it into his mouth. Delighted with the taste, he took another bite. His appetite took over, and he committed his attention to the meal, sampling the vegetables and employing the stiff biscuits to sop up the juices.

For the rest of the evening, Brother Spartacus spoke about gold. He did not speak in terms of value and measure but in themes of migrations and accumulations. Civilization, he inferred, was not the result of man's cultural and intellectual evolution but rather a necessary mechanism to facilitate the collection process. Moreover, suggesting that humankind's true and only purpose was providing a labor force, toiling like bees enslaved by some sentient honey.

He talked of rich Nubian mines plundered by ancient pharaohs, of Pliny's tales of the fabled Las Médulas, and the legends of ancient Sakdrisi. Of Persians, Greeks, and Romans seduced by the same golden bride. Empires rising only to burn, crumbling to pale ash while gold's luster shined on through the ages. Gold, the constant connection across blood-soaked centuries, inherited from the ashes of the past by savage kings emblazing themselves in the image of Charlemagne and embraced by the catastrophic whims of a lustful God. Dark vaults beneath the Vatican were swollen with it, hoarded by a lineage of pious dragons, lording over its multitudes with a crooked cross.

The words of their peculiar host wove a nightmare tapestry of garish images, carrying Alphonso's thoughts along on a polluted odyssey.

"If you say that mankind is nothing but a race of

slaves, existing only to serve some ominous and unknown intelligence, then... To what end?"

"Unknown?" A strange smile wrinkled across Brother Spartacus' face. "No, the end is clearly present and passing through their hands every day! His voice is a compulsion, one that cannot be ignored. The end is the unification of his annihilated self, nothing more."

"Unification? For this, our free will is subjugated?"

Brother Spartacus wiped the chicken grease from his thin lips and smiled, "Ironic, isn't it?"

"What?"

"To serve him, Alphonso, you had to choose to forego your own will. Of course, this is not true. You never held this power, so it was never yours to surrender. What we are is aware. Our service grants us knowledge of our actions. Even in refusal, he would have granted you the kindness of death, for he is good to his chosen."

Helena darkened as the conversation developed, withdrawing into her meal. Alphonso noticed her discomfort but drew no attention to it.

"Thousands of years of art and philosophy are nothing but the product of this *compulsion*? How do you explain that?" Asked Alphonso

"What does an artist use to buy his bread?"

Alphonso did not answer. He had none to give. The conversation turned to the quality of their meal, and the mood lightened. Helena's mood brightened, and she recounted their adventure slaying the chickens. Brother Spartacus listened and laughed with genuine mirth.

That night, Alphonso slept on his artist's block, haunted by Leopold's face and visions of gold. Fits deprived him of meaningful rest, and he woke with images of golden insects blowing, like locusts, across the land.

He rose in the morning to the familiar chiming of the harpsichord drifting down the hall. He followed the sound to the staircase and found Helena already waiting there. The music stopped, and they ascended.

The days passed in this way. Disjointed fragments of history and myth filled his mind during his waking hours, only to be assembled into vivid dreams while Alphonso slept. An understanding formulated, marked by an internal bridge between himself and another, growing intelligence within him. In his dreams, the Other was sitting on a golden throne, speaking to him kindly. He would ask questions, and the Other would answer, every dream lasting a lifetime. While clear and lucid at the time, the memories of these conversations shattered when he opened his eyes. The mornings would find him exhausted but satisfied and eager to return to Brother Spartacus' lectures.

The fear and trepidation he experienced on arrival quickly became enthusiasm and curiosity. The opposite proved to be the case with Helena. She spoke less and became morose. When she looked at him, it was like she was looking at the sun, with careful indirectness. For his part, he paid little attention, being enamored by the wisdom of Brother Spartacus and his nocturnal visitor.

On the tenth night, Alphonso was pulled from his dreams by Helena urgently shaking him.

"Alphie!" she said in a shouted whisper. "Wake up!"

"What is it!?"

"Do you believe me?"

"What do you mean?"

"Do you believe I can see and know things?"

"If I say yes, can I go back to sleep?"

"Do you believe?"

There was an urgency to the question that unnerved him. The distance that had grown between them over the last few days seemed like a chasm, he realized, of his own creation. Helena's voice carried the desperate tones of one abandoned and divided by it.

"Yes, I believe you," he said. "What's wrong?"

"I fear something terrible has happened, something hidden

from me."

Alphonso sat on the artist's block and put his arm around her. She was trembling. The bridge inside him went dark as he touched her, the Other recoiling into the void.

"Everything will be all right, I promise," he said.

"You can't promise that."

"Perhaps not."

Something in her touch brought completion and clarity to his waking state in a way he had not felt since arriving. The presence of the Other receded almost entirely, leaving only Alphonso, leaving him alone with her. The broken moon and its collection of stars cast their silver light across the empty room, and he kissed her. Like castaways on some lunar island, they hid in each other's arms and kissed until her trembling subsided.

He held her close, quietly contemplating the secret meaning of a kiss. Why he had done it and how such a foolish thing could resolve so many human conditions would forever be a mystery to him.

"I'm not one of you," she said.

"What?"

"You can tell him if you want, but he'll never catch me. Are you going to tell him?"

She had drawn away and now sat rigidly on the block, her dark eyes looking through him the way one might look past the glare on a pond to the fish below.

"I won't tell him, I promise. Though I don't understand what you mean."

"I was never chosen." She sat silently as if waiting for some terrible and instantaneous retribution. When none came, she continued, "My mother sent me to learn about him. Brother Spartacus is not his real name. He's a bad man, Alphie."

"How?" Alphonso stammered. "He knows me and what I carry, how could the same not be true of you?"

"Because of my sight. It protects me." She stepped down from the block and paced in the moonlight. "My mother caught one of them coming to this place. She stole his golden token and caused him to become lost in the forest. She brought me here and gave me the gold to show him, he did not question it. When I was sure he did not suspect me, I gave it back to her, and she took it away to destroy it."

"You lied? What do you mean, lost in the forest?"

"Lost in a way you don't want to be lost!"

"Why? I don't understand."

"Because he's evil."

She grabbed both his wrists and held them.

Alphonso found conviction and fear in her eyes. He thought of the malice invoked whenever he had mentioned the name Leopold George, the muttering curses of the ancient Norse sailor, and the malevolence of his night in the forest.

"I'm leaving this place tonight," Helena said. "You're not one of them either, you should come with me."

"How do you know?"

"Because you're not!" She released her grip. "Do you want to see like I do?"

"Yes."

"This is the only way..."

Helena went to the window, gazing at the gibbous moon as if forming some unspoken covenant. She lifted her cream-colored dress over her shoulders and discarded it on the scarred wood floor. The moon, for its part, honored the bargain and wrapped her in its light, revealing her perfection.

"Now you," she said.

Alphonso began disrobing, tossing his clothes to the floor near her dress. His pale, bony shoulders and thin arms gave him the appearance of some starved, flightless bird groping in the darkness. She watched him with a curious detachment, like reliving a memory. When he had finished undressing, she directed him back to the block.

"Lay down. Close your eyes, so you can see."

Her hands settled on his shoulders as she climbed onto him. Behind his eyes, her form burned like a lava sculpture, though her skin was cool and smooth. When he entered her, he began to float on a fathomless black sea, and she was the ship that rested on its dark surface.

"Don't be afraid, it happens fast. You won't fall."

Floating became flying, rising upwards at terrifying speeds. The stars and the moon returned, and the whole university lay below. Strangely, his vision encompassed every direction simultaneously, watching the stars streaking by and the dark Bavarian countryside following beneath. The ocean passed under, and his home in Vermont was gleaming on the shore like a dollhouse on a hill. Then it was gone, and he crossed mountains and forests, with rivers cast over the land like discarded strings of yarn. A sudden focus brought him to an arid land of carved red earth, and he knew he had arrived.

A rocky outcropping rose out of a dry and empty basin like a mountain in miniature. A line of Indians carrying torches wound around its circumference, from its base to its peak. They marched in trance-like synchronicity, each bearing a golden ingot. The vision was so clear. He perceived their faces and heard the shuffling of their moccasin-clad feet. A terrible voice emanated from within the mountain. To whom it spoke, or the meaning of its words, he could not decipher.

The vision exploded in light, and he crashed to earth.

"Did you see?" asked Helena, bathed in starlight and looking down at him.

Alphonso struggled to find his voice. He had forgotten how to use it in the separation from and subsequent return to his body.

"I did..." he said, finally finding the words to speak.

He closed his eyes and listened to her bare feet maneuver across the bare wood floor. He heard the rustling of his clothes as she fished her dress out of the pile. Then, something heavy dropped to the floor and rolled, roaring across the planks like a great stone wheel, causing him to rise in alarm.

The moon betrayed her and withdrew its light, and suddenly, the gulf between them returned. Helena's face was hidden as she picked up the coin, but the gold gleamed proudly in her hand.

"No! No! No!" Her voice quivered, and she dropped the coin, fleeing from the room in tears.

Alphonso did not follow. The chasm between them was complete. The Other had returned. He closed his eyes and let the dreams come.

When he opened his eyes, the sun had replaced the stars, and the delicate hammer strokes of the harpsichord were fluttering in the hall. He dressed quickly, wound his golden watch, and picked the coin up off the boards. Helena wasn't on the stairs that day, nor would she ever return.

He found her room empty, save for two pages torn from her ledger. One was the portrait of himself, aged to an old man, now looking sad and weary. The second was one of the drawings of the blackened tree, with a woman hanging by the neck from its outstretched branch.

When presented with the news of Helena's departure, Brother Spartacus examined the coin with coy familiarity.

"A coin for the child" were his only words on the subject.

THIRTY-THREE

May 20, 1865
Muscogee County, Georgia

"With respect, sir, how far West do you intend to take us?" asked Wallace Reed.

"Hard to say, Mexico, perhaps," said Sheldon. "At least across this river."

"Well, we can't cross at Columbus," said Wallace Reed. "It's occupied by Federal troops."

"What about north? Is there a bridge or a place to ford?" Sheldon asked.

"No, sir. There's a mill not too far from here on the river and, if memory serves, a ferry crossing. I can't say for certain."

"What about south?"

"Past Columbus?" Reed pondered. "With respect, General, an armed band of our sort is lucky to not have meet resistance as it is. Those roads will be watched, no doubt."

"How far to the mill?"

"Two hours without the wagons? Maybe more."

Sheldon looked across the Chattahoochee. All that remained of the crossing were two blackened bridgeheads with swift, deep water in between and Alabama on the other side. Otherwise, the road split north and south in larger thoroughfares than the eastern road from which they came.

"Send your scouts north to the mill, double time."

"Yes, sir!"

Reed strode off, barking orders at his men as Robert

approached.

"It's a fair question," said Robert.

"What?"

"How far West do you intend to go?"

"As far as it takes to get these wagons into Trust hands. Honestly, I'd thought Thomas would have found us by now."

"You're not seriously contemplating Mexico? Your chances are better for Ohio."

"It's not me, it's Him. He's guiding me."

Sheldon again looked to the river as if the bridge would suddenly rebuild itself.

"The gold told you this?"

"Yes."

"Perhaps I should ride out and find Thomas. I don't mean to refute your experience, but Mexico is not on our charts. Leastwise, not with this load!"

"He would have found us if he were meant to," said Sheldon.

"Sam, you're not right. I appreciate your connection as your seed takes hold, but it may be clouding your judgment. You've been leading this troop, wandering the wilderness like some deranged Moses, and if it continues, it can only end badly."

"What of your seed?"

"What?" Robert flinched.

"Your field lays fallow," said Sheldon. "I wouldn't expect you to understand."

"I am not having this discussion with you, I'm riding out to find Thomas."

"Suit yourself, I don't require your blessing or approval. Ride out, I don't care if you come back. But if you try to interfere with this company, I'll have you shot. Remember who wears the star."

Robert did not reply, turning for the tiny clearing off the road, where the wagons and horses waited. Sheldon watched as he mounted his horse and galloped back down the eastern fork of the road from which they came.

Witnessing the spectacle from the cook fire, James Reavis

stood and joined Sheldon at the river.

"Where is he off to in such a hurry?" he asked.

"I don't think he knows," Sheldon answered.

"Is he coming back?"

"I don't know."

"Sir, I'm not sure if this is the right time, but if you have a moment?"

" Why so glum? What's on your mind, James?"

"I want your permission to leave this outfit, I've done all that I can for you, and I can't see a purpose to keep me around."

"A man like you would walk away from a pile of gold like this? Hardly believable," Sheldon smiled.

"On the contrary, that's exactly why I want to go. This gold is cursed, it will carry us straight to hell."

"You strike me as a man with few heavenly designs, why take on such consternations now?"

"I'm a thief, sir, not an acolyte of the apocalypse."

Sheldon laughed and clapped him on the shoulder, "Don't be so dramatic, we're all bound for one hell or another."

"Are you certain that we've not already arrived?"

"Walk with me, James," Sheldon turned toward the riverbank.

They stepped from the road down a slight embankment, following a narrow game trail leading toward the river. It took them through the red maples and tall ferns down to the muddy bank. A woodpecker went silent as they passed, and a pair of blue jays chirped across the river, landing on the Alabama side.

"Tell me about Robert Black, why does he hold such a grip on your soul?"

Reavis did not answer. Distracted, he stepped away toward a large, flat-topped boulder that jutted out from the shore into the river. A cluster of objects sat on top of the stone perch, stacked and arranged in an orderly grouping.

"What the hell..." he said as he climbed up the side of the boulder to investigate.

Sheldon followed and stood with him on top of the rock. A

pair of polished leather boots sat next to a neatly folded pair of trousers, shirt, vest, and hat. A saddle sat near the clothing, the cantle engraved with an ornate floral pattern. A masonic apron lay across the saddle, flecked with tiny dark blood spots. Beyond the saddle, more blood was splattered across the stone. Further, over the opposite edge of the boulder, a thick, red smear tracked down the side and into the river. A naked man floated face down in an eddy, blood clouding the water around his gunshot head. The man's foot was snagged on the branch of a submerged log, preventing him from being taken by the steady current of the Chattahoochee. Sheldon caught a glint of something metallic sticking out of the mud, the barrel of a pistol.

"It would appear he no longer found his place in this world agreeable, poor soul," said Sheldon.

"I'm sure he had his reasons," said Reavis, staring morbidly at the corpse.

They left the items where they lay and climbed down off the rock. Back along the trail, the woodpecker returned to his obsessive tapping. Sheldon's boots slurped in the mud as he reached into the shallow water and retrieved the pistol. He examined the weapon briefly, then slid it into his waistband.

"Well?" said Sheldon. "My question still stands."

"I'd rather not speak of Robert Black," said Reavis.

"Which is exactly why I ask."

"Whatever hell you're driving us toward, it's nothing compared to the devils that ride with that man. I've seen things, sir, things that I will never speak of."

"I assure you, you'll have my protection. Something seems off with him, I need to know if I can trust him."

"And you're asking me!?"

"No matter what you tell me, I won't let him hurt you."

"He took me to meet the devil, and he killed him! With all respect, you cannot protect me, sir."

"I have no fear of Robert Black," said Sheldon.

"It's not him that I fear, it's her!"

"Who?"

"I've said too much already," Reavis was shaking.

Sheldon snapped off a long branch from the half-submerged log and began removing the smaller dead branches from it with his knife. Blood swirled around the eddy and clouded with the mud raised up as he disturbed the fallen tree.

"Can you tell me why you stay with him then?"

"No, I've said too much."

"You haven't said anything. Nothing that makes sense anyway."

"You can shoot me in the head, like that sorrowful bastard. I know what I know, and I know nothing can be worse than Robert Black's wrath."

"I understand, James, believe me, I do. I have my own secrets," said Sheldon.

"I'll never find my way home, will I?"

Sheldon stretched out the freshly pruned branch and prodded the floating corpse on its tangled foot. Freed from the snag, it drifted out of the eddy and into the deeper, stronger current, steadily gaining pace and floating away downstream.

"With a little push, even a dead man can find the sea," Sheldon smiled.

Reavis watched the naked corpse catch the whitewater and disappear around a bend in the river. For a moment, Sheldon thought the man might follow after it.

"I take that to mean, no?" said Reavis, walking deflated toward the camp.

"Take it how you like it," said Sheldon. "But you run off again, you'll regret it."

Sheldon returned to camp and poured himself a cup of coffee. As he sat sipping it on the river bank, the sound of approaching horses broke the tranquility. Wallace Reed's scouts had returned. He dumped his coffee into the river and went to hear their report.

"We found a ferryman sympathetic to our cause," said Reed. "It's a small boat, it will only hold one wagon at a time, but if we hurry, we can be in Alabama by nightfall."

"Excellent news, Sergeant! Let's get these wagons on the road!"

Reed began shouting orders, and the men rushed to break camp, having the entire outfit rolling north in less than twenty minutes. Sheldon rode beside Reavis, tall in the saddle and infested with destiny.

"Robert was right, you know."

"How's that?"

"All you lack is the staff."

THIRTY-FOUR

January 4, 1831
Ingolstadt
Kingdom Of Bavaria, German Confederation

The rains hadn't relented for four days in Ingolstadt, overfilling the gutters and coming down the sides of the house in shifting curtains. Alphonso reckoned that it always rained for funerals and that a man of Brother Spartacus' stature would account for copious amounts of it. He stoked the fire and then drifted to the window, searching the storm for any signs of its intentions.

The Black House was constructed by its namesake, Sir Robert Black of Devon, in 1774. In recent years, the estate had passed on to a trust administered by Helena von Hahn. An anomaly amidst the Bavarian architecture, the classic English manor house was a monstrosity of brick lurking behind an ivy-covered stone wall. It hunched at the end of a lonely lane, lurching with mossy peaks and darkened windows, enjoying the solitude afforded shunned places.

Three years had passed since he took on the Other. It spread in him like metallic petrification, a morbid alchemy developing at a rate he could not arrest. Ensconced in his mind and biology, it also had a heart that beat with a single purpose, the golden, ticking watch he vigilantly maintained. He kept it with him always, fearing the consequences should the ticking ever stop.

Three men joined him in the shuttered halls of Ingolstadt

University. Two of them curiously, and certainly not coincidentally, were students like himself at Yale. They, too, traveled with their own secret passengers, their minds filled with the designs of gold. The third man was an unsettling enigma, dark and filled with Delphic proclamations. He spoke of the world being ravaged by an invisible war, a war that would make them soldiers. This man, Morya, had much to say about their future.

The Black House offered a refuge from Morya and the others, away from the oppression of destiny back at the university. Again, Alphonso went to the window of the sitting room, this time, his vigilance was rewarded. A coach had arrived. The coachman helped his passenger step down to the inundated walk and attempted to ward off the rain with his saturated cloak. The heavily bundled passenger waved him off and walked briskly to the door. Alphonso ran to undo the latch.

Two pairs of eyes greeted him at the door, peering out of the heavy, fur-lined overcoat. He could not be sure whether she was protecting the child from the cold or from, prying eyes, or both.

"Hello, Alfie," she said.

"Helena, come in! Come in!" he said and ushered her to the heat of the hearth.

"I'm sorry I didn't come sooner, I couldn't," she said. "He's been looking for me."

"Who has?"

"You know him. I took a risk to even write you, but we are safe here in this house. We are protected."

"Is this..."

"Oh! Yes, of course! This is your son, Robert." She handed the sleepy child to Alphonso, and he took him in his arms, gently bouncing him.

"Robert?"

"Yes, after Sir Robert Black," she said. "A founding member of our society. A lot has happened, I promise to tell you everything when I can."

"Why not now?"

"Soon, I promise. There is much to discuss in the little time we have."

Robert placed his thumb in his mouth and fell asleep.

"Come, there's a nursery upstairs."

Alphonso followed her up the broad stairs, steadying himself on the worn banister. He laid young Robert in the crib with a soft blanket, leaving him to his dreams.

"This way." She led him to the master suite at the end of the hall.

An enormous four-poster bed sat opposed to another large fireplace, between them lay a bear-skin rug. Various hunting trophies and relics of taxidermy adorned the chamber.

Helena knelt to kindle a fire in the hearth, the opening almost big enough for her to stand.

"Is he really gone?" she asked. "Did you see him?"

"No, it wasn't a proper funeral. I can't say where they laid him. We only discussed his estate."

The fire took hold and blazed in the hearth. She paused briefly, warming her hands, then stood and removed her coat. Alphonso was sure she would reveal the same cream-colored peasant dress; instead, he found her dressed in a simple black gown trimmed with petite black lace and drawn under the bust with a dark maroon band.

"Were there others?" She hung her coat on the protruding antlers of an eternally majestic stag.

"Two, like me, classmates, in fact. A man named Russell and another named Collins and Morya."

"The one who hunts me."

Helena closed the distance between them and took his hand, her eyes passing over him like a sympathetic doctor, lacking the heart to deliver a diagnosis. She smiled and brushed his cheek with her other hand.

"You're one of them now, I can sense the thing churning in you."

"I'm here with you, not them."

"Did you bring it?"

"Of course, if I don't keep it wound-"

"Someone dies," she said, releasing his hand.

"I'm sorry."

"Can I hold it?"

"Are you sure you want to?"

Helena held out her hand, accepting the watch. Her face contorted, betraying her revulsion for the object. She opened the case, listened to it tick, and then read the inscription embossed in gold.

"You understand what this is, Alphie?"

"A curse," he said.

"It's a piece of him, a living sprout of flesh. He's in you now, and he always will be."

"I didn't choose this!" He snatched the timepiece from her hand.

"He's only getting stronger. You won't be able to hide from him while you carry it. You're bound to him, never alone."

"I'll drop it in the ocean, Leviathan take it!"

"And when the ticking stops?"

"Then what am I to do, Helena?"

"Death is the only loneliness left to know."

Alphonso turned to the fire and kicked the grate in frustration. Even now, he was aware of its presence, though it was somehow made dormant in the Black House. Though, as Helena had said, he knew it could not last.

"Is there nothing to be done?"

"I can teach you how to make a sanctuary inside yourself, where your mind can be safe," said Helena. "I can't make him leave."

The fire crackled as the kindling fell to coals and the larger wood settled in its bed. He watched the flames crawl up the sooty brick and wondered if they were hot enough to melt gold. The watch lay cool and smooth in his hand, delicately ticking the answer.

"What is it like, having him inside you? Does he speak?"

"Not with words. If it is his will to command something, then it would seem to be my own will. There is no overt personality, more a passive magnetism that guides me. Emotionally, he behaves like the weather with no correlation to season, if a thing like that can be said to have emotion. When I met the others like me in Brother Spartacus' old chamber, I sensed that he was pleased. Here, there is something that chills him, forcing him, like winter, into hibernation."

Helena listened but made no comment. When he finished, she said, "I want you to take Robert with you. He's not safe here, not with me."

"Then his peril will double in my care!"

"You will find a way, I have no doubt. Tell no one he is your son."

"That is a tall task, I'm still only-"

"You will find a way," she interrupted.

Alphonso turned away from the fire to face Helena and further protest her request. The black gown lay coiled at her feet as if melted from her flesh. The firelight cast shifting shadows over her nakedness and reflected in her eyes as she stepped back slowly toward the bed.

"Are you going to show me how to see?" he asked as he moved closer.

"Not this time."

THIRTY-FIVE

May 20, 1865
Muscogee County, Georgia

Robert had no intention of finding Thomas Rogers. Instead, he set out in search of the nearest Federal soldiers he could find. It took him only two hours to locate a Union Cavalry troop patrolling the same road they had traveled that morning. Considering the war's end and the vigorous hunt for Lincoln's assassin, it was a miracle they had escaped conflict as long as they had.

Robert clenched the teeth hanging from his neck and concentrated. Elizabeth's manifestations were not guaranteed. There was familiarity and convenience with Reavis, which she could manifest at will, much to Reavis' torture. Otherwise, her connection to the physical world seemed dependent on Robert and his ability to reach out to her, a skill he had far from mastered.

"Elizabeth, if you're there, I need you," he said. "Can you see the captain at the head of the column? I pray that you do! I need you to take him."

The approaching troop took notice of him. One soldier trained his field glasses on him and pointed excitedly. The entire troop surged forward.

Robert waited. She had never taken someone from such a distance. The thunder of hooves seemed to fill the forest, and the dust roiled behind them like a storm cloud. None of the approaching soldiers had their weapons drawn, though they appeared determined to capture him. As they became close enough for Robert to make out their faces and hear their shouting voices, the teeth dug into his neck and the captain's brown eyes faded to blue.

"Follow me, boys!" He shouted, turning his horse around and charging down the western road.

Elizabeth rode the captain like a puppet, waving the horsemen on and maintaining the chase.

◆ ◆ ◆

Thomas Rogers followed the dead wind and Aristotle Johnson and Company E followed him. From Richmond to Atlanta, they went on bleak roads crowded with an endless dirge of defeated men. Those who saw them ride observed with prophetic sorrow as if this troop of black men were the very horsemen told of in Revelations. Never could they imagine such a host moving freely through the heart of Dixie.

For Thomas' part, he was near oblivious to the injured and hateful looks cast by vanquished rebels. He rode out front, embraced by fate and confident that he would arrive in the proper place at the time he was meant to. When he closed his eyes, he imagined the golden cage of his bones gleaming brightly beneath his flesh. It was an affirmation of his faith, a reward for his suffering, and a call toward duty.

What was a comfort to him was a perturbation for Lieutenant Johnson, who did not feel the dead wind and could only perceive it through Thomas's bizarre and compulsive behavior. While their orders were simple; find and capture Jefferson Davis, their execution of those orders was, at best, unorthodox. They asked no questions and investigated nothing, driving onward as if their destination was already known to them.

On the muddy banks of the Chattahoochee, Thomas knew

they were close. The sun loomed menacingly over the river as if it might forego the horizon and instead sink into its currents. A golden sheen rippled over its waters, and the beacon fixed in Thomas' mind shone brightly in his path. He turned into the dead wind and called for double time, galloping down the southern road.

◆ ◆ ◆

They found the ferry to be little more than a derelict barge that the owner had modified into his floating home. To the gratitude of Sheldon and the men of the Georgia Company, the destitute ferryman was eager to assist and did not waver in discarding his shelter to accommodate the wagons. Even so, it was a tedious process. The barge was secured to a flimsy dock, where a makeshift ramp was employed to bridge the gap from the pier just above the water line. The entire process took about forty minutes per wagon. Miraculously, and to everyone's surprise but Sheldon, the gold-laden wagons did not sink or capsize the humble craft.

Sheldon understood that his train was going to Mexico. The gold, like the river, had its own course, and Sheldon need only ride it toward its end. He suspected that his road would end at Stallworth's door and that he would just ride through on his golden Trojan Horse. Then he would take back what was rightfully theirs. The sentient whispering chittered with approval as his thoughts played out the possibilities.

The seventh wagon was rolling down the ramp when Robert Black came hollering down the road. His horse was wild-eyed and lathered, looking as if it might collapse with every gasping breath.

"They're coming! To arms! To arms!" He yelled.

Sheldon's brow furled at the sight of him. Half of his men, including Wallace Reed, were on the other side of the river, and the other half was preparing the wagons. A chill went down his spine as he wondered if fate had betrayed him.

"Calm down, Captain Black! What's the alarm?" He asked, meeting him on the road.

"Federal Cavalry, a whole troop of them! They can't be more than five minutes behind!"

Robert's warning was quickly confirmed as a dustup appeared on the road, rolling forward like a cloud of locusts. The Georgia men began forming a buttress with the wagons and preparing to defend.

"Fucking Crow!"

"Would you rather I didn't warn you?"

"Bad luck just clings to you like shit on a boot!" Sheldon said, drawing the dead Mason's pistol, now cleaned and reloaded.

"General! To the North!" One of the men shouted.

"Holy Hell!" Sheldon growled.

Another smaller troop of Federal cavalry was thundering toward them.

Across the river, Reed deployed his men along the bank with rifles. His sharpshooters opened up on both converging forces. Reed's efforts had some success slowing the attack from the south, as several horses fell in the road and tangled with those that followed, creating a temporary bottleneck in the road.

Sheldon closed his eyes and sought refuge in the roots of his tree. This was not the end.

"Back-to-back, men, give them hell!" Sheldon shouted.

Sheldon went to the cook wagon, facing north on the road. With the pommel of his pistol, he smashed several glass jugs of camphine, then lit it with a match. He kicked the blocks out from the wheels and fired his pistol next to the horse team.

The flaming wagon went careening down the road before the terrified horses veered into the ditch at the side of the road and broke free, fleeing into the dense woods to the east. Several bursts of flame consumed the wagon as the remaining stock of lamp oil and ammunition began to combust. The blazing obstacle served to slow the advance of the northern force.

Across the river, Reed's men focused their fire on the densely packed road, inflicting fatal casualties. Those on the eastern shore fired from the cover of the wagons, catching their attackers in a vicious crossfire.

Robert stood with his pistol in his hand, aiming into the chaos. The road was filled with horses and men scrambling to get out of the path of those rushing in behind them. Sheldon joined him, taking aim and unloading his pistol into the scrum.

"I'm going to Mexico, Robert," said Sheldon, calmly turning to face him.

"That's not the plan, Sam! We should surrender here and let Collins and Russell work it out. Mexico is madness."

"Surrender? That's madness!" Sheldon reloaded his pistol.

An ammo crate exploded in the wagon blocking the north road, showering them with burning splinters and bits of canvas. To the south, the troops were forced to dismount and spread out through the trees or along the river bank. One man, a Captain with oddly blue eyes, advanced on foot down the center of the road. His body flinched as he absorbed shot after shot from the defending Georgia men.

"This is it, Robert, I'm taking what we have forded and leaving. Most of the gold is already on the other side, you take the rest and get it to the Trust."

Bullets whizzed by their heads and impacted the dirt at their feet as the Federal soldiers rallied and organized their assault. Robert took cover behind a wagon, snatching a repeating rifle from a fallen man, while Sheldon calmly went to the river and boarded the waiting barge.

From the dock, Sheldon watched as the deranged captain turned his back to the bullets that perforated his flesh and began firing at his own men. He walked back south, dispatching man after man, to the horror of his confused soldiers. When the captain's pistols were exhausted, he drew his saber and began swinging it wildly at everyone within reach. A federal lieutenant put himself in his path and confronted the officer. Finding no sanity in his eyes, the lieutenant shot him in the face, finally bringing him down.

Across the river, Reed's men laid down a ferocious barrage on the attackers, having clear targets on all but the few men who retreated to the woods. To the north, the flames and greasy black smoke blocked all view of the other force.

Robert began shouting orders at the remaining Georgia men, and they began rushing to prepare the wagons while others advanced down the road, routing the forces to the south. Sheldon took a pole and helped push the barge off into the river.

A single rider emerged from the flames, leaping over the burning wreck and charging forward to the dock. Sheldon recognized the man immediately as Thomas Rogers.

Thomas spurred his horse down the bank and onto the dock, picking up speed as if he intended on jumping the distance to the barge. Sheldon reached into his pocket and produced the gold Caligula coin, gripping it between his thumb and forefinger. Holding it up so Thomas could see, he raised his pistol and fired.

Sheldon's shot was well placed, striking Thomas' mount in the head and felling it instantly. As the horse collapsed in a heap on the dock, Thomas flew forward and splashed into the muddy waters of the Chattahoochee. Sheldon still held the coin when he surfaced, gleaming like a second sun in the late afternoon. Thomas understood and crawled back up to the dock.

Sheldon smiled as Thomas and Robert stared each other down across the battlefield. Part of him hoped to see Thomas unsheathe his knife, though it was not to be. Whatever accord was struck between their hateful stares, Thomas returned to the northern road and withdrew his force from the battle.

As the gunfire ceased and the smoke cleared, the Georgia men stood victorious on the eastern shore. After removing the dead from the road, the wagons were reoriented and underway, this time with Robert Black leading them. Sheldon, Reavis, and seven wagons of gold now rolled west, following the setting sun.

◆ ◆ ◆

Lieutenant Aristotle Johnson strained his eyes against the heat and smoke at the battle beyond. Thomas diverted from the primary host and attempted to intercept the wagon crossing. His nemesis, a pale blond captain, stood unconcerned at Thomas' advance. A peculiar countenance to the man, a diabolical kind of confidence, played on his face in the glare of the setting sun. His arms and legs seemed too long, twisted somehow, and he had an unwholesome golden hue. When he fired his pistol, it was like he summoned a lightning bolt to strike Rogers down.

Johnson ordered his men to stand ready, then spurred his horse toward the flames, leaping over the obstruction as Thomas had. He found his captain knelt over his horse, struggling to remove his tact and gear. He seemed utterly unconcerned with the battle playing out on the road.

"Hold your men, AJ," said Thomas.

"Sir?"

"This is not the company we're looking for, it's not worth losing men over."

"But those are our men, dying like dogs in the road!"

"You can't save them, no one can."

Lieutenant Johnson was numb with shock and rage, he took a step toward the wagons, drawing his pistol. Even as he looked to engage, the last Federal troopers fled the field, the others dead or dying. He trained his pistol on the tall, dark-haired captain, seemingly commanding the outfit. He heard the click of a hammer pulling back.

"Don't do it, AJ, that man will get his comeuppance, and it will be me that delivers it, no one else," Thomas aimed his pistol at Johnson's chest.

"I am utterly fucking confounded by this entire operation! Fuck you!" He shouted, returning to his horse and back toward the flames.

The scene on the road played out before him like he wasn't there. The flames were subsiding, and his men stood ready, yet the rebel wagon teams simply turned around and casually drove on south, past the mounded corpses.

To the confusion of E Troop, Aristotle Johnson led them north, turning their backs to the carnage on the river. Each man of that company had seen horror enough to last a lifetime, though none among them had, or ever would again, see a scene so strange.

THIRTY-SIX

May 24, 1865
Lincoln County, Georgia

T he grass near Chennault's Plantation was green and bending over with its own weight. The lush pasture shimmered with the wind in the last light of the Georgia sun. Pink and orange clouds faded into the vignette of the sky's darkening edges, and fires sprung up from the camp of circled wagons resting on the pastoral plain.

Sergeant Bushrod Carter stood next to Robert, feeding whole branches into the fire.

"What's your plan after this?"

"Florida," said Carter. "I got a brother there."

"He didn't take up sides in all this?"

"He took a side, his own. Wendel is a different kind of person. No less noble than you or me, but cut from another bolt entirely."

"I suppose you can't choose your kin," said Robert.

The fire rose, igniting a cluster of dead leaves on a fan-shaped branch. The sun was under the horizon's jagged line, and the night birds and lonely toads began making their first soliloquies of the evening. Another fire blazed up in the camp, rivaling their own light. Around it, the men eulogized over an empty whiskey bottle while someone played a sad dirge on a harmonica. A new bottle was produced, and their spirits were renewed.

"I gotta piss," said Robert, excusing himself from the

fire.

Sergeant Carter nodded as Robert left the ring of firelight and disappeared into the starlit grass. The revelry at the other fire increased as the second bottle of whiskey was drained and employed as a flute in a drunken skiffle band.

Robert crossed the field and turned his collar up against the cold. The days were getting warmer, but the nights had yet to accept the changing season. The road was quiet, only the distant ruckus from his own camp gave any challenge to the night sounds. A solitary light in a window of the Chennault house flickered in the distance. He entered the grove, weaving around the dark posts of trees rising like jail bars placed by some blind or demented warden. Finding a small clearing, he paused, undid his trousers, and released a steaming stream into the foliage.

"Hello, Robert," said Thomas Rogers.

Robert continued to piss, ignoring the salutation until he finished.

"Finally showed up, what took you?"

"Oh, I been around. Mostly trying to make space between you and General Wild. He's the one tasked to bring you boys in. Grant's man."

Thomas stood between two trees, a shadow, vaguely human and almost invisible.

"Well, why hasn't he? The sooner this train goes off the tracks, the better for Sheldon."

"I'm not here to take the prize, that's Wild's job," said Thomas. "I'm here for the gold, what little is left. Collins' orders."

"The real gold is heading west. Don't get greedy and let it slip away."

"Something you want to tell me, Robert?"

The whites of Thomas' eyes, focused on his own, became visible to Black. He became acutely aware of the pistol at his side and silently measured the odds of deploying it.

"I think Sheldon might be compromised," Black said. "I don't think he has any intention of coming north with that load. Maybe Price cut him in. He seemed real keen on Mexico when we split."

"Or maybe he feels the same about you. Either way, I'm taking that gold. That going to be a problem for you?"

"These men aren't here to fight. I don't want them hurt."

"Those men are, how would you put it, 'of no consequence.'"

Thomas drifted through the space between them.

"Are you threatening me, cocksucker?"

Thomas smiled widely, something Robert had never known the man to do, revealing gleaming white blades of teeth lined up like guillotines while his molars radiated the unmistakable luster of gold, displaying impossible luminance in the darkness of the grove.

"I will take a wagon tonight, one that you carefully prepare for me. Green or red, I don't give a fuck what color the grass is when the sun rises."

"Fuck you!" said Robert, but Thomas was already gone.

When the sun came up with pink and orange clouds, General Edward Wild arrived at a field awash with carnage and misery. Six men lay dead, including Bushrod Carter, who had been shot eleven times and dragged through the field in defense of a missing wagon. There were many wounded gathered in triage under improvised white flags. Only the men that succumbed early to the whiskey survived unmolested as they slept through the fray.

Robert Black was not to be found.

June 19, 1865

Edwards Plateau, Texas

Sheldon and company crossed the Mississippi at the deserted town of Bruinsburg and continued west. The dead wind continued to impose its protection, propelling and keeping them unseen. Each mile blurred like a laudanum haze, cast to their hinds like discarded dreams. Their bizarre providence went unquestioned by any man in the company save James Reavis. He largely kept his concerns silent and gave few dissenting arguments, playing the part of Secretary Reagan and maintaining the status quo.

He had made one complaint shortly after Bruinsburg, saying, "I've become acclimated to terror, sir. Robert. Black has left the scars on my soul to prove it. I'll go your way and take this load, but I want your promise that you'll cut me loose before we pass Hell's gates!"

"Sure, James, just let me know when you see those gates swinging."

Deep in West Texas, they came to a small river valley bordered by rough hills patched with yellowed grass and scrub. Sheldon rode out front, guiding them south along a cattle-hardened path beside the river.

They were fording to the river's western bank when Sheldon held his sword up, halting the column. Half the wagons remained on the eastern shore, one caught in mid-passage, water flowing just below its axles. Silhouetted against the sun and the indigo sky, a pair of riders looked down on them from the hillside. The dull thunder of hooves manifested in the distance beyond the riders. Soon, countless others lined the hillside above the valley.

Two riders descended from the west, one of them hoisted a white undershirt tied to the end of a long dowel or stick. Sheldon rode out to meet them. As they approached, their features became discernable from the glare of the afternoon sun. The man holding the flag was a ginger-haired giant who bore the markings of a lieutenant on his dusty uniform. The other rider sat rigid like a thin, bony tree. His long gaunt face was exaggerated by his black goatee and cavalry hat. The stars on his collar displayed the rank of major general.

The men stopped their horses a few feet away from him and saluted. Sheldon returned the salute as he drew his horse up the bank, feeling the heat of the dead wind where a river-cooled breeze ought to have been. He smiled at the general and his aide.

"General Jo Shelby," said the man. "This is Lieutenant Abbot, and that Mongol horde on the ridge is the Iron Brigade."

"General Basil Duke," said Sheldon. "You boys are a welcome sight."

"What brings you so far west?" asked the general. "Strange fortune, finding a friend in this wasteland."

"Indeed, General. These are dark days, but we have been fortunate enough to make it this far. God willing, he'll bring us to Mexico."

"Mexico?"

"Yes, sir! We carry the last vestiges of our Confederacy in those wagons. We intend on taking asylum in Mexico."

"Fortune indeed! We are currently en route to Mexico to offer our service, such as it is, to the Empire."

"I certainly hate to impose, General, but the gravity of my mission necessitates that I insist. We sure could use an escort."

"Those wagons are a concern. They look heavy and slow. We move fast and plan to cross the border in a day or two."

"Speed is not a concern, we'll keep pace," said Sheldon.

"Specifically, what do you mean by last vestiges?"

Sheldon reached into his jacket and retrieved the manifest and the documents Reavis had drafted. He passed them to Shelby and watched with satisfaction as the general absorbed the information. The dead wind blew, and the river hushed its babble.

"It would be my honor, General Duke! Beyond that, I

consider it my sworn duty to see it done. The Iron Brigade is with you."

"Thank you, sir, you're a God send."

Sheldon ordered the wagons forward to the western shore and followed the valley south. The two generals rode together ahead of the wagons, the sun falling warm on their shoulders. The wagons rolled smoothly and quietly over the hard-packed sand. The heat within them flowed like an uplifting wind that inspired an ease of motion utterly void of fatigue.

Shelby spoke of his home in Missouri and the early days of the war while Sheldon rode quietly along, absorbing his words like they were part of the landscape. Shelby boasted of the battles at Carthage and Pea Ridge and his months-long fifteen-hundred-mile rampage across Missouri that secured the legend of the Iron Brigade. Sheldon listened, occasionally asking questions but revealing nothing of his own experiences in the Army of Northern Virginia.

As they rode, Sheldon watched the ridgeline for a glimpse of the general's fabled outfit. The cut of the valley was such that it passed through hills and high grassy plains in a way that rarely afforded him a clear view of his escort. They were several miles downriver before the ridge on both sides of the river dropped enough to offer a complete vision of the Iron Brigade. Sheldon was awed by the size of the host, a force that numbered in the thousands.

PART FOUR
THE DUPLICITY OF SUCCESS

two sides of a coin
even with the sharpest eye
you see only one

-Matsuo Sogi

THIRTY-SEVEN

March 17, 1866
Harlan County, Kentucky

In the morning, it was crows flapping from tree to tree. At night, it was bats, screeching and fluttering like moths against the moon. Their directive was unambiguous; follow, and Thomas obeyed. As he took the high winding road from Black Mountain down to the darkened holler, he clenched the blood ruby in his fist and imagined the day it would turn to stone as the life faded from Robert Black's eyes.

As he urged his reluctant horse along the Black Hollow Road, the ivy-covered trees and odd Japanese house were strangely familiar to him, as if he had visited there in a dream. The rain came when he reached the charred forest of white pine, transmuting the ash into frothy black mud. Ahead of him lay the hulking ruins of Black Ash Manor, confirming the worst fears of William Russell and the Trust.

Reaching the clearing, his horse would go no further, so he dismounted and continued on foot. Six black columns reached skyward, looming above the ruins of a broken temple to some forgotten god. A partial brick facade stood crumbling in front of the stone stairs, rising to the nothingness of the former porch. The rain washed over the flame-eaten beams and timbers, jutting out of the center of the pit and through the surrounding tangle of brick, stone, and tile.

Above the wrecked manor house, rain fell the fiercest, taking on a near-solid form. He stopped at the useless steps and looked up past the towering columns into the growing maelstrom. The clouds above him dissolved, and the sun shone down in beams on the burned mansion. The light-filled in the spaces between the rain and the image was realized. Sculpted in living water, a man's face looked down at him. The rains ceased, and the face fell to earth in millions of heavy drops.

"Morya."

Thomas climbed the heap of rubble and crawled about the debris, searching for any sign of life. Most of the material had settled into concrete piles of fused mud and ash. The larger beams suggested that cavities might exist beneath them, and he focused his efforts there. His fingers dug into the black muck, pulling at bricks and stones that slurped and sucked against the ooze. A wretched sound came drifting with the wind, distant but growing closer. Hundreds of crows were descending on the ruins.

Their wet wings slapped against him as they pressed through the small spaces, and their frantic squawking filled his ears. Some came down directly, while others circled above, waiting for an opportunity to land. Instead, they flapped in frenzied spasms, focusing their frustrations on a single beam in the chaos of brick and refuse. Their wings and claws moved the filth in tiny scoops from around the beam until Thomas could see a deeper darkness below.

His excavation revealed a staircase concealed beneath the beam, leading down into a cellar. The cacophony of crows spiraled above him, cawing triumphantly as he cleared the way. Dropping down into the dark, his feet slid on the slimy stairs, and he tumbled the remaining distance to the partially flooded floor.

A voice spoke out to him, more terrible than the crows, fueled by rent lungs.

"Thomas Rogers, good of you to come."

"Who's there?"

"You know who I am," said the gurgling rasp.

"Master Morya, forgive me."

"There is nothing to forgive! In fact, I find myself in your debt, you have come to me in a rare time of need."

Vague shapes began to define themselves in the gloaming cellar. As his eyes adjusted, another light developed, crimson and dark like dying embers, yet pulsing like a living vein. It moved inside a man-shaped thing, blackened and encrusted with ash like the broken bones of the sunken mansion. At its core, it swirled with smoke, as if the burned shell was merely obscured glass and not the charred remains of a man.

"My pride allowed this to happen," said Morya.

"How do you still live?"

"Live?" His laugh was like steam releasing through a slit throat.

The sunlight found its way to the top of the stone staircase and spread its dull luminance throughout the caved-in cellar. Morya was now clearly visible, impaled through the floor and wrapped in chain. Only the gold orb, set into the translucent jade ring, remained unburned. Morya looked back at him with rusty, coal-like eyes.

"I don't live, neither do I die."

Thomas crouched and waded through the scummy water, gripping the rusted iron post that ran through the center of the burnt figure.

"Yes, do it," said Morya.

The post required him to pivot and swivel to pry it from the floor. Bones and crisp flesh crackled as he vied for play while the muck below surged and slurped with the turbulent struggle. The sick heaving of Morya's perforated lungs wheezed with the efforts. With a final tug, the post came free and clattered against the stairs where he tossed it.

"Good, now help me with these chains."

"What are you?"

"Most never ask," Morya coughed, and black purulence oozed from his mouth and wound.

Thomas found the chains remarkably heavy, tangled and fused with rust. They tore at Morya's arms, breaking off bits like charcoal from a log.

"I'm asking. I want to know."

"With you, Thomas, I believe knowing might reinforce your conviction." His wound seeped and hissed with his contortions.

"Tell me, I want to hear it in your words."

"I came when this world was an unformed ball of magma. I followed him when he fell. Men put names to things, arrogantly believing it gives them power over them. You have no word for what I am."

Another link of rusty chain broke free, and the coil loosened.

"Are there more of you?"

"There is only one of him," he gurgled.

"Who is he?"

Morya's lips cracked and split, shifting on his face like a cooling lava flow.

"His is gold."

Rogers let loose another heavy length of chain. Morya's flesh came off in chunks with the chain, spreading on Thomas' hands like chalky jelly.

"Who did this to you? How is it possible?"

"One of our own, Robert Black."

"Black did this?"

"Yes. He brought something back from Deer Island, something dead."

"Is that how he trapped you here like this?"

"I did this to myself," Morya growled, his voice wet and full of pain. "I allowed myself to be trapped in this flesh, arrogance! It will not happen again."

The final chain broke free and unraveled from around Morya's shoulders, and his arms began to move. Gold reflected off the fetid pool as he slid the ring from his finger and handed it to Thomas.

"Take this," he said. "Send it to the Trust. Tell them I'm coming."

Thomas closed his fingers around the weight of it, then slid it into his pocket.

"Don't tell them about Robert, leave that to me."

"Why?"

"It goes beyond Mr. Black. Taft broke his covenant, ultimately, this lies with him."

"Are you going to kill them?"

"Death does not excuse one from service," said Morya.

"What about Robert?"

"Find him, bring him back alive, if you can. He has a role yet to play."

Morya's flesh began to mold and rot as the sick pool he sat in soaked into his destructed body. The churning smoke and embers inside him grew brighter.

"I don't understand, if Taft betrayed us, why..."

"You can't betray us!" His head rolled off, still speaking as it splashed in the cesspool, crumbling and dissolving in the rancid waters. "I am grateful to you, Thomas Rogers, so I will reveal a secret."

"Tell me, please," said Thomas reaching into the water with his gloved hands to retrieve the mass of gelatinous froth and blackened viscera that was once Morya's head.

"Those who work against us are our greatest servants!"

Morya was gone, only the sedimentary stain of flesh remained, dissolving into the waters under the ruins of Black Ash Manor.

March 23, 1866
Mount Auburn
Cincinnati, Ohio

"Are you prepared for this?"

"Are you?"

"I'm already dead, Robert. There is no more fear in my world."

The oars creaked in their collar and quietly splashed in and out of the Ohio River. Elizabeth's blue eyes shone like two symmetrical stars beneath the darkened hood of the nameless boatman. His shoulders leaned and heaved in smooth, easy strokes as the craft glided across the current, leaving the Kentucky shore behind. The lights of Cincinnati skulked out of the gloom ahead like fireflies in stasis or stars reflected in a calm black lake.

"Can you save him?"

"I can't say," she said. "He still has to die."

"I pray for another way."

"Sogi almost broke me, I don't know what would have happened if he'd won. Would I have been ended? Or would I have been merely returned to the dead place from which I came? He was alone, un-joined by the golden worm. I had only the lunatic gnashing of his mind to contend with. Your father is occupied, albeit weakened by the absence of his mark. Should that artifact be returned, there will be nothing I can do."

Her voice drifted out of the hood, mixed with the boatman's in an unnatural unison. Regardless of how frequent her visits were, he was still not fully accustomed to her unsettling manifestation. Ignoring her peculiarly luminescent eyes, he looked past the chasm of cold, silent water to the opposite shore taking form in the void.

"I suggest shooting him in the head," she said. "Quiet his mind."

"What if you can't separate him? Will death be enough?"

"No, he will drift between our worlds until he finds another to take his place."

"As they believe I was meant to do."

"Yes. A lie that will soon be realized."

The skiff jerked as the oars struck the rocky bottom. Silently, the boatman rose and stepped out into the waist-deep water, dragging the boat onto the beach. Robert stepped upon the shore, pausing to watch the blue lights dim from the hood of his ferryman. He continued up the bank where the gray line of dawn stretched out from the curves of Mount Adams. By the time he reached the vineyard slopes, blues and pinks were bleeding into the dark sky.

He chose to walk through the grapevines, hidden from the quiet streets. On reaching the peak of the hill, he could almost see his father's house. Robert lingered among the grapes and watched the sunrise so as not to arrive too early. The courtesy seemed almost ridiculous. Tact had no place when murdering your father. He ran his fingers over the teeth around his neck.

The lush green lawn welcomed the reluctant killer. As his prints pressed down in the dewy grass, he imagined them wet with blood on his return. The culpability lay with his father, Robert did not choose this crime. The knowledge did not ease his mind nor make the walk less dreadful. Perhaps he would be met with an alternative, some unforeseen salvation to be plucked from Heaven's mana. The teeth weighed heavy, pressing into his chest, somehow monitoring his thoughts to provide an answer. There was no other way.

Killing Morya proved futile. His attempts to curtail Sheldon's indoctrination only galvanized the boy's resolve. One final failure awaited, inevitable even if every other gambit had been successful. He approached it slowly over a grassy lawn. It was supposed to be the last phase of the plan, but now it was the only move left. Robert knocked on the door.

There was no answer.

He knocked without response, eventually resigning himself to sitting on the stairs and waiting. As he sat, half in the sun and half in shade, distant laughter interrupted his morbid meditation. It came quietly at first, like some trick of the wind, then stronger. He stood and listened, following the sound to the side of the house. The laughter became punctuated with a strange conversation, all in a single voice. He couldn't make out the words. Robert came to the back of the house to find the origin of the laughter, young William Taft.

William wore a fine black suit with polished black shoes. A pearl-colored tie hung from his neck, fixed to his shirt with an oversized golden tie pin. He climbed high in the nightmare tree on the arm stretched toward his open bedroom window. His jacket hung strangely from the tree with smaller branches stretched through the arm holes as if it were being worn.

"Hello, Mr. Black!"

"Hello, William. Is your father home?"

William shook his head slowly.

"No, sir, he's still in Washington. He's been gone a long time." He crouched down on his haunches to better make eye contact with Robert.

"Are you alone?"

"Yes, Mama took everyone to church, but not me. I didn't feel good."

"I thought I heard talking."

"I was talking to my friend." William gestured to the branch-filled jacket as the sun shone through the tree. The leaves changed from green to gold in the light.

Gravity shifted with subtle pressure, similar to the experience of slowly sinking in a lake. The tree lurched motionlessly, like it always leaned, close and menacing. The bark shifted to gold, and the trunk twisted into thick coiling roots beneath the guest house.

"I thought you were afraid of that tree?" he asked, stepping into the shadow of the house and shading his eyes with his hand.

"No, not anymore." William giggled, "That's a strange belt buckle. Is it real gold?"

Robert ignored the question.

"Do you think it would be alright if I left a note for your father? I can just go into his study and leave it there for him. You can tell him to look when he comes home."

"What if he doesn't?" William's tone shifted as if he were

speaking from his suspended jacket. "What if you find him first? What then? What then?"

Robert backed slowly toward the kitchen door at the rear of the house.

"I'll just be a moment, no need to come down."

He found the door unlocked and the house empty. William's words left him unsettled. Nervously, he made for the study and closed the door behind him. Alphonso's private sanctuary lay disorganized. Books and an empty bottle of scotch were left on the desk. An ancient-looking sea chest sat on the bricks in front of the fireplace, its latch bent and the lid slightly ajar. The ghosts of half-burnt pages haunted the ashes of the hearth, blackened beyond translation.

He found ink and quill on the desk, though no paper supply was apparent. He opened the desk drawer and found no suitable material on the bookshelf. Lifting the lid of the sea chest, he discovered a stack of bound letters, a frail and frayed charcoal drawing of his father, and a leather-bound journal. The portrait was dated August 1827, though oddly, the likeness was contemporary. He flipped through the book to find a blank page and ripped it from its binding. Robert laid the paper on an empty swath of desk and sat down to write, but curiosity stayed his hand, and he laid down the quill.

The journal's first entry was written in January of 1831. It detailed an Atlantic crossing with a three-year-old boy, his newly discovered son. To find himself on the first page of his father's journal opened wounds, long dormant but festering. Taft, ever elusive on the subject of his absence as a father, spoke through these pages what he had been loath to tell his son. Sadness sank into horror as he continued to read.

It spoke of a self-realized abomination whose struggle to escape damnation achieved only crimes against flesh and family. Every act of defiance or effort to break his Faustian contract with the other yielded tragedies more heinous than his submission could ever have realized. All hope of a meaningful relationship with his father, beyond their joint struggle, died on the yellowing pages of the manuscript. Considering the damning account that remained intact in the journal, Robert cringed to imagine what words lay in the hearth's ashes.

Light and reason failed him, his own words wholly inadequate to express his depth of dread. Finally putting ink to paper, he wrote, "I will see it done," and folded the note inside the journal of Alphonso Taft. He returned it to the wooden chest and sat in the gloom, staring at the crooked lid.

William tapped at the door.

"Mister Black, are you still here?"

A sick pit opened in his core, oozing with loathing. He fought the urge to run and wished himself away to any place other than the Taft house.

"I'm here," the words cracked in his dry throat.

"Oh good!" William opened the door. "This package just arrived for you, what splendid timing!"

William presented him with a rectangular shaped box wrapped in plain brown paper and twine, addressed simply to Robert Black with no return address or postal mark.

"Thank you."

He accepted the package and stepped past the child into the hall. His boots clacked against the hardwood floor, increasing in pace as he made for the front door. It opened without resistance, releasing him into the bright sunlight.

"Goodbye, Mister Black," said William faintly at his hind. Then, less clearly, "Don't come back!" though Robert could not be sure if he heard him correctly.

He walked briskly, not stopping until reaching the shady side of the hill at Mount Adams. He sat down among the grapes overlooking the Ohio River. He no longer doubted the need to kill his father, only that he may be too late. The world filtered through the lens of that futility. From the grapes to the sun to the gray water of the Ohio, every sense suffered the taint of putrid fecundation and decay. He pulled the string on the package and tore the paper away.

It was shaped like a shoebox and made of rough pine, giving the impression of a tiny coffin. To further the image, it emitted a stench partially responsible for the foulness of the air. With trembling fingers, he lifted the lid. A reek of death floated out of the box, rising from the maggot-infested corpse of a crow. One black eye remained, bulging like a blister, the other a writhing window of larva. Its wings and legs were folded carelessly, broken, and forced to fit. The beak gaped slightly open with one fat worm wagging like a tongue. He stared, transfixed by disgust, too affected to drop the thing.

A sudden fluttering of wings burst from inside the box, shaking and shuttering like it was shedding rain. The creature cawed a sick, haunting squawk and took flight over the vineyard. It circled once and dove, striking violently at his head, screaming with dead rage. The screeching took on a voice as it encircled his head like a carrion halo.

"Hope is lost! Hope is lost!" it screamed in the voice of Morya.

Robert drew his pistol and fired, dispatching the impish bird in an explosion of black blood and feathers.

THIRTY-EIGHT

March 24, 1866
Conway, Massachusetts

Every rock in the long walls segmenting the Sheldon property was personally extracted from the rich Deerfield River Valley soil and placed by Jay Sheldon. When the strain of humanity became too great, he would retreat to the land and the sanctuary of his gardens. For thirty years, he pulled rocks from these gardens, creating carefully maintained borders. It was an apt metaphor for how he tried to care for those he loved, meticulously divided and confined by barriers of his own construction.

Jay Sheldon ceased digging and leaned on his spade, turning his head just long enough to see Russell step out of the carriage. Collins and Taft followed him, obscured in the late evening sun. Jay put his boot to the spade and dug.

"Ahoy!" Russell shouted. His cheer fell flat.

The carriage driver hopped down from his seat and unstrapped the collection of small bags and luggage from the back of the cab. His wispy gray hair floated with the wind, reminiscent of one of Fowler's doomed servants.

"Just set them on the porch," Taft said, leaning out of the cab.

"Thank you, Johnathan," said Collins.

The three founding members of the Trust stood on the stone path in front of the large Federal-style house and watched Jay dig in his garden. His hands and forearms were caked with dirt, clumps clinging in the folds of his rolled-up sleeves. He made no indication that he intended to stop.

"There's no speaking to him when he's in this state," said Collins.

"Agreed," said Russell.

The front door squeaked open on its rusty hinges, and Marta, the Sheldons' maid, appeared. The bell-shaped Bavarian scooped up their luggage under her hefty arms, offering only a token acknowledgment of the men, "Ja, Ja," and shuffled back into the house, leaving the door open behind her.

It was clear they were expected as Jay had not abandoned hospitality. The spacious living room was set with several carts bearing a variety of refreshments. Along with a selection of decanters, there were small cakes, bread, cheeses, and several bottles of wine. A tall water pitcher sat on an end table, likely an afterthought to the alcoholic offerings.

The Sheldon's home seemed more like a museum with its diverse, if not bizarre, collection of décor. It was as if Jay had selected one item from each port he visited and forced it into his own unique aesthetic. From old-world luxury to primitive simplicity, Jay had somehow collected the world and deposited it in his living room.

Collins scooped up a crystal decanter, poured himself a healthy glass of bourbon, then sank deep into an over-stuffed chair and kicked his feet up on its matching ottoman. The failing sun found its way through the lead crystal window and lit the gold lenses of his glasses.

"Well, here we are," he said before sipping from his cup.

"So we are," Russell answered, pouring wine into a goblet.

Alphonso paced the room, glancing up the long narrow staircase as if he expected someone to descend at any moment. His boots clacked harshly when he stepped from rug to hardwood, adding an irregularity to his pacing that caused Collins to turn his head whenever he heard it.

"Stop that," said Collins.

"I have a lot on my mind, this is abysmal timing. I can't just drop everything and head east at the drop of a hat!"

"I'm sure Teressa feels terrible, inconveniencing you with her dying!"

"You know that's not my meaning," Taft groaned. "She hates us. You know that, right?"

"It's only fair, she knows us."

"We are a loathsome lot," Russell agreed.

Marta drifted back into the room carrying a small tray of summer sausage and venison jerky. Her dress hung long from her girthy hips, concealing her feet and lending her ambulation the semblance of a sentient dress form on wheels.

"Misses Sheldon is sleeping." She put the tray down on one of the carts. "I will come when she wakes."

"Thank you, Marta," said Collins.

"Ja, Ja."

She floated like an automaton up the staircase.

"We deserve her hate," said Taft, gazing out the window to Jay Sheldon, silhouetted against the pink sky, furiously carving the earth with a pick. "For what we took from her."

"What about what we gave her?" Collins kicked at the ottoman so that it jumped off the rug and gestured with a sweeping hand at the fine objects in the room. "Jay too, for that matter. He was never chosen, never called away to Ingolstadt. He got to live his life."

"And his son?"

"We don't choose," said Russell. "Remember?"

"Teressa most certainly did not."

Collins turned his gold-lensed eyes on Taft. He poised himself to speak, then thought better of it, choosing instead to stand and refill his glass.

"Any word out of Mexico?" asked Russell. "Has Sheldon managed any kind of communique?"

"Only that he's gone after Stallworth."

Collins extended the open wine bottle to Russell and topped off his goblet.

"Well, then, what of Rogers?" Taft asked. "Has he returned?"

"Not yet. He sent this."

Russell produced Morya's ring and held it to the dying light. The milky jade looked like bone in the gloom. "He's coming," he said.

"What about Robert Black?" asked Collins.

"Nothing," said Taft turning back to the window. "The sun is gone, and still he digs."

Russell sat with his right hand tucked in his vest, rigid like a portrait of Napoleon. His other hand combed through his beard, bringing it to a point.

"I have never understood his obsession with that garden," he said.

"It brings him peace," said Collins.

"Peace? If you say so," Taft muttered.

Their shadows grew as Marta and her candle descended the stairs. It occurred to them that the room had gone dark. She stopped halfway down the stairs.

"She wakes. You may come up now."

Alphonso left the window and started up while Collins and Russell topped off their glasses before following. The stairs led to a short hall with Teressa's room directly to the left. Marta entered first, setting her candle down on the vanity. A tall armoire with engraved floral panels stood in the opposite corner. Three chairs sat neatly spaced a few steps from the massive canopy bed. Translucent silk curtains drew back to the sturdy headboard on which the withered body of Teressa Sheldon leaned.

"Sit, I'm not contagious. Unfortunately."

She pulled her long hair back from her pallid face, running her fingers through her tangled blond and gray locks. Crow's feet grooved toward her tired blue eyes, red from tears.

Alphonso sat while Collins and Russell chose to stand, leaning on the high-backed wooden chairs. Marta closed the door behind her as she exited.

"How are you feeling?"

"I'm dying, Danfort. How do you think I'm feeling?"

"I don't have the words to express how sorry I am," said Taft.

Teressa coughed and adjusted herself on the bed. Tiny specks of dried blood spotted the pillow she used to prop herself against the headboard. She sipped from a glass of water on her nightstand, then turned her eyes to the three men.

"Why are you here? Your pity feeds my cancer."

"I'm sorry."

"You said that," she wheezed. "You've taken my son, and your apologies are nothing but a sick reminder of that fact. Clearly, my husband wasn't enough for you."

"We haven't taken anyone, Teressa," said Russell. "Choices were made."

"Lies were spoken, you mean."

"Teressa..."

"I only allowed you here to curse you and what's left of your rotted souls. I hope you burn for your sins! I hope..." Her voice broke, and she fell into fierce convulsions of coughing.

The bedroom door opened, and Jay Sheldon stood at the threshold.

"Gentlemen, that's enough. She needs her rest."

"Rest!" She coughed painfully. "How can any of us rest?"

"Teressa, is there anything you want me to tell Samuel?" asked Collins.

"Burn, Danfort!" she rasped.

Collins sighed and followed the others down the stairs.

The living room was now brightly lit by several oil lamps and sconces. Sheldon's dirt-encrusted shovel leaned against one of the sofas near his muddy footprints.

"We're sorry, Jay," said Taft. "We didn't mean to upset her."

"Twenty years too late for that."

Jay drank straight from the wine bottle. In the lamplight, his eyes were red from tears. Dirt clung to all parts of his clothing, streaking through his light brown hair and darkening his hands. Sheldon stood several inches taller than the men of the Trust, looming over them like a filthy and lachrymose gravedigger.

Collins drained the bourbon decanter into his glass.

"Do you know why I chose this spot to build my home?" Asked Jay.

"Because it's lovely and idyllic," suggested Russell.

"No," he scoffed. "I chose this spot because there was already a garden here."

"How nice," said Collins, breaking off a piece of bread.

"It was an old garden, but well-tended with rich soil."

"You hardly strike me as a farmer," chuckled Russell.

"No, I am not, though the Pocomtuc people were. They lived here peacefully for generations before war with Mohawk, colonists, and other tribes drove them off."

"Things change," said Collins. "The strong survive, and the weak adapt or perish."

"I suppose that's true, but survival comes with a price," said Jay, drinking from the bottle. "As it happens, one of the Pocumtuc people refused to let his land go lightly a warrior named Gray Lock. He fought in the Drummer's War and beat back the French and the English, though the settlers continued to come."

"Like I said, you can't defeat progress," said Collins.

"It wasn't the end. As white men flooded the Deerfield Valley, something strange began to happen. People began vanishing without a trace. When search parties were sent, they, too, went missing. Though he should have been long in his grave, the name of Gray Lock continued to be whispered with reverent terror.

Some believed he haunted the valley, others said he cursed it. None could say for sure until a gruesome discovery was made. One winter, a starving trapper came across a patch of winter gourds. As he thanked the lord for good fortune and continued his harvest, he uncovered the rotting corpse of a missing settler, followed by another, and another."

"More of these gardens were discovered, all over the valley, in areas where people had gone missing. In fact, to this day, folks are still reporting strange crops growing in the forest, though the legend of Gray Lock is all but forgotten."

Jay gulped the remainder of the wine and tossed the empty bottle to Russell.

"A disturbing tale, indeed," said Russell. "However, I struggle to find the point."

"I'm quitting, William, and I am gravely prepared to defend my decision."

"What about Sam?"

"You've killed my son like you've killed my wife."

"We've killed no one!" said Taft.

"You, of all of us, should recognize that lie," said Jay.

"Take some time, Jay, consider the ramifications," said Collins.

"This is all I care to consider," said Jay, snatching up his shovel and turning for the door.

THIRTY-NINE

May 13, 1866
Veracruz, Mexico

When they came, their shadows were as tall as horses, their legs rising and falling like an orchestra of jagged knives. Their dark and glistening carapaces scraped hideously between the decayed doorsill and the hardened clay floor as they contorted their way into the cell. On passing the gauntlet, jubilant antennae tasted the foul air, and membranous wings fluttered like geisha fans in the fragile gray light seeping under the cell door.

Pedro sat, part of the darkness, peering down upon the creatures' plain of putrid existence and welcomed them by crushing them with careful claps before sucking their meat and juices from the star-crossed lines of his palms.

Time was measured in buckets of his own filth. Only when he had filled one, overflowing with piss and feces, did his jailors reluctantly empty it into some undisclosed pit of rancid horrors. How long were these intervals? Pedro could not speculate. Though every time the door opened and the dingy light from the outside washed his cell like a shit-colored sun, he would prick his skin on a jagged piece of stone wall and stamp it with his finger above the pile of filthy rags where he slept. Thirty-two bloody prints marked his days.

His sustenance arrived via a slat in the door. When the bolt was thrown, a ladle would be thrust through the tiny opening, and a guard would count to three. If Pedro couldn't position his cupped hands below the ladle by the end of the count, it would tip, and he would be forced to slurp the foul water off the grimy clay floor. Often, a boiled beef bone with meager shreds of meat or a stale crust of bread would follow the ladle, providing just enough nutrients to keep him clinging to life. These visitations came sporadically, with no sensible methodology. It was as if his survival belonged to the mercy of some failing, geriatric mind, sometimes dispensing several meals a day or, just as readily, forgetting for vast, unknown swaths of time. But the buckets could not be overlooked, as the aggregate stench of untold excretions was something the guards would not endure.

Outside his claustrophobic prison cell, Pedro could only wonder at the conspiring fates whose whims deposited him there. An endless, blindfolded wagon ride from Parral had found him unceremoniously discarded and seemingly forgotten. Chief among his tortured thoughts was the well-being of his daughter, Sophia. The promises of Colonel Miguel Lopez provided no solace; a man of such brutality would lose no sleep after murdering an infant. Perhaps the colonel had followed the map, past the sombrero peak and the Rio Salado to his family's mines. In the small hours, when sleep evaded him, Pedro imagined the intrepid Colonel Lopez cresting the ridge of a particular box canyon, only to find Geronimo patiently waiting for him. Such were the mysteries Pedro brooded upon as he sat forsaken in the perpetual blackness of his cell.

The thirty-third bucket was not yet half-full when the door opened. This time the blinding light of filth stayed.

A vicious, growling shadow addressed him, "Get up!"

Human speech had become alien, the meaning was indecipherable in his language of misery. The guards usually only spoke in grunts or bootheels. He stared blankly into the dirty light, struggling to process the command.

"Now, you wretched shit!"

Pedro rose from his stinking pile of rags, propping himself against the wall. His hand ran over the sharp outcrop of chipped stone, and he pricked himself on the palm. The Black Decree of Maximillian promised death to men like him. Certainly, the promise was now to be fulfilled. Blood pooled in the pit of his palm as he admired its glorious color. Then, when enough blood had gathered, he pressed his hand next to the thirty-two thumbprints and watched it turn black as it soaked into the greedy stone.

"Move!" yelled the jailor, gesticulating with the barrel of his coach gun.

He limped toward the door, hopping on one leg and dragging his atrophied leg behind him. Malnutrition and prolonged confinement had caused his wound to regress, and walking was nearly impossible. Past the door stretched a long hall with many doors like his own, seven of which stood open and occupied by other pitiful prisoners. At least he would not face the gallows alone.

"Up the stairs!" commanded a second guard.

Pedro fell in behind the last prisoner as they slowly ascended the crude stone stairs. Trembling and weeping, the first prisoner reached the top of the landing and fell to his knees at the door, begging for his life. Another guard quickly put his boot to the man's back, grimacing in disgust.

"Open it! Time can't save you!" he screamed.

The man collected himself, returned to his feet, and pushed the latch on the door. White, blue, red, and green light dispelled the gloom in brilliant, luminous glory. The man crossed himself and walked awestruck into the radiance. Calmed by the light, the others followed, and Pedro limped behind.

When Pedro passed into the light, he realized that he had not been incarcerated in a prison but rather in the basement of an ancient and disused cathedral. Beyond the stained-glass martyrs and saints, a fiery sun raged in a sky so large he felt that he was now the roach, waiting to be crushed and sucked from between the fingers of a mad and terrible god.

The guards ushered them past the shattered pews, up and

over the altar with its cracked and leaning Christ, beyond faded and moth-eaten curtains, to the small rear door. The door opened, and they stepped into a narrow, cobblestone alley. A wagon with a caged bed sat to one side. A young white man with a prolific mustache and bushy sideburns leaned against the wagon near the open door. As the guards lined them up against the outside wall, the man pushed the brim of his gray Stetson hat, revealing his dark eyes, squinting under thick dark brows.

"Ocho Pendejos." The white man held up eight fingers to illustrate his meaning.

"Sí," said the jailor who carried the coach gun. "Mr. Reagan asked, and I have delivered."

Mr. Reagan stretched his legs, went to the first prisoner in line, and examined him with a discerning eye. Apparently satisfied, he passed on to the next. When he arrived at Pedro, he sniffed the air and then shook his head in disgust.

"I'll take the seven, but not the last."

"No, no, no! That is not our arrangement!"

"Don't try and cheat me, Noe! You said eight. That one hardly qualifies as half!"

The driver, another white man, hopped down with one hand on his pistol.

"Is there a problem?"

"You take them all, or you take none!" said Noe, waving the shotgun past the line of prisoners.

"No, that's not how it works, you fucking cheat! You said eight, not seven, and a cripple! Look at his leg, it's fucking crooked. He can barely stand! What do you feed him? Shit and cockroaches? I need men to dig a latrine! He looks like you pulled him out of one!"

"Quit complaining! You're lucky to get them!"

"Seven," said Reagan.

"No, you will take them all! I am done with this place! I will not make a prison for one man!"

"Fuck you if I care what you do with him!"

"Is that so?" said Noe, walking down the line of prisoners. He raised the gun to Pedro's face so that the massive bores blocked the sun from his eyes. "Maybe I just fix the problem!"

Pedro closed his eyes, and two black circles remained in the red light of his eyelids. These men were not soldiers, not in Maximillian's army. Whether bandito friends of the nefarious Colonel Lopez or some other foul element of corruption, this would be no state-sanctioned execution. Silently, he said a prayer for Sophia and waited for the end.

"Damn it, Noe!" said Reagan. "I didn't say kill him!"

"Well, what is it going to be then, Blanco?"

"Fine, I'll pay half! Final offer!"

Noe smiled and lowered the weapon.

"We have an accord."

Pedro heard the splashing of coins as the transaction was completed, though he did not open his eyes until the rough hand of a guard dragged him away from the wall to the waiting wagon. The prisoners piled in around him, crouching on their haunches as they jockeyed to find room. As the wagon pulled out of the alley onto the cobblestone street, the full might of the sun glared down like the flaming iris of God, casting shadows of the iron bars like crosses on their faces.

May 1866
Superstation Mountains, Arizona Territory

The top of the mine was funnel-shaped, delving into a crack in the earth, just big enough for a man to squeeze through. Inside, the tunnel sparkled with rose quartz, gold, and silver. At the base of the hill, grown over with scrub oak and peppered with cholla and ocotillo, was a hidden entrance to the mine, dug straight in like a traditional drift. The two tunnels may have intersected at one time, though a cave-in currently separated them. Geronimo could have spent a lifetime chiseling out rich hunks of ore in the upper tunnel if he were so inclined. Instead, he chose to pillage the vast stockpiles of roughly forged ingots and unprocessed ore hastily hidden in the lower tunnel years ago by Pedro's family.

Geronimo carefully stacked the stones in the wall, sealing off the lower tunnel, while Fun and Chihuahua loaded the gold bars onto their horses at the top of the ridge. There was enough gold concealed there to keep him and a small army in guns for the rest of his life. With the end of the White Eyes' great war, guns freely flowed through the trading posts. Life was good.

He considered his promise to Nana and the wishes of Victorio. To his reckoning, he had kept his word; this gold did not belong to the tiny mountain. In fact, if Victorio and Cochise kept their word, the gold he paid the white men for guns would end up in the mountain anyway. Victorio was a fool, fighting against his own interest in a war that wasn't real, at least not to the Apache. War was coming, with or without gold, and he would be ready when it came.

As they led their horses along the crumbling ridgeline and looked across the canyon to where the peak of the great sombrero shone through the mountains, Geronimo could hear the laughter of the Yellow Painted Man. Geronimo laughed with him. The golden man fought his war in the spirits of men, while his own war was of the earth, with flesh and blood. His spirit was mighty, and it was clean.

May 23, 1866
Carlota Colony
State Of Veracruz-Llave, Mexico

"Don't you tell him about your mine," said Reagan. "The general gets real spooky when the subject of gold is broached.

Stick to Stallworth's gold."

Pedro dipped the rag in the pail of soapy water and ran it down his arm, scrubbing the sweat-caked dirt as he went. Satisfied, he rang it out and repeated the process on his other arm, paying extra attention to his pits.

"I wouldn't mention those Indians you're friendly with, either. Not sure how he might interpret that kind of relationship."

Pedro washed his neck and shoulders, then turned the rag to his chest. The soapy brown water rolled down and splashed into the straw and dirt of the stable. Geronimo's slashing scar raised up pink against his brown goose flesh. He plunged the cloth back into the pail, sopped up a fresh load of water, and worked on his lower extremities.

"In fact, be prudent when discussing that business at the fort. Perhaps it's best if you blur the facts of your incarceration a bit. Maybe you stole some chickens or something?"

"Chickens?" Pedro raised a leg to wash his foot.

"Sure, why not?" Reagan shrugged. "It sounds better than you slaughtered the entire garrison and made off with their munitions."

"I didn't kill anyone, the Apache did."

"You don't know any Indians, remember?"

Pedro washed his other foot.

"What should I say then?"

Reagan dumped a second bucket of fresh water over Pedro's head, washing away any lingering suds.

"Stallworth. Best to stick with that."

"I told you everything about Santa Rosalia. Besides, the Apache wiped it out. What more can I say to him?"

"He wants your account firsthand. Tell him about the operations, business partners, security strength, that kind of thing."

"Does he mean to steal from him?"

"Best not to ask what he means to do. Here, put these on."

Pedro took the clean shirt and pants and put them on. He

was pleased to discover that Reagan had also brought him a new pair of boots and stockings. However, his ragged old sombrero remained. In his short time at the colony, his health had greatly improved.

General Duke's house in the village sat among a small cluster of public buildings close to the stables where Pedro bathed. This was one of the smaller settlements of the Carlota Colony, which stretched for miles and included countless homesteads, rancherias, logging camps, farms, and other endeavors the expatriated CSA men were starting up. The spirit of industry and enterprise quickly filled the void in the men hollowed out by the long years of war. Unlike many other villages in the colony, the general labored to keep a semblance of military order here, even if it had been reduced to a largely symbolic mantle as the Iron Brigade and the Georgia men quickly gravitated to postbellum life.

Pedro limped along next to Reagan and listened to his continued warnings. Fear lingered in the fringes of his thoughts, vaguely defined by the suggested omissions. He feared the general; his stark blue eyes were always watching and silently judging. From a distance, he found something unsettling and familiar about the man, like he had inflicted some cruelty on him in a long-forgotten nightmare. The idea that Pedro would now sit under his judgment or that the general would have any interest in his world profoundly disturbed him. With his potential freedom at stake, his consternation only grew.

"Don't worry, you and I are partners now. I'm not going to send you back to the chain gang."

Pedro nodded. The brim of his frayed and filthy sombrero was dipped low to cover his eyes. They walked past the feed store, farrier, and saddler, standing next to the other in a row of irregularly walled, hastily built structures. Everything leaned like it was drunk, and most of the buildings were still unfinished, with colonists or other slave laborers like Pedro busy at work on them. Still, the buildings served their purposes, and business was already thriving as the former Confederates settled into what they hoped would become their new home.

"You'd do well to trust me, Pedro. I know this man, he's not one to trifle with. Just stay on task, answer his questions." He lifted the brim of Pedro's sombrero. "Don't volunteer anything that isn't relevant."

They arrived at a sod cabin, and Reagan banged twice on the crude plank door. An indistinguishable grunt answered the knock. Reagan pushed the door open, and they walked inside.

"Secretary Reagan," said the general. "Mr. Gonzales."

General Duke sat dressed in his Confederate uniform, framed in the dusty trapezoid of light streaming through the cabin's only window, leaning against the sloping wall on the back two legs of his chair. The sunlight fell across his lap and illuminated the book he was reading. A cot sat in the corner with a locked chest butted to the end.

He leaned forward in the chair and set the book down beside him on the hardened dirt floor.

"Thank you for coming."

Pedro stood, anxious and exposed, in the general's gaze. He shifted his weight nervously, finding it difficult to achieve a comfortable stance in the claustrophobic cabin.

"You look well, Pedro. Have you been getting enough to eat?"

"Sí."

He tilted his head slightly so that the brim of his hat prevented direct eye contact. The general's presence was unsettling, his eyes too blue, and they seldom blinked.

"I'll be direct, I need more information on Stallworth."

"Of course, I'll tell you what I can."

"Secretary Reagan shared your story with me. I was so intrigued that I thought it prudent to discuss the matter with you personally. You claim that Stallworth is working with Juárez and the Americans, that he gives gold to Juárez for weapons and, in turn, is granted mineral rights?"

"Sí, but not exactly that way..."

"What do you mean?"

Pedro kicked absently at the dirt floor.

"He never pays in gold, only silver."

General Duke stepped toward Pedro, lifting the sombrero's brim to look into his eyes.

"Only silver? How do you know this?"

"I hear it from the Chinaco who take the silver to buy the guns, from the whores, where they spend the part they steal, and from the priests that end up with the rest. They all tell me he hoards the gold to himself."

"Hoards where? Parral? What about Veracruz? I was told he worked out of Veracruz?"

Pedro looked into Duke's dead doll eyes, and his hands began to shake. It came to him suddenly, surprising him as if he had turned over a rock to find a rattlesnake. He had seen this man before. He seemed much older now, but Pedro was sure. He had witnessed him drag that big Apache to that cursed fort in the New Mexico Territory three years previously. He wore the uniform of a different army, looked fifteen years younger, and was decidedly less menacing back then, but it was him.

"Easy, General," said Reagan.

"I don't know, probably in his palacio by the river," Pedro said to the ground, refusing to make further eye contact. "I know nothing of Veracruz."

"So, Parral?"

"Sí, close to his mine at Santa Rosalia."

"If there is as much gold as you claim, he must have an army to protect it for him, right?"

"Worse. He has Maria Bonita."

"What about this Maria? How many soldiers does she command?"

Duke sat down on his cot.

"I couldn't say, as many as she needs."

"What about the Emperor, does he have men there?"

"There was a fort, but they... They went away."

The general opened the trunk at the foot of his bed and

retrieved a twine-wrapped bottle of mescal. He pulled the cork, took a pull, and offered it to Pedro.

Pedro looked at it like he was being offered a live fish or some other squirming creature. After a moment's pause, he accepted the bottle and drank. Reagan had no such reservations and drank immediately after Pedro before passing the bottle back to General Duke.

"Do the names Virgil Price or Tad Taffy mean anything to you?"

"No, I'm sorry."

"I'm organizing an expedition to the region soon. I would like you to serve as a guide."

"No, I can't," his voice cracked, and his heart fluttered.

"No? Why not?"

Pedro felt the urge to run, to break through the door and sprint for the horses. Escape was not possible, he had to answer him.

"I was arrested there, I cannot go back."

"But you're from Parral, yes? Surely your transgressions are not so heinous that an imperial pardon would not atone for them. What crimes did you commit?"

"I..." Pedro stammered, "I killed... chickens!"

"Chickens?"

"Sí."

"They imprisoned you for killing chickens? We all kill chickens, Pedro. Is there something you aren't telling me?"

Reagan cleared his throat and took the bottle of mescal.

"It's all right, Pedro, I'll tell him. Pedro poisoned the chickens of a neighboring rancher that undercut his prices in town. The rancher butchered the chickens and took them to market anyway, and people got sick. He feels terrible. It's difficult for him to talk about it." He took a strong pull from the bottle and passed it to Pedro. "Isn't that right, Pedro?"

"Sí, many people got sick."

"I see."

Pedro drank the mescal, fire already rising from his belly. If

General Duke intended to kill him, at least he enjoyed the small comfort of a drink first.

"So, then." The general reached into the open chest. "Do you write?"

"Some."

"Take this." He handed Pedro a small notebook and a graphite pencil. "Draw me a map of Parral, as best you can, and make notes of anything you think I should know."

"What things are important to know?"

"Pedro, do you like working in the stables? It's better than digging latrines, right?"

"Sí."

"Well, if you don't want to spend the rest of your time here at Carlota looking up from the pit of one of those latrines, slowly drowning in shit and piss, then you tell me what is important. Do you understand?"

"Sí." He took the pencil and paper.

"Secretary Reagan, I believe it's time to draft another letter to our gracious host, Maximillian. I need that meeting."

Duke took the bottle and swirled the liquid inside; it was less than half-full. He put the bottle to his lips and drank, then set it back in the trunk. The lid of the chest crashed down, releasing a cloud of dust swirling into the long rectangle of light that had elongated across the room.

"Now go, get to it." The general laughed and put his hand on Pedro's shoulder as he opened the door. "And, chickens? Let's have no more incidents with chickens, shall we?"

Reagan and Pedro exited without a word, their eyes squinting against the invading sun.

FORTY

May 27, 1866
The Tomb, Parlor 322; Yale
New Haven, Connecticut

"Rari Quippe Boni," said Morya. His abnormally long fingers slid across the smooth, black marble mantel of the enormous fireplace to a wooden plinth mounted with a human skull. A small gold tag read, "M.V.B ."His lips curled in a cruel smile as his fingers crossed over the strange memento. Below, the Latin quote on the mantle and the engraved emblem of the skull and bones gazed darkly into the cold and windowless stone of Parlor 322.

His skin was dark if darkness could be said to have a color. In the thirty-five years since their meeting in Ingolstadt, Taft had encountered men from all parts of the world, but none shared any semblance to Morya. At times he appeared Moorish, or perhaps as a Kurd in the ranks of Saladin, at other times, a devotee of Krishna. Time had not affected him in the decades since Bavaria, and Taft was no closer to guessing the man's actual age. Standing in the fierce glow of the fire, his slightly elongated forehead, thick brows, and wide, black eyes bore a striking likeness to a hieroglyphic pharaoh stepping out of the stone and into the parlor. In truth, he was none of these things, and Alphonso Taft shuddered to imagine whose image Morya was created in.

Russell, Collins, and Taft sat in tall-backed wood chairs at a finely stained, black oak table, the room's only furnishing. The usual trappings and decorative flourishes of the Bonesmen had been removed, leaving the sandstone walls stark and bare. The men's faces tilted like pallid moons, anchored to the pull of Morya's gravity.

"Why am I here?"

The three men stared blankly, unsure if Morya's question was rhetorical.

"I am here to calm your troubled minds."

Morya paced around the table. He reached into his long, black frock coat and retrieved a small leather-bound journal.

"You are like ships lost at sea, carrying precious freight. The voyage is perilous and the way is long, fraught with the tides of confusion."

Morya raised his ash-gray palms upward to the mock heavens.

Again, the men did not respond.

"Allow me to be the gull on the wind, your promise of land."

Morya brought his hands together in faux piety.

"Salvation is at hand, for you float on a serendipitous sea that rises and falls with an ardent and calculated purpose; to protect and to guide."

He paused and looked directly toward Taft.

"None who sail here may be taken astray."

Taft noted the old leather book clutched in Morya's talon-like fingers. It was identical to the one in his grandfather's old sea chest, sitting on a shelf in his study. Dread stirred in him like something scratching at a cellar door. Across the table, the lenses of Collin's glasses reflected gold fire. Russell's head turned, regarding him curiously.

"Because, my dear mariners, it is a poor captain that discards his compass and sextant. How could such a pitiful pilot hope to chart a righteous course?"

"Why are you telling us this?" asked Collins.

"You are my brothers, or more specifically, my brother's keepers and you should know that I care very deeply for him. Once we were pure, in a place of light, but we fell."

Morya stepped back toward the black marble mantle and

stood between the Trust and the fire. He cast no shadow, though he blocked nearly all the light.

"Now, we are but dormant shadows..."

"You speak of the Other," said Russell.

"I speak of the bridge between you." Morya's voice raised in volume, "Danfort, I see your golden spectacles have endured. Your compass is intact!"

Collins removed his gold-wire glasses and set them on the dark oak.

"William, what of your compass?"

Russell reached into his breast pocket, retrieving a thin golden rectangle the size of a playing card, and laid it on the table. Faint characters caught the light, engraved in a dead and forgotten language.

"A fine captain! Mr. Taft?"

"I lost it. Long ago."

"Oh, Alphie, such things cannot be lost, they will always find their way."

Morya held his hand close to the fire, the ring of Brother Spartacus shining from his thin finger. The bright green jade absorbed the fire's light, and the golden orb shone as if molten.

A new light manifested itself like another sun, casting its light in the place beneath their flesh and bone. Red embers and shifting clouds danced in a fathomless cosmos framed by the windows of their physical forms, with the notable exception of Alphonso Taft. A dark shadow cast across his body, it seethed like an oily vapor trapped inside a prison of glass.

"Poor captain," said Morya. "Your deviancy caused this dissonance, setting in motion the events that we must now discuss."

The curious light faded.

Taft felt the eyes of his partners upon him, silently asking him, "Why?" He could not bring himself to return their gaze. Instead, he watched the space where the fire's reflection outlined Morya's silhouette in the dark grain of the wood. Why? The answers were murky, even by his own reckoning.

He convinced himself his actions were the logical responses to a cruel sequence of tragedies inflicted upon him by his golden shadow. The truth was more complex, more human than the thing inside him, whose eyes he had blinded.

"I was visited by one of your neophytes, Robert Black," said Morya.

Alphonso Taft's face went pale.

"I congratulate you on training such a formidable student, though never meant for our coterie. We do not choose. Isn't that right, Mr. Taft?"

Taft stared blankly back at Morya and remained silent.

"What happened?" asked Russell.

"He razed Black Ash Manor to... ashes, quite literally around me. Then, he dispatched the poet, Matsuo Sogi, with necromancy and left me chained in the smoldering ruins. Hardly the behavior of a responsible captain!"

"Robert betrayed us?" Collins growled.

"He threw his lot in with Virgil Price and his mob of dissenters and apostates. Clearly, Samuel Sheldon was also the beneficiary of Mr. Black's handiwork."

"How far does this go?" said Russell. "Are we undone?"

"Undone?" Morya let out a short sarcastic burst of laughter. "Nothing happens except by his will. This can no more be undone than you can stop the flow of time or change the law of gravity."

"How do we reconcile this?" asked Collins.

Morya paced around the table, back to the fireplace. He ran his bony fingers over the engraved Latin words.

"The good are indeed rare," he sighed. "We do not choose our successors, Mr. Taft. Your son, Robert Black, will die."

"How many of my children have you already killed?"

"How many have you?"

Taft trembled at the question. Morya's words were cold but without malice. He stood with his back to the fire and opened the leather-bound book, thumbing through the pages.

"Do you know what this is?"

"You know that I do," answered Taft.

"I paid a visit to your home at Mount Auburn, your boy William is a lovely child."

Morya chose a page and read:

January 18, 1831

I hear it ticking continuously, waking or sleeping. It is less machine and more a mind, communicating in increments of time. There is a transmutation below my flesh, recreating me as a golden automaton. I imagine cogs and wheels occupying the places where my joints and tendons should be. The ticks of these gears are his voice, compelling me to accept while lulling me to forget that I was ever any different.

Helena, in her grace, taught me how to protect my thoughts, to build a wall inside, a place he cannot find. Maintaining my hidden vault is exhausting but essential to retain my personal sovereignty.

Our son is a stranger to me and doomed to remain so. His safety and the success of our endeavor necessitate it. He shares his mother's gifts, attributes undoubtedly useful to our coming struggle.

With the rhythm of a ticking clock, Morya slowly flipped the pages.

December 20, 1841

A letter arrived today from Helena. I read it while my new bride lay sleeping in the next room. The guilt of imagined infidelity is no less than the actual thing. Exacerbating my culpability is the fact that I cannot decide to whom I am being unfaithful, Franny, Helena, or the ticking monster inside me. My soul is split in three, and my allegiance has no home.

Ten years, nearly to the day since we last met, she writes to tell me of our daughter! Helena, my first and only love, why now? She named the child Helena Petrovna; like Robert, she is hidden. The war is coming, she says, and our children are soldiers.

I wonder if this war is to be fought by or against me.

"Helena, our lost student," sighed Morya. "Pity about her."

"What do you know of pity?"

Russell and Collins leaned in, elbows on the table, eyes fixed on Taft. Morya noted their attentiveness and smiled in saccharine mockery.

"Let's skip ahead a bit, shall we?"

March 15, 1842

Helena came to me! It was a reprise of the vision so long ago in Ingolstadt when we stood, under dark skies, at the base of the mountain. "He's there," she pointed. She took my hand, imparting a deluge of information. The urgency was profound. The knowledge is incomplete, though it directs me to the southern wastelands and the people who roam there. It is clear to me now that I must find this place if there is any hope of stopping this.

When I woke, the watch had stopped ticking. I turned the crown, sure that Helena was dead.

"Tick... Tick... Tick..." Morya smiled as he flipped through the book.

November 29, 1848

I blame my dreams, in them, my mind is unfettered, transparent for the Other to see. I dream of the mountain and he dreams with me. I stand at its base as the sky is burning and He comes, a flaming orb, screaming toward the peak. The light is blinding, then warm nothing. I hear him ticking in the stone.

This morning, I woke from the dream to Franny's inconsolable weeping. Our Mary passed in the night. Poor Peter found her there, lifeless in her bassinet. I could only speculate his thoughts as he waited for her to wake. Again, the watch had stopped.

What possible crime is deserving of such cruelty? Is my knowledge of His secret home some unfathomable threat?

Perhaps my family is an intolerable distraction to the work, and this punishment is made to bring me to task? He does not speak in words, and these deadly messages seem to defy translation into human terms.

Peter is too young to understand; perhaps he is the lucky one. Charles, in his innocence, asked if she had been taken by angels. I could not find the words to answer.

With deliberate formality, Morya flicked the pages to the next entry.

January 15, 1849

The white men call this place Apacheria, presumably after the heathens that dwell here. Somehow, they and the mountain are connected. I know I am near. I employed a former army scout familiar with the Apache. With his guidance, success is imminent.

I keep my mind shuttered, concealed from the Other, though I remain uncertain of my ultimate intent. If I can find the mountain and stand in the place where I dream, perhaps the answer will come. For that reason, I also keep this secret from my partners. While it is in our stock and nature to chase visions of gold, I am confident they would not share my motives.

Regarding my partners, I pray they excuse my absence as I leave them inundated with industry. California gold is pouring east, and I neglect my duties to the Trust every moment I am away. In proxy, I delegated some of these responsibilities to a capable associate of Van Buren, a portly fellow named Price. Even so, if my undertaking is not soon successful, I will be forced to abandon it.

"Now that name does ring some bells! Does it not, gentlemen?"

Taft bowed his head with his hands clenched on the table. He did not need to raise his eyes to know his partner's ire.

"I assure you, the best is yet to come!"

January 17, 1849

I found the mountain, walking as if in a dream. It rose up out of the valley floor like a cancerous blemish. He lives inside. I know that now. I took the winding path to the top to see him and confront him, but I could find no entrance. I'm sure he concealed it from me, the coward. I left the watch, still ticking, at the top of the mountain, looking over the bleak desert plain. When it stops, I hope that this time, it is me it takes; I long for the day and my freedom.

"Do you feel free?"

"No."

"You enjoy the victim's role, but we both know you are far from innocent. Shall I continue?"

"No!" Taft pounded his fists, shaking the oak table. "That is quite enough!"

Morya ignored the outburst and flipped several pages ahead to the next desired entry.

May 23, 1849

I am not alone, and I fear I never will be. The phantom ticking continues, though the watch is leagues away. It haunts my sleep and presents visions of that terrible Indian. I see him looking down murderously at me, my perspective being that of the dial. He does this often, generally before engaging in some violent rampage. Distance has not abated the watch's proclivity toward death.

Though the Other's eye is blind to my thoughts and movements, he is not vanquished. He reaches out from me, affecting changes and exerting his influence. I see the evidence in the curious looks of compromised strangers and hear it ticking always.

He flipped ahead.

March 3, 1851

I have done the unspeakable, and I welcome the hell that

awaits. The golden parasite will not be content in my cage of flesh. With his foul, invisible arms, he touches my family yet again. I don't expect those with sanity to comprehend, just know that it had to be done.

I heard it again, marking the seconds like a hideous, beating heart. The source, this time, originated in the house rather than within the haunted chambers of my mind. I traced it to the bassinet, where little Alphonso lay sleeping. It became louder, undeniable, pounding like velvet hammer strokes beneath his pillowcase. Carefully, I lifted his head, expecting to find that cursed thing returned to taunt me. It was not so. Beneath the pillow, I found the ancient Roman coin bearing the head of mad Caligula.

I smothered my son in his cradle and threw the coin into the river. He will not lay claim to my line! This curse ends with me.

Papa loves you, Alphonso.

Morya sighed and turned to another page.

June 3, 1852
I am a murderer. To any bold enough to read these pages, I confess to the murder of my wife. My culpability extends to the insidious influence of the Other, who took Franny from me long before my desperate act.

It was her that placed the coin. Somehow the coin found its way from the silty bottom of the Ohio into her hands. I caught her placing it under our newborn son.

"We do not choose!" she said, the words of Brother Spartacus. She was a familiar to him, compromised by the parasite exiled from my thoughts.

I strangled her where she stood and then placed her in her bed. I will sew that hideous coin into her funeral gown, let it rot with her in the grave!

What wretched sorcery claimed her soul and allowed that unholy coin to rise from the muck? Now another life may need

to end, another boy that shares my name.
He has taken his last from me!

Taft wept in heaves and gasps, his face buried between his arms.

"Stop! Please! Have mercy and just destroy me!"

"But there's so much more! Don't you think everyone wants to hear about Robert Black?"

Morya laid the book down in front of Taft and put one hand on his shoulder. The fire hissed and cracked while the men of the Trust awaited his judgment. The dark man smiled and released his grip on Taft.

"Don't fear. I did not come to dispatch you, Alphonso. I am not as careless as you."

"What then?" Russell's voice was quiet, his eyes still locked on Taft.

"We continue," said Morya. "There will be a man in El Paso del Norte I want you to meet."

"Mexico?" asked Collins.

"Yes, I'll send word when it's time."

"And Robert Black?"

Morya stepped to the fireplace.

"It's time we righted the ship. We possess a very gifted asset in Mr. Rogers. I have deployed him with full faith in his abilities."

"Pulvis et umbra sumus," said Taft.

Turning to the table, Morya smiled broadly, showing stark white teeth.

"You are not yet worthy of dust and shadows."

FORTY-ONE

June 15, 1866
New Orleans, Louisiana

T he bar at May Bailley's was a dim sanctuary of rich oak nestled in the bosom of a bustling brothel. While most evenings, every seat and table would be occupied by men waiting to have their turn in one of the restless boudoirs. In the midafternoon lull, Robert Black enjoyed the place almost to himself, save for a solitary patron perched a few bar stools away.

"Pardon me, sir, are you a writer?"

"Excuse me?" Robert looked up from his bourbon.

"It's just that I noticed that stack of manuscripts in your satchel, and I imagined that you were either a writer or a book salesman."

"Neither," said Robert.

"Ah, a touch of humility, well spoke," said the stranger.

"Myself, I've long aspired to be a writer. When I was a boy, I left home and became a printer's devil."

"Is sulking about whore house whiskey holes the best way to find a literary career?"

"I'd think not, yet here you are. I suppose I can take inspiration from that."

"I'm not a writer."

Robert waved at the barkeep and tapped his glass.

"Did you write and publish that manuscript?" Asked

the stranger.

"I did," Robert nodded thanks to the bartender and took up his glass.

"Then, you are a writer."

"That is your opinion, sir, not my own."

"No, sir, it is a matter of fact, and I applaud you for it."

"Well, huzzah then."

"Huzzah, indeed," the stranger laughed and extended his hand. "Ambrose Bierce, sir, a pleasure to make your acquaintance."

"Do you often harass strangers in brothels?" Robert asked, ignoring the man's hand.

"Strangers, no. Though, when I recognize a kindred spirit."

"This is the only spirit I recognize at the moment, Mr. Bierce."

Robert turned back to his glass, staring deeply into the depths of his bourbon."

"I meant no offense," said Bierce, sipping from his own glass.

He turned his attention to a fly buzzing about the bar room for a moment. It circled endlessly, persistent through the heat and humidity.

"What's it about?"

"What?" Robert turned again, exasperated.

"The book, what's it about?"

Robert stared off to the buzzing fly, the only noise aside from the stranger's nagging questions. He considered the exhausting and tireless work he had invested in transcribing and narrating his father's journal, Morya's secret book, and his own experience with the Trust. He had labored not to keep the secret but to expose it, an effort so far met with a tepid response from journalists, librarians, and bookstores. Now, with an eager audience, he took a mighty gulp of his whiskey and shrugged away the bitterness of failure."

"It's about a man who mistakenly enters a pact with the Devil and allows that devil to travel within his mind and soul. He gets forced into doing the Devil's work, and when he refuses, the Devil begins to kill his family and destroy everything he loves. The man enlists the aid of his estranged son to help fight the Devil. The son employs necromancy and summons powerful spirits, but the Devil is too strong. Therefore, his own recourse is to murder his father and pry his soul from the Devil's clutches."

"Incredible! Take my money, sir!" Bierce reached into his pocket and retrieved a handful of silver dollars.

"I will give you one free, however, there are two conditions," said Robert.

"Of course," Bierce eagerly agreed.

"One, you must understand that every word in this book is true and act accordingly."

        "True, you say?"

"Yes, very much so. Second, there is a man following me, a very bad man. If you see this man, give him a wide berth and deny all knowledge of ever knowing me. It could be more than your life you lose."

"Sir, you are the greatest book salesman I have ever encountered."

Robert handed the man a manuscript, and he immediately began thumbing through it.

"Barkeep, settle up," said Robert, tossing a five-dollar gold coin on the bar.

"Thank you, sir!" the barman pocketed the generous tip.

"Excuse me, barman, does this establishment have storage available for its guests? I have errands to run this afternoon and would rather not haul this satchel around."

"We do, though it is generally long-term, reserved for our regular customers that wish to discretely store a few sundries."

"Excellent," said Robert, placing another five-dollar coin on the bar and passing over his satchel.

"Sir, a question," said Bierce.

"Yes," said Robert.

"What is this strange writing? The characters are like nothing I've ever seen, and I've seen books printed in dozens of languages."

"I don't know. I copied it straight from the Devil's book."

"I see," he said. "The Devil's book."

Robert left Bierce puzzling over the manuscript and left the shaded confines of May Bailley's for the sun-washed streets of New Orleans. There were arrangements to be made and supplies to be purchased. This leg of his journey was nearly over. It was time to find his father.

◆ ◆ ◆

"We don't serve colored folk," said the barkeep at May Bailey's. "Even if they got captain's bars. You understand."

Thomas smiled wide enough for his golden molars to gleam in the sun pressing in from the doorway.

"I'm not here for service, I'm here looking for a deserter. A man by the name of Robert Black. I have it under good authority that he is a guest here. Point me to him, and I'll be on my way."

"Never heard of him," said the barman. "Even if I had, I probably wouldn't say. Bad for business, you understand."

The tone in his voice was enough to convince Thomas he was in the right place. He had heard from many locals of a strange northerner with a nervous disposition staying with the ladies of the carriage house. He drew his pistol and shot the barman in the face. Blood and brain matter sprayed across his newly polished glassware as he slunk down dead behind the bar.

"I do understand," he said.

Ambrose Bierce stood from his barstool, tucked his new book under one arm, and raised his other, slowly moving toward the door.

"What about you? You see a man that fits that description?"

Bierce contemplated his response while staring down Thomas' pistol.

"I did see such a man, sir. Unholy-looking fellow. He promised to return this very afternoon. Some business with the barman, I believe."

"What business?"

"I couldn't say, just that I overheard him say he would return."

"Hmm."

"May I pass, sir? Please, I have no stake in this, captain."

"Go," said Thomas.

Bierce slid out the door and escaped into the humid heat of the city.

Thomas reached across the bar and selected the bottle of whiskey with the least blood on it, and sat down at the bar to wait.

He was close before; he missed Robert by a day in Tallahassee and only a few hours in Montgomery. In Birmingham, it felt like the son of bitch had just left the room wherever he looked. Now, in New Orleans, he was sure that he had him. He could feel the golden cage of bones singing it to him from beneath his skin. More, the blood ruby was growing brighter. It seemed angry, shining against the light as if it were starving for destiny.

Morya said to bring him back alive. Morya was wrong.

About halfway through his first glass of whiskey, the door creaked open, and sunlight ran the length of the floor. Thomas peered from under the brim of his hat, prepared to spring his trap. It was not Robert, though the young man that stood there did look somewhat familiar. The door closed behind him as the man crossed the distance between them.

"You remember me?" He asked.

"Can't say that I do," said Thomas.

"Well, mayhap you remember this!"

The man drew a hatchet from his waistband and brought it down swiftly toward Thomas' outstretched arm on the bar. Thomas fell back off his stool, stumbling into the dingy gloom of May Bailey's, barely escaping the blow.

"Who the fuck are you, kid?" Asked Thomas, reaching for his gun.

"My name is Aaron Tyler!" he shouted, ripping the axe from the bar top and rushing Thomas.

The kid was on him before he could draw his pistol, moving with uncanny speed and ferocity. Then, with one brutal swing of the hatchet, the blade struck hard on the cylinder of Thomas' pistol, denting, knocking it from his hands, and discharging a shot.

Once again, the door opened, and sunlight flooded in. Robert Black stood there, looking in on the conflict. He looked at the bloody bottles, and the barman's corpse, then recognized Thomas and quickly retreated back the way he came.

"Hold up, you cocksucker!" Thomas yelled at the slamming door.

The axe swung down through his hat. It was a grazing blow, though it left a bloody gash on his bald head. Thomas whirled away from his attacker, drawing his blade.

"All right, you shell-sucking son of a bitch, let's finish this!"

"Give me your best, Mr. Nations!" He said, attacking with a swift but wild arc.

Thomas ducked under the blow and slashed at the Tyler boy's exposed elbow joint, slicing through flesh and tendon. The hatchet sailed over the bar, smashing several bloody bottles. As his opponent recoiled in pain, Thomas wrapped around him from behind, taking him in a choke hold and slipping his blade between his ribs.

"Fuck you," Aaron Tyler gurgled.

"I let you live, you dumb son of a bitch!"

"You killed my pa! But I found you, I sure did, you fuck!"

Thomas sank his blade deeper and waited for the blood-choked wheezing to stop, then let the boy fall in a bloody heap on the bar room floor. His own wound was bleeding profusely, soaking his uniform. He felt dizzy. Was it his wound, or had something changed?

He reached into his pocket and retrieved a small gray stone where the blood ruby had once been. He dropped it into the spreading circle of the boy's blood. It had been his all along.

His dizziness persisted as he stepped out of the bar and onto the street. Curious pedestrians gawked with horror at the steady streams of blood channeling the contours of his face. He had been wrong about the ruby, just as his mercy had been a mistake. Now, doubt seeped into his mind. What would he do when he inevitably caught up with Robert Black?

June 16, 1866

The fisherman, Coleman Rideau, lay dying in Robert's arms amidst the rancid trappings of his dilapidated shack. His eyes, once brown, were now forced into a crystal shade of blue, the hallmark of Elizabeth's manifestation. His only crime had been defending his fishing boat from the theft of Robert Black. Now, the boat, and Rideau, lay perforated with holes, both useless to the world.

"Do you think I've done enough?" Robert asked.

"Who can say," Elizabeth spoke through the cracked lips of Rideau.

"I distributed seventy-two copies, three left behind at May's.

"And if by chance anyone reads your book, will they think it anything less than the ramblings of a madman?"

"I don't know," said Robert, squeezing the hand of the

fisherman.

"It's beyond your control, in any case."

Blood seeped from Rideaus lips, and his body began to tremble. Somewhere behind Elizabeth's eyes, his soul floated like a Chinese lantern, caught in her preternatural sky.

"Yes, you're right. Only El Paso remains."

"Are you certain the wires with your father were not intercepted?" She asked.

"It doesn't matter. In fact, it probably makes it easier if they know I'm coming."

"It won't be like when you killed my father, the evil inside him was his own. The monster inside of Alphonso Taft cannot be destroyed."

"I know."

"There's no guarantee I can separate his soul from that of the beast, you must be prepared for failure," she said.

"I'll save a bullet for myself," he said, stroking Rideau's blood-matted hair.

"If it comes to that, I'll be with you."

"I love you," he said, holding the fisherman tight and kissing his rank lips.

"I love you too," she said.

"Though, I much prefer the girls at May's to this wretch," he wiped the blood and tobacco juice from his mouth.

"Thomas is still out there, he won't stop," said Elizabeth.

"I'm not afraid of Thomas, he has no say in any of this. He just doesn't know it yet."

"Just be careful, my love," she said as the shattered body of Coleman Rideau convulsed with death throes.

Robert applied pressure to the wadded-up shirt he was

employing as a blood stop. The smell rising from Rideau was a noxious mix of sweat, whiskey, and urine. He swept the sweaty locks away from the dying man's eyes and stroked his cheek, but he was dead, and she was gone.

Robert stepped out of the shack into the moonlight filtering through the cypress. Rideau's boat was ruined, eliminating the possibility of escaping into the estuary. He would by land, through the sunken town of Horace, toward Lake Charles and work west from there.

The bayou claimed the town of Horace decades before. It existed near the crossroads of Old Horace Road and the nameless trail that wound through the bayou to the fish shack. All that remained standing of the old settlement was a crumbling bell tower rising like a sick lotus from the swamp-sunk church. Its glassless window gaped like a blinded cyclops, leaning menacingly low above the waterline.

Swaths of blue iris and switchgrass filled the clearing that marked the town's gravesite, almost obliterating the road north. It grew tall and defined the water's edge where the bright moon laid silver on the still, black swamp. Night herons squawked their displeasure as he stepped into their jurisdiction, and the soft splash of nocturnal things escaped his encroachment.

The unmistakable sound of broken glass interjected the nocturnal din, and a faint glow began to shine from the church's crooked window. A moment later, flames licked through, lapping at the dry Spanish moss draping from the roof. Soon the entire structure caught fire like some ghastly candle. The road lit up prominently, further than Robert could previously see. In the center of the weed-choked path, a man stood with a rifle trained on him. The man smiled, and Robert saw the gold teeth gleaming in the fire's light.

"Hello, cocksucker!" Thomas called out.

"I won't be murdered as easily as those men in Georgia."

"You got anything to say for yourself before I serve the gators a candlelight dinner?"

"I do," said Robert. "You're going to let me pass."

"No, I don't believe that is an accurate assessment of the situation."

"I've got a message to deliver. They're going to want to hear it. From me."

"No problem, you can tell me. My memory is outstanding."

"Not that kind of message."

The fire reached its zenith, filling the clearing with flickering light. The water reflected the flames, broken only by the jagged teeth of oak stumps and the glowing eyes of alligators.

"What then? You livin' just ain't on the menu."

"I lied about Deer Island, about Mangas."

The gleam of gold disappeared as Thomas gritted his teeth.

"Yeah?" said Rogers.

"He told me where the mountain is. I know its secret."

"What's stopping me from cutting that pretty head of yours off your shoulders, maybe taking a trip to Deer Island and separating you from your secrets?"

"You won't. That gold in your mouth knows better than your own mind what the truth is."

"And what's that?" asked Thomas.

"Truth is you couldn't handle me in life, let alone death. Just stand aside, Thomas, you know they'll be waiting on me."

"Maybe I put that to the test..."

The broken cross of the church fell hissing into the swamp, and the structure began to lean in on itself. Finally, the light dimmed, and Rogers fell into silhouette.

"No, I don't think you will," said Robert.

"I had you dead, you miserable fuck. I still will when this is done!"

"Maybe it's me that gets you," said Robert.

"I'll see you in El Paso del Norte, cocksucker!"

Thomas Rogers faded into the darkness of Horace Road without another word. The church screamed at the water line as the steeple started to give and sway. Robert watched until the flames turned to embers, and the old bell came crashing through the planks and splashed into the sunken pews below.

FORTY-TWO

June 24, 1866
Chapultepec Castle, Mexico City

T he light was viscous, like something that could be scooped from pools and carried in crystal decanters. It came through the stained glass in waves of gold and blue, washing over gold leaf moldings and intricately carved panels and reflecting off the cool Italian marble floors. The harsh clacking of their bootheels echoed like a team of horses in the lengthy hall, ringing in Sheldon's ears as if to say that this was not a place where ordinary men should walk.

His host displayed no such apprehension and stood entitled in proud appreciation of the hall's eloquent craftsmanship and garish beauty. Sheldon had come to expect these long pauses; his guide installed them regularly throughout the tour to punctuate the significance of some objet d'art or to absorb the majesty of an architectural feature.

As Emperor Maximillian I of Mexico stood in silent admiration of the hall, his fingers curled in a half-fist resting thoughtfully below his lip as if posing for a portrait. His long coat never creased, its epaulets hung perfectly like golden curtains, and his polished boots gleamed from the floor to his knees. Rising above the immaculate uniform was Maximillian's head, awkwardly poking through like a child standing on their tiptoes to fill out his father's clothes. Though well practiced, his noble pose was thwarted by restless, scheming eyes, constantly in motion, like unsettled blue marbles. Enormous sideburns lay on his shoulders like a hairy collar, thwarting any symmetry with his oblong head. Sheldon regarded the man's features as unfortunate, distracting to any sense of stateliness.

"Ah, Athena," said Maximillian, standing before one of the floor-to-ceiling stained glass panels.

"Beautiful," said Sheldon. "I'm grateful for the audience, Your Majesty. Have you-"

"My patron in these difficult times." He moved closer to the panel and paused again in appreciation.

"Sir, have you had a chance to consider my proposal?"

"Proposal?"

"Yes, the proposal I detailed in my letters. It's been weeks, and I have yet to receive a response, hence I finally came to speak to you in person."

The Emperor touched his chin thoughtfully, then moved to the next panel.

"Hera! Queen of the gods!"

"You have, actually, read my letters?"

"General Duke, I previously expressed my position regarding merging our military forces to your superiors, General Shelby and General Price. Even as we speak, American ships prowl the gulf and work to block our ports. If war were not so fresh on their souls, I believe they would not hesitate to march against me. You understand if I am not eager to give them reason."

Maximillian's face darkened, and he stepped to the next panel.

"Your Majesty, it is European imperialism they oppose. James Monroe famously spoke to this long ago. There is no interest in further prosecuting the war between the states."

"American imperialism, then? Pedaling freedom to our poor and unwashed masses? What does America care for these people? I have brought civilization to them, an alternative to the endless juntas, freedom from corrupt warlords and would-be presidents!"

"You are a bastion of justice for the people of Mexico."

"How many could stand here as we do and look to the old gods and know their stories? Would any of them behold this wonder and recognize the face of Aphrodite?" Maximillian swung his arm in a short arc, pointing at the panel. "No, they wouldn't. They would likely smash it to pieces and grind it into cheap jewelry. They lack culture. They possess no law, no justice, and no concept of self-governance. They are savage in every way!"

"Savage or not, they are your subjects. If you wish to show them something better, you must bear the strain of conflict and survive. I see the full troop ships sailing out of Veracruz for Europe while Juárez grows in strength. Soon, France will withdraw her support altogether. You need allies."

"Do I?" His eyebrows furled like two angry caterpillars striking out at his eyes. "Will you be my friend, General Duke? How many men are left in your command, maybe one thousand? Maybe less?"

"Less every day, as your fortunes darken."

"You would know more than I. I might think more of your military pontifications if you had arrived unconquered!"

"My apologies, Your Majesty. I meant no disrespect. Only that our fates are tied to yours. Your generous allotment of land has been a godsend to my men. We love Mexico and consider her to be our home. If Juárez is restored, we will be forced to return north. As you correctly point out, many have done so already. I come to assist in any way possible to ensure your long reign. To that end, I propose assistance that does not require openly marshaling in the field."

"Hmmm." He stepped toward the next sunlit panel. "Enlighten me."

"Apologies for not being more forthcoming in my letters, I thought it prudent to discuss these matters privately. I believe France and your European coalition are abandoning you, undoubtedly under pressure from the United States. Without their support, you cannot hope to win."

"So, get to your point."

"Gold, Your Majesty."

"Do you recognize the goddess depicted in this panel, General Duke?"

"I do not."

"Not many do, she is often excluded from the pantheon of Greek mythology. Ironically, it is this exclusion, this... insult, she is most famous for."

"My apologies, sir, I am not overly familiar with Greek mythology."

"There was a great wedding on Olympus. Truly a magnificent affair to which all the gods were invited. All except Eris, due, of course, to her reputation for creating discord. Her revenge for this slight was to craft an apple of pure gold engraved with the words 'To the fairest one, which she secretly delivered to the festivities. The resulting conflict between Athena, Hera, and Aphrodite was legendary. So fierce was the fighting, Zeus appointed an impartial mortal to judge Paris, prince of Troy. The three goddesses plied him with gifts until finally, he chose Aphrodite, who had offered him the most beautiful woman in the world, Helen, wife of the king of Sparta. A thousand ships set sail to bring her back, followed by years of war and sorrow."

Maximillian turned to face Sheldon, his eyes no longer appearing dim and frivolous but rather keen and far-seeing.

"Are you my golden apple, General Duke?"

"There are many who would misrepresent their loyalty to you, I do not count myself among them. I consider myself a quick study of political landscapes, to that end, I have identified many whose allegiances are far more convoluted."

"Be clear, General."

"Many of your benefactors, so-called conservative party members, bear significant ties to American mining interests. In fact, your failure is anticipated by them, and they prepare for it. Soon, Mexican gold, silver, and copper will be streaming across your northern border to the United States, if it is not already."

Maximillian took a few steps toward the doorway at the hall's end.

"Shall we continue?"

Sheldon followed him into another short hall, then outside to a stone-railed walkway overlooking the expansive gardens.

"Grasshopper Hill. That's what this place translates to in the Aztec language. Not a very regal name. I debated renaming Peacock Hill, though regretfully, I could not secure any of those noble birds. Empress Carlota and I have an island full of them, but none seem to survive the voyage. It's a pity. I created and named that grand boulevard below us for my dear wife. The Paseo de la Emperatriz!"

From their view on the walkway, all of Mexico City stretched before them, bisected by the broad swath of the Promenade of the Empress, which terminated at the castle gates. Lush growths of eucalyptus and ahuehuete cypress covered the hillside and converged on the walls like billowy, green clouds. Meticulously manicured gardens contrasted with the wild growth beyond the wall, contained by black and white marble tile paths. The paths wound around fountains, monuments, and the statues of forgotten heroes of bygone empires. Maximillian's blending of Colonial, Mexican, and modern European designs was both extravagant and flawless. If nothing else, the Emperor had vision and style when it came to design.

"I am profoundly impressed, truly I am, though I profess a certain urgency in continuing our previous discussion."

"Gold."

"Yes, it's vital to your success here. I bring information from reliable sources that a man named Stallworth is serving as an intermediary between Juárez and the United States. Gold for weapons. I believe he has extensive operations in Parral. This is a man you are familiar with, correct?"

The Emperor scowled, his knuckles turning white as he gripped the stone railing.

"I know the man."

"In exchange for his service, Stallworth and his company will receive untold expanses of mineral rights in the Chihuahua region. A region, I might add, you recently withdrew the bulk of your army from."

"Continue, General."

"I would consider it an honor, as would my men, if you allowed us to serve the Mexican Empire by riding to Chihuahua, eliminating this insurgency, and securing these state assets, beginning with the mine at Santa Rosalia. The men who stand with me are a well-equipped and formidable fighting force, and such a task is well within our capabilities. Further, it would save you the burden of allocating your own valuable and greatly needed military resources."

Maximillian brushed his hand through the thin patch of hair where the sweat had weighed it down to his shiny scalp. His brows vacillated between anger and frustration over blue eyes that now found no pleasure in the beautiful things surrounding him.

"This would seem like wisdom, but most folly does. I will allow the expedition under the condition that it is overseen by my trusted adviser and a contingent of men of whose loyalty I am certain."

"Viva Maximillian!"

"Viva Mexico," said the Emperor.

July 13, 1866
Sierra Madre Occidental Mountains
State of Chihuahua, Mexico

The slow, discolored flow oozed out of the volcanic rock and pooled in reddish-brown puddles below the road before disappearing into the same black rock it came from. Sheldon watched with disgust as the Mexican pack masters scrambled down the shale with their tins and cups, scooping the viscous water and sopping it up with scarves and rags.

"Not thirsty?" The colonel removed the silver eagle motif cap from his water skin and drank gluttonously.

Sheldon shrugged.

The colonel never thirsted nor wanted for anything, in fact. An entire wagon, complete with a valet, served as his executive field office, filled with provisions and creature comforts. Despite seven hundred brutal miles of shoddy or nonexistent roads, treacherous mountain passes, and sun-blasted desolation, his pants were ever-pressed, and his boots never failed to shine. Sheldon resented the presence of the Prussian commander, though nothing could be done. He was Maximillian's proxy.

Prince Felix of Salm-Salm considered war his birthright, frequently recounting his glories in the famed Eleventh Husar Regiment or his exploits in the Austro-Sardinian war. Sheldon found him pedestrian and uninspiring as far as soldiers went, with his smallish head and receding hairline. The specks of his eyes sat awkwardly in the pink platter of his boyish face, overcompensated by a prodigious and ridiculously manicured mustache proudly spanning the width of his head. How such a man managed to become aide-de-camp for the Emperor was a point of bafflement for Sheldon. However, his former post as a brigadier general in the Army of the Potomac proved to be his most damning credential, providing a source of contempt between his command, the Confederates of Georgia, and the Iron Brigade.

The pack masters clawed their way back up the crumbling slope, carefully protecting the brown water. They offered it to the wagon teams and pack animals in shallow pans. Sheldon sat on his horse, the sun baking through the wool of his Imperial Mexican Army uniform. It itched and smelled of coal oil from countless louse treatments. Sergeant Wallace Reed rode beside him, sweat rolling down his cheeks and neck, darkening the stiff blue collar of his uniform.

"Water is where you find it," said the colonel, and he spurred his horse forward to the front of the column.

"Pig fucker!" Sheldon sneered.

"You would think he commanded this expedition," said Reed.

"He certainly acts like he does," said Sheldon.

Iron shoes and wagon wheels scraped over the rutted and washed-out road as the column lurched forward. Dark blemishes of turkey vultures circled the sun with spiraling prayers in an otherwise pristine sky. Sheldon and Reed rode on together.

They took the pass below Agua Puerca and followed an ox path through several canyons, skirting the feet of the mountains. At the insistence of the ever-refreshed Colonel Salm-Salm, Sheldon acquiesced to the Prussian's navigational sagacity. However, tactically, he felt the colonel's guidance lacked defensive consideration. Sheldon's eyes continuously scanned the ridge line until the column finally descended through the foothills into the open expanse of Valle de la Vacca Muerta.

The divisiveness of the company was displayed clearly in their camps. Sheldon and his sixty Confederates set their fires near an improvised stone corral built up from the ruins of an ancient presidio. The Imperial Guard, under Colonel Salm-Salm, looped their wagons to the west on the edge of an alkali flat, where the sun sank into distant blue hills. Salm-Salm's bright fires wafted the scent of roasting beef and raved with raucous, mescal-fueled song. Conversely, the Americans sat around dim coals, eating jerked pork and salted offal while coyotes whined and sulked about in the void.

"You trust that son of a bitch?" asked Reed. He leaned against his saddle and pinched tobacco into his pipe.

"I do not," said Sheldon. "But I ain't ready to go home, even if half of Carlota is. This Salm-Salm prick is no different than any other over-starched uniform. We'll make do and get the job done. Don't worry about the colonel, I've bested worse in my day."

Sheldon almost believed his own assurances.

Reed puffed on his pipe, and the cherry swelled, casting its glow on his face. His free hand absently traced through his beard, stroking it toward its point. His eyes drifted to the tiny waves of yellow flame dancing on the fire's coals.

"From where I sit, General, we're providing a service to the Emperor. This colonel goes on like we're some load of chickens he's tasked to bring to market. I don't like it, no sir."

"You're not wrong. What would you expect from a Union lickspittle?"

Reed kicked at the fire, coaxing more heat and light from the tired coals.

"Wishes be damned, it is what it is," Sheldon spat. "By my reckoning, we're about sixty or seventy miles too far west and closer to Parral than Santa Rosalia. That is if we trust Mr. Gonzales' map. I'd be happy to visit Stallworth's palacio and clean the vaults. However, the Emperor's definition of state property is not yet so broad."

"Even if we stacked the wagons up over the bows with gold, you think it would make a difference at this stage?" Reed breathed out a perfect circle of smoke that hung like a silver ring in the moonlight.

"Truthfully?"

"No, sing me a nursery rhyme," Reed chuckled.

"I doubt it," said Sheldon. "Maximillian hasn't the sand to win by his own merits, regardless of his war chest. His only hope sits with Napoleon III. If France became convinced that those mountains were made of gold, mayhap they turn those ships around and risk open war with what's left of them northern boys in blue."

"You want that?"

"Don't you?" Sheldon poked the fire, and the coals reluctantly came to life.

"My father was a candlemaker, my mother a seamstress,"

said Reed. "God-fearing people. They owned a little piece of land just outside of Savannah. When Sherman came, his bummers took everything worth a cent and burned the rest, along with the corpses of my parents. That's a wrong too tall for me to right, but I'll take whatever chance I get to try. If I must wear this louse-infested Mexican hair-shirt across Satan's half-acre for an opportunity to toss a little lead at those arrogant Union sons of bitches, I will most happily comply."

Reed puffed his pipe and stoked the cherry.

"I'm sorry for your loss." Sheldon poked at the fire again, but the ash did not glow.

"I appreciate that."

Sheldon turned up his collar against the night chill and stood over the ghost of their campfire.

"I'm turning in," he said. "Tomorrow, that double-named cocksucker better have his compass straight!"

"Goodnight, General."

"Goodnight, Sergeant."

The sun came out of the crook of two peaks like a strange fire egg birthed by an angry volcano god. Sheldon woke, shook his boots for scorpions, and stared over the salt flat at the Mexican camp. They were already hitching the teams and breaking camp. The smoke from their fires drifted across the gulf between them, carrying the scent of bacon and coffee. His stomach growled.

Colonel Salm-Salm met him partway between the camps, impeccably dressed, freshly shaven, with his mustache gloriously waxed. Sheldon stretched his neck as the man strode over the cracked earth, the dark western sky behind him.

"Good Morning, General Duke!"

"Colonel, I've been reviewing my maps, and our route seems less than optimal. Are you certain you've chosen the most direct path?"

"How very astute, General! In fact, we are taking a slightly longer passage. A late winter storm washed away the road of our preferred course, forcing us to choose an alternative. I assure you, we are quite on course for Santa Rosalia. Just across this valley and east through the pass at Dos Hermanas. We'll be descending very near the canyon."

"Very good, then," said Sheldon. "Another thing, my men, are running short on water and other provisions, is there anything you can spare from your stores?"

"Oh, I'm sorry," the colonel shook his head. "The strain has been great on my men as well. Our stocks are dangerously low. I'm certain that such a seasoned and formidable band of men as yourselves are well familiar with such hardships."

Sheldon turned his back and walked toward his camp. His men already saddling their horses and making ready.

"Fifteen minutes, General," Salm-Salm shouted after him. "Be ready!"

They crossed the alkali flats and took an ox cart trail into a range of rocky hills spotted with yucca plants and tufts of yellow grass. The wagons pitched and lurched over the uneven and crumbling terrain while climbing steadily higher. Colonel Salm-Salm and his dozen Imperial Guardsman rode two by two at the vanguard, a hundred feet in front of the lead wagon. The Americans went single file outside the wagons or brought up the rear.

The pass appeared more like a wash than any traversable passage. Smooth, round rocks peppered the path, occasionally narrowed by boulders the size of men. Sheldon doubted a return trip would be possible with gold-laden wagons unless the dead wind desired to sweep them like leaves across the mountain. In their present state, they barely managed and only with determined effort.

The back side of the pass descended between a shear mountainside to the left and a near-vertical cliff to the right. The riders fell in between the wagons so as not to plunge to certain death. After several miles of steep grade, the path softened, and the mountainside became a rocky ridgeline spotted with scrawny, dry pines. The cliff below dropped to even more treacherous depths. Sheldon tossed a small stone and counted five before it hit the canyon floor. By late afternoon, they seemed no closer to open country. He feared they might find no plausible location to camp and be forced to ride through the night.

As the sun began to slip behind the peaks, they came to a crude bridge, barely more than a couple of split pine logs, spanning a deeply washed-out section of the trail. Salm-Salm and his Imperial Guards easily crossed the bridge on horseback and continued up the subsequent rise. The colonel paused, looking down on the lead wagon as the team stopped short of the span.

Sheldon and Reed carefully passed alongside the wagons to assess the viability of the crossing. The lead pack master climbed down from his rig and looked up the rise at the colonel. He shouted something back at the next wagon in Spanish, which in turn was repeated by the other teams in sequence. The lead wagon's teamster shot a nervous glance at Sheldon before disappearing to the opposite side of his wagon. Sheldon and Reed rode to the bridge, intent on crossing over to Salm-Salm, only to find that the colonel and his men had vanished over the hill. The shouting from the column became frantic, and they turned to see the entire entourage of Mexican packers clambering up the hillside.

"What the hell..." said Reed.

Shapes of men rose from the rocks above the road, men armed with long rifles. Sheldon looked across the bridge to find the road occupied by a woman mounted on a sturdy bay roan. She rode naked to the waist and bore hideous mutilations, viciously contrasting with her otherwise feminine form. The scarred corners of her mouth pulled back in a terrifying smile that exposed her dirt-encrusted teeth. He knew her name immediately.

A cacophonous explosion erupted from the trail behind him. Wagon pieces rained down on the trail and sailed over the cliff. Two riders thrashed wildly, blown over the edge by the blast and suspended in horror above the chasm, legs churning for purchase over the abyss. A second wagon vaporized, then a third. In the chaos, the horses ran mad with fear, one team pulling its wagon over the precipice, only to detonate halfway through its plunge. The hillside erupted in rifle fire, gun smoke rolling like a cloud through the pass. Bullets pinged and reverberated through the rocks around them. Sergeant Reed wrestled with his reins as his horse made a circle and bucked wildly.

Consumed with terror, the lead wagon team charged mindlessly toward them.

"Ride!" Sheldon bellowed.

He charged across the bridge and drew his sidearm, the thunder of hooves close behind. Ahead of him were Maria Bonita and two other riders. He extended his arm and fired. Six shots squeezed out of his gun in what seemed to be a single breath. The two riders panicked at his charge, turned their horses, and galloped over the rise. Maria, with a lunatic grin, stood her ground and drew a blade as long as her forearm.

Blood sprayed up his chest and face as a bullet ripped through his mount's head, followed by awkward weightlessness. The rocks caught him hard, his momentum carrying him tumbling like dice across a deadly game board. He hadn't stopped rolling before he felt the sweaty nakedness of the deranged killer pinning him to the ground.

"Blue, like Naica," she said, holding the blade to his throat. "It must be you!"

Her words floated to him on an ocean of thunderous hooves and rifle fire, cresting in a violent tide. Reed was screaming, shots booming from his Dragoon. Smoke flowed like foam on the wave of chaos, enveloping him and the naked murderess. Complete and all-consuming silence took him, and he was lost in the swirling fire of flesh and shrapnel as the lead wagon exploded over the bridge. He tumbled with it in a tide of blood and splintered wood, coming to rest face up to the sulfur-tainted sky.

"Get up!"

The words didn't mean anything, they faded into the ringing in his ears. Maria was gone, replaced by a man and his horse standing in the sky.

"Take my hand, General!"

His face stung from the pieces of wood protruding from it. Nothing made sense. What a beautiful sunset. Why is the man screaming?

"Now!"

He took his hand but did not know why. He planted his foot on the hind of the horse, pulled himself up behind the man, and embraced him. The clouds went racing by.

FORTY-THREE

July 13, 1866
El Paso Del Norte
State Of Chihuahua, Mexico

T he venerable old church was visible from the river. Its bone-white walls and sensible angles struck out from the drab dirt hillside. A thin and modest cross of wood adorned its bell tower, advertising salvation to the seekers of Christ. Between the men of the Trust and the mission, the streets careened out from the old Spanish bridge like a drooping spider's web, lacking a distinct purpose. Sloping mud buildings popped up like mushrooms in clusters and uneven rows, interrupted by the occasional colonial-era buildings with orderly, tiled terracotta roofs and symmetrical proportions. The entirety of the city was an unappealing and arbitrary jumble of architecture. The thought occurred to Taft that the city planners were either drunkards or suffered from some terrible palsy.

They walked uphill, coursing through crooked streets washed in filth. Wild, careening hordes of rag-wrapped peasants swarmed through morning markets where merchants offered strange, stinking meats drying from sticks or laid out on rickety tables. Black corn and wormy apples lay on woven blankets with yucca, mealy lemons, and sorghum piled in woven baskets, peddled by farmers whose eyelids hung like droopy curtains. The whole town stank of nameless filth, marinated in centuries of hygienic indifference.

They paused in the shadow of a war memorial, now home

to incontinent pigeons and proud Juáristas who slung their rifles like trophies or wore them like prayers. Juárez's soldiers congregated in the small plaza with its dry fountain, drinking mescal and pulpy wine fermented from unknown fruits. The stones nearby were stained with blood where a barber employed his practice and had no qualms about removing teeth or performing other mundane medical services. His chair was a gruesome thing, tacky with blood and cut with curiously worn slots on the arms, implying the necessity for restraint. A whiskey-drunk American occupied the chair as they approached. He sat naked above the waist, one purple eye swollen shut. He sang the songs of Steven Foster while celebrating his expatriation by having a Mexican eagle tattooed across his chest.

"A fairly good rendition of a goose," remarked Collins. "Considering it's being administered with surgeon's tools!"

The barber sneered as they passed and blew a wad of snot toward their feet. He wiped his nose with his blood-stained sleeve and returned to his art.

The mission sat on a lonely and unused slope of the hill. A relic of the old empire, it had fallen from favor among the faithful who had moved on to join more wholesome congregations. The priest was said to be a Chinaman, secretly responsible for all of Chihuahua's opium trade. Whether truth or hyperbole, Taft did not know, though no devotees of the dragon lingered to offer evidence.

The heat became oppressive as they crested the hill to that detested place. As they approached the dark oak doors, an old familiar nausea came to Taft. The sick feeling when *he* worked through him when the Other would state its directives. Alphonso seldom felt such violations since dispensing of the watch, typically occurring only where gold lay in quantity or, lately, in the presence of Morya.

"Let's meet our secret celebutante," said Russell, opening the double doors. "Shall we?"

Alphonso stepped into the cool, fragrant darkness, haunted

by some strange incense. Whatever piety the place had once contained was relegated to the high-arched altar, which still housed its dusty and neglected spiritual paraphernalia. The pews sat piled in the back of the room, and the few existing windows were covered with heavy fabric or curtains. Only a high window above an ancient crucifix remained unblinded, slashing through the gloom with a single, brilliant beam of light.

Morya stood before the altar with another shorter man beside him, both in silhouette.

"Gentlemen, excellent of you to come. You will not be disappointed. Allow me to introduce my friend, General José de la Cruz Porfirio Díaz Mori."

General Díaz stepped into the square of light, his ceremonial finery constellated with gold buttons, gleaming like polished stars.

"Are these your accountants?" he asked, waiving his gold-fringed arm toward the men of the Trust.

It occurred to Alphonso that they all wore nearly identical black suits. In fact, they did resemble a ghoulish pack of bankers.

"No, my friend," laughed Morya. "These are the most powerful men in the United States. They have come to Mexico to share their power with you."

"If that is the case, perhaps I should turn my army north."

Russell stepped across the defiled church, observing the general as he walked. He ran his thumb and forefinger through his beard in contemplation.

"Judging by those muskets your so-called soldiers carry," he said, "you might want to march back in time a hundred years while you're at it."

"Guns are no match for heart." Díaz struck his chest with the heel of his palm.

"Heart is useless without a brain," said Collins.

"Yet none are a suitable replacement for friendship," Morya interjected.

Díaz stepped toward the altar.

"You seem to forget. I already have friends. Formidable allies, as you know."

"Yes, of course," Morya sighed. "Allow me to expedite our discussion and get to the point of things."

"By all means, proceed!" said the general.

"We find ourselves at a unique and serendipitous crossroads, each positioned perfectly to benefit the other. General Diaz has just been offered the prestigious position of commander of Frederick Stallworth's private army," said Morya.

"Let us be clear, it is my army, not his," interjected Diaz.

"Yes, of course," said Morya. "You, gentlemen, have been lamenting the wrongs done to you by this very same individual, have you not?"

The men of the trust listened with rigid focus.

"General Diaz, for all his strengths, lacks capital and perhaps influence. I am certain he would appreciate friends such as yourselves."

"I lack for nothing!" Said Diaz.

"Really?" Morya laughed. "Tell me you would not enjoy an infinite line of credit from the American bank of your choosing, access to the best armaments money can buy, or the endless and invaluable political connections resting at the fingertips of the Trust?"

"These are all things Mr. Stallworth has already offered, why should I choose you over him? Perhaps, I just kill you and bring him your heads. I'm certain the reward would be great."

Díaz drew the pistol from his hip and stepped back so that Morya and the Trust stood within the arc of his aim.

"Yes," said Morya. "That is one choice."

"Well?" Díaz pointed his weapon at Morya.

"It may be easier to show you rather than explain. Shoot me. Please."

"You think that I would not?" Diaz sneered.

"I'm asking that you do. Please."

"As you wish."

Díaz took careful aim at the center of Morya's face and fired from a few steps away.

Morya's skin rippled with light, exuding a golden-red corona. The depth of matter that composed his presence became flux with an otherworldly quality. No trace of the bullet penetrated the space where he stood, and the report of the weapon faded like a scream in the darkness. Díaz fired repeatedly, taking careful aim between shots, edging closer until the pistol barrel was inches from Morya's forehead. Díaz kept firing as the gun clicked on empty chambers, his bullets lost to the void of Morya.

"May I continue?" Morya asked.

Díaz searched the wall of the church for traces of bullet damage and double-checked his chambers for some evidence of misfire. He found neither.

"As your eyes have surmised and your mind is undoubtedly processing, we are no ordinary collection of accountants."

Díaz stood slack-jawed and silent. His pistol dangled from a single finger like a useless tassel or a broken ornament.

"We haven't come to suggest a partnership or some banal business arrangement." Morya's flesh continued to pulse with its strange interdimensional fluctuations. "This is an invitation to become something more than human, to join us in a timeless endeavor."

"I don't understand, what does that mean?"

"It means, Porfirio, never being alone," said Morya.

Alphonso cringed. For forty years, his only conscious desire was to be alone, away from the ticking darkness. Agonizing months and two thousand miles had passed since New Haven, where Morya poured out the contents of his life like some sack of vile and vexing objects. Exposed to his peers, he waited for consequence, salvation, anything. Even his secret postman had forsaken him until Morya's irrefutable summons. Now, in a nameless and desecrated church, at the forgotten altar of an indifferent god, no time or miles remained between himself and judgment.

He could only believe that the ascension of Díaz into their covenant implied his own expulsion. It was an event that was certain to come with maximum prejudice, payment in full for his hubris and treachery. Images of dark and hitherto unknown rites fluttered through his imagination, for such a wretched task necessitated some diabolic protocol. He looked to the crooked wooden cross and the square beam of sunlight and despaired at the futility of prayer. The mercy of a simple death, a lonely and extinguishing step into oblivion, was all he hoped for, but Morya's words haunted him. *It means never being alone.* Never was a long time.

"I'm listening," said Díaz.

Russell and Collins stepped closer to the altar while Taft stood in the middle of the pew-cleared church with his head bowed.

"What if I told you that Cibola is real and many other things besides?" Morya reached into his jacket pocket. "We can show you these things; all you need to begin is this."

Alphonso lifted his head to face his fate. He looked to Morya, expecting to witness Díaz being offered his long-forsaken and despised gold pocket watch. But, instead, Morya's hand contained something else, a small, roughly cast and pitted gold cross. There at the precipice of the abyss, he was denied destruction. Instead, he was filled with the rotting warmth of the dead wind, mercilessly blowing over the raw and severed tendrils where the other lay sleeping. In that hollow place, he heard its terrible ticking, counting down to an inevitable reckoning.

"This once belonged to Francisco Vázquez de Coronado y Luján. I now offer it to you."

"Coronado," Díaz murmured as he reached for the cross.

Morya's long dark fingers closed around it.

"This is more than a piece of gold. Accepting it is accepting your place among us."

"More?"

"It is a seed," said Collins.

Morya's fingers unfolded like spider legs. The cross lay in the black of his palm, alive with luster.

"I accept."

Díaz delicately lifted it from his hand as Taft turned away, trembling.

"Shall I kill him for you then?"

"Stallworth? No," said Morya.

"What then?"

"When the time comes, do absolutely nothing."

July 15, 1866
Hidalgo Del Parral
State Of Chihuahua, Mexico

Stallworth did not come to the balcony. The tradition, begun in distrust and carried on habitually, was now broken. Maria preferred to negotiate this way, with her assembled killers' protection and full diplomatic transparency. She could only opine that her failure to secure the head of the American general was the cause for this breach of protocol. Now the door to the mansion was open, the luminous splendor visible within, radiating its invitation.

An invisible army of crickets sawed mindlessly to the misshapen moon, haunting the sky like a bleached and broken skull. Maria came off her horse and handed the reins to the killer at her side. She pulled the layers of scarf from her face and tossed it over her saddle, looking out past the gate to the dozens of riders lingering in the shadows along the road and river.

"If I don't come out," she said, "burn it."

Maria stopped by the fountain before approaching the

house. With cupped hands, she scooped water into her damaged mouth. Brown streams rolled down her chin and onto her thin cotton shirt. With her index finger, she scrubbed her front teeth and spit into the fountain. Satisfied with her hygiene, she strode to the open front door and into the shimmering light.

Crystal chandeliers, candles, and sconces blazed in every room of Casa Stallworth. Servants appeared from adjacent rooms to escort her, leading her down a long hall adorned with portraits, presumably of the Stallworth clan. The corridor intersected another short hall that was bisected by a grand staircase. The mystery of where Stallworth secured his gold was at least partially answered by the massive iron gate that blocked the lower flight of stairs and the heavy steel doors that lurked beyond.

Maria's tour ended in the lavish reaches of Stallworth's formal dining room. Though the table was fit to serve her entire band, only three settings were present on the vast plane of embroidered linen. Stallworth sat at the head of the table, dressed in a fine black suit with a billowy pink tie. His beard was freshly trimmed, and his hair neatly secured with pomade. A young general sat directly to his right, attired in his ceremonial finery. He had cruel, hawkish brown eyes that were in no way softened by his gallant mustache and goatee. His body was thin and ridged, poised like a vicious weasel or badger. Maria recognized the man immediately as Porfirio Díaz.

"Welcome, Maria." Stallworth raised a crystal goblet of dark red wine in her direction. "Join us, please."

A servant pulled out her chair for her, guiding her to Stallworth's left and directly across from General Díaz. Maria drew her hair back from her shoulders, securing it in a loose knot, and removed her Bowie knife from her side, laying it across the setting of formal flatware. The servant waited stoically for her to sit before pushing in her chair behind her.

"You look like you want to fuck." Her eyes were fixed on the general. "Is that true?"

General Díaz curled his lips in the slightest smile.

"Well, don't look in this direction. I don't fuck rodents," she said and spread her napkin across her lap.

"Maria, are you acquainted with the esteemed general?"

"I choose not to associate with such base individuals."

She plucked a roll from a silver basket. Beside her, a servant filled her glass with wine.

"Ah, such eloquent praise, like pearls falling from the lips of the queen of murderers," said General Díaz. "Or, should I say, from the lip?"

The scarred corners of her mouth turned into a begrudging smile before her teeth ripped into the crust of the dinner roll. Stallworth observed the exchange, a gleeful voyeur to their contempt.

"How long have we been friends, Maria?" asked Stallworth. "Three years? Maybe more?"

"In such matters, I can only count as far as the last bag of silver. You understand, friend. Currently, my memory is foggy on this subject, it's been a long time since I counted any silver."

"I do not envy you, Mr. Stallworth," said the General. "Such fickle friendships must be the source of great uncertainty in these dark times. I could not bear the strain of such doubts. Thankfully, our friendship is built upon a rock of truth and mutual respect."

Maria ignored Díaz, her attention solely devoted to Frederick Stallworth.

"The world is changing," said Stallworth. "A new age is called to order. No longer will savage winds blow across these brutal lands. Civilization will prevail. We will all have to learn to change with it, to adapt. Even you, Maria."

"And in these turbulent times, I am going to need friends." She took half the glass of wine in one gulp. Grains of dirt washed to the bottom of the glass. "Friends like you, is that right?"

"Precisely."

Three servants moved behind Stallworth and his guests, delivering roasted tomato bisque with clock-like synchronicity. The bowls were shallow and wide, with delicate blue floral patterns around the bone-white lip. Stallworth sat with his head slightly tilted as if anticipating further acknowledgment of the subject.

Maria ignored the spoon under her blade, lifted the bowl, and tilted it toward her mouth, slurping the soup as it flowed over the edge. It ran from the hole of her mouth, down her chin and splashed on the tablecloth. Her exposed front teeth glistened with grit and blood-red tomato pulp.

"I killed many Americans for you, friend."

"Yes, but you did not kill *the* American! It's a crucial distinction."

"You call for scalps and heads, and I'm the savage?"

General Díaz chuckled as he spooned soup into his mouth.

"His head was the only relevant detail that you either ignored or were incapable of achieving!" Stallworth slammed his spoon on the table with an unimpressive clank.

Maria sopped the remaining soup with her roll and pushed the bowl away. She washed it down with wine and gestured to the servant. Silently, he refilled her glass.

"I am a forgiving man, a benevolent man, a man that recognizes the value of friendship," said Stallworth. "I'm going to allow you to rectify your mistakes, to mend the broken fibers of our relationship."

She drank deep from the crystal glass, suppressed a belch, then killed the remaining wine.

"So, what you're about to suggest is an opportunity to provide friendship without receiving friendship. I cannot say that such an opportunity appeals to me. No, I think it would be best if I considered our future friendship while I counted silver. Perhaps such reminiscences might lead to a more favorable and fortuitous future for both of us."

"Ah, such gratitude," said Díaz. "I can't imagine how you've managed."

Stallworth's gaze trailed down the length of the table, passing over the silver settings and service. He stroked his beard with his thumb and forefinger for a moment before breaking his own trance by snapping his fingers. The domo came to his side, and he whispered instructions in his ear.

"You're right, Maria," said Stallworth. "You're right." He raised his glass to her with a sigh, "To your health!"

"Salut!" said Díaz, joining the toast.

Maria tilted her empty glass.

Two servants appeared at the far end of the hall carrying heavy canvas sacks in each hand. Stallworth smiled a serpent smile and gestured toward the men.

"Shall I have them secure it to your mount?"

"I will go with them."

She crumbled her napkin on the table and rose from her seat.

"And miss the main course? No, please stay!"

Maria ignored his invitation, secured her knife, and joined the men with the silver.

"Fuck yourself!" she said as she passed through the door, the servants following behind with the jangling sacks.

"It's a cold world," Stallworth called after her. "You will not stay warm by the fires of your burning bridges!"

FORTY-FOUR

July 16, 1866
Chapultepec Castle, Mexico City

"**I** bet it was that wall," said Pedro. "It looks to be the tallest."

"What about it?" said Reavis.

Pedro stepped to the rail and leaned over, rising on his tiptoes. The effort was futile as he could not see beyond the castle wall from his vantage on the second-floor walk. His attention was soon seized by a winged profile washed in the sun's brilliance.

"Look!" he said. "Ha! A sign! It was there, I'm sure of it!"

"You're raving."

"That's an eagle!"

"Still raving. Care to clarify your ramblings?"

"That is the wall that Juan Escutia leaped from, draped in the flag of Mexico. It was an act of incredible bravery."

"Bravery?"

"He would rather die than let the flag fall into the hands of the Americans, he was a hero!"

"Wouldn't a hero have won the battle?"

Pedro shook his head and looked down to the black and white checkered tiles of the terrace.

"Do you believe the men who died at the Alamo were heroes?"

"No, they're dead," said Reavis.

"Bahhh!"

Reavis smirked and turned his head back toward the tall

glass doors of the castle. Inside, the servants rushed up and down a long hallway, urgently engaged in undisclosed tasks. Concerned that he and Pedro may have been forgotten, he walked to the door and tapped on the glass. Two men carrying a steamer trunk turned in unison. One of them acknowledged him with a nod before returning to their task.

"I don't like this," said Reavis.

"I am accustomed to disappointment. Count yourself among the privileged to be fed shit straight from the horse's ass. An audience with the emperor is a rare honor."

"At least the view is remarkable."

"On that, we agree," said Pedro.

Reavis returned to the rail and gazed over the gardens and the distant Caballero Alto. Near the main gate, wagon teams jockeyed in the courtyard, positioning to be loaded. Argumentative shouts and demands were exchanged in Spanish, though Reavis could not interpret what was being said.

The tall doors opened, and one of the servants beckoned them to enter.

"Sígueme," he said.

The man ushered them across the hallway into a garishly designed antechamber and closed the door behind them. Reavis took off his jacket and draped it over the back of a deep blue velvet chair. Pedro toured the room with his eyes, admiring the gold leaf molding and paneling. He ran his fingers over the blue and gold motif of the wallpaper, and his eyes widened with each fantastic object he discovered.

For all its opulence, the room was in considerable disarray. The purpose of the chamber was likely meant as a lobby or sitting room, but it was stacked with items that clearly did not belong. Among them were folded linen and several boxes in various stages of being packed. An oak writing desk at the far end of the room made a strange altar. A piece of velvet had been laid across the top, on which was a large gold crucifix, a silver inlaid jewelry box, a portrait of Maximillian in Mexican military garb, and a delicate, jewel-encrusted crown.

The second door to the room opened, revealing a larger suite that appeared to be a private office. This room was in greater distress than the first, lacking any semblance of order. Standing in the doorway was a pale-skinned woman of striking beauty, her dark hair curled neatly in a bun and secured with gold hairpins and black lace. Her dress was simple black silk with a modest bustle and subtle flourish around the shoulders. She stood motionless, her golden-brown eyes like the sad pistils of a human lily.

"Secretary Reagan," she said in lightly accented English. "Thank you so much for coming, I am Carlota."

Reavis and Pedro bowed.

"Your Majesty," they said in tandem.

"I do not know your companion," she said.

"Pedro is my secretary."

She smiled and nodded, stepping into the antechamber.

"I apologize, gentlemen, for the circumstances in which we meet. My husband deeply regrets his absence. Unfortunately, pressing military obligations necessitate that I act in his place. As you can see, you have arrived at a time of some chaos."

Unsettled by her grace and beauty, Reavis searched his mind for something clever to say.

"Thank you," he managed.

"Secretary Reagan, again, I apologize, for I am also obligated elsewhere. As you find me, I am preparing for my own diplomatic assignment. I leave for France in two days." She stepped forward into the room, locking eye contact with Reavis. "It is with deep sorrow that I must report to you the death of General Duke and his entire expedition."

"No, tell me there is some mistake?"

"I'm afraid that it is true," said Carlota, taking Reavis' hand and squeezing it between her delicate fingers. "Colonel Felix of Salm-Salm, aide-de-camp to my husband, barely escaped with his life. He reports that the Americans gave a fine account of themselves, but they were hopelessly outnumbered by Juárez's soldiers."

"Who is this Sam Sam? I would very much like to speak to him!"

"That is not possible, he left this morning with the emperor."

Pedro once described to Reavis the feeling he experienced emerging from his incarceration at the cathedral, how the world became so immense and terrifyingly bright. As he absorbed Carlota's words, he began to understand how Pedro must have felt. Freedom was at hand and honorably won. He had kept his word to Robert Black and fulfilled his service to the enigmatic Samuel Sheldon. Every tether between himself and this insanity was now severed. He looked down at the tiny pale hands embracing his own, observing the genuine empathy of the Empresses. He wanted to embrace and kiss Carlota, not in any romantic overture, but out of pure relief and joy.

Carlota released his hand. She retrieved a rolled document from the desk drawer and presented it to Reavis.

"My husband had this drafted and instructed me to deliver it to you."

Reavis took the document and broke the seal.

"That writ will release your gold and valuables secured in our vaults in the city. We can no longer offer you protection in the colonies. We recommend you return to the safety of the United States at your earliest convenience. If you hurry, you may be able to charter a ship from Veracruz before the American blockade is permanent."

Reavis examined the document. It was written and signed in the emperor's own hand and bore his official stamp. His mind was a maelstrom of thoughts.

"Is the war going so poorly?"

"My husband would claim otherwise, but candidly? Believe me when I say the situation is dire."

"You're pulling out of Mexico City, aren't you?"

Carlota did not answer at first, her lips betraying a subtle frown.

"I know this is a great burden to place upon you, my deepest sympathies," she said. "Regretfully, I must return to my preparations. Take as much time as you need to collect your thoughts."

"Thank you, Your Majesty," said Reavis.

Carlota exited through the door that they had entered. Immediately, she began issuing orders in Spanish to the servants, her voice fading down the hallway.

"This is terrible news," said Pedro.

"For who?" Reavis smiled.

"I don't understand."

Reavis stood staring into the document, analyzing the pen strokes. His eyes were portals to the inner machinations, spinning like clock gears in his head. A culminating epiphany came over him as he returned the document to its rolled form.

"What is it?" said Pedro.

"General Price and the governors have fled the Juáristas, and General Duke is dead."

"Sí ."

"I am the highest-ranking active officer of the Confederate States. I'm President!"

"If you say so," sighed Pedro.

"Not bad for a deserter! Pedro, there's a lot of work to do. I will stay in Mexico City and handle arrangements here. I need you to carry the news to the colony and rally as many as are willing. We are riding north! Tell them to bring as many wagons, horses, and provisions as can be mustered."

"This will take time. These men, they are scattered across the valley!"

"Do what you can, enlist the others to help. Make this happen, and I promise I will help you find your daughter."

"Why would they follow me?"

"Well, they can stay and fight Juárez or return home rich men. Just present those options. I'll be at the Grand Hotel."

"I will do my best, Mr. President, sir," laughed Pedro.

He stepped out into the hallway and stood admiring Chapultepec's lavish décor and architecture while Reavis retrieved his jacket from the velvet chair and tucked the writ into its inner pocket.

"I know this isn't very presidential," Reavis said, folding the jeweled crown, golden crucifix, and jewelry box into his jacket. "My apologies."

July 1866
Hembrillo Basin, New Mexico Territory

Loco was right. Victory against the White Eyes could not be won in battle. War was in their hearts, and they came eagerly to the fight, thirsty for vengeance. No sooner had they finished the war with themselves than they turned their rage toward the Indeh. With the names of Cochise, Victorio, and Juh, on their lips, soldiers came by the hundreds to the hills and mountains, eager to have their war.

Once as plentiful as the sky, the yellow metal now eluded them. More often, their raids produced only lead and blood. They stacked countless heaps of it in the Tiny Mountain, though it did nothing to abate the tide of settlers, prospectors, and soldiers. The Chiricahua were exhausted from this war, and all agreed it was time to end.

Cochise rode to the west and the safety of his stronghold in the Dragoons. Concealed in the fortress of treacherous peaks and secret valleys, his people would be safe indefinitely. Loco returned to Ojo Caliente to live peacefully with the whites, a dubious prospect among the other Chiricahua. Still, many weary of conflict chose to join him.

Victorio and his band traveled with Juh and his warriors,

eager to return to his stronghold in the Blue Mountains. Like Cochise, he trusted the natural fortifications that had kept his people safe for generations. Juh hoped Victorio would accept his invitation to stay with him on the high mesa, where their united forces might keep the Mexicans and the White Eyes away.

For Victorio, the dreams became worse, visiting him nightly. He confided only with Nana, telling him of the Yellow Painted Man's curse upon him. In his dreams, the further he went from the mountain, the heavier his legs became until he could only crawl. When he could crawl no more, a strong wind or heavy rain would come and carry him back to the peak.

"It is not done," Victorio told Nana.

"We are done with it," Nana replied.

"I will leave this place and gladly die before I return, but it is not done."

FORTY-FIVE

July 30, 1866
State Of Chihuahua, Mexico

G ray smoke trailed up in thin columns against the
shifting blue gradient of the sunrise, and tiny pricks
of firelight twinkled like dim stars in the shady smear of the
town perched on the horizon. Seventeen wagons stretched the
road, stacked to ridiculous heights with crates, chests, barrels,
and literally anything capable of hauling gold. Loaded beyond
reason, the wagons did not creak or groan, nor did the horses
strain at their burden.

"This road will take us through Santa Barbara," said Pedro.
"It's a bad place, and bad men live there. We should go around."

"Is it a good route?" asked Reavis.

"For travel? Yes. For safety? Not so much."

The two rode together, next to the lead wagon, on a smaller
trail parallel to the main wagon road. They were eleven days
out from Mexico City, and Pedro could not remember the last
time they ate or slept. The favor of the dead wind carried
them, crossing the tall, grassy mesas of Durango, through high
forests of oak and pine, skirting the dry and foreboding Bolsón
de Mapimí. The horses did not thirst, the men did not hunger,
and all rest had been forsaken. They were as ghosts, passing
beyond all meaningful human contact, like some Flying
Dutchman of the desert wastelands.

Life had always been a scale for Pedro, and this strange
journey was nothing but more ballast. The man who called

himself John Reagan was a grifter and thief. He held no claim to any office, let alone president. Why the seventy-five men in the company were oblivious to this baffled him. Still, the man had honored his promises and brought him closer to the trail of Donna Sophia and, in the process, earned his friendship.

"What kind of men live in that town?"

"Bad ones," said Pedro.

"Yes, you said that! Bandits? Soldiers? Juaristas? Something else?"

"Yes, and worse."

"You're hopeless!"

The sun fully hatched over the horizon, causing them to squint and hold their palms against the blaze. Santa Barbara was lost in the glare where the road stretched into mirage. As their eyes adjusted, two long black shadows stretched westward, like a pair of giants striding toward them. Pedro pulled a spyglass from his saddle bag and trained it on the men.

"You're not going to believe this."

"What is it?"

"It's your friend, the general."

"It can't be!"

Reavis snatched the glass and aimed it toward the men.

The light went out of Reavis, the man claiming to be John Reagan. Whatever grandeur his artificial mantle of power and freedom provided withdrew from his soul like water turned to vapor. Pedro was not immune to the mystery of the dead wind; he felt it filling their sails and saw its power painted in the dread on Reavis' face. Whatever the nature of this power, it possessed both will and mind, and it had led them to that very place at that very time.

Sheldon and Reed stood like disheveled beggars in the road, smiling like idiots as Reavis and Pedro spurred their horses. Their uniforms were torn and stained with blood and all manner of filth. Sheldon was hatless, with torn fabric bandaging his wounded head.

"They told me you were dead!" Reavis called out, halting his horse.

"Sorry to disappoint them," said Sheldon.

"It was that dandy Prussian Colonel, Salm-Salm," said Sergeant Reed. "He sold us out to that mangled witch!"

"If he did so, it was without the emperor's consent," said Reavis. "Otherwise, I doubt he would have treated the rest of us with such kindness nor released the gold from his vaults."

Sheldon looked to the approaching wagons, counting them in his head. A puzzled look crossed his face.

"Why so many wagons, so heavily laden?"

"Ah... about that..." Reavis stuttered. "I may have made some altercations to the bank document and... Well, I... We might have acquired some of Maximillian's gold as well."

As the wagons got closer, Sheldon counted them with astonishment.

"How much of Maximillian's gold?"

"All of it."

A smile widened on Sheldon's face, "Well done, Secretary Reagan, well done!"

"You defrauded a foreign government?" asked Reed.

"I prefer to say that I renegotiated the interest rates on our deposit."

The Sergeant frowned.

Samuel Sheldon stood in wonder. The design of his secret architect had been revealed. He required no further evidence. His reward had come, and the golden tree was in bloom. Years away from his family, the murkiness of purpose, the tedium of his charade as General Duke, in the end, it was all justified. His mission was a success. If only Collins were here to see it.

"You've done well, John," said Sheldon. "There's a town up ahead, it's practically abandoned. We can hold up there long enough to plan our next move."

"Pedro said it's full of bad men," Reavis said, looking side-eyed at Pedro.

"It may have been, but something happened there. The shops are all closed, some buildings are burned, and the streets are empty. Reed and I have been sneaking in at night to steal water and food."

The lead wagon reached them and came to a halt. Cheers went up among the remaining Confederates at the sight of Sergeant Reed and General Duke. Reed hopped up on the wagon and exchanged a hearty handshake with one of his men.

Pedro dismounted his horse and handed the reins to Sheldon.

"I'll ride the wagon for a while, General." He chuckled, "I'm sure you and El Presidente have much to discuss."

Sheldon and Reavis rode out ahead, and the wagons began to roll. He recounted his ill-fated expedition to Santa Rosalia and the treachery of Salm-Salm. Since the attack, they had been hiding in the mountains and foothills, evading bands of Maria's men. Three days earlier, they came out of the mountains and found the town.

"We saw the wagons across the flat, and I knew," said Sheldon.

"I believe you. I think you could suss out a gold tooth if it sank in a lake! There's something I forgot to tell you. This was waiting at the bank." He reached into his shirt pocket and retrieved a small envelope.

"It's opened."

"I thought you were dead!"

Sheldon opened the letter. It bore no signature, only the words El Paso del Norte.

"Listen, Mr. Sheldon, if that letter is from Robert Black, I don't want to go. You hear me? I've done more than my share for whatever dark business the two of you are up to. That man scares the hell out of me, and I'd just as soon stay here if it's all the same to you."

"Well, sir," Sheldon smiled. "If the South is to rise again, it will need its President!"

"Look, I barely held this thing together. To be honest, I'm mystified why these men haven't slit my throat and split up this trove! Talk among the men is to meet up with Shelby in Missouri, maybe start some sort of resistance to the occupation there."

"Where have you been leading them?"

"I told them I knew a place in Arizona where we could safely stash the gold, then we could figure it out from there. I might have told them I intended to build a castle out of it. It wouldn't have mattered as long as we had the wind at our backs. It's evil, you know that. It fucks with their minds. It's fucked with mine. We don't eat or sleep, and neither do the horses. Just like when we left Georgia. I can't do it anymore, Sheldon, I can't."

"I asked you once to warn me when you saw the gates of Hell swinging on the horizon. Is that time now?"

"I don't know about that. I sure hope not. But I can't anymore. That's all I know."

"Get me into Texas, and that will do, James."

"Thank you, Sam. I mean that. Thank you."

A dozen men rode into Santa Barbara with Sheldon ahead of the wagons. They found the main street running through the center of the settlement entirely unpopulated, apart from a three-legged dog that came lobbing out of the livery to growl and bark along after them. Low adobe buildings with terracotta roofs lined the street and housed most of the town's businesses. Many bore signs of violence; kicked in doors, broken windows, and, in some cases, fire. Pitted craters speckled the stucco where bullets had left their mark. The columns of smoke, at first mistaken as chimneys or cookfires, snaked skyward from the ruins of shanties on the town's northern edge. The structures, mainly constructed of wood and scrap, were densely packed and thus consumed en masse.

To the west, a colonial-age monastery loomed behind tall stone walls. The sprawling complex's central feature was a white brick church topped with twin spires, standing free on a hillock. On top of the towers, Sheldon observed the first human residents of Santa Barbara, eight or ten children, and a black-frocked priest. The young ones hid when Sheldon waved up to them. He turned his column west and stopped before the chained iron gates.

"Hello up there!" Sheldon yelled in English.

"Go away!" the priest shouted back.

"Come down here, please! I only want to talk. We mean no harm!"

The priest shook his head.

Sheldon dismounted and approached the gate. Beyond it lay an open courtyard, broken only by a dry fountain guarded by a one-armed statue of Saint Francis.

"Oh, this is perfect!"

"Leave now!" yelled the priest. "You are not welcome!"

"I'm coming in, don't be afraid!"

Sheldon drew his pistol and shot the lock off the gate. The priest yelled something further that was lost in the creaking of the iron hinges.

Sheldon sent a runner to guide the wagons back to the monastery, the others rode in and hitched their horses. After securing the mounts, they began investigating the other buildings. In the fountain basin, Sheldon found the missing arm of the saint, a broken bird on its stone sleeve.

"Put it down!" demanded the priest as he burst from the church door. "Go away with your men! We have suffered enough!"

The wind changed as the agitated priest carried on with his dissenting tirade. It came out of the north, bringing the scent of the burnt slum. It was an unwholesome aroma, sickly and sweet, a foulness reminiscent of a cauldron Sheldon had once tended after robbing a grave. The fate of the absent population became more apparent.

He carefully laid the saint's arm back in the basin and stepped out of the fountain toward the advancing acolyte.

"Easy, Padre, we won't be long. Less than a day."

"Putos pendejos Americanos blancos!" blurted the priest, who then quickly crossed himself in exasperation. "El mundo esta lleno de asesinos."

"Excuse me?" Sheldon did not comprehend the words of the priest.

Several tiny faces crowded in the shadow of the church door. Sheldon waved calmly at them, causing them to dart back into the darkness.

The agitation of the priest became increasingly frantic. He waved at the children to stay inside while slowly backing away from Sheldon.

"Killers! You're all killers!" he shouted as he retreated to the church, slamming the door behind him and setting the heavy bolt.

The wagons began to roll into the compound. They circled the fountain, reaching their assigned spaces under the expert direction of the red-haired Lieutenant Abbot. He started unhitching the teams and leading them to feed and water in an improvised corral. Sheldon ordered sentries on the wall and outside the church and set up a temporary command post in a small administrative building. They would wait out the night and devise a plan in the morning.

It had been weeks since he slept in a real bed, and the straw-stuffed sack he laid on felt like a feather mattress. Within moments, he was asleep.

Sheldon felt the blade at his neck before he heard the words, "Do not call out."

His eyes blinked open to reveal Maria Bonita perched over him, naked like polished wood in the candlelight. Her long black hair was loosely braided, hanging like a thick snake over her shoulder.

"To think, after everything, I find you here!"

Her words hissed through her lipless teeth. Her body came down lightly so that her knees pinned his arms to the mattress. She reached between her legs with her free hand, deftly undoing Sheldon's belt buckle. His eyes widened, both startled and concerned.

"Do what you came to do," whispered Sheldon. "It will not end well for you, I promise you."

"No, this is not the end." She pulled his cock out of his pants. "This is where we begin."

His muscles tensed, and her weight shifted effortlessly to compensate.

"I came to this town, this pit of scum and depravity; I darkened every door looking for you. None would confess, so I heaped their bodies like trash." Her hand squeezed and tugged at him while she spoke. "I left them burning so God might smell them rising to Heaven."

"You killed these people, looking for me? You should have killed me when you had the chance."

"Ah, that is the problem." Her hand moved faster, succeeding in its intent. "My former employer would agree. Now he has found another army to do the job. He must truly hate you."

Sheldon squirmed and bucked his hips, causing the blade to cut into his flesh. Thin, warm streams of blood flowed through the week's old stubble and down to his chest. Maria's eyes flashed a fatal warning, and he made himself still.

"I knew when I saw you, just as the Lady of Bone foretold." She took him inside, working her hips and thighs like a python strangling its meal. "Of course, I could not kill you!"

Her scared chest moved with the tide of her breath, gently whistling through her gritty teeth.

Sheldon lay in a paralytic state of erotic horror. Candlelight writhed across the blade and flickered in the slate of her eyes. Somewhere in the town, the three-legged dog voiced his lamentations at the sickle moon.

"What?" he managed.

"She knows what you are, and so do I!" she growled. Her wetness was spreading. "Beneath your skin, I see your master!"

She leaned in close, allowing her sex to systematically grind downward. A tendril of drool descended like spider silk from her damaged lips.

"Our gods are violent ones."

"You're mad!" he grunted.

Blood flooded from beneath the blade, down his neck to the straw mattress. The tension built in his body, and it occurred to him that his virginity had been stolen. He hadn't prized his chastity; in fact, it existed because of his own indifference. Now that it was gone, he found the indifference remained, tainted only by anger at the audacity of its theft.

"My golden sapling!" Her body contracted around him as he climaxed as if to extract every drop. Sweat dripped from her nose, splashing on his cheek. She smiled, her face bearing a deranged skeletal countenance.

"*Like a seed...*" Sheldon repeated the words once spoken to him by Thomas Rogers.

"I have a gift from my saint to yours. You will do this."

She put her mouth against his ear and nibbled. The softness of her perfect lower lip pressed his lobe into the dirt-stained upper teeth, then she whispered her secret.

"How do I know this isn't some trap?"

He felt her convulse with laughter from inside.

"You're still breathing!"

She lifted her hips, and he slid out of her, soft and useless like a drowned slug.

"Be there before sunrise, he will be unguarded. As we speak, Díaz is preparing to ambush my men. It will not be an evening he soon forgets!"

The blade vanished from his neck, and he heard the soft pad of her feet as she leaped backward from the bed to the hard-packed earthen floor. For a moment, she paused at the window, her lithe silhouette framed against the starlight.

"Tell me I'm beautiful."

"You're..." he started, but she was gone. "Insane."

Sheldon quickly stepped into his trousers and out of his quarters into the darkness of the compound. His sentries were in place, the wagons accounted for, and nothing was a miss. He sent for Abbot and Reed.

A plan was conceived.

Two hours later, he passed under the abandoned fort at Cerro de la Cruz with twenty-five heavily armed soldiers of the Iron Brigade, including Abraham Abbot. They crossed the river unimpeded and rode along the path that led to Stallworth's mansion. If there were witnesses, they stayed sensibly concealed, shuttered in darkened houses.

Their horses' iron shoes rang out against the cobblestones and echoed along the riverfront. A light blinked on in an upper window of the mansion, then another. A shadow moved in the balcony apartment as the glow spread. Finally, the French doors opened, and Stallworth stepped out on the terrace.

Sheldon rode ahead, stopping before the fountain.

"Good evening to you!" Sheldon tipped an invisible hat.

"So, you're the pigfucker!"

"I suppose that's a matter of perspective."

"You know I'll hunt you down to the ends of this earth. You cannot conceive of the horrors I will lay on you."

"Bold talk for a man standing at the end of his days."

Stallworth leaned on the stone railing and looked down at Sheldon and the Iron Brigade. They were dressed in commoners' clothes, bearing no signs of allegiance. His majordomo stepped up beside him, brandishing a double-barreled shotgun. Stallworth said something quietly to the man, and he lowered the weapon.

"You're not going to kill me, Captain."

Stallworth tossed down an iron key ring.

"General, actually." Sheldon scooped the ring with his cavalry sword.

"Is it, though?" he chuckled.

A shadow crossed Sheldon's heart. Stallworth smiled at him smugly, wrapped in his silk smoking jacket and angora slippers.

"What's he prattling on about?" asked Abbot.

"I hope you brought enough wagons! Also, try not to track any dirt through the house," Stallworth said before returning to his apartment, the majordomo closing the doors behind him.

"What the hell?" Abbot was mystified. "He's just going to give it to us?"

"He thinks his men will run us down, take it back," said Sheldon. "He's going to be disappointed."

The approaching wagons crossed the river bridge, the clacking of the wooden wheels echoing down the river. Somewhere in the shadows, a stray dog's rebuke harangued them. Sheldon wondered if it was missing a leg.

"Let's get to it!"

He tossed the keys to Abbot, who led the first men into the Stallworth house. Sheldon took the opportunity to relieve himself in the fountain while he waited for the wagons to arrive.

The night passed like a peyote dream as the cold blade of the moon reaped the field of stars. They stacked the six wagons full of gold bullion and several heavy sacks of silver in assorted specie. Stallworth remained in his chambers, and his staff stayed hidden, nor were they interrupted by other interlopers. Dawn found them a mile west of Parral, watching the sun rise right out of the town. They turned north at Santa Barbara, where the rest of the wagons were already prepared for departure and waiting on the road for them. Sergeant Reed was the first to greet him and shake his hand.

Twenty-three wagons took the road north, sailing under the steady current of the dead wind. It was as if they stood still, and the world traveled through them. Hills and valleys passed effortlessly like painted landscapes on a theater canvas. They went in a haze of half-light and shade, where even the sun was afraid to look at them.

It was sunset when they came to the strangely sloping town of Naica. An army of saguaro stood in sentinel, their shadowy arms stretching morbidly in crooked prayer. Sheldon stopped the lead wagon and removed the sacks of silver Spanish and Mexican coins, stacking them by the dilapidated, broken wall.

He pinned a small note to one of the bulging sacks that read, "Because you're beautiful."

FORTY-SIX

August 1866
Big Burro Mountains, New Mexico Territory

O n the third day after the council at Tiny Mountain, the skies blackened. Rain was coming. The Apache kept to the high ground and avoided the washes and arroyos while looking for a place to shelter. Recently, the monsoon season had produced several haboobs, including a blinding storm of dirt and sand on the day they left the Tiny Mountain, but very little rain. The wind whipped over the ridgeline and whistled through the rocks. The storm was imminent.

"We should make for the pines across the valley," said Geronimo.

Juh nodded.

"It is too far," said Victorio. "If the storm comes, we may get caught in the wash. We have small children. They may be lost."

"We cannot stay here," Juh said with deliberation so as not to aggravate his stuttering.

"We might go down the western valley, but the road there is well traveled by soldiers." Victorio pointed his rifle.

"I do not fear the soldiers," said Geronimo.

"We have many women and children," Victorio repeated. "We should not look for a fight."

"If there are no soldiers," Juh said, peering into the distance, "it would be safe."

Three hundred Apache stretched across the length of the vast, rocky ridge. They traveled light, with few skins and without horses, carrying only enough food to preserve them until the next storage cache. They crouched among the boulders and waited.

"I say we go west," said Geronimo.

Juh tilted his head and considered the roiling clouds.

"West," he agreed.

"Where is Lozen?" Nana scanned the line of Apache on the ridge.

"Yes, my sister will know if the enemy is near."

Nana turned up the mountain and sought out Lozen. He found her sitting on a flat rock, stitching a tiny moccasin, not far from the head of the group. The owner of the shoe was a young girl named Gouyen. She watched Lozen with intense focus, memorizing the patterns in her stitching. Lozen finished and slipped it on the foot of the child. Gouyen smiled widely and embraced her.

The dramatic change in weather caused an aching in Nana's foot, exacerbating his limp.

"You are needed," he said, sitting down on the rock as Lozen stood.

The sky swirled black, pregnant with violence. Lozen hurried to where her brother stood with Geronimo and Juh. She closed her eyes and began to sing. Slowly her feet began to lift and fall, then faster. She began chanting with her arms outstretched, dancing in a slow circle, entranced with her song.

"What is that?" asked Gouyen.

Nana gazed west over the ridgeline as if his eyes could see the valley beyond, "What, child?"

"What is that in your hand?"

Unconsciously, Nana had removed the gold timepiece from his pouch. Its luster did not fade, even under sunless skies.

"White Eyes medicine." Nana made a mock scary face.

"Can I hold it?"

Nana handed the watch to the child.

Gouyen's tiny fingers explored the device. Surprised to find the case opened, she was fascinated by the bone-white face beneath the glass.

"What are these marks?"

"Powerful magic!"

Her thumb and forefinger pinched the crown and twisted. A faint, ticking pulse began deep inside the case, and the delicate second hand began to move.

"It's moving!"

Nana snatched up the device and observed the slow rotations of the hand. He felt the strange ticking in what previously had been lifeless metal. Instantly, he regretted his mockery and considered smashing the thing on the flat rock where he sat. Something warm dropped on his forehead. Heavy drops of rain began to fall.

"To the west! To the west!" cried Lozen, her arms stretched out, palms facing the western valley.

The rocks began to hiss as the rain crashed on the mountain. Nana slid the watch back into his pouch and ran to retrieve his rifle.

The Apache made ready for battle.

Sonoran Desert
State Of Chihuahua, Mexico

They passed on roads and over alkali flats, through sandy dunes and hills of volcanic rock; everywhere the company rode, a path availed itself to them. At times they saw the dust of massive armies moving like ignorant clouds on the horizon. Outside the great city of Chihuahua, they traveled among an enormous herd of cattle and went unnoticed by the vaqueros and all other human eyes. No man questioned their luck save to praise the leadership of the brave and wise General Basil Duke.

On the third night out of Santa Barbara, they made their first camp near the ruins of Casa Grandes in the broad valley of the San Miguel. They roasted rabbits and ate salted beef for supper, sleeping out on the plain under a jeweled blanket of stars.

Sheldon was restless; Reavis found him pacing by the riverbank. Shrieking bats tumbled wild and reckless through the blackness above the babbling stream, gorging on insects.

"It's time, Sam," said Reavis. "Are you good on your word?"

"Are we in Texas?"

"Pedro has friends in Janos who can help find his daughter. I want to go with him."

Sheldon sighed and bent down to retrieve a small pebble.

"What's in Janos for you?" he said and lobbed the pebble over the river. A bat shrieked in pain and disappointment as it swooped in and caught the stone with its hungry jaws.

"Does it matter?"

"No, but indulge me..."

"Pedro has some work lined up for us, maybe even a claim we can work."

"Silver, I hope," Sheldon smiled.

"Are you going to let me go or not?"

"When the men ask, and they will, tell them I'm sending you to California to secure friendly banking arrangements and to develop a west coast network."

"Thank you, Sam," said Reavis, he turned to leave, but Sheldon grabbed his arm and stopped him.

"What does Black have on you?"

"Excuse me?"

"You've lived in fear of that man's shadow as long as I've known you. Why?"

"He's the fucking Devil, sir. He put ghosts in my head!"

"Ghosts?"

"I don't have words to describe the Hell, only to say Robert Black is a man in perfect comfort there. He's got a demon that rides with him and lives in those teeth around his neck. I already said more than I should, can I go now?"

"Go," said Sheldon, releasing his arm. Reavis' words soaked in as he watched the man vanish in the cool night.

Sheldon returned to camp as the predawn glow lit the sky, sleepless and eager to be moving. Pedro and Reavis were gone. The company was already breaking camp, hitching wagons, and rolling by sunrise.

They followed the river north through farm and cattle country, veering east when the land became dry, and desolation replaced the fertile valley. Through strange canyons and forgotten paths, over dead rivers and ancient lava flows, the wagons rolled. That night, from the crest of a cholla-covered ridge, they saw the fires of a great army camp lying between them and El Paso del Norte. Sheldon turned the wagons away to the northwest, and before dawn, they crossed the border east of Palomas.

The sun came up behind a sheet of gray clouds that darkened as the wind continued carrying them to the northwest. By noon, the sky was black, and the sun was no longer visible. They were gaining elevation, and, for the first time, the animals showed signs of fatigue. The deprivation of rest and rations began to manifest itself next in the men of the Iron Brigade, and their weariness threatened to overcome them.

"When I was fourteen," said Abraham Abbot, the massive ginger. "I rode mail for the Pony Express. They had outposts all along this route, later incorporated on the Butterfield line. We're not far from one of those old stations. The place hasn't been used since before the war, likely in ruins now. They used to call it Soldier's Farewell."

Sheldon nodded, and they turned to the north.

They pushed the wagons further, and the horses frothed with sweat. The dead wind had relented. Nature swarmed in to fill the void. It took all of their collective wills to manage the final miles as if the entire distance they traveled accumulated and descended on them at that moment. In the U-shaped turn out of the station, horses began collapsing in exhaustion before they could be unhitched. Panic seized the affected teams, spreading chaos through the company and jamming the road for the last wagons in the column.

The station itself was reduced to its foundation and overgrown with weeds. The crumbled remains of a corral and other buildings lay abandoned and decayed, spread across the rubble of the small settlement. The totality of it sat above the main road, concealed by rocks, mesquite, and ironwood trees. Several tall hills rose to the east on the other side of an arroyo where a faint trickle of brown water flowed.

Sheldon spurred his horse up the loop to where the soldiers struggled with the horse rigging. Wallace Reed hitched his mount to an ironwood and tried to calm the horses of the lead wagon. Several other soldiers of the Iron Brigade joined him, their efforts in vain. His head felt light as the air pressure fell, and the first heavy drops of rain darkened the rocks.

The sky broke open, and the deluge began. Fear spread among all the horses, throwing riders and bolting. The cries of horses and men came to Sheldon through the hiss of rain, his vision restricted to a few paces in front of him. He pushed forward to the edge of the arroyo, the stream there now a steady river. Thunder ripped the sky, and another rider fell; he did not get up. The thunder came again, closer, rolling again and again. Sheldon looked to the ridge. An avalanche of men was descending upon the station.

"Reed!" Sheldon screamed into the maelstrom. He could only hear the Apache's war whoops and the rain's perforating violence. "Abbot!"

He drew his pistol, took aim at the descending horde, and pulled the trigger. A flash of fire erupted from the weapon, and the Colt Navy revolver lurched painfully from his hands, splashing into the wash. Chain fire had set off nearly every chamber. Sam sat dumbfounded, staring at his bleeding, empty hand. The statistical improbability was not lost on him. The dead wind had changed. The serendipitous favor of his golden patron was now set against him.

It was a paralyzing reckoning. He looked on, powerless to stop the tide of savage humanity. The Georgia men and the soldiers of the Iron Brigade fought as if in stasis, held in place by the downpour. Their dark shapes acted out death scenes like some shadow theater tragedy.

Lieutenant Abbot stood in the wash, bent over a young Apache warrior. His hands were locked around the warrior's neck as he simultaneously throttled and drowned the boy in the stream. Tiny blood clouds erupted from Abbot's chest even as an arrow left a jagged trench across his forehead, deflected by his giant skull. Life faded from his pale blue eyes, and they took on the color of dirty water. Finally, he fell on the young Apache, who writhed out from under the fallen soldier.

Sergeant Reed appeared high above the fray, standing on the bench of one of the stalled wagons. Horses without riders thrashed like salmon carried by the current of their own mindless terror. Reed leveled a rifle, laboring to navigate a shot through the chaos. Desperately he directed his fire toward the wash and the heathen onslaught. A horse reared up to throw its rider, and Wallace's shot found the friendly target, drilling his own man through his side. Blinded by the rains, Reed's lips screamed silent curses, and he strained to line up another shot. A female warrior, part of the vanguard, fell with the rain upon him. She plunged her slender blade between his ribs and into his thundering heart. Instinctively, he drew the rifle close to his chest, holding it like some cherished thing as he fell dead from the cab of the wagon.

One of the surviving Georgia men came to Reed's aid, arriving only in time to catch his fall. He tumbled to the ground with the corpse of his sergeant, putting himself between the woman warrior and his comrade. With empty chambers, he brandished his pistol like a club and stood to defend himself. The woman advanced. Reed's blood dripped from her knife and saturated her right arm. The Georgia man swung the gun downward, like a hatchet, toward her head. It glanced off her left shoulder as she side-stepped and thrust the blade into his neck. Her compromised momentum caused her strike to divert, slicing up through his neck and breaking the thin blade off under his chin. Blood came in thick streams, strong enough to resist the rain. The soldier danced wildly in a circle, pulling at the shard with bloody fingers. Like a declining wind-up toy, he spun down, leaning against a wagon wheel as the Apache woman shrieked in triumph.

The faces of Sheldon's men were like cattle at slaughter, eyes wide in disbelief and fear. Their gasping mouths filled with blood and rain, muting the violence of their screams. Blood flowed through the turnabout in sickening depths, completing the slaughterhouse imagery. The first volley of arrows and rifle fire proved devastating, killing with an efficacy only possible through the will of the dead wind.

Sheldon shook with rage, screaming into the hellscape, cursing the complete and profound betrayal. The rest of the Apache reached the arroyo, throwing themselves into the torrent, one of them particularly fixated upon him. He was older than the others, and his foot dragged behind, turned almost sideways. Sheldon knew this Apache. He had seen him years before at the side of Mangas Coloradas. He carried a long rifle, and a bone-handled knife was tucked into his waistband.

"Venganza!" the aging Apache howled into the rain. He broke from the others and charged toward Sam with a speed that seemed impossible, given the man's lame, club-footed leg.

Sheldon's horse bucked, struck by a bullet, sending him splashing into the path of his attacker. The Apache was on him instantly, bashing him with his rifle. Sheldon attempted to stand, but the increasing flow through the arroyo caused him to slip further downstream. His attacker had no such problem, wading along with him, intermittently kicking him, and pummeling him with the rifle butt. Sheldon heard the stock crack as it fell hard on a rock near his head. The elder Apache howled and drew his blade, leaping on Sheldon as the waters swiftly carried them down the arroyo.

His limbs became entangled with his enemy's as he struggled to keep the blade away and his head above the raging water. Sheldon's head emerged as the rocks beneath him vanished, and they fell. The face of his enemy was briefly framed against the violent sky. He could see the knife descending like the solitary fang of some abysmal wolf. He felt it cut into his chest as his head cracked against a boulder below. He was swallowed by the black and silent sky.

FORTY-SEVEN

August 8, 1866
Near El Paso Del Norte
Texas-Mexico Border

Dust slowly swirled in a cosmic parody, floating in the sunlight streaking through the windows of the Stevens House. For Sheldon, the brightness was something akin to the afterlife, saturating his senses with its strange serenity. Outside, the sun lurked like a thwarted killer, passively raging against the dry grass and hapless cattle surrounding the farmhouse. Further supporting the imagery of some hereafter were the assembled colleagues of the Trust, silently regarding him like a lab specimen or some meteor suddenly fallen to earth.

Taft, Collins, and Russell sat curiously silent across the cherrywood dining table like a trio of morose and solemn undertakers. Whether by design or morbid accident, their black suits were nearly identical. Sheldon wondered if, by some involuntary act of haunting, he was participating in his own funeral. Also present was the enigmatic Morya he had met on the road so long ago. Like the men of the Trust, he wore all black, though the cut of his suit seemed finer and somehow more exotic; the lapels a bit more flanged, the tail slightly longer, and the pants immaculately pressed and tapering down to the fine gloss of his leather shoes. He wondered where Thomas Rogers and Robert Black were. It seemed fitting that they should be here for this.

"Sam," said Collins. "Before we continue, we have something we need to tell you."

Sheldon turned his head to Danfort, almost surprised that the man could see his ghost. His neck creaked, and his joints felt fused with rust. He took a sip from the glass in front of him, the warm water soaking into his throat like a dry riverbed before it could reach his stomach.

"What is it?"

"Your mother," Collins said. "She passed."

"I'm sorry," said Sheldon.

The news fluttered around his mind like a piece of some lecture from a forgotten history professor. He struggled to find the relevancy. It occurred to him that his mother was in discussion and that he should have feelings. Searching for traces of her face or memories of her love, only the night under the Mayo Bridge in Richmond came to him. That night he chose the golden coin over the silver key. Somehow, every memory that preceded that moment was divorced from meaning, antiseptically cleansed of emotion.

"I'm sorry," he repeated.

"Sam?" asked Collins, concerned.

"We are also concerned about your father," said Russell. "He's become somewhat... unhinged."

"It's true, Sam. He's been making certain threats."

"I'm sure you deserve them. I wouldn't push the man."

"He intends on leaving our service," said Russell.

"Considering the sensitive and secret nature of our work, you understand what a liability he would be," said Collins.

"Then, of course, there is the Guild to think of. That is one asset he must not be allowed to depart with. That is if he is allowed to depart..." added Russell.

"My father is no fool. He is perfectly capable of negotiating his own terms."

"Enough of that for now, gentlemen," said the Morya. "I'd very much like to speak with our Odysseus. What a marvelous tale he must have."

The heat was stifling; the curtains hung still over the open windows. Morya slowly paced the room's perimeter, pausing from window to window, observing the bleached and sterile grass surrounding the Stevens Estate.

"You can trust him, Sam," said Collins.

"Can I?" Sheldon drained the glass of water and refilled it from the calico ceramic pitcher resting on Mrs. Stevens' hand-embroidered doily. "Trust is not my long suit."

"Trust is meaningless," said Morya. "What I require is faith."

Sheldon considered the statement absurd. Both his eyes were webbed with broken vessels, and his pupils were like robin's eggs in a field of red. Blood seeped through the breast of the shirt he wore and had dripped down to stain his borrowed trousers. Even his hair was matted with blood. In his assessment, faith was responsible for his miserable condition.

"Is faith so hard to accept?"

"I woke up naked, bathed in my own blood. My company murdered, stripped, and eviscerated, split open for the vultures. Millions of dollars in gold gone, and not so much as a single fucking coronet head left behind! What lessons of faith do I take away from that?"

"How did you survive?"

"I fell into a wash..." Sheldon said, straining to recall the last moments of the attack. "That crippled bastard with the club foot beat me with his rifle until it broke. I remember his knife coming down on my chest as we fell, and then darkness."

"Perhaps he believed that he had killed you. Luck? Or did fate intervene, how are we to know?"

"His blade hit bone, then the rock knocked me cold."

"Tell me of your golden sigil, did you lose it?"

"No. I found it up the wash, near where I fell in, lost among the rocks." Sheldon produced the coin and handed it to Morya, who held it to the dusty sunlight and admired its luster.

"What *luck* indeed!"

A pitiful sob percolated from Taft, exhaling into whispered mutterings of "The coin...the coin... the coin..."

Sheldon ventured an exhausted glance at the weeping man, too inundated in his trauma to process Taft's bizarre reaction.

"There's something more, something I cannot explain," he continued.

"Please, tell us, Mr. Sheldon," Morya smiled, offering Taft a patronizing pat on the back.

"The Apache I fought was older, a chief, I think. Instead of cutting me apart, he left this shoved in my mouth. It almost choked me. However, the part I cannot reconcile is this," Sheldon retrieved the gold pocket watch, opened the case, and placed it on the table. "The interior inscription bears the name of Mr. Taft!"

Alphonso Taft convulsed in horror, gripping the table's edge as if it threatened to send him spinning through the room with the atoms of sunlit dust.

"It's not real, none of this is real!" Taft moaned.

"Outstanding, our *faith* is restored. Isn't that right, Alphonso?"

Taft trembled on the edge of tears. Two perfect reflections of the watch framed in the gold of Collins' lenses. He and Russell looked on like witnesses to the final act of a stage magician, an impossible yet wholly anticipated prestige.

"I believe, Mr. Sheldon, your enemy intended to defile you with that object, but as you are a man of faith, the act transmuted into a blessing!"

"I never expected..." said Taft.

"This is exactly what you should expect!" said Morya.

"Take it," said Collins.

"Yes, take it!" Morya's smile stretched across his face with frightening mirth.

Sheldon's head throbbed from his wounds. Through the sunlit fog, the edges of objects became fuzzy, and the faces of the Trust were washed with golden light. Only Morya remained, rigidly outlined in black, his features cool and defined. His eyes turned down to the table, and the meaning of the golden watch became profoundly clear.

"From the start, none of this was chance," said Sheldon.

"Correct, Mr. Sheldon. It is important that you understand your will is forfeit. As Mr. Taft can testify, even in resistance, the only possible ends are by His design."

"The butchering of my men and the vanishing of countless tons of bullion?"

"Absolutely."

"Why?"

"It hadn't occurred for me to ask. There are none he owes answers to."

"Who is he?" demanded Sheldon.

Taft brought his gaze to Sheldon and met him with lunatic eyes.

"What did you hope to find, you fool? Did you think it was *your* flesh made gold? Tell me, Sheldon, does the knowledge of your insignificance lessen or strengthen your resolve? How does it feel to forge your own chains? "

Russell and Collins turned their eyes to Taft. Morya's pacing ceased, he stood like the living shadow of the sun, pondering the outburst.

Morya took a step toward Sheldon and extended his hand, the Roman coin rested in his ash-gray palm.

"His flesh is our mark."

He placed the coin in Sheldon's hand.

Sheldon ran his fingers over the worn edges of Caligula's image, then returned the coin to his pocket. Morya now stood by Taft, his long charcoal-colored fingers clenching his shoulder like a perched raven.

"Take up your mantle."

"I curse you all!" Taft wept.

"Of course you do," said Morya.

Alphonso Taft took the watch in his hands and looked upon the face as if it were a portal to another world. Then, his face became calm, and the tears ceased. Decades of grief drained from his eyes as they became filled with something, or someone, else.

"Mr. Sheldon," said Taft, his voice perfectly composed and clear. "There is one final matter to resolve."

"Of course," said Sheldon, extracting a strange form of comfort from Taft's new demeanor.

Taft put his thumb and forefinger on the crown of the golden watch and twisted. It began to tick with the cruel stratagems of time.

Morya's smile was a chasm of ivory.

FORTY-EIGHT

August 9, 18666
Texas-Mexico Border, Near El Paso Del Norte

"**D**o you like this one?"

"What?" Robert sipped his mescal and pretended to miss her meaning.

Lupe had gone away. At the age of twenty, she was already a veteran of the harsh streets and filthy saloons, intimately familiar with the violence of the soul. The place inside, where Lupe went, was safe and insulated like a ship's cabin, and she did not seem to mind that Elizabeth was at the helm.

"I love the eyes," he said.

She smiled and placed Lupe's hand over his.

The place was a nameless rat hole with a single door that had come off its hinges. On the rare occasions that the bar would close, the barman would simply nail it shut. A solitary lantern hung from a piece of hemp cord hooked to the ceiling; it wasn't clear whether for ambiance or an attempt at utility. The floor was uneven, and the furniture all had legs of different lengths, so when the whores danced, everything rocked. It was a haven for degenerates wanting to quench their thirst for cheap booze or to have their cocks jerked under wobbly tables.

Robert sat at the table furthest from the bar with his back to the wall. He wore the grubby clothes of a prospector and had grown his beard long. She sat across from him, her blue eyes like an oasis in the desert of Lupe's face. A streak of sunlight ran from the door down the middle of the room, illuminating half of his face.

"You're going gray, Robert," she said, running her fingers through a patch of his beard.

"Nonsense, it's merely silver dust."

A shadow of a man stood in the doorway, casting his long dark limbs across the room.

"He's come," said Elizabeth.

"Robert," the shadow said.

"Sam."

"Your father sent me," said Sheldon.

"Is that so?"

Sheldon wore Union dress blues, clean and pressed, with captain's bars pinned where he once displayed a fraudulent star on his Confederate uniform. He looked down the iron sights of his gun at Robert in his ragged state.

The degenerate patrons were silent.

"I know it was you in Richmond. You sold me out to that bloated prick Virgil Price."

"I'm sorry about that, Sam."

Sheldon fired his pistol.

Lupe threw herself up and backward over her chair, taking the first shot in her neck, severing her spine. Her eyes were brown and blinking in confusion when she came to rest amidst the straw and swill. The barman raised a coach gun, his greasy black hair falling over Elizabeth's eyes. Sheldon's gun was thunderous as the blood mist spread from the man's chest and painted the back bar, the coach gun falling useless in a rain of broken glass.

Robert rolled out of his chair and squeezed two shots from his Colt. The first went wide, and the second bullet caught Sheldon in his left hand, removing his pinky and part of his ring finger.

A blue-eyed vaquero flung himself from his place at the bar, deeply gouging Sheldon's eye with a broken bottle neck. Sam shoved the man back into the hanging oil lamp, knocking it to the floor in a blaze of blue flame, then put a bullet in the vaquero's head.

Robert's next shot went wild and struck the falling vaquero in the back, shattering bone and boring a hole through his heart. His blood hissed as it mixed with the burning oil. Black emptied his chambers in rapid succession through the waves of flame. The bullets escaped harmlessly through the front wall of the tavern, creating holes instantly filled with sunlight.

Drawing a knife from his boot, Robert rushed through the flames. He felt the dead wind blowing foul across the puke-stained floorboards.

Sheldon's next shot was true, and Robert fell, gut shot, to the floor.

Elizabeth screamed in anguish, flying across the burning floor in the skin of a toothless old man, brilliant blue shining from the wrinkled caverns of his eye sockets. Sheldon raised his weapon again and dispatched him. He fell half in the fire at Sheldon's feet, the old man's crab-like hands clutched at his ankles.

Another bar wretch became filled with Elizabeth's rage. She snatched a bottle from the bar and advanced through the expanding fire. Robert slumped in a spreading pool of blood, his knife pointing at Sheldon. He backed away, sending his final bullet into the chest of the demented prostitute, then struggled to reload with blood-slick fingers, managing only one round before the pain made the attempt futile.

His left eye was blind, he could feel the shards of glass protruding from the soft flesh above his cheek. Blood poured steadily from his missing digit, his pants dark with it. He stumbled backward as the fire increased its fury, his pistol trained where the streaking sun met the rising flames.

A woman pushed through the fire, her blouse and hair consumed by the blaze as she stepped over corpses to reach him.

"Burn with us, coward!"

Sheldon used his lone shot to silence her.

He turned his back to the fire and made for the sunlit

portal. A sharp pain and sudden force seized his momentum and brought him tumbling to the ground. Robert Black had one hand on his ankle, the other furiously grasping for the knife that protruded from Sam's calf. Sheldon struggled but could not gain any purchase on the blood-slicked boards as Robert dragged him back toward the flames.

Robert wavered on his knees in the apex of the fire. Much of his beard and hair had already been consumed, leaving blackened flesh in its wake. Blood oozed freely from the hole in his abdomen, the wound mortal. With an animalistic display of strength, he jerked Sheldon back to the floor as he fought to reach the exit.

Sheldon watched as the unhinged door somehow began to eclipse the opening. His hands slipped in the blood, and his nails bent back as they clawed the boards for purchase. He caught a glimpse of the blue-eyed drunkard who had been unconscious at the bar. The man now set the door in its frame and began hammering nails, entombing them in the burning structure.

"Stay with me, Sam," said Robert, withdrawing the blade from his calf and raising it to strike.

The bar was now fully engulfed, as were the shelves of rotgut. A grizzled old miner ceased his panicked pulling of loose floorboards. Calmed by his newly blue eyes, he abandoned his attempts to escape and advanced on Sheldon.

"Yes, stay with us, Sam," said the Mexican miner in eerily perfect English.

"I'm trying to save your soul, man!" said Robert, lunging on top of him as the bloody knife arced down at his chest.

Sheldon closed his eyes as golden fire surged through his bones, and he felt his body twisting like a tree in the wind. The leg of a chair filled his hand, and he swung it without thought, bringing the back across the side of Robert's head. Robert's knife blow landed hard, missing Sheldon and sticking deep into the bloodied planks. Robert fell away, and Sheldon quickly found his footing. Brandishing the broken chair, he stepped out of the flames and braced for the miner's attack.

"You were never meant for this, Sam." The miner spoke in a new but familiar voice. "I hate them for what they made you, for taking you away from me! It's not too late, don't let him into you!"

"Mother?" Sheldon wiped the blood from his destroyed eye, desperately trying to see through the flames engulfing him.

"Let it go," said the miner. "Let it melt here in this fire, let the tree burn!"

He brought the chair down hard on the bar, smashing it to splinters. The sharpened stake of a chair leg remained in his hand.

"I chose this!"

Sheldon drove the splintered wood through the miner's throat. Confusion and terror consumed the man's face as his eyes darkened to muddy brown. His hands clutched at the wood in his neck as the blood gurgled and hissed through his esophagus.

Robert reached out with a bloody hand and caught Sheldon's pants leg.

"You chose wrong."

Robert's voice had a curious choral-like quality as if several voices were speaking at once. Fire crawled up his arm, and the burning fabric meshed with his flesh. A strange peace had come over his face, and one eye turned from brown to blue.

Sheldon jerked free of his grasp but did not answer, walking directly to the sealed portal. The ceiling and walls now crawled with flame, and the smoke and heat became overpowering. He gathered his strength and thrust himself against the wooden door. He could hear the nails squeal and bend. He struck again and again until the door burst loose, falling shattered to the ground. Sheldon stepped out of the inferno and into the street. He looked back, and the doorway was a crooked mouth, drooling fire. Robert was nowhere to be seen.

He crossed the street and waited, expecting Robert or some blue-eyed maniac to emerge from the flames. None did.

A bucket brigade formed, but it was too late, and soon they became spectators. Sheldon tied his undershirt around the gash in his calf and washed his wounded hand in one of the buckets. He pressed it with a handkerchief, but the bleeding persisted. Finally, when the roof gave in, he cauterized the wound with coals from Robert's pyre.

The influence of Danfort Collins ensured that no soldiers from either side of the border paid any mind to the greasy black stain in the sky. Eventually, the men crossed themselves, took their buckets, and went away. Pedestrians, though curious, gave the half-blind gringo his space. By late afternoon, the coals had cooled enough to navigate, and he began sifting through the ashes.

He found Robert where he fell, blackened like jerky. The cord he wore around his neck was partially fused into the remaining flesh, and the three clean white teeth were embedded in his clavicle as if he were bitten. Sheldon pried them out with his knife, placed them on a flat rock, and smashed them with another. Then he scattered the dust in the piss-drenched gutter. With two fingers, he reached into Robert's charred eye sockets and lifted as he pried the skull free with his knife.

The following morning, Sheldon rode out. The cool gold disk of the Caligula coin pressed soothingly against his blinded eye, firmly secured under the black felt of his eye patch. The leather sack tied to his saddle horn bulged with a curious load, one that sang a familiar song as it bounced along to the horse's gait. Sheldon tucked his bandaged hand into his jacket and settled for the long ride north to Deer Island.

Turkey Vultures circled the column of smoke in an unholy

halo. The greasy plume rose high in the empty sky like death's umbilical cord, tethering this world to the next. Thomas followed it through the narrow streets of El Paso del Norte, the stench of charred flesh wafting above the typical squalor. At the blackened source, the corpses sprawled in a tangle of wood, bone, and flesh. Rats and dogs worked from the perimeter, competing for carrion as the shadows of buzzards circled lower.

Thomas lashed his horse to a post and examined the carnage. Fresh boot prints cut through the charcoal and ash, leading to a single corpse. The body was headless and mangled beyond recognition. One singular object identified the corpse beyond doubt in Thomas's mind: a belt buckle sunk into the center, not gold at all but a semi-melted piece of lead. Its design was darkened by fire but still visible, an embossed crow pecking at a heart.

"Never was a seed," he said, bending down to pluck the buckle from the seared leather belt. He slid the melted artifact into his pocket and spit on the corpse.

PART FIVE
POSTHUMOUS RECKONINGS
AND
UNREQUITED REMORSE

of what use is gold
dead star watching empty skies
claims nothing at all

-Matsuo Sogi

August 19, 1866
Mount Auburn
Cincinnati, Ohio

Alphonso Taft stepped out of the carriage, grabbed his bag, and thanked the driver. His Mount Auburn home sat like a white monolith on the grassy slope of his lawn as he strode across the grass to his front porch, ignoring the plethora of strange, unmarked packages. He found the door unlocked and swung it inward, setting his luggage down in the hall.

"Hello!" he shouted.

Receiving no answer, he made his way through the house, repeating his greeting. The house was quiet and empty. Standing in the kitchen, he heard faint voices drifting through the open window. Alphonso followed the sound out the back door to the side of the house and the twisted trunk of the old tree. William sat on a swing, newly hung from a high branch, slowly swinging back and forth. He wore his Sunday suit sans his jacket, which hung from a low-hanging branch nearby. His black tie struck out against the white of his shirt, ornamented with a gleaming gold tie clip.

"Hello, father, it's good to see you."

"Yes, William. I'm delighted to be home," he said. "Where is everyone?"

"Away at church."

"You didn't go with them?"

"I don't like church," said William.

"Oh, I see."

"Besides, I knew you were coming. I wanted to welcome you home."

"How did you know?"

"He told me," William nodded toward his jacket.

Alphonso smiled, "That is a very nice tie clip,"

"I know," said William, "It's gold."

"Ah, but do you know? Of what use is gold?"

August 31, 1866
Baltimore, Maryland

D anfort Collins removed the stopper from a bottle of
Kentucky bourbon and poured out two fingers. The
moon was magnificent, beaming through the window and
illuminating the engravings on Danfort's favorite table, like
abstract and ancient runes. He sat alone in the Gabby Saloon
and Mercantile. Ultimately, he decided to keep the name after
he purchased it.

He sipped his bourbon and reread the letter he had just
written. Satisfied, he sealed it and addressed the envelope.
After blowing the ink dry, he stacked it with the others and
bound them all with a string. His boots rang out on the historic
floorboards, on which more famous drunks than himself had
stumbled across throughout the ages. He deposited the stack
of letters in the safe behind the bar, below the shelf where a
wooden case, the size of a hat box, and his father's pistol sat on
display, then returned to his lonely bottle.

He set his gold-framed glasses down and admired the
moon through the trees. When he reached for them again, they
were gone. Suddenly, Collins was alone in a way that he had
not known since his youth.

He finished his drink and poured another. The silver light
became gold as it sifted through the glass of bourbon. Danfort
Collins put his head down on the table to admire the moon's
magic. The wind was swaying in the leaves.

September 2, 1866
Janos
State Of Chihuahua, Mexico

"Pedro, there's something I've been meaning to tell you," said Reavis.

"What is it?" he asked, plucking the feathers of a recently slain chicken.

"My name is not John Reagan, and I was never a member of Jefferson Davis' cabinet."

The hacienda was quiet but for a few surviving chickens clucking dangerously close to Pedro, the Killer. From the shade of the covered porch, they looked north to where the valley ended, and the road wandered into the hills. They drank cool well water with freshly squeezed lemon and enjoyed sopaipillas made by Leticia. Marco Antonio Guzman, the old patriarch, napped nearby in a chair made of deerskin and cholla bone.

"I know," said Pedro, dropping the chicken into the cast iron pot.

"You don't seem surprised."

"I've known for a long time. I always thought you were an exceptional liar."

Pedro reached for the blood-rusted hatchet and contemplated further slaughter.

"That I am."

A charcoal-gray cat with white streaks emerged from its hiding space along the low stone wall. It crept in slowly, stalking the ignorant chickens. Pedro looked for something to throw, though nothing seemed immediately useful.

"Go!" said Pedro, tossing the only thing at hand, the decapitated chicken's head. "My supper, not yours!"

The cat bounced to the side, then snatched up the head and absconded to a shady place.

"Do you think they will find her?" Reavis asked.

"Don Marco Antonio is a friend to the Gonzales and Peralta families. His family is large and connected throughout Mexico. With the chaos of war, it will take time, but I will see my Sophia again." He squinted his eyes to the north. "Do you have your spyglass?"

Reavis disappeared into the house and returned with the device, handing it to Pedro. He trained the scope on the winding north road. Half a dozen Apache riders approached. Pedro recognized several members of the band, Geronimo among them.

Pedro took up the hatchet and stepped into the yard.

"We're going to need to kill more chickens."

September 8, 1866
Conway, Massachusetts

Teressa's stone sat in the shade of a tall red oak just off the main path on Cemetery Hill. Jay lifted the stone himself from a quiet eddy of the Deerfield. It was an anomaly among the slate and greenstone and bore none of the typical funerary imagery familiar to the other graves. The simple inscription, graven into the flat granite stone, read:

Teressa Sheldon, Wife and Mother

Jay laid a cluster of Purple Aster across the stone. The shadow of the oak was almost pink, with the sun bleeding through its leaves. There were no words left to speak. He turned his back to the shady spot and followed the path to the old north road toward Shelburne Falls.

The South River tagged along the road like a lonely puppy, its steady babble washing out the plodding of his horse. When he cut east on the ferry road, the river turned with him, following him almost to the carefully stacked stone wall surrounding the Sheldon house before cutting south to join the Deerfield. Jay frowned at his gardens, now overgrown with weeds and vines. He hitched his horse to the wall at the edge of the property and walked the final distance to the door.

He did not linger long within his former home, only long enough to retrieve his pack and confirm that Marta had departed with her belongings. The first plumes of smoke came up through the house's three chimneys, rich and black in the warm, late summer sky. Jay was heading west on the Conway Station Road with Boston on his mind, and he never saw the flames. His thoughts were on his ship, the Albatross, and the wind that would carry him south. As if to answer, the wind changed, and the black smoke streaked after him, high in the blue, like a lost and mournful apparition.

September 27, 1866
The Vatican, Rome

Giovanni let his vestments fall. His pale and spotted flesh hung loose from his venerable bones. He extended his arms and stepped forward into the expanding pool of gold. The Ring of the Fisherman coiled around his bloated finger and writhed like a golden worm. Breasts, thighs, hands, and mouths rose and fell from the cool yet molten mound of living gold forming from the Papal treasury. Metal limbs lifted his swollen, hairy belly, and golden mouths sought out his withered cock.

Outside the chamber, an urgent knocking persisted. He shut it out of his mind as perverse prayers spilled from his lips. Glistening golden orifices presented themselves, inviting his deviant alchemy. The knocking became louder, increasingly insistent.

"Christ! What is it?" he shouted at the ancient chamber door.

"Your Holiness, forgive me!" said the muted voice. "She has returned, demanding an audience. She is inconsolable. The disturbance is becoming a problem!"

"Very well, I will receive her in my private office!"

The golden manifestations withdrew to orderly stacks of coins and ingots. Giovanni was alone. He restored his vestments and smoothed the stray hairs of his balding head. When he had collected himself, he extinguished the candles and locked the massive door behind him. Pope Pius IX followed the sunken catacombs below the basilica through the secret passages and ascended the steep stairs to his private offices.

Carlota prostrated before him, taking his hand in hers and kissing his ring. Her hair was disheveled, and her eyes swollen from tears.

"Holy Father! I avail myself to your infinite mercy!"

"Rise, my child. What troubles you?"

"Dark forces are at work against my husband. Napoleon III refuses to hear me! If you do not intervene, I am afraid all will be lost."

"What can I do to change the fate of nations?"

"There is gold beyond measure in that land, any brave enough to provide aid would be greatly rewarded," she said. "But it must be soon, time is perilously short!"

"All will be well, child, you are safe here," he said. "Now, tell me of this gold."

December 25, 1866
The Tomb, Parlor 322; Yale
New Haven, Connecticut

P arlor 322 was vacant of Bonesmen, as was the Tomb itself. Outside, light snow dusted the campus and threatened accumulation. Samuel Sheldon entered unobserved, his boots clacking against the marble floors. In his hands, he carried a square package similar in size to a hat box.

"Rari quippe boni," he said, reading the words engraved into the black marble mantel. "The good are rare," he sighed.

Sheldon set the box on the expansive black oak table. He lifted the lid and removed the contents, a human skull mounted upon a small gold pedestal. The bone was clean but charred and blackened in places. Sheldon placed the skull on the mantel of the massive marble fireplace where it could stare over the empty parlor.

He reached into his jacket, withdrew a flask of bourbon, and took a pull. With his other hand, he spread his fingertips over the blackened skull. He closed his eyes and listened to the vibrations rising through his fingers. He could hear the weeping softly echo against his bones. From within himself, emanating from his golden roots, laughter was the answer.

"Merry Christmas, Robert," he said, sliding the flask back into his pocket.

February 7, 1867
New Haven, Connecticut

"H e found a printing press?" Russell marveled, flipping through the roughly bound manuscript.

"It would appear that he did," said Rogers.

"How many of these have you recovered?"

"These make fourteen." Thomas laid two more manuscripts down on the table.

"The others?"

"Burned," said Rogers.

The rain pattered against the dining room windows of Silas Goodrich's former home. In the end, Russell had chosen to strip the place to its bones and remake it to his own taste. Nothing remained of the former owner's decor or furniture, save the haunting portrait of a young woman Russell had never known though had heard a great deal about.

"I take it this is some kind of map," Russell posited. "Complete with clues and legend."

"That is what the text claims," said Rogers. "In the common language anyway. The bulk of it is indecipherable marks and symbols. It's like no language I've ever seen."

"Nor will you," said Russell.

"The rest of the narrative is a damning indictment of the Trust. He describes you, Taft, and Collins as apocalyptic beasts bent on man's ruin."

"Half right," sighed Russell.

"I have no idea how many more of these are out there sitting in bookshops, randomly inserted in library bookshelves, or even distributed."

"It's an outrageous tale, the ranting of a lunatic, easily refuted," said Russell. "Still, we should endeavor to remove them from circulation."

"I've been retracing his steps, it led me to New Haven," said Rogers. "The copy you're reading was mailed to The Palladium."

"Fucking Crow!"

"I resolved the problem of the journalist," said Rogers.

"Good."

Russell scooped up the other copies and carried them to the hearth in the living room. He tossed them into the fire and watched the flames crawl over them, slowly sinking into the paper.

"Whatever it takes," he said, pulling the bench away from the Harpsichord on the adjacent wall and sitting down at the instrument.

"Understood."

"Thank you, Thomas," said Russell as he fumbled through the opening measures of a Bach fugue, but his scion was already gone.

March 20, 1867
Naica
State Of Chihuahua, Mexico

The storm was pushing toward the mountain. From above, the haboob looked like a wave of filth crashing upon the desert. Soon, it would be upon them.

"We must hurry," said Pascal.

He led the horse by its reins up the rocky trail. He wore only a breechcloth, sandals, and a heavy water skin slung over his brown shoulders.

Her silk scarves lifted with the wind, fluttering like ribbons or flags around her. She felt the warm release of water flowing over the saddle and down her legs.

"It's time," she said.

They reached the cave as the full force of the sandstorm raged against the mountain. The horse broke free from its hitching and vanished into the swirling chaos. Pascal took her hand and led her deeper into the cave.

Massive white crystals jutted out from all angles, gradually replacing the granite and limestone. They protruded from the floor of the cave at all angles. Thick and enormous, they rose dozens of feet in the air like the crooked and falling pillars of some alien kingdom that muted the grandest designs of men. Their steps became labored as the oppressive heat and humidity sapped their strength and deprived them of oxygen. The cave expanded in majestic depths of infinite facets and bizarre formations, reflecting and radiating light from otherworldly sources.

They came to a roughly rectangular chamber, the floor covered with ice-blue water. A series of flat stones rose out of the shallow water, creating an improvised bridge. The center stone was a large island of smooth, slightly rounded granite. When they reached it, Pascal laid a blanket down and made her as comfortable as he could.

She gulped at the noxious, hot air and endured the contractions with stoic grunts. Pascal held her hand and prayed.

A thin, frail cry echoed over the granite walls and cyclopean crystals as the child took its first breaths. Pascal wrapped the boy in one of Maria's scarves and placed him in her arms. His cries subsided as his glacial blue eyes looked upon his mother for the first time.

April 1867
Santa Rosalia
State Of Chihuahua, Mexico

"Not that one!" said Jorge. "That drift is barren and dangerous!"

The man ignored him and disappeared into the darkness of the partially collapsed tunnel. Jorge was sure he spoke no Spanish, leaving him uncertain why General Diaz had inflicted him on his crew. The man was clearly insane and, as such, a danger to all those around him.

"Bah!" he said, continuing down the well-supported main

tunnel. "Maybe it will cave in and solve my problem!"

The man walked along in his curious straw sandals, twirling his pick in the darkness. He stopped where the drift narrowed, and the timbers had partially collapsed and remembered the lantern that hung from his hemp rope belt. With the darkness dispelled, he contorted his thin body through a gap in the rocks and into the void beyond.

He went further, sometimes on his knees, down the collapsed tunnel until he came to the end. It was there he heard it the strongest, calling from the rock and quartz. He hung the lantern on an ancient spike and pulled his long, black hair back in a ponytail. The man's face was hideously scarred by fire, the burns trailing up into his scalp where patches of hair did not grow. Similar scars marked his hands. He took his pick and began carving out chunks of rock.

A wide slab of stone gave way and fell at his feet, revealing a brilliant swath of quartz studded with gleaming specks of gold. It was rich ore, some of the richest he had ever seen.

stand at my right hand
all these things will I give thee
make bread from these stones!

Matsuo Sogi put his hands to the brilliant vein and listened to the rocks speak.

May 15, 1867
Santiago De Querétaro, Mexico

Lieutenant Colonel Jose Rincon Gallardo stood at the gate of Templo y Convento de la Santa Cruz. His watch read four-thirty, and the night was at its quietest. Five hundred Juáristas waited patiently in the darkness. They stood in formation, fully visible from the wall if there had been any guards there to see. Colonel Lopez had sent them all away.

"I have done as I promised," said Colonel Miguel Lopez. "Will you honor your word?"

Lieutenant Colonel Gallardo did not hide his disgust for Colonel Lopez, "Here are your pieces of silver!"

"You mock me, sir, but I only wish to save lives! To put an end to bloodshed!"

"You wish to save your own."

A tiny shadow materialized at his side and wrapped her arms around his knees. The child was teetering on the edge of tears.

"No, I do it for her, my daughter, for Donna Sophia!" said the colonel.

"Whatever allows you to sleep. Produce the key."

Colonel Lopez took the key from his pocket and unlocked the gate. Gallardo's aide pushed it open quietly and waved his arms to the waiting squads. The soldiers quietly began filing through the gate. He lifted the young girl out of the path of the men.

"You will find him in the chapel with his countryman, the Prince Salm-Salm."

Gallardo placed a heavy coin purse in his hand, then followed his men through the gate.

June 19, 1867
Cerro De Las Campanas
Santiago De Querétaro, Mexico

"It's very early," said Stallworth.

"Nonsense," said Díaz. "It's a small inconvenience to witness such a momentous occasion!"

Stallworth looked past the crowd to the clearing where the firing squad assembled. Maximillian stood flanked by his two generals, Miramon and Tejia. He was shouting some noble last words about freedom and viva Mexico, though the exact phrases were unclear from their vantage.

"Poor Bastard," Stallworth muttered.

"Inbred Hapsburg clown, he deserves worse," said Díaz.

A half-eaten corn cob sailed from the crowd, landing at Maximillian's boot. An apple soon followed amidst boos and jeers.

"I forgive you!" he shouted, though it was barely audible above the rabble.

"Why are we here?" Stallworth asked.

"You have been so kind to me over our time together, showing me the hospitality of your home. I wanted to show my appreciation and reciprocate by inviting you to a soiree of my creation. What do you think so far?"

"Is this a joke?"

"Joke? No, señor, I do not joke," said Díaz.

Smoke billowed into the clear morning sky. Maximillian and his two generals thrashed against the stakes they were bound to, finally slumping forward as gravity took them and their souls departed.

"Come with me, there's one more thing I'd like to show you."

They walked past the gathered masses to a less crowded area of the hill where scaffolding had been erected. A blindfolded man dropped from a noose through the trap door just as they arrived, legs kicking as the life fled from his body.

"Perfect timing," said Diaz. "It's your turn."

"What?"

Diaz waved to a pair of guards in detail, who immediately

joined them and took Stallworth by his arms.

"What is this?!"

"An execution, of course. Adios, Mr. Stallworth."

July 29, 1867
Baltimore, Maryland

S heldon ran his fingers over the initials engraved in the corner window table of the Gabby Saloon and Mercantile. The trees swayed in the wind outside, and the rain filtered through the leaves. Wood creaked and groaned as workmen pried the ancient bar away from the floorboards. The men grunted from the strain of lifting the sturdy oak, finally separating in a cloud of two-hundred-year-old dust.

"Easy!" said Sheldon. The men set the bar carefully back on the floor.

"What are your intentions for this place?" Edwin Stanton asked, softly rubbing the lenses of his glasses with a kerchief.

"I'll renovate it, then reopen. It will remain a public house, but the name has to change."

"Any thoughts on that?"

"Something to honor Collins, dropping the Mercantile. Just saloon, There's no mercantile here."

Stanton returned his glasses to his face, mulling over the name.

"Look, Mr. Stanton, I didn't bring you here to discuss my future business ventures. We need to discuss how we're going to proceed."

"Proceed?" Stanton looked down his nose. "You didn't bring me here at all! I came out of respect for your former employer and professional courtesy. You may have inherited this termite trap, sir, but you have not inherited my services!"

Sheldon smiled. He rose and retrieved a wooden case, the

size of a hat box, from a shelf next to the old pistol belonging to Collins' father. He slid the strange case across the table to Secretary Stanton.

"Go ahead, open it."

Stanton lifted the lid, gazing inside with horror. Sweat beaded on his forehead and sideburns and streaked down his pale, pudgy face.

"It is no small task to remove the head of a president," said Sheldon. "It's a far greater one to watch the tissue and hair separate from the skull while it roils in a kettle. I count myself among the few who possess the morbid acumen to tend such a fire, hissing with the frothy tufts of hair and globs of flesh that spill over the side. The attention to detail required to scrub the brain jelly and clots of flesh away, to polish the bone to a fine white finish, is a rare gift. You, Mr. Stanton, will bring me one thousand skulls in this manner should I require them. Is that understood?"

Sheldon adjusted the leather patch over his eye. Somewhere through the clouds, a golden sun prowled the heavens. Edwin Stanton trembled.

"Of course," he said. "What can I do for you, sir?"

"The western territories are crawling with hostiles," said Sheldon. "I need a rapid solution to the Indian problem."

"That will take time!"

"If time is the answer, the question is pain. Is that what you're asking for?"

"No, sir. I will organize an immediate response to the threat."

Sheldon drummed the table with the ghosts of his missing fingers.

"Good," he said, fixing one dead, blue eye on the Secretary. "Now, go."

August 1866

Hembrillo Basin, New Mexico Territory

T he air inside the mountain was bad. Every breath
tainted with a festering humid stench, though that is
not what distressed Victorio. The spirit of the place had gone
bad, taken and occupied by something he could not imagine. It
was a rot of memories coaxed from the dust by some horrible
mind that had only just awakened.

The torchlight died in the abyss of the stoped ceiling and
faltered before it reached the chiseled walls of the chamber.
Even the luster of the endless stacks of yellow metal seemed
to suck up the light and exhale darkness. Nothing stirred
save the motionless, dead wind. It was the strongest in the
consolidated heaps of yellow metal, leaving no doubt about its
source.

"It is done." Victorio's words were swallowed by a growing
ring of darkness.

When the light returned, the stacks of yellow metal were
gone, and the entire contents of the cavern were reduced to a
single occupant. Stepping from the darkness into the circle of
light, an enormous man appeared. The entirety of his flesh was
of the yellow metal, and it rippled like water where the light
touched him. His head was strangely elongated, though the
face was that of a man, seamlessly flowing into the insect-like
shell of his skull. While his arms and legs shared the curious
disproportions of length, the constant movement of his flesh
challenged Victorio to define the exact joints and musculature
of the being.

"Are you the god of the White Eyes?" asked Victorio.

"I am what you see," he said in the Apache tongue.

"Then you are their devil."

"If that is what you see."

"You do not deny it?"

The man's eyes shimmered in prismatic golden spirals, and

the flames of the torch distorted across his body like a warped mirror. He smiled as much as his face could be said to smile.

"When the sun shines, you say the sky is blue," he said. "When there is no moon, you say the sky is black. In truth, the sky is neither of these things. I am not here to deny anything."

"Then why are you here?" Victorio said.

"I show myself so that you may know that this place is closed to you. Go in peace, with my thanks."

His forgotten dreams returned, their clarity complete, and he knew the man was not a stranger. He was the mind in the metal, he was the dead wind.

"You poisoned my dreams."

"I have one final dream for you," said the man. "Shall I show you?"

"I want nothing from you!"

"Yet I want something from you, one small favor. Will you promise?"

"I will give you nothing!" Victorio shouted.

"If you wish for me to leave this land, then at Tres Castillos, you will betray me."

"I will betray you with every breath."

"Then we are agreed."

His torch flickered and faded. Darkness encroached to fill the void. When the flame stabilized and the circle of light expanded, he found the cavern returned to its previous state, with the yellow metal settled back to its stacks and piles.

Victorio walked in a haze of doubt and disbelief, ignoring the jeweled array of stars and cool silver moon as he descended the mountain to the plain below. He found Lozen sitting vigil over the fire, a mere collection of rust-colored coals.

"What is it, brother? You seem troubled."

"I'm tired, I need to sleep."

Victorio went to his wikiup and fell into a dreamless sleep.

ABOUT THE AUTHOR

Jason Roberts is a lifetime resident of Seattle and the Pacific Northwest. When not clacking out tales of profound cosmic importance at his kitchen table, he may be found meandering through the mundane oddities of his richly satisfying existence. Such activities might include, but not be limited to, testing his guitar against the sonic thresholds for collapsing buildings, teaching proper swear words to his daughter, intrepidly exploring dive bars for lost relics of hidden bourbon, occasionally running for mayor, and annoying his beloved wife with soap box soliloquies on long car rides to no place in particular.

You may have seen him across the card table, forcing you all in while holding deuce-seven or displaying a middle digit in your rearview mirror in appraisal of your driving skills. Perhaps you've caught a glimpse of him behind the bar, mournfully muddling the mint and lime of your mojito and, not so silently, judging as you sip on your utter lack of gumption.

Yes, he is an asshole. However, he will never shame you for your apostrophe placements or other grammar mistakes. Those people can suck it.

Made in the USA
Middletown, DE
07 October 2023